Deborah Challinor has a PhD in history and is the author of eighteen bestselling novels, including the Children of War series, the Convict Girls series, the Smuggler's Wife series and the Restless Years series. She has also written one young adult novel and two non-fiction books. In 2018, Deborah was made a member of the New Zealand Order of Merit for services to literature and historical research. She lives in New Zealand with her husband.

Books by Deborah Challinor

FICTION
THE RESTLESS YEARS Series
Fire
From the Ashes
The Jacaranda House
The Leonard Girls

THE SMUGGLER'S WIFE Series
Kitty
Amber
Band of Gold
The Cloud Leopard's Daughter

CONVICT GIRLS Series
Behind the Sun
Girl of Shadows
The Silk Thief
A Tattooed Heart

CHILDREN OF WAR Series
Tamar
White Feathers
Blue Smoke

Union Belle

Isle of Tears

My Australian Story – Vietnam

NON-FICTION
Grey Ghosts
Who'll Stop the Rain?

BLACK SILK
& *Sympathy*
DEBORAH CHALLINOR

HarperCollins*Publishers*

HarperCollins_Publishers_
Australia • Brazil • Canada • France • Germany • Holland • India
Italy • Japan • Mexico • New Zealand • Poland • Spain • Sweden
Switzerland • United Kingdom • United States of America

HarperCollins acknowledges the Traditional Custodians
of the lands upon which we live and work, and pays respect
to Elders past and present.

First published on Gadigal Country in Australia in 2024
by HarperCollins_Publishers_ Australia Pty Limited
ABN 36 009 913 517
harpercollins.com.au

Copyright © Deborah Challinor 2024

The right of Deborah Challinor to be identified as the author of this work has been asserted by her in accordance with the _Copyright Amendment (Moral Rights) Act 2000._

This work is copyright. Apart from any use as permitted under the Copyright Act 1968, no part may be reproduced, copied, scanned, stored in a retrieval system, recorded, or transmitted, in any form or by any means, without the prior written permission of the publisher. Without limiting the author's and publisher's exclusive rights, any unauthorized use of this publication to train generative artificial intelligence (AI) technologies is expressly prohibited.

A catalogue record for this book is available from the National Library of Australia

ISBN 978 1 4607 6366 7 (paperback)
ISBN 978 1 4607 1602 1 (ebook)

Cover design by Darren Holt, HarperCollins Design Studio
Cover images by shutterstock.com
Author photograph by Anne Challinor
Typeset in Sabon LT Std by Kirby Jones
Printed and bound in Australia by McPherson's Printing Group

For my excellent friend Ngahuia Te Awekotuku

Prologue

April 1868, Sydney

Tatty Crowe sat near the back of the crowded room at the Printer's Arms Hotel, attending the inquest of her late husband, Titus, who had died seven months earlier. The cause of death, as stated by his physician on his death certificate, was perforated stomach ulcers. Titus had been an undertaker, and not always well regarded by customers or colleagues, and Tatty could see plenty of people in the crowd she knew hadn't liked him who, she suspected, were there hoping to hear any salacious secrets about him.

She was doing her best to appear calm and confident despite being anxious to the point of feeling sick. She owned Crowe Funerals now, making her Sydney's first woman undertaker, but if things went badly she stood to lose everything. Though she was popular with her customers, especially the poorer ones, she knew that she most certainly had an enemy or two. She was grateful she had her friends around her, but if the inquest went against her, they would not be able to help. She squeezed her assistant Cora's hand and received an encouraging squeeze back. To one side of the room stood the rest of her faithful crew – Ben and Robert and Henry. It hurt her to think that, if things did go awry, she might never work with or even see them again.

And then there was Elias Nuttall, her nemesis, sitting near the front of the room, just waiting for his opportunity to tell

Coroner Shiell, the audience, and anyone else who would listen that she had poisoned Titus to death. It was *his* fault the inquest had been convened, it was *his* fault Titus's body had been exhumed, and it was *his* fault she was in such a perilous position. She should have realised how far he would go to ruin her and done what she could to stop him, but now it could be too late.

She turned to the back of the room to make sure Friday and the others were still there. They were, and she was grateful. If the coronial jury found that she had poisoned Titus, and Coroner Shiell referred the matter to the criminal court, she would very likely be hanged at Darlinghurst Gaol if found guilty. She would most definitely need the help of every friend she had if that were to happen. But if the jury's decision favoured her today, it was still good to know she could call on associates with resources: she would certainly need assistance to put a stop to Nuttall's vendetta against her.

Tatty sat very still as the coroner called prominent surgeon Mr George Montague to the front of the room to report on the postmortem he had conducted on Titus's exhumed body. Her shoulders ached with tension and her fingernails dug into her palms as he impassively read out a summary of what he'd found.

And then she held her breath.

Coroner Shiell said, 'Thank you for your findings, Mr Montague. Is it your opinion then, as a senior medical professional, that Mr Crowe died as a result of perforated stomach ulcers or of deliberate arsenic poisoning?'

Part One

1864

When I am dead, my dearest,
Sing no sad songs for me

Christina Rossetti, 1862

Part One

1864

*When I am dead, my dearest,
Sing no sad songs for me.*

—Christina Rossetti, 1862

Chapter One

Early September 1864, London, England

Tatiana Caldwell lay in bed, suspended between sleep and wakefulness, half dreaming of a time little more than a year earlier when she had been sixteen and her loving family was whole and happy and life was good. Then she awoke completely and realisation hit her like a physical blow: none of that was true any more. Her beloved father, Hector, was dead; her mother, Betsy, had been cheated of the ongoing allowance Hector had so cleverly left her in his will; and to stop the bank from foreclosing on their five-bedroom house, the only asset they had left, they'd had to take in lodgers. Worst of all, Betsy was extremely ill herself now.

With a sigh Tatiana pushed back the bedclothes and sat on the side of the bed, her bare legs dangling. Her bedroom smelt stuffily of the beeswax Mrs Seddon used on the furniture, and the stale water in a vase containing a decaying arrangement of delphiniums and hydrangeas she hadn't had time to replace. The clock on the mantel read just past six: time to get up, go downstairs and help Mrs Seddon and Lorna prepare the breakfasts for Mr Denham, the young and quite nice lodger, and Mr Wooten, the middle-aged, not-nice one. But first she'd pop into her mother's room and make sure she was all right, and that Lorna had taken her a cup of tea.

She used the chamber pot then poured a few inches of cold water from a jug into its basin, stripped off her nightdress and had a quick wash and cleaned her teeth, shivering slightly in the cool air. Summer was on its way but the north-facing side of the house rarely warmed up before midday. Then she dressed – chemise, stockings, drawers, stays, camisole, petticoats, gown (black, as she was still in mourning for her father), and boots. No crinoline. Doing housework in a crinoline was almost impossible. She unplaited her long coal-black hair, gave it a quick brush, then tied it back in a low ponytail.

Next door she knocked gently and waited for Betsy to call out. When she didn't, Tatiana immediately thought the worst and pushed the door open, stepped inside and stood in the dimness, gripping the knob, her heart pounding, listening desperately for her mother's laboured breathing. And then, to her knee-buckling relief, she heard it – slow and shallow and raspy, but reasonably regular.

'Ma?' she said in a loud whisper, not wanting to wake her mother if she needed to sleep. 'Are you awake?'

A sigh from the bed, then nothing, then a grunt followed by a snotty sniff. 'Tatty, love.'

Tatiana crossed to the bed and kissed her mother's forehead. Her skin felt sweaty and strands of her hair stuck to her face. There was an unpleasant smell about her, like rancid milk, though she was bathed in bed at least once a day. Tatty had decided it was the smell of illness. She'd heard Lorna say the other day it was the smell of death, which had earnt Lorna a sharp smack on the arm from Mrs Seddon, but she was choosing to ignore that. Lorna said all sorts of silly things.

'Do you want some light?' Tatty asked.

Betsy indicated yes, so Tatty lit the oil lamp on the nightstand as the sun hadn't yet quite risen. 'How do you feel this morning?'

'Not so bad,' Betsy said, rolling onto her back with a groan.

Tatty thought her mother looked awful. Her skin appeared grey and slack, and enormous bags like bruises darkened the skin beneath her eyes. She was forty-three but looked at least a decade or more older. Her appearance frightened Tatty badly. 'I'll fetch you some tea, shall I?'

'Have you started on the breakfasts?' Betsy said, then exploded into a horrible, bubbling fit of coughing. Tatty quickly handed her a cloth but not before a small spray of blood had stained the bedclothes.

Tatty stared at the mess, then pulled her mother up into a sitting position and secured her there with pillows.

Betsy wiped her mouth with the cloth and said, 'Shit.'

'Do you want your laudanum?'

Betsy nodded and Tatty passed her the brown bottle from the nightstand. Betsy took a good swig, closed her eyes as it went down, then handed the bottle back.

'I'll get that tea,' Tatty said and hurried out of the room before her mother could see she was about to cry.

She met Lorna at the top of the stairs, the tip of her tongue sticking out as she concentrated on not dropping a tray loaded with a teapot, cup and saucer, spoons, extra hot water, and a plate of biscuits. Lorna wasn't the brightest or most competent of housemaids, but she was Mrs Seddon's niece and if you employed Mrs Seddon, which Hector and Betsy had since Tatiana's birth, you also employed Lorna. She had been fifteen then and was thirty-two now and no brighter, but Tatty loved both her and Mrs Seddon and considered them part of her family.

When Lorna saw the tears in Tatty's eyes, her own face crumpled.

Tatty knew what would come next, forgot about her own misery and thought, Rats.

'Oh no, she's dead, isn't she?' Lorna wailed. 'Oh no, oh Lord save us, what will —?'

'No!' Tatty reached up and gently rearranged Lorna's house-cap, which was slipping down over one eye – a slightly awkward manoeuvre as Lorna was five inches taller than her own five feet two. 'No, shush, it's all right, she hasn't died.

Really, she hasn't. I just felt a bit sad, that's all. It's all right, you can take her tea in.'

Lorna's face relaxed. 'Can I?'

Tatty nodded. 'Go on. She's sitting up, waiting for you.'

Lorna's smile was radiant as she headed off down the hallway towards Betsy's room.

Downstairs, in the kitchen at the rear of the house, Tatty found Mrs Seddon stoking the range and getting the breakfast things together.

'Morning, dear. Have you been in to see your mother?' she asked.

Tatty nodded. 'She's not very well. Lorna's just taken in her tea. She was a bit upset. She got it into her head that Ma had died.'

Maggie Seddon looked at Tatty beadily through her wire-rimmed spectacles. 'Had she? Why was that?'

Tatty looked away. 'Perhaps because I came out of Ma's room nearly crying.'

'Mmm?'

Tatty knew Mrs Seddon was waiting for her to go on. She was in her early fifties and, unlike Lorna, not remotely simpleminded. In fact, she was as sharp as a boning knife. 'Ma had a coughing fit and brought up some blood.'

'A lot?' Mrs Seddon looked concerned.

'Not a huge amount but we'll have to change her sheet after we've done the breakfasts.'

'You do know that isn't a good sign?'

Tatty swallowed down a surge of panic and willed herself to keep calm. She didn't want to talk about any of that. She took the lid off the breakfast teapot to see if there were tea leaves in it yet. No, there weren't.

'Don't ignore me, Tatiana,' Mrs Seddon said. 'You're going to have to face facts.'

'I have.'

'Have you? Really?'

Tatty had, sort of. 'I *know* she's sick. Of course I do.' She reached for the tea caddy and spooned leaves into the teapot. 'But as she's refused to ever see a doctor we don't even know what's wrong with her, do we?'

'How do you know she hasn't seen a doctor?'

'Because every time I've asked her to, she says there's no need.' Tatty added more leaves to the teapot.

Mrs Seddon said, 'That tea will be undrinkable. Tip some of those out. And she *has* seen a doctor.'

This was definitely news to Tatty. 'When?'

'After your father passed away, and again four or five months ago, when her cough started getting worse.'

'Why didn't she tell me?' Tatty didn't know whether to feel angry, relieved or jealous because she'd been excluded.

'I expect because she didn't want to worry you.'

Well, that was pointless, Tatty thought – she was worried anyway. 'What did the doctor say?'

'*I* think your mother should have told you this by now,' Mrs Seddon said, sounding grumpy, 'and I don't think not telling you is doing anyone any good. So *I'll* tell you. She has consumption.'

Tatty was still for a moment. She knew what consumption was, and that it was common, and that most sufferers died from it. 'There's no cure for that, is there?'

'I'm really not sure.'

Tatty looked at Mrs Seddon and saw she was in fact sure of the answer to that question. So was Tatty. She tried to speak but only a squeak came out. She cleared her throat and tried again. 'When will she die?'

Mrs Seddon sighed and scooped the excess tea leaves out of the teapot herself. 'I don't know, love. Let's just make the best of what time we have left with her, shall we? It could be months and months, even years, for all I know.'

Tatty didn't think Mrs Seddon really believed Betsy would live on for years. 'Will I get it now?' she asked. 'Do I already have it?'

Mrs Seddon shrugged. 'Who knows? Do *I* have it? Does Lorna?'

'Does Lorna have what?' Lorna said as she entered the kitchen.

'Fleas,' Mrs Seddon said.

'Fleas!' Lorna looked horrified. 'I don't have *fleas*!'

'Well, that's all right, then, isn't it?' Mrs Seddon said.

'Did Ma drink her tea?' Tatty asked.

Lorna nodded. 'Some of it.'

'And did she have a biscuit?'

'No. She said maybe later.'

'Well, I'll take her up some breakfast,' Tatty said, knowing her mother probably wouldn't eat that either.

Mrs Seddon said to Lorna, 'Go and look in the downstairs linen cupboard for a clean cloth for the breakfast table, there's a good girl.'

Lorna was back in five minutes. 'I can't find one. We must have run out.'

'Don't tell me they're all in the washhouse?' Mrs Seddon exclaimed.

'We probably have run out,' Tatty said. 'They're bad enough at the table as it is, Mr Denham and Mr Wooten, but I'm sure Mr Wooten's been making messes on purpose since Ma's been sick and not able to ... you know.'

Every single morning, it seemed, either Mr Denham or Mr Wooten managed to slop porridge, egg or their beverage on the cloth. This meant it had to be laundered, dried, starched and ironed before it could be used again, a process repeated with every dirty supper cloth. It was as galling as Betsy providing the lodgers with porridge and ham and eggs for breakfast, just so she could charge them more. The Caldwell family hadn't even eaten that well when Hector was alive. Tatty didn't really mind Mr Denham getting ham and eggs, but Mr Wooten certainly didn't deserve such bounty.

'Not able to what?' Lorna asked.

Mrs Seddon said, 'Never you mind. We'll use one of the

cloths from the big table and fold it in half. Fetch one of those, will you, love?'

Off Lorna trotted again.

'In fact I know it's Mr Wooten,' Tatty said. 'The other morning I saw him deliberately wipe his eggy knife on the cloth.'

Mrs Seddon said, 'How uncouth.'

'I think it's my fault.'

'How can your mother's illness and Mr Wooten's conniptions regarding her unavailability be your fault?'

'Because after she took to her bed, I had a talk to him in the parlour. You know how he likes to read his papers and smoke his smelly pipe in there?'

Mrs Seddon nodded.

'Well, I was very polite, to start with, anyway, and I informed him that due to her ill health Ma would no longer be providing him with any manner of personal services. And he said, "Oh, I see." And then he said, "I don't suppose you'd be interested? You're young and quite pretty and your mother *is* lacking a little ..." And I can't remember the word he used, but it was something like radiance or vitality. Something he intended to be insulting. And then he said, "I pay well."'

'The rude bugger!' Mrs Seddon said. 'Has he not looked in a mirror in recent times?'

'Clearly not,' Tatty said. 'So I said, "No, I'm *not* interested, and how dare you say that about my mother?" And then I thought I was going to be sick because of how nasty he'd been about Ma and had to rush out of the parlour.'

She glanced over her shoulder to make sure Lorna wasn't hovering within earshot. She was practically twice Tatty's age, but too naive to understand why Betsy had done what she'd done, if she'd even noticed what had been going on, which Mrs Seddon said she very much doubted.

Tatty had known when her mother had first commenced her arrangement with Mr Wooten, and so had Mrs Seddon, and she'd known before that of Betsy's history as a prostitute.

Because her little family had been so insular and self-contained, she hadn't realised her parents were an odd couple even though, when she was old enough to hear it, they'd shared with her the story of their courtship. So she knew that her mother had been a pretty twenty-five-year-old croupier and sometime 'demi-mondaine' when she'd met and married Hector, who'd been forty-six, stout and balding, a successful accountant with his own business, and addicted to the card tables. However, she hadn't known what a demi-mondaine was until at the age of sixteen she'd attended Mrs Belvedere's Academy for Young Ladies, a finishing school where she'd been nastily informed by a clique of girls that her father had married well beneath his social standing and that her mother had been a prostitute – another word for a demi-mondaine. But over the years she had seen for herself that her parents' union was a very happy one, so she decided that if they didn't care, why should she?

And then everything changed when halfway through her year at Mrs Belvedere's her father dropped dead of apoplexy in his office, his death revealing the devastating news that he'd remortgaged the house and there was no money in the bank – all apparently spent on gambling. But as the law dictated that wives couldn't inherit property, businesses or money in any case, he'd evidently tried to make amends for his failings (and flout the law) by making arrangements in his will for his senior clerk, at that time Selwyn Boyd, to direct funds from the accounting business into a trust, which would afford her mother a regular allowance and pay the mortgage on the house. Mr Boyd, however, soon drank the business into bankruptcy, leaving her and her mother penniless, hence their need to take in lodgers to pay the mortgage. The only good thing to come out of that awful year was that she'd had to withdraw from Mrs Belvedere's because there was no money for the fees.

The lodgers' board payments didn't cover everything – expenses, salaries, taxes and the mortgage – so Betsy had reluctantly made arrangements with Mr Wooten to provide the sort of services that didn't usually come with bed and board. Tatty hadn't much liked the situation when Betsy told her, but she knew they needed the money and she trusted her mother to know what she was doing. And it was never mentioned again until Betsy fell seriously ill.

Mrs Seddon said, 'Well, Mr Wooten can always find board elsewhere if arrangements here are no longer to his liking.'

'Yes, he can.'

Lorna reappeared then, clutching a white silk damask tablecloth stiff with starch. 'What about this one? It's a bit big but we could fold it lots of times.'

'That's perfect, Lorna,' Tatty said. 'Would you like to set the breakfast table? The lodgers will be down soon.'

When she'd gone yet again, Mrs Seddon said, 'Tatty, I know I said it could be quite a while before God takes your mother, but are you prepared for when he does?'

Tatty said, 'Where are the oats?'

Mrs Seddon said, 'Will you not answer me?'

'I don't really want to talk about it. Not right now.' Tatty thought the kitchen was getting horribly hot and she felt like going outside.

Mrs Seddon pushed her spectacles up her nose. 'Why not?'

'Because it's going to be soon, isn't it?'

'I really don't know, love. I wish I did.' Mrs Seddon shook her head. 'No, I don't wish that at all. That would be such a curse, to know when someone's life will end.'

Tatty felt tears prick her eyes, and pressed her palms against them to stop any renegade tears.

'Do you need to pray?' Mrs Seddon asked.

Not really, Tatty thought.

'Would you like to take a few minutes in your room? Or perhaps outside in the fresh air. You look flushed.'

Tatty nodded and went out into the backyard, where it was definitely cooler. She walked past the privy and the clothesline and down the path to the apple tree that was covered in moss and produced sour little apples. And then she prayed, asking God for peaceful rest in heaven for her father, and for her mother to be saved from her illness and to be returned to good health as quickly as possible.

As usual, she didn't get any response.

Or relief.

*

In the third week of September, Tatty took up Betsy's tea tray, setting it on the hall floor before she knocked.

'Ma,' she said as she slowly – apprehensively – opened the bedroom door. 'Ma?'

It seemed that nothing at all was moving in her mother's room, not even time. She crossed the floor and set the tray down on a side table.

She stared down at her mother, who was lying on her side, one hand resting near her cheek. Her eyes were closed.

She seemed very still. *Very* still.

'Ma?'

Blood suddenly pounded in Tatty's ears and she didn't want to but she knew she had to: she touched her mother's face. It was as cold as if Betsy had been outside on a winter's night.

'Oh no, Ma, please don't.'

Tatty stood still for a moment, then, walking as though she were in a dream, opened the drapes to let in the weak dawn light, then returned to her mother. Her face was extremely pale and her lips, eyelids and fingernails were tinged with blue.

She was dead.

Her mother had died.

Tatty pulled up a chair and sat beside the bed. Her head throbbed and her heart felt as though it had burst, but, now that the time had come, she couldn't cry. Everything was jammed in her throat. There, the pain was excruciating.

She wasn't sure how long she sat there but eventually she heard someone tapping on the open door.

It was Mr Denham.

'I do beg your pardon and I'm so sorry to interrupt but, well, the door ...' A pause. 'Is everything all right?'

In a voice that sounded to her altogether like someone else's, Tatty said, 'My mother has died.'

'Good God, that's dreadful! May I be of help?'

'I ...' Tatty began, then gave up.

'Can I fetch someone for you? Mrs Seddon, at least. Family? Or the undertaker?'

Tatty cleared her throat. 'Thank you, but I'll tell Mrs Seddon and Lorna, and there really isn't anyone else to inform.' She stood. 'If you don't mind, I don't think we can prepare your breakfasts today. Could you please make your own arrangements?'

'Of course. I'll tell Mr Wooten he'll have to spill his food somewhere else this morning. I'm so sorry, Miss Caldwell. Please accept my condolences.'

'Thank you.'

Tatty left him to knock on Mr Wooten's door and made her way downstairs. By the time she reached the kitchen she'd started to cry, which really was a relief, physically at least.

Mrs Seddon knew immediately. 'Oh, Lord, she's gone, hasn't she?'

Tatty nodded and suddenly she was wrapped in Mrs Seddon's plump, immensely comforting arms, which reminded her of Betsy's hugs before she'd lost so much weight through illness. She cried even harder, and not the tidy, lady-like weeping that had been recommended at Mrs Belvedere's finishing school, but noisy, ugly bawling. Mrs Seddon held and rocked her, getting tears and snot all over her shoulder. Eventually Tatty's crying slowed and devolved into teary sniffs, and she messily blew her nose.

'Where's Lorna?' she asked.

'Stripping our beds. Laundry day today.'

'Oh. So it is.'

'But that will have to wait,' Mrs Seddon said. 'And so will the lodgers, this morning.'

'I spoke to Mr Denham. I sent them out for their breakfasts.'

'Well, you *are* a clever girl. Shall I go and tell Lorna or would you like to? She'll be very upset.'

Tatty knew that. 'Would you? Please?'

'Of course. And then would you like to lay your mother out? Lorna and I will help you.'

No, Tatty thought, I would not like to lay my mother out. She would like her mother to still be alive and healthy and happy, with a husband who was also still alive, but that wasn't the way things were. *Nothing* was the way things were. She felt as though she had no control over anything now. 'Yes, please. I'll get everything ready,' she said, her voice breaking on the last word.

'Everything' meant hot water, soap, washcloths, towels, muslin and scissors, which Tatty had learnt were required for laying out when her father's body had come home. She began collecting things and taking them to Betsy's room, wincing when she heard Lorna's wails start upstairs in the servants' quarters. She'd taken Hector's death badly, too. Poor love.

She took the hot water up last, then sat beside her mother and waited. Finally, Lorna's howling stopped and she and Mrs Seddon appeared.

'Is she in heaven now?' Lorna asked, eyeing Betsy's cold, still body.

'She will be soon, dear,' Mrs Seddon said. 'Come on, let's get her sorted.'

Between them Tatty and Mrs Seddon rolled Betsy onto her back and removed her nightdress. Tatty thought she must have died some time earlier in the night because blood had gathered all down her right side and stained her skin purple, and rigor mortis had begun, stiffening her hands, feet and ankles, and her jaw. They lovingly washed her from top to toe and dried her, and Tatty brushed her hair until it lay in pretty waves and tied her jaw with a strip of muslin to keep her mouth closed. Then Tatty asked Lorna to choose a gown for Betsy to wear.

This set off Mrs Seddon, who made a noise between a sob and an oink and said, 'You can be very kind, you know, Tatiana Caldwell.' And then she said, 'Oh Betsy, how did things go so wrong?' and burst into tears.

This upset Lorna again, and also Tatty, who laid her head on her mother's cold, bare breast and sobbed and sobbed.

Eventually they all ran out of tears, Lorna picked a dress – a lovely purple taffeta gown, one of the few that hadn't been sold – and they dressed Betsy, although the gown was too big now, and covered her to her waist with a clean sheet.

Mrs Seddon said, 'You'll have to engage an undertaker.'

'I know, but I'm definitely not going back to the one who did Pa's funeral,' Tatty said.

'Good Lord, he was a shyster, wasn't he?'

'No, that's not right,' Lorna said. 'Mrs Caldwell said he was a fucker.'

'That will do, dear,' Mrs Seddon said.

Tatty wanted to laugh and cry again at the same time at the reminder of her mother's colourful language. The undertaker *had* been deeply unpleasant. At the time of her father's death she and her mother had had no money at all, and thought they'd have to bury Hector on the parish. That would have meant no funeral, burial in a mass grave with no headstone, and the most devastating social shame. But then Betsy had sold her jewellery and they'd scraped together enough for mourning clothes and a very modest funeral with the bare minimum required for respectability. The undertaker, however, had badgered them to spend more, then belittled their financial position, insisted on payment in advance and tried to overcharge them. Her mother's assessment of him had been very apt.

'I'll definitely go somewhere else,' Tatty said.

Mrs Seddon said, 'I would. And I know you won't have had a chance to think about this, or maybe you have, but what will you do? You can't stay here running a boarding house to pay the mortgage on a property that will forever be owned by a trust. You're an educated young woman, Tatty. Make something of yourself.'

Tatty nodded in agreement. She was definitely educated. When she was aged from six to fifteen her father had employed a governess to teach her arithmetic and how to read and write to quite advanced levels, and he himself had taught her the principles of accounting, which he said everyone should know. Of course her enrolment at Mrs Belvedere's, learning to paint and arrange flowers and embroider samplers and plan a menu and so forth, hadn't been terribly successful, as she hadn't found any of her classes to be particularly useful. And despite all her education, as far as she could see, her choices were limited: she could either become a governess or get married.

She'd already decided she didn't want to spend her life teaching children their times tables and the difference between 'rain' and 'rein'. She hadn't had much to do with children and, although she didn't actively dislike them, she couldn't see herself spending her life surrounded by them, and that included any of her own. Betsy had been a wonderful mother but Tatty suspected she was going to take after her father – preferably regarding his professional competencies rather than his gambling addiction. So that took marriage off the table for her as she had no intention of working like a lackey to support a husband and/or his business only to end up with nothing if he died – unless, of course, by some twist of fate that business really might benefit her in some way. And if that were the case, she would have to find a way to avoid producing children, if the husband that came with the business insisted on them.

There was a third possibility, but she'd barely thought about it – hadn't really *let* herself think about it – hoping instead that her mother would recover and all would be well again: she could start her own business, perhaps in London, or maybe somewhere else altogether. She really didn't know yet.

'I know you've a lot to think about right now,' Mrs Seddon added, 'but you'll possibly have to make some decisions fairly soon. Especially regarding the lodgers.'

'I know,' Tatty said.

Mrs Seddon said, 'Good girl. Now, your mother told me she'd put money aside for you, and for her funeral, but that you weren't to waste it on anything fancy. Some of the proceeds from Mr Wooten, I gather. It's in a tea caddy in the bottom drawer of her dresser. The key's in the nightstand.'

Feeling hurt, Tatty stared at her. 'She talked to you about dying and not me?'

'Not much. Your mother believed she was going to die, she just didn't know when, and told me she was preparing for it, that's all. I couldn't tell you because she didn't want you to know. She didn't want you to worry.'

Again Tatty thought how needless that had been, when she'd been worried sick anyway. She found the small key in the nightstand while Mrs Seddon fetched the tea caddy. Inside was a paper packet full of cash. Tatty tipped the wad of notes and handful of coins onto the end of the bed.

'Hell, she must have been charging him the earth!'

Tatty looked at Mrs Seddon, who shrugged. 'Your mother was just as savvy as your father, in her own way.'

Tatty counted the money, then counted it again. 'There's almost a hundred and nine pounds here!'

Lorna gasped. 'You're rich, Tatty!'

'Well, not really, but it is quite a tidy sum.'

'Which is not to be spent on a fancy funeral, remember,' Mrs Seddon said. 'It's for you.'

*

Tatty engaged the services of Dunn and Dunn Ltd to arrange Betsy's funeral. On the day of her death they supplied a coffin fitted with a small pillow and lined with white cotton crape, and Tatty ordered a wood-panelled hearse pulled by two black horses – black velvet drapes only, no ostrich plumes – a four-person mourners' coach, and no attendants, paid for in advance. Mr Dunn did his absolute best to bully her into booking more mourners' coaches, because surely family and many close friends would want to attend the funeral of such a well-respected widow as Mrs Caldwell, but Tatty resisted his chivvying and refused to budge.

She knew for a fact there wouldn't be mourners at Betsy's funeral, just as there hadn't been at her father's. When they'd married, Hector's family had completely disowned him, and Betsy had severed ties with her side to avoid the inevitable eventuality of certain members knocking on her door with their hands out. One coach was ample for her funeral, as there would only be Tatty, Mrs Seddon and Lorna in attendance. And Mr Denham, who had unexpectedly asked Tatty if he might also attend. Of course she said yes.

The burial was at Bow Cemetery, where her father had been interred. The fee to open Hector's grave and lay Betsy's coffin on top was a little over half the cost of buying a new plot. She felt a *very* odd sense of déjà vu: the only difference between this interment and her father's was that Mr Denham was attending, and this time she was burying her mother.

It was raining and the wind was up. The skies had been heavy with clouds the colour of dirty pewter all morning and she'd hoped the rain would hold off until after the burial, but it hadn't. By the time they arrived at Bow Cemetery it was pouring, and the hearse followed by the carriage splashed through large puddles in the thoroughfare through the cemetery. Arriving at Hector's grave, a very wet Mr Dunn, who had been riding on the open seat of the hearse, opened the carriage door with rain running off the brim of his top hat and asked what she wanted to do.

'Get on with it, I suppose,' Tatty said. 'We can't sit here all afternoon waiting for the rain to stop.'

Mr Dunn nodded and stepped back, holding the door.

Tatty got out, ignoring Mrs Seddon's exhortation to remember her umbrella. What use would an umbrella be when she was standing in a muddy puddle and the wind was blowing the rain almost sideways?

Mr Denham clearly thought the same as he alighted from the carriage umbrella-less, and Lorna didn't have one either. Mrs Seddon's blew inside out the moment she unfurled it. The reverend made a mad dash from the tree under whose boughs he'd been sheltering, his vestments flapping, and met them as they removed Betsy's coffin from the hearse and carried it to the grave. The gravediggers had done the best job they could, given the weather, and covered the pile of dirt next to the newly opened grave with a tarpaulin in the hope it wouldn't turn to mud and ooze everywhere. Tatty had a quick peek but all she could see of her father's coffin was a glimpse of the lid, though she didn't know what she'd expected, or even why she'd looked. Planks had been laid along the sides of the grave and across it. Betsy's coffin was rested on those while the reverend administered the last rites and rain dripped off the noses of the little group of mourners.

Finally, Betsy was lowered into the ground to join Hector, and the gravediggers, looking exactly like a pair of drowned grey rats, began to shovel the excavated soil back into the grave. Altogether, Tatty thought, the entire business had been utterly miserable.

After the funeral, when everyone had returned home and changed into dry clothes, Tatty decided to take stock of what was in the house and asked Mrs Seddon to help. Very little had been purchased since Hector and Betsy married, with the result that most items – furniture and furnishings – looked rather worn.

'You probably wouldn't get much for the contents if you wanted to sell them,' Mrs Seddon said, 'which you can't do because you don't own them. They'd be considered chattels.'

'It would be easy enough, though,' Tatty said. 'To sell them, I mean. People who buy house lots don't tend to bother about the legal side of things.'

'Who told you that?'

'Ma.'

'Well, she was probably right,' Mrs Seddon said. 'Do you want to sell it all? Have you an idea germinating in that clever head of yours?'

Tatty did have an idea, one she'd been thinking very hard about for several days.

'I've decided I want to own a business. I want to make money.' Tatty hesitated, then added, 'And I want to be independent. I don't want what happened to Ma to happen to me.'

'Brave words and I'm sure you can achieve that, but you'll lose it all if you marry,' Mrs Seddon warned.

'I'm not going to marry.'

'Never?'

'No. Well, probably never. I don't want to work hard then have to give everything I own to a husband, not necessarily even a decent one like my father. That must have annoyed you, handing over everything you'd earnt, before you were widowed.'

Mrs Seddon said, 'I've never had a husband, love, and I've never been widowed. I'm a spinster. All cooks are called missus. It's tradition. What sort of business are you thinking of?'

'I don't know, but definitely not running a lodging house.'

'So you'll have to get rid of Mr Denham and Mr Wooten?'

Tatty nodded.

'Do you want me to do that?'

Tatty said no thank you, she'd do it. She was quite happy kicking Mr Wooten out into the street but she'd rather come to like Albert Denham. He'd been kind and never a bother and she wanted to explain to him her reasons for ending the boarding arrangement.

'And then what?' Mrs Seddon asked.

Tatty said, 'And then I'm going to emigrate.'

Maggie Seddon looked so astonished that Tatty laughed.

'*Emigrate?*' Mrs Seddon exclaimed. 'Good Lord, girl, where to? And what on earth for?'

'To New South Wales in Australia, so I can start again. I don't have any ties here, do I?'

'You have me and Lorna.'

'Yes, I do, and you and Lorna have your own family.'

Mrs Seddon made a face. 'Yes, well, I have mentioned them now and then I must admit, but like a lot of people we don't all get on.'

'Oh.' Tatty felt disappointed. She'd always thought Mrs Seddon's sprawling family sounded lovely.

Mrs Seddon sighed. 'There's no harm in telling you, I suppose, but you can't ever tell Lorna this. She thinks she came to live with me because her mother, my younger sister, Olive, already had too many kids. Lorna was her ninth baby and she got stuck during the birth and by the time the midwife finally got her out she was blue and floppy and barely breathing, the poor little thing. I was there. It was winter. Olive told the midwife to put her behind the privy under a sack in the snow and let her die. Well, an hour or so later I crept out for a look and she was still alive so I took her home and she became mine, though she grew up a little daft, as you well know. I never spoke to my sister again. The whole family knew what happened and it caused ripples, I can assure you. Some of them think I'm a she-devil for interfering with God's will and they've never let me forget it, and the rest think I did the right thing saving a defenceless infant.'

'They left her in the snow to die?' Tatty didn't know whether she was horrified at what Olive had done, or stunned by her pragmatic solution to limiting her already large family.

'It happens far more often than you might think,' Mrs Seddon said. 'Anyway, Lorna's my constant responsibility and I love her, so, yes, I do have her, but I'm not quite so attached to some of my family.'

'Well, I've made up my mind,' Tatty said. 'I'm forgetting about this house, scraping together all the money I can, and I'm buying a passage to Australia. Look at this.'

She passed Mrs Seddon an advertisement cut from *The Daily Telegraph*, which read:

Notice to Young Women Desirous of Bettering Their Condition –

Female Emigration to Sydney, New South Wales:

A Free Passage
In New South Wales (and Victoria and Tasmania), there is a dearth of Women compared with the whole number of People, so that it is impossible to obtain Women enough as Female Servants, other Female Employments, and even Wives. The consequence is that desirable employment situations, with good wages and living conditions, are abundant, and opportunities for industrious and resourceful Females abound. Enjoy favourable year-round Weather, share in the prosperity of the Colonies, and be rewarded for your Labour.
   Every information may be obtained on application (personally or by letter) at the Emigrant Depot, 15 Fish Street, London.

Mrs Seddon said, 'That's all very well but what about me and Lorna?'

'Come with me. Please,' Tatty said with fingers and toes mentally crossed. 'That would be wonderful.'

Mrs Seddon snorted. 'Don't be ridiculous. I'm fifty-two and I'm *far* too old to be gallivanting around the world. And poor Lorna: she'd have a conniption the minute she saw one of those bungaroos they have over there.'

'I think they're called kangaroos and I doubt they hop up and down the main street of Sydney. And even if they did she'd get used to them.'

'I'm not sure she would. No, we're staying here, thank you.'

Tatty felt hot tears well up again at the thought of quite possibly never seeing Lorna and Mrs Seddon again. 'I'll miss you horribly.'

'And we'll miss you, love.'

Tatty blew her nose. 'What will *you* do?'

'Oh, we'll find another position easily enough.' Mrs Seddon looked at the advertisement again. 'And it's free? Someone else pays for you to go?'

'Apparently the British and Australian governments both do, but I'm paying my own way,' Tatty said. 'I don't want to owe anybody anything. A completely new start, that's what I want.'

Part Two

1865

*Strange secrets are let out by Death,
Who blabs so oft the follies of this world*

Robert Browning, 1835

Chapter Two

January 1865, Sydney, New South Wales, Australia

Having arrived in Sydney on the last day of December 1864, Tatty had now been staying at the Sydney Female Immigration Depot for over a week. Evidently the depot had once been a convict barracks, and now the top floor of the three-storey building was an asylum for elderly, destitute, and mentally and terminally ill women. Female migrants newly arrived in New South Wales and looking for work like Tatty lived temporarily on the floor below, in dormitories furnished with iron beds and hard mattresses. The dormitories were clean but rats nested under the floorboards and skittered out to steal food and anything else tempting that wasn't carefully hidden away. That was all right as far as Tatty was concerned – anything was infinitely better than the last thirteen crowded, stinking and airless weeks she'd spent wedged in steerage class below decks at sea. She *had* paid her own way, but not nearly enough for a private cabin.

It had been a hideous experience, made worse by extreme seasickness – hers and almost everyone else's – and one she hoped never to repeat. The sickness had subsided after a week or so, which had improved matters in the sense that she had no longer actively prayed for death. Instead, she'd just felt empty – physically from prolonged vomiting and lack of food, and emotionally from grieving, the knowledge that she'd left behind the last people who knew and loved her, and the realisation that she was truly alone. She wondered then if she had made a terrible mistake leaving London. But as she'd rested in her narrow bunk, watching other single girls and women mingling, and mothers with babies and small children helping one another, and single young men sharing a joke at mealtimes, she came to the conclusion that being alone was very likely the result of a frame of mind. If she didn't want to be alone, she had only to decide not to be and then act on that decision.

When she finally felt well enough to go up on deck she took a book because there was only very dim light below decks and she couldn't see to read. On the third day of sitting tucked into a corner (passengers were only allowed on deck if they kept out of the way of the crew) absorbed in her well-thumbed copy of WM Thackeray's *Vanity Fair*, another steerage passenger approached her and asked if she would teach her four children to read and write. They were aged from six to ten, she said, and she could pay Tatty a shilling per session.

Tatty had left England with a substantial nest egg of one hundred and twenty-one pounds and sixteen shillings (which was the money her mother had earnt, less the funeral fee, her passage, and a gift of twenty pounds to Mrs Seddon and Lorna for their service on behalf of her parents, plus seventeen pounds she had made flogging her house-lot of used furniture). She didn't need work teaching children to read and write.

'I don't have experience as a teacher,' Tatty said, her hand shielding her eyes so she could see the woman against the sun.

'You can read and write, though,' the woman said. 'You're reading a book now. That's enough, isn't it? I thought it'd be good if my kids could even just write their names by the time we get there.'

Tatty noted the woman's clothes – worn and old but carefully patched and darned. Her children's clothes would no doubt be the same, yet the woman was willing to spend considerable money she probably couldn't afford on them learning the basics of writing and reading so they were less disadvantaged.

'All right,' she said. 'I'll teach them, but we'll need to find some scrap paper and ink pens, which is unlikely, or chalk so we can write on the deck.'

The woman grinned delightedly and clapped her hands.

'And my fee is tuppence per session,' Tatty added.

'But that's nothing.'

'No it isn't: it's my fee.'

At the midday meal, which steerage passengers ate at long tables below deck, Tatty felt disconcertingly as though she was being stared at. At first it was just the woman she'd met on deck, sitting farther down the table with her brood, waving gaily to her. She waved back. Then she realised others were also sending glances in her direction. Then a woman across the table and down a few places tentatively raised her hand to attract her attention.

Unfortunately, Tatty didn't know her name. 'Hello?'

'Mrs Cox says you're going to teach her kids to read and write. Will you teach mine as well? I can pay.'

'And mine as well?' another woman said.

'And ours, too, please?' a man added.

And that was how Tatty ended up teaching twenty-six children the very basics of reading and writing for not much pay – because it was something to do and it took her mind off being packed into steerage like a sardine in an extremely smelly tin, and she thought that everyone should be able to at least read and understand a written agreement, and sign their own name. The experience of teaching children wasn't quite as challenging as she'd previously assumed – although there were plenty of short attention spans and outbursts of cheekiness to deal with – and was even rather satisfying in its own way. However, after three months of doing so she nevertheless remained convinced that she wasn't destined to pursue a career as a governess.

And now she was here at the Immigration Depot with other single girls and women recently arrived in New South Wales.

Tatty found Sydney to be very, very different from London, though so far she hadn't had much opportunity to explore. It was a much smaller and newer town – only eighty-five or so years old, they said – and built on a very beautiful harbour rather than a river. And the light! Tatty thought it sparkled. Perhaps it had something to do with the never-ending aquamarine sky. And there were so many gorgeous birds Tatty had never seen before. They reminded her of jewels, adorning the trees. They were noisy, though, surprisingly so. There were horrors, too – in particular the spiders, monsters she'd never have conjured even in her worst nightmares and enough to send girls running from rooms, screaming hysterically, including her. Perhaps the hardest thing to adjust to was the heat. At home, the summer her father had died had been hot, but here the heat was *utterly* enervating and apparently nothing out of the ordinary for an Antipodean January. She sweated all day long, drank cup after cup of tea, spent her evenings sponging sweat stains out of her black mourning dresses (worn for her mother now, rather than her father), then went to bed and suffered through nights sometimes not much cooler than the days. The heat was something she hadn't reckoned with, and she hoped she'd get used to it. She was never at her best in the mornings and was even worse if she hadn't had a good night's sleep.

This, she thought, was unfortunate, because prospective employers came to the Immigration Depot in the mornings, usually to hire girls in positions such as nursemaid, kitchenhand and housemaid. Tatty was grateful she'd paid her own way to Australia, as girls who'd opted for the 'free' passage would be indentured, whereby their employers were required to train them in some sort of skill and pay them for their labour. On the other hand, an employer could end an indentured employee's contract for bad behaviour, or if both parties agreed on the termination. Tatty felt this gave an employer the upper hand, as the employee couldn't herself decide to leave.

Also, she hated the hiring room because potential employers, usually men, came in and wandered about staring beadily at the girls on offer as though they were fillies at the saleyards. (She'd never been to a horse sale but imagined there was a similarity.) Now and then employers came in looking for girls to fill more elevated positions such as milliner, dressmaker, senior cook, supervising laundress, and at one point she was offered a position as an actual governess but turned it down. It didn't fit in with her plans: she couldn't see how she could develop the position of governess into a business, unless she eventually established a company that hired out governesses, which didn't seem likely. If *she* were a governess she'd rather work for herself.

Finally, after almost three weeks, when she was beginning to worry she might have to take a position she didn't want then find something more suitable later, the right employer walked into the Immigration Depot's hiring room.

He too wandered about inspecting all the available girls – an almost entirely new group by now except for Tatty and a few others – but his gaze kept sliding back to her. It was still very hot and she was tired and had a headache from inadequate sleep, and she wasn't in a particularly good mood. She watched him as he approached.

He appeared to be somewhere in his forties, so not young, and neither was he handsome. His cinnamon-coloured hair was greying, he had a wide mouth, a big nose, a raw complexion and deep frown lines between his brows. He wore black from his hat to his boots: Tatty checked for signs he might be clergy but saw none. His hands were bony and so, probably, was the rest of him.

'Good morning,' he said. 'My name is Titus Crowe. Are you Miss Tatiana Caldwell? The matron here has recommended you to me. She says you are an educated girl.'

Tatty didn't know whether to be pleased about that or not. 'Good morning. Yes, I am.'

'And how old are you?'

'Seventeen.'

'When will you turn eighteen?'

'In March.'

'I assume you can read and write?'

Tatty thought it was time to rein him in. 'Excuse me, Mr Crowe, but would you mind telling me what sort of apprentice or employee you're looking for? Because I could well be thoroughly unsuitable, and I don't want to waste your time.' And I certainly don't want you to waste mine.

'I am an undertaker and I'm looking for an assistant, specifically a female. Obviously.'

Tatty eyed him as she mulled the possibilities.

'I see that has silenced you,' Mr Crowe said.

Tatty said, 'Yes, I can read and write. What duties would this assistant be expected to ... undertake?'

'Quite a variety, including most of the funereal arts, so I'm looking for someone who isn't squeamish. Are you?'

'I don't think so.'

'Good. It's occurred to me that having a woman on my staff would provide a compassionate touch I believe many customers may appreciate during times of bereavement. To my knowledge no other undertaking business in Sydney has a female on staff. I feel it would be of real benefit to Crowe Funeral Services. I also want someone to manage the paperwork – the correspondence and accounts and bookkeeping and such. I don't have time to keep track of it all these days. Are you numerate? Are you capable of managing accounts? The matron here said she thought you might be.'

Tatty confirmed she was.

'Excellent. Finally, there are domestic duties. I already have a live-in housemaid. Her name is Cora. She cleans, cooks and also looks after my mother, Mrs Lydia Crowe, who is bed-bound and suffers from senility. It's a lot for Cora to do. I'd expect you to help her from time to time. My mother can be somewhat demanding.'

Tatty wasn't sure she particularly liked the sound of that. 'May I ask, is there a Mrs Titus Crowe?'

Because if there was, why wasn't *she* looking after Mrs Crowe senior?

'My wife died when lying in, along with our child.'

'Oh, I'm so sorry.'

There was an awkward pause, then Titus said, 'Are you interested in the position? I can pay you a reasonable wage, which I think you'll find is higher than what you might have expected in England for similar duties, diverse though they are. And of course accommodation and meals will be included.'

Tatty thought she was unlikely to get a better offer, at least in the short term. And she would learn a trade she could possibly use to her advantage at some point and that she suspected she might enjoy, earn a steady income (and keep her nest egg), and have somewhere safe to live.

'Thank you very much, Mr Crowe. I accept.'

'Good. You will be indentured, so if we both find the arrangement unsatisfactory we can end the agreement. If I find your performance unsatisfactory, then I can end the agreement. Is that understood?'

Tatty shook her head. 'I'm afraid *you've* misunderstood, Mr Crowe. I paid my own way to this part of the world and I don't owe any government anything, therefore I am not subject to indentured employment. I'm a free agent.'

Titus looked at her, his face impassive, and for a moment she thought he might just walk off.

Then he said, 'Then I will revise my offer. The details pertaining to duties, wages, accommodation and meals stand. If we both find the arrangement unsatisfactory we can end our agreement. If I find your performance unsatisfactory, then I can end the agreement. If you are dissatisfied, you of course may leave. Is that acceptable to you?'

'Yes, it is, thank you,' Tatty said.

'So you accept the position?'

'Yes.'

'Good. I have my cart outside, so if you would have your belongings brought down?'

Tatty went upstairs and packed her things, said goodbye to Matron and her dormitory mates, then watched as Titus Crowe loaded her trunk onto his cart. He might be thin but he was obviously strong. She took a seat beside him, glad of the first tiny breeze she'd felt in days as the horse moved off across the square in front of the depot.

'You're wearing black,' Mr Crowe said. 'May I ask why?'

'My mother died recently.' Tatty wondered whether to tell him her father was also dead, then decided she wouldn't.

'Please accept my condolences. I'll mention now that we wear black as a matter of course at Crowe Funeral Services. Day and night. I believe it's more respectful to our customers. And we *are* undertakers.'

'How many staff do you have?'

Mr Crowe told her and it was fewer than Tatty expected for a business likely to be open all hours. He and his staff must be run ragged.

'Are you leaving family behind in England?' he asked.

'Yes,' Tatty said, and she was. She just didn't know them.

'What made you choose to emigrate?' Mr Crowe reined in to let a coach and four exit Hyde Park. Tatty had been for several walks there and hadn't been impressed: the park wasn't nearly as nice, or as big, as Hyde Park in London.

'The same reasons as anyone else, I'm sure. Opportunities. A new life.' To stop him asking more nosy questions, Tatty said, 'Where are we going?'

'To my business premises on George Street, which is the town's main thoroughfare. I have stables, and accommodation for myself, my mother, Cora, and now, of course, you. Henry, my ostler, lives over the stables, as does Robert, my other assistant.'

As it happened George Street wasn't far away, so neither was Crowe Funeral Services. Tatty had already noticed that the streets of Sydney were befouled with almost as much horse and bullock shit as were London's, and open drains were filled with human waste, rotting vegetable matter, and fish and animal offal, all of which absolutely reeked in the summer heat. Her nose also told her the town had its share of tanneries and candle factories and butcheries and overflowing graveyards, all of which also contributed to the smell. She imagined that when it rained, if it ever did rain because in the weeks she'd been in Sydney nothing more than a few random spits had fallen from the sky, all the filth would be washed from the streets and the drains and perhaps even the cesspits, down the hills on which Sydney sat and into the harbour from where it would be swept out to sea, and everyone could breathe freely again in a clean, fresh town. If only it *would* rain.

Titus drove the cart down a narrow carriageway off George Street that culminated in a stable yard behind a two-storey weatherboard building facing directly onto the street. The roof was of corrugated iron and the whole appeared recently constructed. At the rear were a stable block and a double carriage house. A nice-looking, well-built man Tatty thought was probably in his early thirties appeared from the stables and took hold of the horse's reins as Titus jumped to the ground.

'Henry, this is Miss Tatiana Caldwell, who is now working for us. Miss Caldwell, this is Henry Dodds. He looks after the horses and vehicles, drives the hearse and does various other duties.'

Henry Dodds reached up and helped Tatty down from the cart. 'Morning, Miss Caldwell. Very nice to meet you.'

'Good morning, Mr Dodds.' Tatty brushed dust off her dress. She was *covered* in it.

Mr Dodds had a moderately deep, slightly gruff voice that she might have found attractive if she was noticing that sort of thing, which she wasn't. He also had dark blond hair and was without sideburns, a beard or a moustache, some combination of which the majority of men seemed to favour.

'It's Henry,' he said. 'No one calls me Mr Dodds.'

'Thank you, I appreciate that,' Tatty said, realising immediately that she sounded a little frosty and arrogant. She cast about for something more cordial to add, and failed.

Titus said, 'You'll find this is a very dusty town in summer, I'm afraid. Henry, take Miss Caldwell's trunk upstairs, will you?'

In the kitchen at the back of the house – a space even hotter than the yard because it was dominated by a merrily burning cooking range – Titus introduced Tatty to Cora, whose surname was Billings.

Cora had a red face, though Tatty suspected it wasn't red all the time, sweat-damp hair the colour of hazelnuts, ears that stuck out somewhat, and a pretty smile.

'Morning and welcome!' Cora said as she stirred a pot. 'It'll be nice to have someone else to talk to. But I'd better get on with this. Her ladyship'll be wondering where her dinner is. Or maybe not. She might think she's already had it.'

'That's enough of that, Cora. She's referring to my mother,' Titus said to Tatty by way of explanation. 'Would you care to meet her now, or after the midday meal? She doesn't leave her room.'

Tatty didn't really want to meet Lydia Crowe at all but she might as well get it over with. 'I'd like to meet her now, please.'

She followed Titus into the house proper, having a good look at the modest furnishings as they went, then upstairs and along a hallway to a closed door at the far end. He knocked: a thin, scratchy voice called out in response.

He opened the door, entered, then backed out again immediately, bringing the stink of human faeces with him. For an awful, confusing moment Tatty thought he'd suddenly soiled himself, then realised the source of the smell must be his mother. He shut the door behind him, his lips pressed together with annoyance and his face flushed with embarrassment.

'You'll have to meet her after dinner. Perhaps you could unpack your trunk now. I'll show you to your accommodation. Your room is next to Cora's.'

He ushered her down to the other end of the hallway and around a corner. Tatty was faced with two more doors. One was closed – probably Cora's room, she thought – and the other open to reveal a small room containing a bed, a chest of drawers, a narrow robe and her trunk sitting in the middle of the floor.

'I'll leave you to organise your possessions,' Titus said. 'I expect Cora will serve the midday meal in about an hour, once she's attended to my mother.'

Tatty thanked him, feeling like a guest, which he ruined (not unreasonably) by saying, 'You will start work after that. Once you've met my mother Cora can show you where everything is kept in the house. We have a funeral this afternoon so I'll familiarise you with the business facilities downstairs tomorrow morning.'

An hour later, at the table in a dining room furnished with little more than an enormous sideboard, the dining suite and three insipid and badly executed watercolours of local landscapes (Lydia Crowe's efforts? Tatty wondered), sat Titus, Henry and a boy Tatty hadn't met. Cora served and sat down.

Titus said, 'Miss Caldwell, this is Robert Edmonds. He works for me full time and as I said earlier he also lives with us. He does more or less what you'll soon be doing, except you won't be permitted to do the roles that are specific to men. Robert delivers coffins to the homes of the dead; discusses with the bereaved what services they would like at the funeral, encourages them to pay for more, naturally – I *am* running a business here, after all, not a charity – sometimes walks at the head of the funeral procession if we're doing without mutes, which as a female, Miss Caldwell, you will *never* do; helps load bodies on and off the hearses; now and then fills in as a mute himself, again not a role for you; can drive a carriage if necessary; does general jobs around here; helps Henry with the vehicles, and so on. We do hire extra staff from time to time when required, for example, when an elaborate funeral is requested, but that's only ever a temporary arrangement.'

'Hello, Robert,' Tatty said. 'You sound rather busy.'

Robert looked like he wasn't much older than she was – perhaps nineteen or twenty at the most. He was tall and had wide shoulders, nice eyes, thick hair and quite a spotty face, and he seemed shy.

'Good afternoon, miss,' Robert replied.

'It's Tatiana. Tatty, usually.'

Cora shrieked with laughter. 'Tatty! That's really funny!'

Tatty wondered if Cora was a bit simple, or just easily amused.

Titus said, 'That's enough, Cora! I've already warned you once today.'

'It *is* funny, though,' Cora insisted.

'I suppose it is,' Tatty said. 'The story of how I was named that definitely is. My mother once saw a performance of Shakespeare's *A Midsummer Night's Dream* and really liked Titania, Queen of the Fairies. When I was born she was desperate to call me that but misremembered the name and christened me Tatiana, and my father didn't have the heart to tell her. So Tatiana I am, or more often Tatty.'

As if she hadn't spoken, Titus said, 'You may think it unusual, Tatiana, staff taking meals with the master of the house, something I'm sure you never saw in London.'

'Actually our staff did eat with us,' Tatty said, stopping herself before she said, 'Especially after Pa died.'

'You had staff?' Titus said.

He seemed surprised, which puzzled Tatty. How did he think her family had managed to educate her without money and the comforts that money afforded? She nodded in reply and concentrated on her tough boiled mutton, suet dumplings and carrots.

'When Mrs Crowe senior was more physically capable she and I ate here in the dining room,' Titus said, 'and the staff ate in the kitchen, but frankly it wasted time. We can get very busy, especially in winter. So now we all eat together so we can discuss our work. And social conventions aren't quite the same in New South Wales as they are in England.'

'I have heard talk along similar lines,' Tatty said.

Henry said he'd finished putting new shoes on Spirit (whom Tatty assumed was a horse) and now he wasn't limping at all, and Cora said Mrs Crowe had seemed to enjoy her mushed-up dumplings, carrots and shredded mutton. Robert said he'd delivered the extra flowers to the Gaynor house, and informed Titus that they'd changed their minds about the third mourners' coach. They'd decided they only wanted two now.

Titus said, 'I hope you told them two instead of three isn't going to make much difference to the overall fee?'

'I did.'

'Damned Jews,' Titus muttered and shovelled down the last forkfuls of his meat and carrots.

Robert said, 'No, I don't think they are Jews. I think they're Welsh.'

Titus grunted, wiped his mouth on a napkin, stood and left the room.

'He's annoyed because Lydia shat herself again,' Cora said. 'I don't know why: he doesn't have to clean her up. I do.'

Tatty imagined the hands that had prepared their meal also tending to Lydia Crowe, and retched.

'Are you all right?' Cora asked.

'Yes, it's just ...' Tatty made a face.

'Jesus, girl!' Cora exclaimed. 'I washed my hands! Did you think I'd serve mutton, dumplings, carrots and shit for dinner?'

'For God's sake, Cora,' Henry said.

Cora laughed. 'Well, she did, look at her face!'

Tatty carefully blotted her mouth with a napkin, noting it was beautifully laundered – spotlessly clean, starched and ironed. Presumably Cora took care of the table linen (because who else would?), demonstrating a level of skill and very likely close attention to cleanliness. However, the housemaid's assumption that she knew what Tatty was thinking really irritated her and she was tired and feeling altogether quite overwhelmed.

So she said, 'You *might* not have washed your hands. I don't know what sort of pig you are, do I?'

Silence descended. Robert and Henry froze in their seats.

Tatty glared at Cora: Cora glared back.

Then Cora said, 'I'm not any sort of pig. If you could take the time to climb down off your high horse, I think you'll find I'm a very clean person. Anyway, *you're* the one who'll be handling stinking corpses and shoving bloody great needles in them and draining their blood. I'll stick to scrubbing pots and pans and Lydia's dirty under-drawers, thanks.'

Tatty had no idea what Cora was talking about, but now she was quite regretting being rude. She let out a huge, wobbly sigh. 'I'm sorry I said you're a pig. I didn't mean it.'

After a short and suspenseful pause, she and Cora shared a quick smile.

'That's all right,' Cora said. 'I'm sorry I said you're on a high horse. It's probably more of a donkey, a small one.'

From the corner of her eye Tatty saw Henry and Robert exchange a 'that was close' glance.

'Do you need help with the dinner things?' she asked Cora.

Cora said yes, and by the time Titus came looking for her, between them they'd cleared the table, salvaged any leftovers for supper, put the mutton bone aside for soup, and started to wash the plates and cutlery.

'Leave that for Cora,' Titus said. 'I want you to meet my mother.'

Once again Tatty followed him upstairs. This time the door to Lydia's room was open but Titus knocked on it anyway before he entered. Again that reedy voice. He beckoned to Tatty and she went in, not realising until she felt dizzy that she wasn't breathing. The window was open so she cautiously took a small breath, gratefully discovering that the air was now fresh.

An old, old woman lay in bed, propped up against a pile of lace-covered pillows, a single sheet pulled up to her chest and tucked into the mattress as if to keep her prisoner, though she looked far too frail to even think about escaping. Her face was deeply creased in all directions by age, her eyes were pink and rheumy, she was toothless and any hair not hidden beneath a lace-trimmed mob cap was snow white and wispy. She wore a high-necked, long-sleeved nightgown and a bib of sorts tied loosely around her neck so that it lay over her chest and disappeared beneath the bed sheet.

Titus said loudly, 'Mother, this is my new assistant, Miss Tatiana Caldwell.'

Lydia Crowe screwed up her face. 'What?'

Tatty heard Titus stifle a sigh. He raised his voice even further. 'This is Tatiana Caldwell. She's come to work for us.'

Lydia said, 'Speak up.'

Titus fetched an ear trumpet from a side table and handed it to his mother. She placed the wide end over her mouth and repeated, 'Speak up.'

Titus took the trumpet off Lydia, turned it around, put the narrow end in her ear and said into the other end, 'Mother, this is Tatiana Caldwell. She's come to work for me and she'll be helping Cora with you, too.'

Lydia said, 'Where's my dinner? I want my dinner.'

'You've had your dinner,' Titus said. 'Cora gave it to you. She said you enjoyed it.'

Lydia shook her head wildly, nearly dislodging her cap. 'She's *lying*. I didn't get it and I'm so *hungry*. I'm *dying* of hunger.'

Shocked at the old lady's theatrical accusations, Tatty looked at Titus but he didn't seem at all disconcerted.

'Don't fret, Mother, I'll get her to bring you something up.'

'She'll steal it for herself! Gobble, gobble, gobble!'

'I'll talk to her now,' Titus said, and left the room, gesturing for Tatty to follow him. 'Pay no attention, she's having one of her bad days.'

Tatty could see that. 'How old is Mrs Crowe?'

'Seventy-seven.'

Tatty was horrified – she'd thought she was at least ten years older than that. The old lady could possibly go on for another decade. How awful for her, and everyone else.

She helped Cora finish off the dinner dishes, then went outside to the yard and watched while Henry and Robert prepared the hearse – a very beautiful vehicle with four glass sides embellished with gold accents and otherwise painted a gleaming black – and the two magnificent horses pulling it. Their names were Spirit and Phantom, which Tatty thought were splendid names for funeral horses, and they were cloaked in black velvet drapes and wore tall head-dresses of thick black ostrich plumes. They were Belgian Blacks and had, according to Henry, cost Titus an absolute fortune to import to New South Wales from England.

That night as she was preparing for bed, a knock came at her door. Her heart sank as she remembered what Mr Wooten had once asked of her, and she hoped that Titus Crowe didn't have the same sort of expectations.

'Who is it?' she called.

'Only me, Cora.'

Tatty let her in.

'Sorry to interrupt,' Cora said, setting her candle down.

'It's all right, you haven't.'

Cora said, 'I just wanted to say sorry again for the high horse comment at dinner. I've been trying to work out why I said it and I think it was because you put my back up when you said your family had staff. My family didn't even have food some days. I thought if you're that well off, why are you taking a job some girl might really need? But afterwards I thought, well, you'll have your reasons.'

'I do. And *I* was angry because you made an assumption about what I was thinking and who I am and because I'm tired and I miss my family, and that's why I called you a pig, not because I think you're dirty. I just wanted to hit out at you.'

'*I'm* not the pig: mad fucking old Lydia's the dirty one around here.'

Tatty laughed. 'You sound just like my mother, swearing like that.'

'Your mother? But you had *staff*!'

Tatty wasn't sure if she was being serious, then decided Cora might be someone who used sarcasm a lot. 'My mother was uneducated and a croupier in a casino, and my father was twenty years older than her and a professional man with a successful business. Not the sort of match you see often but they had a very happy marriage.'

Cora raised an eyebrow. 'Had?'

'They both died recently.'

'Well, I won't pry but I'm sorry to hear that. My mother died thirteen years ago, when I was six.'

'That would have been hard for you,' Tatty said. 'And that makes you nineteen now?'

Cora nodded. 'Thomas, my father, married again just about straight away so there'd be someone to look after me and my brothers and sisters. My stepmother, Agnes, is an ex-convict like Da, except she earnt her ticket of leave. Da never did. He could never stay out of trouble long enough. He served his entire fourteen years. He and Agnes both drink. A lot. I'd rather be here than at home any day.'

Tatty didn't know what to say. At least her father had tried to make amends for his mistakes.

'Anyway, I just wanted to make things right with you,' Cora went on. 'It'd be terrible having to work together if we didn't get on, don't you think?'

'A nightmare,' Tatty agreed. 'Thank you.'

'Oh, and I forgot to mention this to you earlier. Titus isn't on the square.'

Tatty's heart plummeted for at least the second time that day. She knew what that meant because her mother had told her.

Titus was dishonest.

'In what way?' she said.

'Robert and Henry reckon he bullies people into paying for services they can't afford —'

'But don't all undertakers do that?' Tatty interrupted.

'Probably,' Cora said. 'And his burial club's a con and he's blackmailing folk who provide other funeral services, like the haberdashers and the coffin-makers and the bakers.' She picked up her candle. 'So if you don't think you can look the other way while all that's going on, you might not want to stay here. But I hope you do.'

After Cora had gone, Tatty sat in bed in a circle of lamplight and thought about her revelation. It was certainly disappointing news, but she knew she was being naïve expecting Titus Crowe to be completely above board in all his business dealings. He was, after all, an undertaker, and everyone knew undertakers made their money from the misery of others. Cheating the bereaved seemed almost to be the logical next step.

Did she really want to be tarred with the same brush as Titus?

Or did she want to try to make some changes?

*

The following morning Titus showed Tatty around the business premises downstairs. Several rooms were dedicated to Crowe Funeral Services, including two knocked into one with a large window facing the street in which a range of coffins was displayed, and a smartly furnished room where Titus sometimes talked to the bereaved about what services they wanted, though, he said, this was more likely to happen at the home of the deceased. The last two rooms weren't open to the public – Titus's private office and the room where he performed the new art of embalming. This, he explained, was a technique of preserving corpses, a modern version of which had been developed as a consequence of the civil war in America and to date was rarely requested, but that was the absolute latest thing in the funeral industry in civilised societies, including Australia.

In the coffin showroom, as he described the virtues of the various models and how to sell them, Tatty began to see what Cora had meant about him not being on the square. Then again, she thought, he was a businessman, and she felt he should be able to make as much money as he could, as long as customers weren't cheated.

'First of all, try to get them to come into the showroom to see the coffins for themselves. They're more likely to go over their budgets if they see something they really fancy. Always start out with the most expensive model.' Titus ran his hand along the side of a gleaming coffin made of dark wood. 'This is imported mahogany. Beautiful, isn't it? It was made by Eliza McBride, the best cabinetmaker in Sydney. Well, she and her son make them. He's crippled in the legs but very gifted with his hands. We also have native blackwood, red cedar and jarrah, all very nice, and of course plain pine for those reluctant to spend money.'

Tatty stared at him, thinking about her parents' cheap funerals, and in particular her father's plain pine coffin. 'But not everyone can afford an expensive coffin. I expect lots of families can only afford pine.'

'Unfortunately,' Titus said. 'These smaller white ones – painted pine – are for children, of course, and the tiny models are for infants. And at the very bottom of the ladder, and it really irritates me every time I have to sell one of these, are the fabric coffins. See, they're just a wooden frame covered with rigid cloth dyed black. You might as well bury the corpse in a plain shroud, in my opinion. But people buy them: you'd be surprised. They're not lined of course, not like the wooden models.' He stuck his hands in his pockets. 'Now, the way to convince folk to spend more than they want to is to appeal to their vainglory. You say to them, "Do you want your friends and family to know this is all you can afford? Do you want them to think that this cheap little box is all you think of your sadly deceased husband or wife?" You're an educated girl, Tatiana, so you probably have a reasonably good idea of how society operates. I'm sure you know what I'm talking about.' Titus shrugged. 'Now, you might think I'm taking advantage of folk in their hours of need, but I've got a business to run and bills of my own to pay. And it's human nature, isn't it? You can't appeal to a person's social pretensions if they're not already pretentious. And in the end I *am* providing a service people need, and a quality one at that. They don't have to come to me, but plenty do. And if they *do* pay more for funeral services than they intended, well, then that tells me they probably wanted to, and *could* actually afford it. I expect they thank me when everything's over and done with.'

'*Do* they thank you?' Tatty asked.

Titus looked nonplussed. 'My customers? Sometimes they do, yes.'

His private office was in a bit of a mess. Tatty thought it might take her a while to sort out his paperwork, though he insisted that his accounts were all up to date. He showed her his 'system' and eventually she saw the logic of how he ordered and kept track of his finances, and realised he probably was just short of time, not mired in debt as she had at first feared. He showed her a ledger book labelled *Burial Club*.

'Do you know what a burial club is?'

'I've heard of them.'

'I think they're an excellent arrangement for people on meagre incomes who otherwise might have to give their dead paupers' funerals. I started a local club five or six years ago. Robert passes out handbills at every funeral we conduct and our numbers are growing all the time. But there are a number of other burial clubs in town. Other undertakers operate them and so do churches and community associations and even some workplaces.'

'So people pay money into the club …' Tatty prompted.

'Yes, every week, just a small amount, depending on the age of the insured person and the type of funeral they want. And then when the time comes there will be a nice sum available to cover the costs of a funeral, and no one has to go into debt or suffer the shame of burying their dead on the parish. I have a couple of men go round and collect the payments on payday, before the money's all spent. I certainly don't have the time to do it.'

That didn't particularly sound like a con to Tatty, but perhaps Titus wasn't telling her the whole story.

The last place he showed her was what he called the embalming room. It was fairly bare except for a wooden table the size of a door in the middle of the room, and several shelves against the walls holding large glass jars of various fluids and powders. Next to the table sat a tiered wooden trolley. On the bottom tier was a big, narrow-necked jar with a rubber stopper and a long tube coiled around the base. An identical jar sat on the top tier together with a leather case with brass latches, currently closed. The flagged floor was without coverings, and the single window featured a heavy curtain held back by a tie. On the trolley and along the shelves were placed enough lamps to brightly light the room, probably even at night, Tatty thought. She stepped closer to the jars on the shelves to read the labels: turpentine, aluminium, creosote, zinc chloride, lead, arsenic, ethyl alcohol and methyl alcohol.

'What are all these chemicals for?' she asked.

'They make up the embalming fluid,' Titus said. 'You won't be embalming any bodies. I've only done two myself and it takes great skill.'

Tatty thought, Really? So how did you manage to acquire the necessary great skill if you've only done two?

On Titus went: 'I believe there is an undertaker in Melbourne doing the occasional embalming, and I heard the other day someone in Tasmania might also be starting up. It's the way of the future, especially when the deceased needs to travel before burial.'

'How does the procedure work?'

'The corpse is laid out on the table here,' Titus said. 'Incisions are made in the neck, and as embalming fluid is fed into the carotid artery via the tube from this jar on the trolley, it pushes blood out of the jugular vein via a tube and into this other jar. Blood rots and breaks down so best to have it out of the body.' He glanced at her. 'You're not feeling faint or ill, are you?'

'No.' Tatty thought Titus looked almost disappointed.

He went on. 'The embalming fluid going in is coloured and gives the corpse's skin a pinker, more life-like appearance.' He clicked open his embalming case and took out what appeared to be an enormous sewing needle. 'This instrument is called a trocar. It goes through a small incision into the corpse's belly, and the chest and abdominal organs are punctured to drain them of gas and fluid, otherwise the body will swell and possibly burst before it's buried. I've seen that happen and it's most unfortunate.' He put the trocar back in the case and picked out a large, curved needle. 'This is for sewing the jaw closed. Not strictly necessary to preserve a body but it does improve the appearance after death. All that is needed now is something to keep the eyelids closed, though I imagine they could be sewn, and perhaps devices to prevent purging. I suspect, however, that purging is a force of nature and therefore not stoppable. But so is decay, of course, and now look at what can be done with embalming.'

Tatty thought the whole idea sounded quite grotesque: blood drained, organs punctured, mouths sewn shut. Shouldn't dead bodies be left alone to do what they did naturally? On the other hand, people did die away from home and families probably were desperate to have them returned.

She said, 'May I ask, how much did you charge?'

Titus looked confused. 'What?'

'You said you've done two embalmings. How much did you charge?'

'Oh. Well, it's a very expensive procedure. I had to send all the way to America to acquire the embalming kit, which itself was extremely costly,' Titus said. 'And there's my expertise, of course. And time. It does take quite a while.'

He wasn't going to tell her. Never mind — she'd probably be able to find out by looking at his accounts and receipts.

Titus glanced at his watch — a rather nice gold one on a heavy chain. 'I'm delivering a coffin to a widow straight after dinner,' he said.

'To the Welsh family?'

'No, someone else. I'd like you to come with me. It's time you started to earn your pay.'

'Of course.' And that pay, which at one pound fifteen shillings was not quite as generous as Titus had initially implied, would be welcome because it was still a reasonable weekly amount, and meant she wouldn't have to touch the money she'd brought from home – currently very carefully hidden in her room in the lining of her trunk.

Dinner was boiled fish, sauce and boiled potatoes.

Tatty spooned some sauce over her fish, then hesitantly tasted it. 'What sort of sauce is this, Cora?'

'Fennel.'

'It's quite unusual.' Tatty really did miss Mrs Seddon. 'Is this your recipe?'

'It's Mrs Beeton's,' Cora said. 'I couldn't make something like that up!' She burst into laughter. 'I'm not the best at cooking, am I?'

'It's ... nice,' Tatty said, knowing she probably couldn't do much better, day after day for six people, as well as tending to all of Cora's other duties.

After dinner Titus and Robert loaded a cedar coffin onto the cart, wrapped in a blanket so it wouldn't be scratched if it slid around. The horse pulling the cart wasn't a Belgian Black, but an attractive bay named Shadow.

Tatty and Titus took the seat on the cart. Tatty thought Robert would settle himself in the back but he didn't.

'Isn't Robert coming?'

Titus flicked the reins and off they went. 'No, he's busy. You can help me get the coffin out. You're going to have to build up a bit of physical strength for this job.'

Tatty didn't know what to say to that so she changed the subject. 'Who names the horses?'

'Henry. He lives for them. Fool. Horses don't need names.'

Nothing else was said during the journey, which took about twenty minutes. Tatty was relieved as she didn't feel much like talking, happy to just look around. She thought they were going north but wasn't sure — she didn't know the town well enough yet. She could smell the sea — a scent with which she was all too familiar now — and then she could see it, both in front of her and to her left. Also ahead were several windmills turning lazily on the skyline, looking as though they couldn't be bothered to move much in the heat. The street they travelled along wasn't paved and dust puffed up in small clouds from Shadow's hooves as he walked briskly. Tatty could feel it grittily on her teeth and her dress was powdered with it, as were Titus's black suit and Shadow's rump and legs. She wanted to spit but refrained.

'What's the name of this street?' she asked eventually.

'Kent.'

There were houses of all styles on both sides — grand edifices of two and three storeys with extensive verandahs, small cottages and comfortable-looking villas with dormer windows, and at one point some new-looking tenements.

When they stopped, it was in front of a smart three-storey house made of the pale stone that also seemed to be the building material of many of the town's civic buildings. Tatty climbed down from her seat, thinking that if she owned Crowe Funeral Services she'd deliver coffins to the bereaved in a vehicle much smarter than Titus's ordinary old black-painted cart. A fashionable dog-cart, perhaps, though she'd still have Shadow pull it: he was so pretty.

At the rear of the cart she leant forward to grab the end of the coffin and as she did she pressed the front of her crinoline against the tailgate, sending the back of her skirt flying out and up. Rats. She imagined a strong gust of wind flipping her over into the cart, or even picking her up and flying away with her, and pressed her lips together to stop a giggle from escaping.

'Something amusing?' Titus asked as he joined her.

'No.'

She'd do away with her stupid crinoline altogether if she could, and perhaps she would, especially if Titus expected her to heft coffins and possibly even bodies around. As far as she understood he wanted her to be a helpful, discreet and sympathetic addition to his staff, not a fashion mannequin.

Together she and Titus hauled the coffin off the cart, took an end each, and carried it to the front door of the house. All the drapes were closed in the windows along the front and a wreath made of black grosgrain ribbon hung on the door. Tatty thought they should have taken the coffin to the back door, but said nothing.

They put the coffin down. Titus knocked. A housemaid wearing a black armband answered, revealing a dimly lit hallway.

Titus merely pointed at the coffin, as though the maid wasn't going to understand anything he said.

She opened the door further. 'Please come in. Mr Abernathy is laid out in the parlour. Mrs Abernathy is keeping vigil with him.'

Titus clicked his fingers at Tatty, which she took to mean she should pick up her end of the coffin. She did. Titus picked up his, and as they passed the housemaid, she widened her eyes very slightly at Tatty. Tatty responded with the briefest of eyerolls and they exchanged tiny smiles.

'Ma'am, the undertaker's here,' the housemaid said at the parlour door.

Mrs Abernathy, Tatty presumed, rose from her chair. The well-appointed room was very hot and stuffy and lit by lamps. Black cloth covered two mirrors, the mantel clock appeared to have been stopped at half past ten, and two photographs on a side table – presumably depicting Mr Abernathy – had been turned face down. Near Mrs Abernathy the body of an elderly man was laid out on a chaise in what were possibly his finest clothes, and surrounded by an abundance of flowers. Roses, lavender, lilies, gardenias and plenty of other varieties Tatty didn't recognise were arranged along the floor beside the chaise, behind it on tables, and at the man's feet. Their perfume was lovely; nevertheless the air was still faintly tainted by the smell of what she recognised as decomposition.

'Mr Crowe,' the woman said.

She was elderly, her silver hair a lovely contrast against her black gown, Tatty thought. She and Titus placed the coffin on the floor beside the chaise. The dead man was sunken-eyed with jaundiced-looking skin and lips turned almost black.

'Good afternoon, Mrs Abernathy,' Titus replied. 'This is Miss Tatiana Caldwell, my assistant.'

'A girl?' Mrs Abernathy said. 'How novel.'

'Please accept my condolences regarding your bereavement,' Tatty said, unsure whether Titus expected her to say anything or not. She glanced in his direction but he didn't seem perturbed.

'Thank you, dear.'

'Is this a suitable moment to transfer Mr Abernathy?' Titus asked.

Mrs Abernathy said, 'Yes, but I don't wish to observe.'

'Where would you like him placed once transferred?'

'In front of the hearth, please. But not on the floor,' Mrs Abernathy said and glided out of the room.

Titus turned to Tatty. 'Tatiana, please fetch the trestles from the cart.'

'What are trestles?'

'Wooden legs that fold up. They're in the compartment under the seat.'

Tatty brought them into the parlour to find that Titus had moved most of the flowers away from the dead man.

'He smells a bit, doesn't he?' she said.

'Of course he does. He's been dead for three days and it's the height of summer. Grab his feet,' Titus said, taking hold of Mr Abernathy under his arms. 'The ankles, not the shoes, they're likely to come off. And on three, lift. One, two, three!'

Tatty lifted and manoeuvred her end of Mr Abernathy out over the coffin, almost over-shooting it.

'For God's sake!' Titus cursed.

'I'm sorry, he's not as heavy as I was expecting,' Tatty said.

'You must be stronger than you look.'

Titus aligned Mr Abernathy in his coffin – head on the centre of the pillow, legs together, arms bent at the elbows and hands one on top of the other and resting on his stomach. He was well past rigor so his limbs were easy to manipulate. Then he and Tatty set the coffin on the trestles before the empty hearth, propped the lid against the wall and surrounded Mr Abernathy once more with the flowers, Tatty arranging the blooms attractively on the floor and in a manner that partly hid the trestles.

'Very nice,' Titus said as he yanked on the bell pull to summon the maid.

Mrs Abernathy came instead. 'You've finished, I assume?'

'We have. Would you care at this point to discuss options for Mr Abernathy's funeral? I'm sure you want only the very best arrangements for a man of your husband's social and commercial stature.'

Mrs Abernathy sighed and sat down – not on the chaise, Tatty noticed. 'I suppose I'd better get things organised, hadn't I?'

'Do you have family to assist you?' Titus asked. 'Sons, daughters?'

'Not here in Sydney. I have two daughters back home in England, a son in South Africa and one in New Zealand. However I am expecting my eldest daughter and her family to arrive tomorrow from Victoria, with luck.'

'That's some consolation. Family are *such* a support in times such as these.' Titus sat beside Mrs Abernathy – but not too close, Tatty observed – and produced a notebook.

She also looked for somewhere to sit, chose the chaise (after quickly checking nothing had leaked out of Mr Abernathy) and settled down to watch Titus at work.

'Now,' he began, 'you'll be wanting our best hearse, I assume? Glass-sided and finished with gold leaf and etching?'

'I expect so. Is there another choice?' Mrs Abernathy asked.

'We have our basic model — wooden sides and painted a very nice polished black. No one on the street will see the magnificence of the late Mr Abernathy's beautiful coffin and accompanying floral tributes as the funeral procession passes by, but very smart all the same.'

'The glass hearse, I think.'

'Well chosen. Two horses or four? I think four, all with feathers and drapes of course, imparts a greater sense of grandeur, don't you?' Titus waited expectantly for Mrs Abernathy's nod of agreement, which duly came, then made a note in his book. 'Good. Now, mourning coaches. I'd suggest two of our larger models. Each is pulled by a pair of our magnificent imported Belgian Black horses, the same breed that pulls our hearses, and each coach can accommodate up to six passengers.'

Tatty frowned. As far as she was aware there weren't six Belgian Blacks stabled at Titus's premises. Neither were there two coaches — of any size — just his glass hearse and the wooden one, and the little cart. He must hire them.

'I really don't know if we'd need two coaches, if one coach can take six people,' Mrs Abernathy said.

Titus made an 'mmm, I don't know' face. 'Two adds weight to your husband's passing. Observers will see the coaches, know they carry his family and assume he must have been a very beloved man for so many to be attending his burial. One family coach could appear a little ... forlorn? Is that the word I'm looking for?'

Tatty thought if Titus had said that to Betsy regarding Hector's funeral, she might have given him a good smack across the face. It seemed to her he was pushing Mrs Abernathy because he thought she could afford to pay a tidy sum for her husband's funeral, and looking around at her home she probably could, before her access to her husband's money disappeared. But Tatty thought Titus was getting very, very close to conning her, and it was uncomfortable to watch.

There was a short silence, during which Mrs Abernathy's mouth slowly settled into a straight line and the vertical wrinkles on her top lip deepened. 'Two then,' she said.

'Very good!' Another note in Titus's notebook. 'Now, attendants. I recommend two mutes to lead a procession involving a glass hearse, two mourning coaches and eight Belgians. One mute could appear a little ... unbalanced.'

Mrs Abernathy raised a hand then let it fall to her lap again.

Titus took the gesture as a yes. 'Excellent. Would you like a dozen or so professional mourners?'

'No! No, I would not like professional mourners, thank you.'

Tatty felt like cheering.

Titus seemed unperturbed by Mrs Abernathy's rebuttal. 'Well, then I highly recommend you consider purchasing a mortsafe. I *truly* believe one can't put a price on one's own peace of mind when it comes to the eternal rest of one's nearest and dearest.'

Tatty saw this hit home as a flicker of fear crossed Mrs Abernathy's face. She had seen the iron frames known as mortsafes or mortcages in London cemeteries, anchored over graves to secure them from the grave robbers whose reign of terror had reached its awful peak years before her time, but probably not Mrs Abernathy's.

Without thinking Tatty blurted, 'But surely there aren't any grave robbers here in Sydney?'

Titus gave her a sharp look, but said lightly, 'Oh no, nothing like London's resurrectionists of thirty years ago. I do apologise, Mrs Abernathy, I certainly didn't mean to imply that. Heavens, no! But with this colonial fad for collecting the remains and body parts of diverse racial specimens, who knows what will appeal to today's anatomists?'

An awkward silence fell. Tatty looked across at Mr Abernathy's coffin. He had been a smallish man, elderly, obviously Caucasian, and appeared perfectly ordinary except that he was deceased. She thought he would probably be safe from postmortem interference.

Evidently so did his wife. 'I really don't think a mortsafe will be necessary, thank you.'

Tatty took the opportunity to ask, 'How many years were you and your husband married, Mrs Abernathy?'

'Oh.' Mrs Abernathy looked somewhat nonplussed though not displeased by the query. 'Fifty-nine years. We would have celebrated sixty years together this coming August. And I don't regret a single year with him.'

'What a lovely thing to say and a wonderful tribute to Mr Abernathy,' Tatty said. 'That must be of some comfort to you, having had such a long and rewarding life together.' Her parents, she knew, would have killed for a marriage lasting fifty-nine years. Instead they'd had to make do with not quite seventeen.

Mrs Abernathy blinked, as though that fact hadn't occurred to her. 'Yes, actually, it is. I've been fretting about what remains of my life without him and I should be looking back on all the many marvellous years we did have, shouldn't I?'

'You must miss him terribly, though.'

'I do. Of course I do. However, nothing stays the same, does it? No matter how much we might wish it would.'

Tatty was aware of Titus observing her conversation with Mrs Abernathy, but he was obviously keen to get back to business, butting in with, 'Have you considered funeral biscuits, Mrs Abernathy? Crowe Funeral Services has contracts with suppliers of every funeral provision, you know.'

'I'm sure I can see a baker about that myself, thank you.'

'Stationery?'

'No, thank you.'

'A dressmaker or a milliner for your weeds?'

'I have a personal dressmaker.'

'A jeweller?'

'No.'

'A monumental mason?'

'It's too soon for a headstone.'

Bereaved or not, Tatty could see Mrs Abernathy was losing her patience with Titus, and that this had probably started around the 'forlorn' comment. But finally he said something that piqued her interest.

'Perhaps a final photograph or two, then, of your beloved before burial, to keep and treasure forever? And for other family members who sadly cannot be with you to share your grief and to farewell Mr Abernathy?'

Mrs Abernathy looked at him, her head tilted to one side.

Titus forged on. 'The quality of photographic images really has improved in these modern times. I'm certain you wouldn't regret it.'

'Perhaps that would be a good idea,' Mrs Abernathy said.

Tatty didn't think so. In her opinion a photographer should have been summoned the moment Mr Abernathy had died, not now he was a three-day-old corpse with a discoloured face. Or better yet, several months before he'd succumbed to death, when he might have looked moderately healthy. But then his wife might already have several of those, judging by the overturned picture frames on the side table.

Titus made another note in his little book. 'Very good. I'll send Miss Harvey along to see you with her camera equipment later today.'

'*Miss* Harvey?' Mrs Abernathy looked pleasantly astonished. 'The photographer's a woman? Goodness me. A female undertaker's assistant and a lady photographer both on the same day? What *is* the world coming to?'

Titus misinterpreted her. 'Oh, please, don't worry, I've seen Miss Harvey's photographs and she really is quite competent. Now, if you'll give me a moment, I'll work out my estimate. And you were hoping to bury Mr Abernathy tomorrow or Thursday? At Camperdown Cemetery or Devonshire Street?'

'Thursday preferably, and at Camperdown. We're Church of England.'

After doing a quick calculation in his notebook, Titus announced, 'The fee mounts to approximately seventeen pounds. To wit, five pounds for the hearse and four horses, three pounds for the two mourning coaches plus horses, seven shillings each for the mutes, two pounds eighteen shillings in total for the flowers, four shillings for pallbearing duties, a shilling each for the gravediggers' fees, seven shillings and tenpence for the burial fee, two pounds eighteen shillings for the coffin, lined, and between one pound twelve and two pounds for Miss Harvey's photography.'

If Mrs Abernathy thought that was a lot of money — and Tatty certainly thought it was — she didn't say so. 'Why wouldn't I just pay Miss Harvey directly?' she asked.

'You pay Crowe Funeral Services and we pass the money on to Miss Harvey,' Titus said. 'We have an arrangement. And we require payment immediately after the funeral. I'm sure you understand.'

That was nice of Titus, Tatty thought, having had to pay the fees for both her parents' funerals in advance. But outside, as she climbed up onto the cart, she wondered if Mrs Abernathy had got what she really wanted for her husband's funeral. The procession would certainly be worth watching with the elegant hearse and fine horses and the mutes, and people on the street would no doubt assume someone really quite important was heading to their final resting place, but was that worth seventeen pounds? Perhaps it was to Mrs Abernathy. Betsy would have loved something like that for Hector, and Tatty would have, too. But most people couldn't afford to spend that on a funeral.

'I hope you were paying attention in there,' Titus said as he took up the reins. 'Did you note how a technique of subtle persuasion can be applied to our benefit? My father, who was also an undertaker, always said that people often don't know what it is they want in times of bereavement until someone else tells them, and as undertakers that job falls to us.'

'May I ask, when did your father die?' Tatty said.

Titus said, 'Seven years ago.'

Tatty considered asking whether Mr Crowe senior had had the mutes, the glass hearse and four Belgian Blacks with feathers, but decided it would be better if she didn't.

Chapter Three

October 1865, Sydney

Over the next ten months, Tatty came to appreciate Sydney. If pressed she probably wouldn't be able to say she loved the city because she desperately missed England's cold winters, but she believed she was happy enough. Regardless of the wonderful opportunities promised in the emigration advertisements in the London papers, she'd been warned before she left home – by Maggie Seddon – that New South Wales was a colony established by degenerate, ne'er-do-well convicts (even though those convicts had mostly come from England), so she shouldn't expect much in the way of society, culture and law enforcement. And also that the streets were unpaved, the buildings often flimsy and temporary, and the parks undeveloped, and that the weather was appallingly hot in the summer and barely cooler in the winter, giving rise to all sorts of bizarre flora and fauna including lethal snakes and insects. And then there'd been the gossip on the ship out about the race of primitive black people who'd been cleared off the land around Sydney Cove, but apparently you still saw some of them from time to time begging on the streets or lying about on the ground drunk because none of them could hold their liquor.

But Tatty had already known that England had stopped sending convicts to New South Wales by 1840, and that by the time of her arrival all sentences had been served and everyone had blended into Sydney's population so it was almost impossible to tell who'd been a convict and who hadn't. There was a social hierarchy not dissimilar to England's, which Tatty had discovered as a result of providing funeral services to most castes within it. She suspected, however, that Sydney's hierarchy was less immutable than England's ancient tiers of privilege and most definitely parochial – something she was sure no one would ever dare to say to those in its upper echelons. Except perhaps those in its lower echelons.

Sydney also offered plenty of culture – theatre, singing clubs, balls, libraries, art and music schools, museums, advanced educational institutions (for some), etc. Much of the character of that culture had of course arrived with immigrants, the majority of them English, though certainly not all. And there was plainly no lack of law enforcement, just as there was no lack of crime. However, as Tatty told Maggie Seddon in one of her frequent letters, she thought the level of crime in Sydney was lower than it was in London. But then she'd been rather sheltered until her mother and father had died, so perhaps she wasn't a good judge of such things.

Maggie had been right about few streets being paved and the parks being immature, but not about the architecture. There were plenty of good solid buildings, many made from the local sandstone, in the centre of the city around George, Pitt, Hunter, Macquarie, Harrington and Elizabeth streets. She was accustomed to grand buildings but there were some quite impressive examples in Sydney. She admired the Post Office, and Government House in the Botanic Gardens, which she thought resembled a castle. And she rather liked St Mary's Cathedral and St James and St Patrick's churches, but less so the monolithic Free Presbyterian and Congregational churches. The Police Office she thought ugly with its forbidding square walls and high railings. It looked all out of proportion, and what was the point of the roof dome crowned with the small cupola? There were, of course, and as predicted by Mrs Seddon, in the narrow laneways and closes where the poor lived, plenty of hovels and sheds likely to blow down or wash away in the next storm. Tatty saw those, too, because it was often the folk who lived in them who paid into Titus's burial club.

And yes, she had found it extremely hot in the summer months – almost unbearably so at times – but she thought she was acclimatising as the city warmed slowly for her second hot season. She had come to terms with most of Sydney's strange insect life, except for the larger spiders, her fear of which she still hadn't quite conquered. There was a particularly enormous species called a Huntsman that often lived inside houses. Luckily Cora was quite happy to stamp on them, resulting in a stomach-churning mess. The ear-splitting buzzing of cicadas drove Tatty to distraction in the summer and she wasn't too keen on the cockroaches either, but she could live with those. To date she still hadn't seen a snake.

As for the primitive black people, she hadn't seen many of those, either. When she arrived Titus had warned her to keep away from them if she saw any on the street and certainly not to give them money or food. She'd wanted to say how unlikely that would be as she didn't often carry money, and even less often walked about with dinners in her reticule, but Titus had seemed serious. She'd asked if they were dangerous and he said no but they were unpredictable. Every time she'd encountered any since his comments – perhaps a woman and a child, or maybe a lone male – the last thing they looked was unpredictable, sitting on the dusty ground, wearing a ragged assortment of European clothing and draped in blankets, barefoot, skinny legs sticking out. Sometimes there had been drunkenness and sometimes there hadn't, but what had struck Tatty was the hopelessness in their faces, as though they had nothing left to live for. And sometimes she saw wariness and even hate, and that was when she walked quickly on.

In that ten months Tatty also learnt a fair bit of what there was to know about undertaking. Naturally she also encountered scores of folk in various states of bereavement – some utterly inconsolable, some stoic, others blatantly keen to get the burial over and done with so the will could be read, and still others grieving as well as mortified because they could barely afford the most basic of funerals. Tatty empathised enormously, and found deep satisfaction in being able to provide the comfort and practical support that neither she nor her mother had received when Hector had died, and that Dunn and Dunn Ltd had failed to deliver when Betsy's time had come. And the more she learnt about the business, the more she grew to enjoy her new profession in general, despite its undeniably unpleasant aspects. But she'd always had a strong stomach and had managed the ugly sights and smells initially with barely a retch, and now they didn't bother her at all.

She was fascinated by the many different trades and services that contributed to the funeral industry, and it certainly was an industry. There was far more to a funeral than grieving people following a hearse to the cemetery, then watching as the coffin was lowered into the grave. There was everything that came before that, and everything that came after. Grieving was a way of life that lasted for several years, perhaps a lifetime, especially for women.

Early on in her apprenticeship Titus took Tatty to meet some of those tradespeople and artisans. She met a shroud-maker who worked from her little house on Cumberland Street on The Rocks making beautiful gowns that were half-dress and half-nightgown in which women and girls could be buried. Tatty had had no idea: when her mother died, Mrs Seddon hadn't said a word about the possibility of Betsy wearing a shroud. Mrs Arnold, the shroud-maker, told her women had traditionally made their own when they made their wedding trousseaus, but that was fading now and often women were buried in their best dresses, or else a shroud was bought for them when the time came.

Tatty was fascinated by the garments. Most were made from pale lawn or crepe or extremely fine merino. On the front they were long-sleeved and high-necked and as fancy as any proper gown might have been, with ruching, pleats, pintucks and satin bows, but at the back they were plain and open for ease of dressing, which Tatty thought was extremely sensible.

She said, 'These are absolutely beautiful. I've never seen such quality. I'm so impressed. Do you make anything else other than shrouds?'

Mrs Arnold tucked an errant strand of hair under her house cap. 'I make christening gowns. Would you like to see some?'

'No, she wouldn't,' Titus said.

'Could I come back another day and see them? Perhaps I could bring a cake and we could have tea. Now, I had another question. That's right, do you make shrouds for men?'

'Some, but it's the fashion these days for men to be buried in their best suits. God knows why. Have you tried to dress a corpse in a full suit yet?'

'I have, actually, including my father.'

'Oh, I am sorry, dear,' Mrs Arnold said.

'That's all right. And it *was* rather difficult with my pa, especially as he'd reached the rigor stage.'

'Oh dear, you poor thing.'

Walking along Cumberland Street afterwards, Titus said, 'I think you'll find you won't have time to be having tea and cake with the likes of Mrs Arnold.'

We'll see, Tatty thought. 'So do you refer customers to Mrs Arnold, as you do with Miss Harvey?'

'I do.'

'And then Mrs Arnold pays you a commission if they buy a shroud?'

'Yes.'

'Couldn't customers just go to Mrs Arnold of their own volition?'

'They could,' Titus replied, 'if they know about her, and not everyone does. I do Mrs Arnold a service by informing them.'

Tatty wondered why Mrs Arnold didn't just advertise her shroud-making services in the newspapers.

A few minutes later Titus said, 'You didn't tell me that your father has also passed. Just your mother.'

Tatty nodded.

'Well, please accept my condolences.'

'Thank you.'

Next, Titus took Tatty to a shop on George Street he suggested she might enjoy visiting.

'Might I?' she said as she read the writing on the shop window, which advertised: *Louis A Coverdale, Manufacturing Jeweller.*

'All women like jewellery, don't they?' Titus said. 'My wife did, and my mother's certainly got enough of it stashed away in her room.'

'I'm not sure *all* women do.'

'Do you not?' Titus glanced at her hands and her ears. 'Actually, no, you don't wear any, do you?'

Tatty said, 'Some of it's pretty, I suppose.'

'Well, Louis Coverdale is particularly good at crafting mourning jewellery. Half of Sydney comes here for their mourning rings and brooches and jet beads. We have the usual arrangement. I refer my more prosperous customers to him and if he makes a sale, and he invariably does, I get a commission. There are other jewellers in town, of course, but Louis Coverdale is one of the best.' Titus paused, looking sour. 'There is a woman who also does very nice work, though it pains me to admit it. However, I don't deal with her because she's generally really quite disagreeable.'

'Is she? How so?'

'She can't hold her tongue and she thinks she knows better than people who actually *do* know better. She's a damn troublemaker, in my opinion.'

'Goodness, she does sound awful.'

'She is.' Titus opened the shop door, activating a bell that summoned a short man with a neat beard and moustache from the rear of the premises.

'Titus, how delightful to see you,' the man declared, though Tatty didn't think he sounded or looked particularly delighted.

'And you, Louis. Let me introduce my new assistant, Miss Caldwell. I'm taking her around to meet some of my colleagues.'

'A young lady, in the undertaking business?' Mr Coverdale looked vaguely startled.

'I'm hoping to add a certain level of feminine grace and compassion to my services. No other undertaker in Sydney is offering that.'

'That's true. Well, it's very nice to meet you, Miss Caldwell.'

'And you, Mr Coverdale,' Tatty said.

There was a short and awkward silence before Mr Coverdale said, 'Are you familiar with the different styles of mourning jewellery, Miss Caldwell?'

'Not in any detail, no.'

'Mourning jewellery has a fascinating history but I won't bother with a lecture. It isn't necessary that you know all that if you're only referring your customers to me so I can sell them a rope of jet beads and you can claim your commission, is it?'

Tatty shook her head, somewhat surprised by Mr Coverdale's candour.

He beckoned. 'If you'd care to step over and look at the items in this case, I'll tell you a little about them.'

Tatty did as she was told.

'Here you have your rings,' Mr Coverdale said. 'For ladies and men, black enamel on eighteen-karat gold, inlaid with *In Memoriam* perhaps, or we can add the deceased's name and date of passing. Alternatively, those details can be engraved on the inside of the band. We also have black enamel and seed pearl rings – they're considered very fashionable at the moment.'

'The seed pearl rings are lovely,' Tatty said. 'The pearls do look pretty against the black enamel, don't they? And I can definitely see the quality of the work.'

'Thank you. Or we can do a gold ring inset with braided hair from the deceased, or a bracelet, a brooch, ear-rings, or an entire watch chain for a gentleman. Jet is very popular, of course, being black. We only import and sell Whitby jet – it's the best quality. I can fashion almost anything out of Whitby jet because it's so hard and doesn't split or flake.' He took a pair of jet ear-rings from the case and held them so they caught the lamplight. 'You'll find widows will wear jet even before their first year of mourning ends because it's such a glorious, deep black, and while yes, it does glitter, a vanity which is supposed to be prohibited for recent widows, here in the colonies nobody worries *too* much about that sort of thing. Well, perhaps only at the very top of the social pile. Onyx is popular, too. That doesn't reflect the light quite so much.' He pointed at some jewellery containing gems. 'These jewels are for when widows have moved into half-mourning. We have garnets, always popular, and also amethysts, neither of which are too garish. Perfect really, especially the amethysts as they complement the lavender shades permitted in half-mourning.'

'They're lovely. My mother was fond of garnets and she had a very nice amethyst ring, although they weren't mourning jewels,' Tatty said, though she wasn't going to admit they had to be sold to pay for her father's budget funeral. She pointed at a couple of large and ornate crosses. 'What are they made of? Wood?' Behind her she heard Titus let out a slightly irritated sigh.

'No, that one's made from gutta-percha, which is latex from a tree in Malaysia, I believe, and the other's vulcanite. That's rubber mixed with sulphur, which renders it solid. They're known in the trade as poor man's jet and they're both a lot cheaper. I import them from England, too, though I deliberately don't sell a lot of either, but it's better than not making a sale at all, isn't it? I'll not stoop to selling pinchbeck, however. People can go to the market if they want to buy fake gold baubles.'

'And you make jewellery for custom orders, obviously?'

'Obviously. I make all sorts of jewellery, not just mourning pieces, and anyone can bring me a design they might have taken from a magazine or a newspaper, or even something they've dreamt up, though I have to say that doesn't always work out and then I find myself offering advice on what might better suit the customer.'

'How interesting,' Tatty said.

'We should move along now, Tatiana,' Titus interrupted.

Mr Coverdale said, 'A word before you go, Titus, if you will. In private?'

Titus looked at Tatty. 'I'll meet you outside.'

Tatty went out, the bell ringing behind her, and stood looking at the window display: a selection of necklaces and matching ear-rings arranged in a tiered horseshoe in front of a red velvet curtain. After a minute or so she heard raised voices coming from inside the shop, but unfortunately she couldn't quite hear what Titus and Louis Coverdale were saying. Perhaps if she pressed her ear against the window? Would that help or would they see her? Would passers-by on the street think she'd lost her mind? She closed her eyes and concentrated but it was no use – the details of the argument were lost to her. Rats. She suspected it wasn't about her, however, but about the commission Titus was demanding from Mr Coverdale's sales to their shared customers. If she were Mr Coverdale she'd be telling Titus that particular arrangement had come to an end. Mr Coverdale made quality jewellery – surely bereaved folk would shop at his store without a referral from Titus? Perhaps he was saying that very thing now.

Titus exited the jeweller's looking deeply displeased.

'Is everything all right, Mr Crowe?' Tatty asked.

'Yes,' Titus said and strode deliberately off up the street so Tatty would have to trot to keep up with him.

So she did.

*

Visiting the baker Titus had an 'arrangement' with was fun, especially as Tatty hadn't even known what funeral biscuits were before he mentioned them to Mrs Abernathy. But then she'd only ever attended Hector's and Betsy's funerals and there had certainly been no suggestion of funeral biscuits then. Had their poverty been that obvious?

The bakery was on Harrington Street on The Rocks, and the baker was a man named Crumb. Titus told Tatty this just as they were about to enter.

She looked at him to see if he was joking. 'The baker's name is Crumb?'

'Yes. What about it?'

Tatty stared at Titus a moment longer, looking for the remotest flicker of acknowledgement that Crumb was an amusing name for a baker, couldn't see one, and followed him into the bakery.

Titus did his usual introductions and Mr Crumb, a broad man with a red face, welcomed Tatty and introduced his wife, also chubby, and two grown sons. In fact the whole family was large, but Betsy had always told Tatty not to trust food made by a skinny cook or baker. Then Mr Crumb gave her a tour of his bakery. She saw the enormous sacks of flour, bags of sugar and wooden tubs of butter, the troughs where the doughs were mixed, the marble slabs on which they were kneaded and formed into loaves, pastries and biscuits, and the very hot brick ovens at the back of the shop. Then he showed her specifically how he made his funeral biscuits from a basic dough similar to shortbread and flavoured with lemon zest, rolled out and cut into rounds. He then pressed the shape of a cross into each biscuit with a wooden mould before putting them into the oven, inviting Tatty to stamp crosses into a few herself. She did, thoroughly enjoying the experience and feeling as she had as a five-year-old, doing 'baking' with Mrs Seddon using a lump of her own grubby dough and her set of animal stamps.

'These are for a funeral later today,' Mr Crumb said, lifting a rack of biscuits off a shelf. 'I'll show you how they're wrapped.'

Tatty wondered how cheeky she could be. 'You don't have any spares, do you? I'd love to taste one.'

'We've always got spares,' Mr Crumb said, reaching for a large bowl of broken biscuits and passing it to Tatty. 'You don't think we all got this big eating spinach, do you?'

Tatty took a piece and bit into it. The shortbread had a lovely crumb, almost melted in her mouth and was delightfully lemony. 'God, it's de*lic*ious! I could eat those forever!'

Mrs Crumb laughed. 'Then you'd end up looking like us.'

From a box Mr Crumb took a pile of printed papers. 'This is the sort of thing we wrap the biscuits in.'

Tatty held out her hand. 'May I see what's on them?'

Mr Crumb passed her a paper. It was off-white and edged in black, and printed with a short obituary of the deceased person covering the top half of the paper and a verse from the bible on the bottom half.

'Do you print them yourself?'

'No, we send out to a printer for that.'

'And they're all the same?' Tatty asked.

'These are. Sometimes we're asked to provide invitations to a funeral but these biscuits are for folk to take home afterwards.'

Tatty watched as Mr Crumb's wife swiftly wrapped each biscuit individually then closed the little parcels with black wax and a seal depicting a skull, all apparently without breaking a biscuit.

'You must do a lot of them,' she said to Mrs Crumb.

'We do. About a quarter of what the people of the town want?' Mrs Crumb looked at her husband. 'Maybe even a third?'

'Which reminds me,' Titus said as he took an envelope from his pocket and set it on Mr Crumb's bench. 'Next week. I'll not wait any longer.'

Oh dear, Tatty thought, wondering what that could be about. Mr Crumb was another one who really should be telling Titus to go to hell. Really, why wouldn't they?

Tatty's absolute favourite visit, however, had been to the magical emporium of draper and haberdasher Mr Rodney Burton. The store itself was huge, covering the floor space of almost three normal-sized shops: a wonderland of an enormous range of fabrics, and notions including buttons, trims, nets, ribbons, beads, paillettes, artificial pearls, lace, artificial flowers, crinolines, boning, busks, threads and needles. What's more, at least a third of the emporium was dedicated to mourning materials. As well as the ubiquitous black crape there was also bombazine, parramatta silk, merino, delaine and velvet, and for half-mourning a head-spinning range of fabrics with a little more lustre and life in black, grey, purple-mauve, lavender, violet and white. Burton's also sold a huge selection of handkerchiefs edged with black lace, black gloves, umbrellas and sunshades, black lace fans, black shoes and boots, and a good selection of shawls. Customers could ask for the help of experienced assistants regarding what fabric to choose and how many and what style of gown to have their dressmaker sew for them, or have the dressmakers at Burton's make the gown in less than a week. They could even choose a garment 'off the rack', which Mr Burton said was becoming more popular these days, even in Sydney among ladies who were determined to prove they were as fancy as women back home in England.

Tatty thought Mr Burton was well qualified to talk about fancy, in snug cream trousers, a teal-green velvet jacket and a rather gorgeous floral-patterned silk waistcoat, all contrasting beautifully with hair the colour of a fox tail and bright blue eyes.

'Did your dressmakers make your outfit?' she asked. 'I love your waistcoat and jacket. I *do* like velvet. Unfortunately I couldn't really sew if my life depended on it. I can darn a sock and replace a missing button, but I'm afraid that's about my limit.'

'It's never too late to learn, dear,' Mr Burton said. 'And yes, my ladies did make my ensemble: they squeezed the work in between our usual bespoke orders. And speaking of "the rack" we really do struggle to find the time to make dresses to actually put on it, I must say, we're that busy.'

Tatty said, 'You mean making just bespoke mourning dresses?'

'Well, we do make quite a lot of those, but we make a lot of everything.' Mr Burton pushed out a hip and jammed his hand on it. 'You'd think in a city of nearly a hundred thousand people there'd be a few more dressmakers, wouldn't you? Even ten more would help. That's not a lot to ask, is it? I'm thinking of starting up a school, I really am. Rodney Burton's Academy of Dressmaking. I like the sound of that. What do you think?'

'I think it's an excellent idea.'

'And you, Titus?' Mr Burton said. 'What do *you* think?'

His top lip curling, Titus said, 'Dressmakers? Like you? No, I *don't* think we need any more in this town.' Then to Tatty: 'It's time to go.'

Mr Burton said, 'It was lovely to meet you, Miss Caldwell. Do come and visit again soon, and if you're thinking about something a little more elegant and modern to wear for work, I'm sure we can help you.'

'Thank you and it was lovely to meet you too, Mr Burton!'

Tatty waved at him then Titus took hold of her arm and propelled her out of the store, which was not only painful but annoying, as she'd wanted to have a good look around. She loved fabrics and notions, even though it was starting to look as though she might be wearing black for some time. That wouldn't be too trying, she supposed, but if she was, she definitely was going to have a new dress or two made, and they weren't going to be plain. She'd had enough of plain.

Next door they popped in to meet the milliner to whom Titus referred his customers: an older woman who employed three girls to fashion confections of net and feathers and ribbon Tatty thought her mother would have absolutely loved, as well as the more modest black straw and crape hats and bonnets and veils a woman in mourning would choose. There were, however, a selection of elegant black hats with slightly larger brims featuring ostrich feathers and small pearl decorations, for women in later stages of mourning keen to demonstrate that they hadn't lost touch with the latest fashions.

Again Titus received a less than enthusiastic reception from the proprietor – a nuance to which he seemed completely oblivious. She was polite but Tatty gained the distinct impression that the sooner they left, the happier the woman would be. And once again the atmosphere generated during the encounter wasn't one of fear, it was more a lack of respect towards Titus. He was demanding a commission from these people and they were tolerating that. Why? Was he blackmailing them? Surely they hadn't *all* done things so bad that Titus had power over them?

As she walked behind Titus back up George Street, dodging rubbish and nuggets of dogshit on the footway, she decided that was very unlikely. By this time she had been thoroughly through his accounts and hadn't seen any evidence that he was blackmailing anyone in his ledgers, and although she knew it seemed unwise, it *was* probably the sort of transaction it would be a good idea to keep track of, especially if there were multiple payments involved.

No, she didn't think he was blackmailing anyone (or at least she sincerely hoped he wasn't), and his demand for commissions from others in the funeral industry was just his way of making extra money where he could. Henry said he'd heard some of the other undertakers did it too, in particular Elias Nuttall of Nuttall Undertakers, whose name Titus had told her she was not permitted to say out loud because he hated Nuttall's guts.

Aside from meeting some of Sydney's interesting and talented artisans, Tatty quite early on discovered that one duty that fell to undertakers was something she'd never considered, probably because there had been no mystery associated with the deaths of either of her parents. As was the case at home, in Sydney when a death was sudden, strange or suspicious, or the cause of death wasn't immediately clear, a coronial inquest was required within days. The body in question couldn't be buried until after the inquest, at which it must be presented, and until then it was kept at the most convenient morgue, which was either North Sydney Morgue at Circular Quay (commonly referred to as the Dead House it was such a noisome little building), South Sydney Morgue at the Benevolent Asylum, or the morgue at Sydney Infirmary. The morgues were no more than small chambers capable of holding only a limited number of cadavers, built with very thick walls against warm weather in an effort to slow decomposition. The undertaker engaged by the coroner – and that was whichever of the town's undertakers was rostered on for that duty – was charged with moving the body to and from the venue of the inquest, usually a public hotel. In summer, and on the rare occasion that there was a delay in holding the inquest, this was not an appealing job. If a corpse really was very badly decomposed, then the jury selected for the inquest viewed it at the morgue to spare the sensibilities of everyone else gathered for the occasion.

To Tatty's annoyance the only task Titus wouldn't allow her to do as part of her training, even after nearly a year, was embalming. This was particularly galling as she knew he'd offered to teach Robert how to do it. Robert, however, had begged off after his first lesson, disgusted by the violence of the procedure. No offer for Tatty though: embalming was a man's job. Titus had embalmed three more bodies now, but would only allow her to watch, and now and then pass him the trocar or thread the curved needle with waxed black thread. However, she followed his movements like a cat tracking a mouse as he carried out the procedure, and she knew by now exactly how much of each chemical was required to make up the embalming fluid.

She would test herself, saying, 'It must be really challenging to find the right vein,' as Titus sliced into the corpse's carotid artery with a scalpel. Not much blood would come out. It couldn't – the heart was no longer pumping to push it out.

'It's not a vein, it's an artery,' Titus would reply without looking around.

Tatty did actually know that. Titus had several books on human anatomy and a slim manual that had come with his American case of instruments, and she'd read them all in her room at night by candlelight.

She'd comment again as he cut into the jugular vein. 'Which vein is that again?'

'The jugular, but you don't need to remember that. Move the trolley a bit closer, will you?'

She did need to remember everything though, she thought, because one day he just *might* let her embalm a body.

Tatty wouldn't flinch as Titus jammed tubes into each cut, the corpse's head rolling about as he did so. Soon, as the embalming fluid entered the body from the jar on the top tier of the trolley, gravity began to push blood out of the other tube and into the jar on the bottom of the trolley. It took time, some tilting of the upper jar and a bit of cursing from Titus, but eventually he'd be satisfied that most of the blood had been replaced with embalming fluid. Tatty wondered whether massaging the limbs to encourage the spread of the fluid might give a better result, but it wasn't her place to comment.

Then came the really smelly bit – draining the abdominal organs of gas and fluid with the trocar and injecting them with embalming fluid. Frequently Titus stabbed the large intestine as well, filling the room with a dreadful stink from a combination of flesh beginning to decay and, often, partially formed faeces, which would be washed out of the bowel as the embalming fluid was forced in via a foot pump.

'This is where you really need to use your special expertise, isn't it?' Tatty would say, trying not to breathe through her nose.

And Titus would say, 'Yes, it is. Pass me the needle and thread.'

Over time, what really began to amaze Tatty about Titus was that he was quite open about his transgressions – about his disrespect for the bereaved despite what he said to their faces, and how he took advantage of folk when they were at their lowest. But perhaps all undertakers conducted business like that? She'd certainly not seen any evidence otherwise. And he either had no perception of how his behaviour might look or he didn't care that she might be aware of it, because her presence never stopped it.

His burial club, for example. He absolutely had to know she knew he was cheating at least some of the people who paid into it, because she balanced the club's books. The members were mostly folk who didn't have large incomes and who paid perhaps a shilling a week, sometimes more, and after several years would have accrued at least five pounds minimum and sometimes significantly more to go towards the cost of a funeral. But the funeral Titus gave them when the time came was only ever worth around four pounds, no matter how long the deceased person had been a club member, so he usually made money on the deal. And he always visited the club member once, early on when they signed up, and if he thought their state of health was such that they wouldn't last long enough for him to make money, he rescinded their membership. Tatty was surprised that anyone belonged to his club at all because people talked, and they didn't like to be cheated. Or perhaps they were too embarrassed to talk if they had been cheated, or they didn't even realise they had been because Titus obfuscated about costs so much, and that was the problem.

And yet Titus went to church every Sunday morning, just as they all did in the house except for bedridden Lydia, and he stood around afterwards chatting to past customers and potential new clients, handing out business cards, bold as you please, shaking hands with folk as if he were a close personal friend of the vicar, which he wasn't.

He never, it seemed to Tatty, stopped working.

*

January 1866, Sydney

Some things had changed since Tatty had started work at Crowe Funeral Services. When she'd suggested to Titus that he purchase a dog-cart big enough to carry a coffin underneath, which would look smarter than the plain old cart he was using, he'd said no and she'd forgotten about it. But then he'd breached the padlock on his purse and bought an elegant dog-cart and had it painted gleaming black, which Tatty thought was a vast improvement. Henry, Cora and Robert were amazed, telling Tatty that Titus hadn't forked out for anything new for several years.

But Tatty's pay didn't increase after twelve months and neither did anyone else's, and she still didn't get any specified time off work: she was expected to be available seven days a week and had to snatch the odd couple of hours of rest or play when she could, which is what Henry, Robert and Cora also did. Cora went out with admirers, which Tatty couldn't decide was indecorous of her or not; Henry called on friends or went fishing; and Robert visited his fiancée, although he seldom returned home in a cheerful mood. Cora had told Tatty early on that Julia, Robert's betrothed, didn't want him working in the undertaking trade and was forever on at him to resign from Crowe Funeral Services. But so far Robert had stood his ground, hoping – according to Cora – that Julia would relent and see that undertaking was a good solid profession for a young man.

'She won't give up nagging him, though,' Cora said. 'You mark my words. She's only eighteen, but she's as tough as old boots.'

Tatty attended a chamber music concert (Sydney was without a full orchestra) and an exhibition of local artists (landscapes, mainly), and she enjoyed visiting the fledgling Australian Museum on William Street. She had also tried to join the State Library, which she had discovered possessed thousands of books, but membership was by subscription only and subject to committee approval, and her application was turned down.

That had annoyed and offended her, because she could have afforded to pay the not inconsiderable fee from her nest-egg, but thinking about the situation later she realised it was probably more prudent that she hadn't been accepted, and her money remain a secret. She settled instead for buying second-hand books, or the occasional expensive new title from a bookstore. She also went for walks through the Botanic Gardens and, when she had the time, went as far as Mrs Macquarie's Chair and sat on the sandstone bench and looked out across beautiful Sydney Harbour. Occasionally she simply wandered around George Street market and The Rocks among the sort of people she often worked with — folk who didn't have a lot of money and who had to toil hard every day to earn what they did have. It was nice to see them looking generally cheerful and bright and busy, rather than crippled by the loss of a loved one.

Cora and Robert and Henry thought she was odd, wandering around the town by herself and going to the museum and to look at 'boring paintings of gum trees' (Cora's description), which Tatty knew because they told her so. In response she invited them to attend the next music recital with her and they all declined: Cora and Robert because they didn't like that sort of music, and Henry because he thought he'd be busy, even though Tatty hadn't provided a date and time. Titus, on the other hand, never commented once on where she went in her rare spare hours, presumably because he didn't notice when she was absent or he just didn't care.

Another thing that happened in the new year was Mr Crumb the baker and, surprisingly, Ruth Arnold the shroud-maker, took a stand and each separately informed Titus they no longer wished to work with him, and if that meant customers boycotted their businesses, so be it. Cora heard Mr Crumb talking to Titus in his office (by pressing her ear against the door), and Tatty had hurried down George Street after Mrs Arnold when she'd left the premises because she'd looked really quite distraught, and had got the story directly from her.

First, she'd steered Mrs Arnold into a tea shop, sat her down and ordered a pot of tea and two slices of Madeira cake.

'I'm sorry,' Tatty said. 'Not a whole cake I know, which is what I promised.'

Ruth Arnold waved away her apology. 'Another time, perhaps.'

In the bright sunlight streaming through the shop window, the lines on Mrs Arnold's face looked particularly pronounced and her skin was pale. Tatty thought she looked as though she could do with several very long, deep sleeps, and the weight of the world being lifted from her shoulders.

They waited in slightly awkward silence until the tea and cake came. Tatty poured, then said, 'I followed you because you looked so upset after you'd spoken to Mr Crowe. Is there anything I can do to help you?'

'I expect you know why I came to see him?' Ruth Arnold said.

'Not exactly. I assume it had something to do with the commission you pay him when he refers customers to you?'

Ruth stabbed at her Madeira cake. 'Yes, and his threats to blackmail me.'

Tatty's heart sank. 'Oh, I'm so sorry,' she said. 'No, I wasn't aware of any matter of blackmail. You might know that I look after the books for the business? I have to say I've never seen any actual evidence of Titus blackmailing anyone.'

'Well, he wouldn't keep records of that with his ordinary accounts, would he?' Ruth said. 'And it was only a threat, but one I wasn't prepared to tolerate any longer. I was transported to New South Wales and served a sentence of fourteen years here and earnt a ticket of leave, and although that was a long time ago there is still a stigma attached to being an ex-convict. If I refused to keep paying him a commission, Titus Crowe was threatening to tell all my potential future customers that my work is inferior, that I over-charge and that I can't be trusted as a businesswoman, which would probably have been ruinous on top of the fact that I'm an ex-convict.'

'That's not very nice,' Tatty said.

'No, it isn't. You need to watch out for Titus Crowe, he's not a pleasant man,' Ruth replied. 'And I've had enough, so I told him today I'm not paying his damned commission any more and he can spread what lies he cares to make up about me, I'll take my chances. Folk can see the quality of my work and if they care to treat with me they'll see I'm honest. To hell with your boss.'

'I think that's very brave of you, Mrs Arnold,' Tatty said, 'and I'm so sorry you've had to work under such unpleasant circumstances, I really am.'

'Thank you. He must be awful to work with,' Ruth said. 'Is he?'

'Titus?' Tatty thought for a few seconds. 'He can be, especially when he's in a bad mood, but I enjoy what I do so I focus on that.'

'Well, do come and see me,' Ruth said. 'You still owe me a cake.'

'I'd love to,' Tatty said.

Titus didn't ask where she'd been when she returned home, though she was certain he must have looked out the window when she'd run out the door after Ruth Arnold. Or perhaps she was flattering herself and he hadn't even noticed. She didn't raise the subject of blackmail with him, though she had a more thorough look through the office paperwork and again found nothing.

He was surly, though, and his bad humour lasted well into the following day when he took her with him to visit a bereaved family named Flood who lived on Little Riley Street off Foveaux Street in Surry Hills, an area noted for its poverty.

'Damn it,' Titus said when he discovered the address. 'Three of us will have to go.'

'Why?' Tatty asked.

'Surry Hills is like a rabbit warren and Little Riley Street isn't much more than an alley. If we leave the cart outside the Floods' house it'll block the way, and if we leave it parked at one end or the other of the alley I'll guarantee both horse and cart will disappear. So Robert will have to come with us and sit in the cart twiddling his thumbs until we're ready to leave. God *damn* it.'

So off the three of them went, a white-painted coffin secured in the dog-cart's compartment for the Flood child who had died.

Titus had been right, Tatty observed; Little Riley Street was narrow – and unpaved and pot-holed – and barely accommodated the new cart. No hearse was ever going to fit along its confines: the coffin would have to be carried out to Foveaux Street or Cooper Street. Titus and Robert unloaded it from the cart, unlatched a gate in a rickety wooden fence and carried the coffin the five or six feet to the Floods' door.

It was opened by a bleary-eyed man who stepped back and let them in. Tatty followed into a tiny foyer with a flight of stairs, then a single downstairs room beyond which she glimpsed a skillion containing a rudimentary kitchen. The house smelt rancid and stale and of damp and dog and old cooked food, the walls and ceiling were stained with smoke and unadorned except for pictures of Jesus and the Virgin Mary and a crucifix, the furniture was old and shabby, and the single window was closed and draped with a black cloth for mourning even though it was January and stinking hot.

'Good morning, Mr Flood,' Titus said. 'One child's coffin as requested. Where do you want it?'

Tatty thought that was rather rude and insensitive, as though Mr Flood had ordered a baked potato, not a coffin for his recently deceased child.

'On the floor, thanks,' Mr Flood said. 'She's upstairs. I'll bring her down.'

Titus said, 'Do you need a hand?'

'No, there weren't much to her by the time she went.'

Titus said to Robert, 'You can move the cart out of the alley now, and do *not* leave it alone for a second, do you hear me?'

'Yes, Mr Crowe.' Robert doffed his hat to Mr Flood and said, 'Please accept my condolences, sir,' gave Tatty a quick glance to indicate his disapproval of Titus's foul mood and behaviour, then disappeared out the door.

'And mine too, Mr Flood,' Tatty said. 'I'm so terribly sorry. It must be so difficult to lose a child. May I go upstairs and speak to Mrs Flood?'

Mr Flood said, 'She'd probably like that but I'm warning you she's likely to bawl.'

Just like you, Tatty thought, noting his red and swollen eyes.

She made her way up the narrow steps to the two small rooms upstairs, one of which was obviously where Mr and Mrs Flood slept. The other room also contained a double bed, which Tatty assumed was shared by a number of the children, and in it lay the wasted body of Martha, their eleven-year-old daughter. Martha's face was as white as cauliflower, her cheekbones, chin and nose sharp, her eyes sunken beneath the lids, and her hands resting on the faded bedcover like two little bunches of sticks. Her hair had been beautifully brushed and her jaw tied and it looked like she was wearing her best dress, though Tatty could see a large repair to the shoulder and a patch in a different fabric on one sleeve.

Mrs Flood sat beside Martha, her back supported by the wall behind the bed, an arm curled protectively around her daughter's head. Mrs Flood's face was a mess: blotchy, red and badly swollen from crying. Six other young children also sat or lay on the bed around their sister, all somehow touching her body. Tatty immediately wanted to cry herself.

'I'm sorry to barge in,' she said. 'Mr Flood said it was all right to come up. I'm Tatiana, from the undertakers? We've brought the coffin for Martha. I'm *so* sorry she's died, I really am. It just seems so desperately unfair when it's children, doesn't it?'

Mrs Flood swung her legs around so she was sitting on the side of the bed, then blew her nose. 'Have you ever lost one? A child?'

'No,' Tatty said. 'I haven't.'

'Well, I hope you never do. The pain is ...' Mrs Flood hesitated. 'The pain is like God tearing out your heart with his bare hands.'

One of the children gasped. 'Ooh, Ma, you'll get in trouble at church for saying that.'

'Well, actually, Peter,' his mother said, 'I don't rightly care about that for the moment.'

Tatty ventured hesitantly, 'The pain does fade. After my parents died I eventually learnt to live with the grief. It's really never gone away and now it's part of me, but it doesn't get in the way any more. But then my parents weren't my child.'

'Thank you, love,' Mrs Flood said. 'That's kind and I hope you're right. I can't be doing with feeling like this for the rest of my life. And neither can my family.'

The stairs creaked and Mr Flood appeared in the doorway. Two of the smaller children ran to him and clung to his legs. 'Hop off now, go on,' he said, unsticking them. 'I'm taking your sister downstairs to go in her coffin.'

This made every child burst into loud tears. Tatty bit her lip. Mr Flood folded back the bedclothes and lifted his daughter into his arms. She was profoundly thin and her legs dangled from beneath her dress like birch canes. She had died from consumption and Tatty suspected there could be more deaths in the Flood family before too long.

Downstairs Mr Flood settled Martha in her coffin, declining Titus's offer of help. The coffin itself was set on the floor in front of the empty fireplace. There were no flowers to arrange around it, and no lace or satin cloths to drape over it. Instead the children sat on the floor, each with a hand inside the coffin, resting on their sister. Tatty reflected that what the Flood family lacked in financial means they made up for with love.

Titus sat at the dining table that dominated the room and withdrew his notebook from his jacket pocket. Tatty's heart sank as she realised he was no doubt about to try and talk the Floods into paying for funeral services they couldn't afford. She sat next to them at the table.

'You'll want our glass coach, I assume?' Titus began.

'Just a moment,' Tatty interrupted. 'What church and cemetery are you considering?'

'We go to St Peter's Catholic Church just down the road,' Mrs Flood said. 'We'll have a small service there and she'll be buried along at Devonshire Street Cemetery.'

'Then why don't you just carry Martha in her coffin?' Tatty suggested. 'Neither destination is far from here and if you can ask another couple of men to help, Mr Flood, I'm sure the task won't be too taxing. Then you can save the cost of hiring a hearse and horses, and also a mourning coach because most mourners can probably also walk that distance. But that's entirely up to you, of course.'

Titus gave her a hard look. 'That's a very practical and economical idea, Miss Caldwell, but the Floods may prefer our glass hearse, or at the very least our wooden option. What might the neighbours think if there is no hearse and no mourning coaches at all?'

'They'll think we're skint,' Mr Flood said, 'and we are, but our neighbours already know that. Everybody round here's skint.'

'But she's our girl, Pa,' Mrs Flood said. 'She deserves a hearse and a couple of those pretty black horses, don't you think?'

'I can do you a deal,' Titus said. 'I can offer you our wooden hearse and two of our best horses at a discounted rate of three pounds ten.'

Tatty opened her mouth then closed it again: that was their normal fee for that combination.

'And I recommend you *do* consider providing at least one mourning coach for mourners of frail disposition,' Titus went on, 'which again I'll discount to one pound eighteen shillings, and also arranging for postmortem photographs. I can tell you now you really won't regret having those taken. Mutes and pallbearers – I admit probably not necessary. And the fee for the coffin is two pounds twelve. Have you considered flowers, or funeral biscuits? Mourning outfits?'

Mr Flood rubbed his hand across his face. 'No, no and no. If we accept what you've suggested, how much will all that cost?'

Titus did a quick calculation. 'Including the photographer, which I can arrange for you, around nine pounds.'

'No photographs,' Mr Flood said. 'And no mourning coach.'

'We *have* to have the hearse,' Mrs Flood said. 'Please.'

Titus recalculated. 'Six pound two.'

Mrs Flood said, 'I'll ask my sister for some money.'

'No you won't,' her husband said. 'I'll take care of it.'

Tatty felt embarrassed and sad for the Floods and didn't know what to say to them, especially knowing that Titus hadn't given them discounts at all.

'We'll have the wooden hearse and the two horses and I'll pay for the coffin, but that's it,' Mr Flood said to Titus. 'I can't afford anything else. I still have to pay for the burial and gravediggers' fees.'

Titus nodded. 'I'll be needing payment in advance, if you don't mind.'

'I'll have the money for you when you come with the hearse tomorrow,' Mr Flood said. 'That's the best I can do.'

'That will be wonderful,' Tatty said, getting to her feet. 'Thank you very much. Mr Crowe, I believe we need to be on our way? We'll see you tomorrow, Mr and Mrs Flood. And again, please accept our deepest condolences.'

Titus looked slightly disconcerted at being hurried along but put his notebook away, stood, and bid the family farewell.

Outside, in the dog-cart at the end of Little Riley Street, Tatty said to him, 'You didn't give them a discount at all, not on the hearse or on a mourning coach. That was deceitful of you. Why did you do that?'

She turned to Robert, who had hopped into the back of the cart, and energetically raised her eyebrows at him, trying to convey the message, 'Yes, he actually did that!' Robert responded by pulling an incredulous face of his own.

Titus said, 'They don't know they're not actually getting a discount, do they? And they'll never find out: they don't have the mental capacity. Also they were dithering. I thought the prospect of getting something on the cheap might hurry them along. It usually does with people as down at heel as they are. And it stank in there. That house was a hovel.'

'Yes, but it was tiny and nine people live in it,' Tatty said.

'Eight now,' Titus said, and flicked Shadow's reins to move him on.

Tatty said, 'Well, I think it's wrong, lying to the bereaved like that. That's the last thing they need, to be cheated when they're trying to organise a funeral.'

'You may, of course, hold any opinion you like,' Titus said. 'But *I* own Crowe Funeral Services therefore *I* decide how the business operates, and I don't see the harm in the occasional white lie.'

But Tatty knew it wasn't just the occasional white lie, or in fact white lies at all – it was much more. After that the trip home passed in silence.

*

In the Crowe household Lydia Crowe had turned seventy-eight and become even more addled in the head. The more she deteriorated the less tolerant of her Titus became, though at times Tatty didn't blame him as Lydia was difficult to manage. Her behaviour was surely due to senility – it had to be, it was that bizarre – but Titus frequently accused his mother of being deliberately obstructive and obdurate. It often took both Cora and Tatty to tend to her now as Titus, naturally, refused to have anything to do with feeding or bathing her, or cleaning up her messes. He would only enter her room and speak to her when she was clean, the room was clean and everything smelt prettily of oil of lavender or lemon and bergamot.

Today the old woman had thrown a good handful of her mashed broccoli, pumpkin and gravy supper at Cora, tipped the rest over her sheet, then knocked her supper bowl onto the floor. Tatty retrieved it.

'Did you not want your supper, Mrs Crowe?'

'Bugger off!' Lydia said.

'I can get you something else. Cora made bread and butter pudding. Would you like some of that?'

'What?'

'Do you want some bread and butter pudding?'

Lydia said, 'I want my window back.'

'Can you help me get these bedclothes off her without us getting covered in mashed veggies?' Cora said.

Tatty said yes to Cora, then to Lydia, 'What do you mean, you want your window back?'

'I want my window back,' Lydia repeated.

'I don't understand what you mean,' Tatty said, turning back Lydia's vegetable-smeared bedding and getting some on her dress. 'Oh, *rats*.'

'For God's sake,' Cora muttered, yanking the bedclothes right off and making Lydia shriek.

'Don't,' Tatty said. 'She can't help it.' But she didn't think Cora was being deliberately unkind, just ... short-tempered.

'She bloody can. She makes messes on purpose just to make work for everyone. For *me*. I've been here nearly six years and she was always a bit of a hard taskmaster, even before she went barmy.'

'She can hear you, you know.'

'No, she can't: she's deaf as a post.'

Tatty said to Lydia, 'Could you please lie back so we can change your bedclothes?'

'What?'

'Could you please lie down?'

'No. I want my window back.'

Sighing, Tatty said loudly, 'What's wrong with your window?'

Lydia waved a skeletal, blue-veined hand in the general direction of the window at the end of her bed. 'That one's not mine. I could see out of the one that was there before, but I can't see out of that one.'

Cora and Tatty exchanged a glance.

'Well, yes,' Tatty said. 'You could see out of it when you could get up and move around. But you can't see out of it from where you are now, in bed.'

Lydia hit her mattress with closed fists. 'No! That's not it! Someone's taken my old window and put that one there instead and now I can't see out of it. I want my old one back!'

'See? Cracked,' Cora said, twirling a finger beside her ear.

'Look, first we'll get you tidied up,' Tatty said, 'and then I'll help you over to the window and you can look out, and then you'll see it really is yours. Would you like that?'

'No point,' Lydia said. 'It's *not* mine and I know it.'

Tatty felt her patience ebbing further. 'Cora, can you fetch a clean sheet from the linen cupboard, please?'

Cora trudged off, grumbling.

Tatty said to Lydia, 'Mrs Crowe, I did ask you if you were happy with pumpkin, broccoli and gravy for your supper, and you said yes. If you'd changed your mind you should have rung your bell and told either Cora or myself that you wanted something else.'

Lydia stared at her, made some pouty shapes with her lips, sniffed, then said, 'What?'

For God's sake. 'Ring your bell when you want something!'

'I don't have a bell.'

'You *do*. Here, see, right at the head of your bed.' Tatty tugged the bell-pull to prove its existence.

'I can't use that,' Lydia said.

'Why not?'

'That summons the Lords of Shouting.'

'I'm sorry?'

Lydia said, 'And there isn't room for them all in here.'

'What?'

'And Titus wouldn't approve, the little bastard.'

Tatty was completely lost now, and slightly shocked – and amused – to hear Lydia call her son a little bastard.

Cora arrived with the fresh sheet. 'Here we are. What's so funny?'

*

February 1866, Sydney

Since she'd arrived at Crowe Funeral Services, there had been one thing for which Tatty was extremely grateful – none of the male staff had shown any romantic interest in her. Robert was betrothed, of course, if unhappily and apparently quarrelsomely. Tatty felt sorry for him and doubted the relationship would last, though at nearly nineteen and never having had a sweetheart herself, she knew she was no expert. Cora agreed with Tatty that Robert's betrothal was definitely doomed. Henry appeared content as a single man, although Tatty found him to be unfailingly friendly, accommodating, considerate, and always willing to go out of his way to help her. Titus couldn't have seemed less interested in her.

But that changed one day early in February. She and Titus were on their way home from delivering a coffin to a bereaved family in Woolloomooloo when Titus made a detour to the Botanic Gardens. He brought Shadow to a halt, dropped the reins and stared intently at his hands for almost a minute. Tatty wondered what was wrong with him.

Then he said. 'Tatiana, I have a proposition for you.'

Tatty sat very still, not entirely sure what was coming.

'Hiring you to work for Crowe Funeral Services has been beneficial. Customers seem to appreciate your presence and our revenue has increased. You will have seen this for yourself in the books. Also, on a personal level, I think we are generally in accord. So, on that basis, I am asking you to be my wife, if you consider that a suitable arrangement.' Titus took something from a pocket and presented it to her on his palm. 'Will you agree?'

Tatty regarded his offering — a gold ring with three stones: a large blue gem flanked, she thought, by diamonds. It sparkled intensely in the sun and was quite spectacular.

'I recall you said you don't particularly care for jewellery,' Titus added, 'but I thought you might like this piece.'

Tatty took a deep breath and looked for a moment at Shadow's velvety ears flicking about, then at some rather large bats hanging in the shade in a nearby tree like black umbrellas blown messily inside-out, and at a little creature she didn't recognise darting about under a bush. New South Wales was *teeming* with strange, furry creatures.

She knew she had to be very careful about what she said next.

'Will that arrangement include me working as an equal partner to you in the business?'

Titus blinked several times. 'I don't know if I'd use the term "partner". The business is mine and always will be. But as I said, your presence has already made a difference. I am amenable to discussing ideas with you about the business.' He frowned, as though perhaps he really wasn't. 'Yes. Yes, actually, I am. As my wife, I will value your opinions. So in that sense our association will change from employer and apprentice to a partnership.'

Tatty couldn't think clearly with Titus sitting only inches away, staring at her and waiting for an answer.

'I'm very flattered, Mr Crowe,' she said. 'But truly, I would like a few minutes to gather my thoughts. Would you mind terribly if I went for a very short walk in the gardens here? Just to clear my head? I would hate to give you a response that isn't going to benefit us both.'

Titus whipped out his watch. 'Ten minutes, fifteen at the absolute most. We've the Beardsley funeral this afternoon.'

'Yes, I know. Thank you.'

Tatty climbed down from the cart. Titus didn't help her, but then he never did. She passed the bat trees, illogically hoping she wouldn't accidentally wake the flying foxes from their daytime sleep, then walked deeper into the shade past palms and fern beds, wanting only to be away from Titus's gaze so she could organise her thoughts. Some considerate landscaper had provided a bench seat in a grotto surrounded by inviting greenery, and she sat down, relishing the silence. She thought of all the good things Crowe Funeral Services could do for bereaved families if she could just convince Titus to make some changes. She'd seen plenty of savings that poorer folk could make by avoiding unnecessary funeral extras, if Titus could be encouraged not to promote them with such vigour. However, she'd already suggested a good number of those changes and he'd ignored them. Would he listen if she was his wife and not just an employee? He'd just said he would when he'd proposed, but would he really and would he actually *make* any of those changes? Also, the burial club – that could be reorganised, too, so that no one ever paid more than they needed to. It would *have* to be reorganised: she really couldn't countenance Titus's blatant cheating of the poor, in particular, of their very limited funds. As an employee all she could do was suggest to him that his practices concerning the club were unfair, which she had and he'd also ignored, but as his wife she ought to have more influence.

But even as respectably married Mrs Titus Crowe of Crowe Funeral Services, the business wouldn't be hers, Titus had made that very clear not twenty minutes earlier. And when he died – which, with luck, would be quite a lot sooner than her because of the difference in their ages – it *still* wouldn't be hers because of the property laws. Marrying Titus might take her a few steps closer to her goal, but she would still be faced with quite a journey before she reached her destination. Was she prepared to travel all the way down that road?

She didn't love Titus, of course, but that was all right: marrying a man she loved hadn't been part of her plan. In fact, marriage hadn't been part of her plan. The obstacle liable to be most challenging regarding a life with Titus was the fact that she didn't even like him. He was dishonest, frequently mean, and not particularly personable. Fortunately he was a man of relatively few words so it wasn't as though she would be constantly conversing with him, but she was worried about the physical side of their union if they did marry. Tatty recalled Betsy's intimate arrangement with Mr Wooten to help pay the mortgage, and reluctantly conceded she would be prepared to do the same, albeit within the sanctity of marriage, to attain her own goals. If she married Titus she would have to yield to his sexual demands anyway: she wouldn't have a choice.

But if she didn't marry him, she would remain that much farther from opportunities to make Crowe Funeral Services the sort of undertakers she thought could better serve the bereaved.

Tatty noticed an insect crawling across her skirt. It was a variegated brown colour and she thought it might be a stink bug. Cora had warned her not to squash them as they absolutely ponged when you did. Instead, she carefully but deftly flicked it with her index finger and it went sailing off into the undergrowth.

That was easy, she thought, and realised she'd *almost* made up her mind.

She retraced her footsteps back to the dog-cart, and climbed up next to Titus.

'What will happen if I forgo your offer?' she asked.

Titus said, 'Then I'm afraid you'll have to look elsewhere for employment, and I very much doubt any of the other undertakers in this town will be inclined to take on a female assistant. In fact, I'll make sure of it.'

Shocked and dismayed by his response, Tatty felt suddenly breathless and faintly disoriented: she knew now of course he was blackmailing other folk in the funeral industry but she hadn't considered for a moment he'd try it on her. What a *bastard*. However, she very much didn't want to lose her job as a professional undertaker or have to relocate. She was putting down roots in Sydney and her new life was starting to blossom: she didn't see she had a lot of choice.

'Then I will agree to your proposition,' she said. 'I will marry you, on one condition.'

'And that is ...?'

'I would like to receive a regular allowance,' Tatty said. 'It doesn't have to be a lot. I'm accustomed to being financially independent and I'm not prepared to go without my own money even if I am a married woman. Put it through the books if you like.'

Titus made a cat's bum with his lips. Then he said, 'That is acceptable. So you will become my wife?'

'Yes, I will,' Tatty said, hoping she wasn't about to make the worst mistake of her life.

Titus said, 'Excellent. Then with your further agreement I'd like to arrange the nuptials as soon as possible. I see no reason to wait, do you?'

'No.'

Tatty looked at Titus expectantly.

He stared back, said, 'Oh,' and put the ring on her finger. It fitted nicely.

'Would you want a church wedding or will you be satisfied with a visit to the Registry Office?' he asked.

Tatty thought about that, and came to the conclusion that she didn't much mind either way. Once, she would have thought she could *only* have married in church, but that was before she'd decided God's presence was everywhere, and certainly before she'd started to suspect, after the deaths of her parents, that he might not be anywhere.

'The Registry Office is acceptable. And probably quicker.'

Titus gripped the reins, then said as Shadow moved off, 'That's settled, then. I'll have the banns posted immediately. And now that we're to be married I do not require you to address me as Mr Crowe. Titus is probably more appropriate. Unless of course we're in the presence of customers.'

Tatty wondered what Mrs Seddon and Lorna would think when she put this news in her next letter.

Cora nearly died when Tatty told her. 'Jesus Christ, girl. *Titus?* Do you know what you're doing? It'll be like screwing a stick insect and you won't even be getting paid any more. And ... ha! Your name, I just realised! You'll be Tatty Crowe!'

Tatty quite liked that. When she was small her mother had told her several times that crows held funerals when one of their number died. Tatty had found the idea charming and had never forgotten it and now here she was, an assistant undertaker named Crowe and a Tatty one at that. The notion was quite amusing, though she didn't expect Titus would see that.

Titus didn't seem to see the funny side of anything.

But that was all right. It wasn't her job to entertain him.

*

Leaning on the windowsill, his back to everyone passing below on George Street, Titus said, 'Mother, are you paying attention? Are you listening?'

'What?'

'I said, are you listening?'

'No.'

She must be, Tatty knew, because she'd answered her son's question with a semblance of logic, if annoyingly. She must be having one of her better days.

He said, 'I have news.'

'So do I,' Lydia said.

Titus sighed. 'Very well: what's yours?'

'I can't remember.'

'Then I'll tell you mine. I've asked Tatiana to marry me and she's agreed.'

Tatty waited for a response but Lydia simply stared at Titus and ground her gums together.

'Mother? Did you hear me?' Titus demanded.

'Yes. I'm not deaf. Who's Tatiana?'

Titus drew a deep breath in through his mouth and let it out slowly via his nostrils. Tatty could see he was running out of patience already.

'Tatiana works and lives here, and has done for over a year. She's helped look after *you* for all that time, so you must remember her.' Titus moved across to the bed and sat on the end of it. 'She's spooned food into that disgusting toothless maw of yours and cleaned up your *endless* stinking messes and listened to your lunatic jabber, and she's a smart, hard-working woman and I'm going to marry her. I want a son and I want one before I'm too old.'

Tatty stared in alarm at the back of Titus's head. True, his comments to his ailing mother were extremely cruel, but even worse was his statement about wanting a son. It was the first mention she'd heard of *that*.

'She doesn't love you, you know,' Lydia said. 'She's only after your money. And mine.'

'How do you know that if you don't know who she is?' Titus said.

'What?'

Tatty watched as Titus clenched his hands into fists and thought, Oh God, he's going to hit her. Then, slowly, he forced himself to relax.

'I said, how do you know that if you don't know who she is?'

His mother tapped her head. 'A woman knows these things. A woman *sees* these things.'

'There's no point tapping your head, Mother. There's been nothing in it for years.'

'Oh, yes there has. I have a world of ... a world ... I have a whole *world* in my head.'

'Oh, stop rambling. I've already posted the banns and we're getting married at the Registry Office. And you can't come.'

'I'll tell her,' Lydia said.

'Tell her what? Tell *who* what?'

'Tatty.'

Titus's face flushed a deep red. 'So you *do* know who she is?'

'I just remembered. The one with mouse hair.'

'No, that's Cora,' Titus barked. 'Tatiana's hair is black. *This is Tatiana!*'

His mother cackled. 'Tatty is as Tatty does.'

Titus lurched forward, making Tatty gasp, then appeared to gain control of himself and sat back again.

'Her name is Tati*ana*,' he said, 'not Tatty.'

'Whose name?'

Titus shook his head wearily and got to his feet.

Lydia said one more time, 'Well, I'm going to tell her.'

'You do that,' Titus said, heading for the door. To Tatty he said, 'Ignore her, she's rambling again.'

'I'll tell Tatty you beat Maria all the time and that's why she died.'

Titus paused in the doorway, then stepped back into the room, and leant over the bed until his face was only a foot from his mother's. 'But that's not true, is it? That isn't why she died. She died giving birth to my son. As usual you've got everything twisted in that stupid, demented head of yours, you nasty old witch.'

'Titus!' Again Tatty was shocked at his treatment of his mother.

'It *is* true!' Lydia insisted. 'You kicked Maria after she gave you a dead baby and it killed her.'

'That is *not* true,' Titus snapped. 'And it won't matter what you say, to anyone, because no one listens to you.'

'Tatty does.'

'No, she doesn't.' Titus looked at Tatty. 'You don't, do you?'

'I do listen, but I've never heard her say that.'

'Well, *don't* listen.'

And with that, Titus stalked out.

Chapter Four

There weren't many preparations to make for the wedding. The forthcoming marriage was referred to in the Crowe household, but not constantly, though Lydia had to be frequently reminded that her son was soon to marry his assistant as she forgot, it seemed, daily.

One day while Tatty and Cora were changing Lydia's bedclothes – happily because clean sheets were due, not because they were soiled – Lydia made an accusation.

'That's my ring.'

Tatty paused, mid flap of a fresh sheet. 'I'm sorry?'

Lydia pointed. 'Give me a look at that ring.'

'It's my engagement ring.' Tatty presented her hand so Lydia could see. 'Titus gave it to me. We're getting married in a week, remember?'

'You stole it. That's my ring. Diamonds and a ... a ... blue like the sea. My husband gave it to me.'

'Oh, give it a rest,' Cora said. 'Tatty's not a thief.'

'You shut up, you hedge whore.'

'Well, that's charming language from a lady, I must say.'

Lydia said, 'You're not a lady.'

'No, I meant you're not. Christ!'

Tatty said, 'This is my ring, Mrs Crowe, and I don't want to hear any more about it.'

'It's *my* ring.' Lydia looked at her skeletal, liver-spotted hands and her face fell. 'Where *are* my rings?'

'We took them off and put them away,' Cora said. 'A long time ago. You kept scratching yourself with them, remember? Anyway, they got too big.'

'You *stole* them. I'm telling the police and I'll get them to change my will so neither of you *nor* that son of mine will get anything.'

Tatty said, 'I'm not sure the police can change wills. And I'm fairly positive we're not in yours anyway.'

Cora laughed. 'But Titus will be and I bet he'll be thrilled to hear you want to disinherit him!'

Outside in the hallway Tatty asked Cora if the ring really was Lydia's.

'I think it might be. It looks familiar but I didn't want to say. Titus took her rings off her not long after I started here and put the cheaper stuff in her jewellery box and hid the best bits because he doesn't trust us. He doesn't trust *me*. Does it matter?'

Tatty thought about that for a few moments. 'Not really. Do you really think she dislikes Titus that much, or is it the senility talking?'

'I really think she doesn't like him,' Cora said. 'She could be pretty short-tempered with him even when her mind was still more or less all there. I know I say she's always been hard work and I'm a bit mean about her now, but before she got sick she was actually a clever lady and quite popular on the social scene.' She paused, then laughed. 'Not mine, of course, hers. And she did a lot of good things around town with charities and the like, and I'm told that as a result the undertaking business was doing very well, even though no one likes an undertaker.'

'Everyone needs one, though,' they both said together.

Cora went on. 'I wasn't working here then so this is all according to what Lydia told me after I did start and before she got sick, but for years Elias Nuttall had the most profitable undertaking company in Sydney but after a while he started losing his goodwill customers to Mr Crowe senior and Crowe Funeral Services, which pissed Nuttall off no end, hence the rivalry. But then Mr Crowe senior died and Titus took over, and according to Lydia, Titus isn't quite as good as his father at being an undertaker and a businessman. I think she tried to manage things but they clashed and then she gradually lost her mind, and Titus's wife dying didn't help. I think Lydia quite liked her.'

'Did Titus really ... kick her to death?' Tatty asked. 'Were you working here when she died?'

'I was and it was all very sad, it really was, because I liked Maria, too. And that poor little baby boy. But I wasn't with her when she died and I didn't see anything that made me think Titus might have caused it. No, I think Lydia's made that up or she's dreamt it or something. I mean, he's not *that* awful.'

'No, he's not,' Tatty said. 'Surely.'

Titus married Tatty at the Sydney Registry Office at the end of February. There were no guests, just Cora and Robert as witnesses. Tatty spent her own money on a new gown even though Titus said he'd be happy if she wore one of her black work dresses. Cora said good old Titus – you couldn't get more romantic than that – but Tatty wanted to wear a colour that wasn't black, even if it was just for one day.

She'd gone to see Rodney Burton of the flamboyant waistcoat and he immediately tasked one of his dressmakers with making her a new gown, which he insisted on discounting. Tatty had been popping into the emporium whenever she could over the past year for a cup of tea and a gossip with Mr Burton, and the discount, he said, was his wedding gift to her. He and Tatty discussed some design ideas and she settled on pale-blue shot silk with a modest round neck, a fashionable new round waist, fitted three-quarter sleeves and a full skirt over a cage crinoline that sat almost flat at the front with most of the volume at the back. Mr Burton said the gown would no doubt look stunning on

Tatty, but would be absolutely wasted on Titus Crowe. On the day of the wedding Titus did actually notice, and informed her she looked pleasing. Tatty wished her mother and father could have seen her in the dress, but suspected they'd have asked why she was marrying someone like Titus.

When they returned home from the Registry Office, Tatty carefully packed her beautiful pale-blue gown away in the tin trunk she'd brought from home. She'd worn black every day except one since her father had died in July 1862, and it looked like she was going to continue wearing it.

And after she'd done that, Titus asked her if she'd managed to put aside any money while she'd been employed by him.

'I had saved some, but I did spend quite a lot on my wedding dress.'

Titus nodded. 'And that was reasonable. A bride is entitled to a pretty gown. But you do realise that as my wife, any money you might still have is now mine?'

Tatty stifled a sigh, and nodded.

'Well, I'd like it, please.'

Up in her room again Tatty retrieved the six pounds eleven shillings she kept in a drawer, and took it downstairs to Titus.

'It's all I have,' she said while trying not to think about the other hundred-plus pounds hidden far more carefully in her room. 'The dress really was quite expensive.'

Titus grunted and tucked the money into a pocket. 'I've considered the matter of an allowance and I think it's appropriate I pay you twenty shillings per month. I expect you to purchase all of your personal requirements and significant clothing repairs out of that, although I will contribute to a new black costume every few years.'

That's very generous of you, Tatty thought without enthusiasm. It was *much* less than her salary. She was going to have to be thrifty if she wanted to conserve her nest-egg. In retrospect it was lucky she *hadn't* been accepted as a member by the State Library.

To her enormous relief, Titus didn't insist on sharing a bed or even a bedroom. He stayed in his and she was able to keep hers at the end of the hallway next to Cora. Titus didn't come to her for marital relations, though – he summoned her to his bed by slipping a note beneath her door. Tatty presumed he didn't want Cora to hear his performance, not that she was likely to because he didn't make much noise. Did anyone? She wondered. She had nothing with which to compare her very limited experience.

Her first time with Titus, the night of their wedding, was ... underwhelming, but again she didn't really know what to expect. Betsy had told her what a wife could and should expect from a husband, and Tatty's imagination had boggled at the thought of her father providing her mother with that sort of pleasure, but Titus didn't do anything like what Betsy had described. He pulled up her nightgown as she lay on his bed, raised his own nightshirt, exposing thin legs, a flat hairy belly and a penis that stuck straight out, and then lay on top of her and tried to push it into her. At first it wouldn't go in and he spat on his fingers and thrust them into her, which hurt, but not as much as his penis did once he finally forced it in. She felt like she was being split in two. And being almost a foot taller, he nearly suffocated her by pressing his bony, sweaty chest against her face while he thrust in and out. She had to move her head to the side under his damp armpit so she could breathe, and raise her knees to take the pressure off her pelvis. But, mercifully, once he did start thrusting it only took him a minute before he shuddered, groaned and, to Tatty's horror, died. A moment later, when he dragged in a great breath and let out another moan, his heart thumping wildly against Tatty's cheek, she realised he was still alive, but he didn't roll off her. She wished he would: her legs, back and private parts hurt. Finally, he did.

Staring at the ceiling, he said, 'Thank you, Tatiana, you can go back to your room now.'

Tatty did and that was when she discovered she had blood on her thighs and the back of her nightgown. She had a wash, put on a clean nightgown, took the dirty one downstairs, scooped a bucket of cold water from the water barrel outside and sloshed the gown around in it.

'Leave it there overnight to soak,' Cora whispered, stepping out of the shadows.

Tatty almost shrieked. 'For God's sake, Cora!'

'Sorry. I heard you come downstairs. I thought you might need some help. If it's still stained in the morning I'll have a go at it with some vinegar or lemon juice. How did it go?'

Tatty felt embarrassed. 'You're very nosy.'

'I know. Your first time?'

'Yes.'

'You poor thing. Did you know what to expect?'

'I did but I didn't get it.'

Cora snorted out a laugh and had to wipe snot off her top lip. 'Ew. Who told you?'

'My mother,' Tatty said, and burst into tears.

Cora hugged her. 'It's all right. Things will get better. Maybe.'

*

The next morning Tatty was a little sore when she peed, and still bleeding. Initially this worried her, until she realised that her courses had probably started a day or two early. If that wasn't the reason for the blood, she feared she may have been grievously wounded the previous night. She'd have to ask Cora. She also felt discomposed when Titus took a seat at the table for his breakfast but treated her as he always had – with polite indifference.

As she and Cora were cleaning up, she said, 'I'm bleeding. Should I be?'

Cora said, 'From down below?'

Tatty nodded.

Wiping congealed egg yolk off a plate with a crust, Cora said, 'You're asking me as if I know all about these things.'

Tatty felt her face burn. 'I'm sorry, but you've had beaus. I just thought ...' She trailed off.

Cora threw the eggy crust out into the yard for the birds. 'Beaus? I've never had *beaus*. Girls like me don't have beaus. But I've definitely had fellows. How much are you bleeding?'

'It's reasonably heavy, like the start of my courses.'

'Are you due?'

'In a couple of days.'

'That's probably it then,' Cora said. 'The excitement of marrying Titus probably brought it on.'

Tatty looked at her. 'There's no need to be sarcastic.'

Cora did one of her snorty laughs. Tatty couldn't help it: she laughed too. 'Why *did* you marry him?' Cora asked. 'You don't love him, do you?'

'No.'

'So why?'

Tatty hesitated, unwilling to say too much. 'I have a plan and it involves running a business. Titus owns a business. I think I can make a difference to how he does things, you know, make funerals better for the bereaved folk we work with. And I like being an undertaker. I didn't think I would, but I do.'

'Undertaker's assistant,' Cora reminded her. 'I hope this plan also involves kids, because you're likely to end up with one before a year's out.'

That had occurred to Tatty, and it was a real concern. 'I *was* hoping you might know how to avoid that. There are ways, aren't there?'

'Your mother didn't tell you?'

'She said she didn't have to worry about it, and that I shouldn't be worrying about it at that stage either. And she was right, I was only fifteen. I was an only child, not that my parents didn't try for more. Ma was still young but my father was getting on. He was as old as Titus is now when I was born.'

'Lots of women use sponges,' Cora said.

Tatty blinked. 'What?'

'You know, sea sponges. You can buy them from the chemist – well, some chemists – and every midwife sells them. You get one and soak it in lemon juice, squeeze most of the juice out and put it high up in your fanny just before you do the deed. He can't feel it's in there and afterwards you just hook it out with your finger, rinse it and put it away for next time.'

'And that stops you falling pregnant?' Tatty was astonished. 'But how does it work? And does it *always* work?'

Cora shrugged. 'That's what I've always used and I've never got into trouble. Something to do with the acid in the lemon juice, apparently. And I've heard a douche of diluted zinc sulphate afterwards works quite well too, which I've never tried – too much mucking around – and there's always withdrawal, which I wouldn't trust at all.'

'What's withdrawal?'

'God, girl. It's when he pulls out before he finishes.'

'Oh.' Tatty felt vaguely stupid.

'And condoms,' Cora went on, 'though I hear the new rubber ones aren't nice at all. Do you not want to have babies? Because I'm fairly sure Titus wants a son to carry on the business.'

'How do you know that? I only just discovered that myself.'

'By standing in the hallway near Lydia's room when he was in there, shouting his head off. I wasn't even trying to eavesdrop. You know how deaf she is. *Don't* you want kids?'

'Not really. And definitely not now.'

Cora said, 'That's going to be a problem, then, isn't it?'

The rest of Tatty's day went on as her days usually did. She thought she might feel different now she was married and wore rings on her wedding finger, but she didn't, except for that vague tenderness in her groin. Also, she really had thought Titus might change his behaviour towards her, but that didn't happen either, except for his earlier concession regarding her use of his Christian name. In spite of his comments on the day he'd proposed about the pair of them being in accord and working in partnership, she was starting to wonder if he might have married her just to avoid paying her a salary – and to secure an heir. It felt to her as though Titus had decided he needed another wife and had chosen her because she was easy to work with, could do accounting, and was healthy and likely to be fertile. And now that they had married, he could focus on his two principal goals – to operate and expand Crowe Funeral Services and father an heir.

He didn't love her, that was clear.

But then, she didn't love him.

Their marriage seemed to have had more of an impact on Henry and Robert, who both kept calling her Mrs Crowe. It seemed ... laboured, and by supper it was getting on her nerves.

When Robert addressed her as Mrs Crowe while asking her to pass the salt, it was the last nail in the coffin.

'Robert, I think among friends and colleagues I'd prefer to be called Tatty,' she said more sharply than she intended. But only *slightly* more sharply. 'Is that all right with you?'

Poor Robert looked crushed at being reprimanded and turned to Henry for help, which made Tatty feel mean. Henry, however, merely shrugged. He'd been in a strange mood for weeks now, quite unlike his normal cheerful self, and Tatty couldn't be bothered even trying to talk to him at the moment.

Titus had to have the last word. 'You will all refer to Tatiana as Mrs Crowe when we are with customers. Otherwise, she may dictate how she is addressed.'

The rest of the meal was eaten in silence.

Afterwards Tatty and Cora were in the kitchen quite late, giving the pots, pans and roasting dishes their six-monthly scrub with baking soda and hot water, when the bell rang on the board.

Cora said, 'That'll be Titus wanting his bedtime cup of tea. You can do that. You're his wife now.' She made a 'whoops' face. 'Sorry. If you don't mind, that is. You should be giving the orders, not me.'

'His bedtime cup of tea? But that's —' Tatty stopped. 'I was going to say that's for old people, but I suppose he nearly is old, isn't he?'

'Forty-four isn't *that* old,' Cora said. 'But compared to you it is. He must think he's in heaven.'

'I'll be nineteen next month,' Tatty said. 'Anyway my father was twenty years older than my mother and they had a wonderful marriage. Pa drank tea in bed and my mother loved taking it up to him, every night. Well, when he was home. Quite often he was out at the casinos losing all our money.'

'So anyway, he likes a cup taken up to his room to drink while he's reading,' Cora said. 'It's usually the last thing I do before *I* go to bed.'

'I'll take it up,' Tatty said. 'Though I hope that *is* what he wants. I'll ask him first.'

She felt vaguely uneasy as she climbed the stairs. Surely Titus couldn't be summoning her for sex, not by the bell – how profoundly rude if he was – but if he was she couldn't think how he'd know she was still in the kitchen. She knocked on his bedroom door.

'Come in.'

Titus was sitting in his armchair in his nightgown, robe and leather slippers, legs crossed, reading a newspaper. 'Oh. I was expecting Cora. No matter. Would you be a good wife and fetch me a cup of tea?'

'Of course,' Tatty said.

Even more relieved than she'd expected, she returned to the kitchen, made the tea, took it upstairs and set it on the side table next to Titus's armchair.

'Thank you.' He picked up a teaspoon and tapped it slowly on the table, apparently thinking. 'Tatiana, has my mother ever mentioned anything to you about her will?'

Bloody Cora, Tatty thought. Always stirring the pot. She must have said something. 'She may have. I think she said something about going to the police about it.'

'The *police*? About her will?'

'She was quite confused.'

'When is she not?' Titus sipped his tea. 'Did she mention me?'

'She possibly said something about having you removed from it. And Cora and myself. She was *very* muddled.'

Titus said, 'Mmm.' Then, eventually, 'You may go now.'

'I hope you sleep well, husband,' Tatty said.

Titus glanced up at her, an expression of genuine surprise on his face. 'Thank you, Tatiana.'

In the hallway Tatty stood outside Lydia's door for several minutes. The old lady was talking, perhaps in her sleep, perhaps not. Her words were indistinct, but she was clearly distressed. Very distressed.

*

April 1866, Sydney

Tatty, Robert and Henry sat at the table, waiting. It was nearly one o'clock and Tatty was extremely hungry. She'd breakfasted along with everyone else at seven that morning but there'd been no time for morning tea.

Someone's stomach rumbled loudly. Tatty knew it wasn't hers.

Robert's face turned bright red.

Henry laughed. 'Hungry, eh?'

Robert, who everyone was aware had recently had the most gruelling argument with his fiancée and was almost at the end of his rope regarding courtship, snapped, 'Yes, I am, actually. I could eat a horse.'

His smile disappearing, Henry said, 'Well, there's no need for that.'

'Then don't state the obvious,' Robert said.

Tatty thought Robert must be very upset indeed to speak like that, Henry being so senior, and a bit of a hero to him. She was sure Henry hadn't meant anything by his innocuous comment about Robert's rumbling belly. And Robert himself was normally so placid and inoffensive and quietly spoken. She wished he'd get rid of his sweetheart, if 'sweetheart' was in fact the appropriate word. She seemed to be causing him nothing but misery. But it wasn't Tatty's business, so she kept her thoughts to herself.

Cora came through from the kitchen, her face sweaty from cooking and a cloth in her hand. 'Bloody hell, where is he? Everything'll be ruined if I don't serve it soon.'

They were waiting for Titus, and had been for forty-five minutes.

Tatty thought he might be in Lydia's room. She'd knocked on the old lady's door twenty minutes previously and there'd been no answer and when she tried to open it she'd found it to be locked. Perhaps Titus was having a private discussion. Perhaps they were talking about Lydia's will.

'I'm sure he'll be here soon,' Tatty said.

'I bloody hope so. My cooking tastes like crap as it is, never mind having it sit in the oven for an extra hour,' Cora said as she stomped off.

Silence for several minutes, then Robert said, 'I'm sorry, Henry. I'd never really eat a horse.'

Henry said, 'That's all right. I know you wouldn't.'

Tatty thought they'd probably all eaten horse at some point. She was sure some of the meat they'd been served on the ship out from England had originally had a mane and a long, flowing tail on it.

Titus finally appeared. 'My mother has died,' he announced as he sat down at the table.

Tatty, like everyone else, gaped at him. For a deeply silent few moments no one said anything. Cora came in from the kitchen.

'Did you say your mother has *died*?' Tatty said.

Titus said, 'Yes.' Then added, 'Sadly.'

'But ... why? What's happened to her?'

'I believe she's had some sort of fatal apoplectic attack. I went up to talk to her and found her like that. Most distressing.'

'She was all right when I took her dinner up at a quarter to twelve,' Cora said. 'She started eating right away.'

'Well, perhaps she choked, but I really don't think so,' Titus said. 'I see no need to send for a doctor. I'll certify her death. I've seen enough examples of death by apoplexy. And I'll register it in the next week or so.' He sighed. 'Perhaps it's for the best. She was clearly suffering, the poor woman, and at last God has called her home. I'd like to bury her in the next few days. Tatiana, could you check our schedule, please? Naturally I want my mother to have the best funeral we can give her.'

'Can we go up and see her, please?' Cora asked. 'Should we lay her out? Or would you rather do that?'

Titus said, 'I'd consider it an honour if you laid out my mother, Cora. Thank you. But don't tie her jaw, because I'll be embalming her. I haven't done a female corpse yet and this is a good opportunity for me to practise setting the features. We all want her to look her best for her last appearance, don't we? Oh, and I should warn you, unfortunately she seems to have lost control of herself during the fit.'

Then he helped himself to a big plateful of veal and ham pie (with burnt pastry) and boiled potatoes.

*

Opening the bedroom window as far as it would go, Cora said, 'Did you see his face when I asked him if he wanted to lay her out?'

'Men don't do the laying out, though, do they?' Tatty said. 'That's women's work.'

'True. They especially do not participate when the body belongs to the mother they couldn't stand.'

'He didn't like her much, did he?' Tatty said. 'I wonder if he ever did. I wonder if he liked his father?'

'I wasn't working here then but I gather they got on better than he did with his mother. But then Lydia lost her mind; his father didn't.'

'Where shall we start?' Tatty said, looking down at Lydia's body. She looked even smaller now that the life had gone from her, but then people usually did.

Cora said, 'Where we always do. Sheets off, then her clothes, then we'll wash and dress her. At least she can't argue with us any more. What shall we put her in? Shall we ask Titus?'

'We'd better,' Tatty said. 'He might have something in mind. We'll put her in a fresh nightgown until she goes down to the embalming room, then dress her properly after that.'

So off came the sheets from the bed, then Tatty and Cora stripped Lydia's body of clothing and took all the dirty laundry downstairs. Then they thoroughly washed her, cleaned her fingernails, carefully brushed her hair, and tucked her into fresh bedclothes until Titus was ready for her in the embalming room. Finally Cora bent over Lydia with a pair of scissors and cut the whiskers off her chin.

'There. Much better. I've been dying to do that for *years*.'

Tatty stared at Lydia's dead face for a moment, a dreadful possibility occurring to her. 'Cora, have you noticed? You must have.'

'The bruise on her lip, like a purple moustache?'

Tatty nodded. 'How do you get that just from having a fit?'

'Well, I don't know, I'm not a doctor.' Cora scratched her own face contemplatively. 'Her eyes look funny, too. They're all bloodshot.'

Tatty said, 'No, well, I have seen that before on people who've had fatal fits or choked to death. It's not that unusual. But the bruise ...' She lifted Lydia's top lip and turned it inside out – where it was equally bruised. 'I've seen this before, too. This is what happens when something is pressed down hard over the face. And Lydia didn't even have any teeth.'

Cora said, 'Something like ... a pillow?'

Tatty and Cora looked at each other.

Tatty felt sick. 'Oh God, I think he might have killed her,' she said. 'I think he might have smothered her.'

Cora said, 'Bloody hell. I suppose we'll have to tell the police.'

Tatty stared down at Lydia's body for a long time. 'Will we?' she said eventually. 'Why?'

'Why?' Cora said. 'Because it's murder. It's patricide.'

'Matricide. Patricide is when you kill your father. And if we tell the police then Titus will be arrested and probably convicted of murder and hanged, and I'll end up with nothing and all this ...' Tatty waved her arms at the room '... will get dispersed because God knows what's in his will, and you won't have a job and neither will Henry and Robert and we'll all have to start again. What's the point of that? And for all practical purposes this is my *husband* we're talking about, Cora.'

'But if we don't go to the police Titus might lose his temper one day and murder one of us. You, even.'

Tatty said, 'Do you really think so?'

'No,' Cora said. 'I don't know.'

'I don't know either.'

'But why do you think he killed Lydia, if he did?' Cora said.

Tatty said, 'I think it was her endless truculence and belligerence and her illogical rambling. I think it really irritated him. I think perhaps she might have taunted him or she became extremely confused and pushed him just that little bit too far, and he lost his temper. There have been several times I've been truly worried he might hit her. I think he's lashed out on the spur of the moment.'

'Are you defending him?' Cora looked astonished.

'No, I am not. But if that is why he's killed her I can't see why he'd want to kill anyone else, can you?' Before Cora could answer Tatty added, 'And if we tell the police about it and Titus hangs for murder we all lose. Let's just bide our time and see what happens, shall we?'

Cora looked at her. 'So you're happy being married to a murderer?'

'Of *course* I'm not.' And Tatty really wasn't.

'Well, I hope you know what you're doing.'

'I don't, not really,' Tatty said, but the vague shape of a plan was beginning to form, one that would not only benefit her but also Cora, Robert and Henry.

That afternoon Titus embalmed his mother, which Tatty initially found perverse because when Lydia had been alive he'd refused to clean or even feed her. But then when she thought about it, she decided it wasn't that odd after all. Titus had hated his mother enough to murder her — and she was sure he had — and now Lydia was just a corpse, albeit with a bit of novelty value because she was female. It was, however, another deeply unpleasant discovery to make about her new husband.

She knew she shouldn't, but she had to say something to him.

While he was setting Lydia's face, she said, 'That's quite severe bruising on Mrs Crowe's lip.'

'It is, isn't it?' Titus tugged a length of thread through his mother's upper jaw to hold her mouth closed.

Tatty waited for a minute and when he didn't say anything more she ventured another little prod. 'What do you think caused it?'

Titus completed his sewing, gave the thread a good jerk to make sure it was tight, then pressed his thumb into the bruise on his mother's face. It stayed the same vivid purple, and would until her flesh rotted off her bones. 'Perhaps she hit herself, flailing around during the apoplectic attack. She really did have such delicate skin.'

'Perhaps that was it,' Tatty said.

It was then that it occurred to her that Titus might have killed two women now — Maria, if what Lydia had said was true, and Lydia herself. What would he do to her when he realised she wasn't going to give him an heir? Cora might be right after all.

'Possibly we should cover it,' Titus said. 'Do you have face powder?'

Tatty said, 'I don't wear cosmetics.' In fifteen months of working with her, had he not noticed that?

'Does Cora?'

'I don't think so.'

'Damn. Will you go to ... where does one buy that sort of thing?'

'A chemist, as far as I'm aware.'

'The chemist then. And can you get some of that red business?' Titus made rubbing motions on the apples of his cheeks.

'Rouge?'

'Whatever it's called. That should perk her up.'

Marginally, Tatty thought. And then: I must get some lemons while I'm up the street.

The following day she was up George Street again, visiting Rodney Burton in his fabric emporium and haberdashery with one of Lydia's gowns – musty-smelling and with a touch of mould scattered here and there – rolled up in a carpet bag. She *had* asked Titus what he'd prefer his mother to wear in her coffin, and he'd replied he wanted her in her best gown, currently in a clothespress and not worn for years. It was now far too big for her, and once Tatty saw the gown, which was very elaborate, she suspected Titus was more interested in how it would complement his embalming work than in honouring his mother. But he wanted it to fit her, and it just wasn't going to, so here she was.

She found Rodney Burton sitting on a purple velvet-upholstered chair, eating dates with a silver toothpick.

'Hello, dear,' Mr Burton said. 'I hear you've had a bereavement. My condolences. Care for a date? They're imported and *very* delicious.'

Tatty tried one: they were nice but quite sweet.

'We *have* had a bereavement. Yesterday. Titus's mother. I have a gown of hers with me,' Tatty said. 'Very lovely but far too big for her now.' She paused. This was the awkward bit. 'Titus is insisting that the gown fits her properly and he'd like you to take it in. Tonight, please. And he says he doesn't expect to have to pay for the work. He says you'll know why. I'm so sorry, Mr Burton. Can I take you to tea the next time I get a couple of hours off to make up for it?'

Rodney Burton's mouth made a moue of distaste. 'You do realise, Tatty, that you've married a solid gold shit, don't you?'

There wasn't much Tatty could say in response to that. Not now.

Rodney stood and balanced his bowl of dates on a roll of black taffeta. Then retrieved it. 'No, I won't leave that there. Some unpleasant little child will come along with its mother, steal my dates then wipe its sticky little fingers all over my beautiful textiles, and I'll only have myself to blame, won't I? When's the funeral? I suppose the alteration *has* to be done tonight, does it?'

'It's in three days but Titus wants everything ready by tomorrow morning. He's embalmed her and she's the first female corpse he's done.'

'Truly the greatest gift a grieving son could give a beloved mother,' Rodney said, dabbing at a non-existent tear. He set his dates on top of a tall cabinet. 'Let's see this gown.'

Tatty removed Lydia's dress from the carpet bag and unrolled it. It was all in black — silk taffeta, with a high, round collar, long semi-fitted sleeves ending in cuffs secured by jet buttons, and a fitted bodice overlaid with lace, the panels defined by velvet ribbon. The skirt was full, but possibly only full enough to accommodate petticoats and not a crinoline, Tatty thought, and featured an overskirt of more lace picked up and held by bows to reveal the silk underskirt, and at the collar of the gown and around the waist glittered more jet beading. Altogether it was a very lovely mourning dress.

'Actually, I remember this one,' Rodney said. 'We made this about …' he screwed up his face as he thought '… four years ago? Five? She didn't want anything designed for a crinoline. A lot of the older ladies don't. They like what they're used to. And once they go into black after the husband goes they often stay in black, especially if they're getting on. Where did I put my dates?' He found them and ate one, offering the bowl to Tatty again. 'Even ageing spinsters often wear black. How many old women have you seen wearing sky blue or crimson?'

Declining another date, Tatty said, 'Not many. Will it be difficult to take the gown in? There's a lot of embellishment on it. I've noticed some mould on it here and there, too.'

'Yes, I can see that, and smell it. Well, it's certainly an inconvenience because we're so busy,' Rodney said. 'But then we're always busy. What size was Mrs Crowe? Now, I mean. She used to come in here a lot when she was working alongside Mr Crowe senior, but I haven't seen her for years. Her illness, I presume.'

'She was skin and bones. She hadn't been eating at all well for a while.'

Rodney tut-tutted and shook his head in commiseration, then said, 'Er, I'm not one to gossip – well, not often and *certainly* not maliciously – but what was the cause of death?'

'Apoplexy.'

'Dear me. Oh well. I expect we can get the alterations done tonight. Quite possibly this afternoon. We'll just put a couple of huge darts into the back of the bodice. I'll have the dress delivered as soon as it's ready. We can't have poor Mrs Crowe lying in her coffin in her under-garments, can we?'

'That's very generous of you, Mr Burton, especially as Titus isn't going to pay you.'

'Bugger Titus. I'm doing it for Lydia. She wasn't a bad old duck, you know. And stop calling me Mr Burton. While your husband is blackmailing me you can at least call me Rodney.'

Tatty was desperate to ask what it was Titus had over Mr Burton, but was too polite. However, she did say, 'Would you mind telling me, is it just Titus extorting people and demanding commissions from funeral industry folk, or is it all of Sydney's undertakers?'

'No, it's not all of them. Out of all the undertaking businesses in town, I've only ever been, shall we say, *menaced* by about half, and I've managed to see off most of those. The undertakers who are on the square have been perfectly reasonable to deal with. I have to say, however, that your husband and that thug, Elias Nuttall, are in a different league. They really have mastered how to dig up the worst dirt on people, and if they can't find any, they'll threaten to make it up. And because of that, they wield the most power. I honestly don't know how they manage to sit in church on Sundays, I really don't.'

Tatty wondered the same thing but Titus and Elias Nuttall did attend church every Sunday – St James's on King Street, which was fortunately big enough that they didn't have to sit anywhere near each other.

Rodney Burton and his dressmakers worked a miracle and Lydia's beautifully altered and cleaned gown was delivered to Crowe Funeral Services late that same day. Tatty and Cora eased the dress onto Lydia's cold body and arranged her in her coffin, restful and ready for visitors.

Titus went out and when he returned an hour later he had Nellie Harvey, the photographer, in tow. Her eyes were a little red and swollen: Tatty thought she might have been crying.

Titus said to Tatty, 'Miss Harvey will be capturing some photographs of my mother. I'd like you to assist, please.'

'Of course,' Tatty said, 'although I don't know the first thing about the art of photography and Miss Harvey knows that.'

'She might want the body in a sitting position or posed in some other manner,' Titus said. 'You're accustomed to handling corpses. You could help her do that.'

Tatty did know that some people liked to have final photographs of their deceased loved ones arranged in a natural pose rather than in a coffin – sitting in an armchair, for example. Perhaps Titus was thinking of something along those lines.

'Is that what you want, Nell?' Tatty asked Nellie. 'Help with posing Mrs Crowe?'

Nellie gave Titus a look that was almost a glare. 'You're the customer, Mr Crowe. Is that what *you* want?'

Tatty was very slightly shocked. She hadn't expected that from meek, quiet Nellie Harvey.

Titus flapped a hand irritably. 'Look, do whatever will best show off the plumpness of the skin and the fact that it isn't turning dark. I want people to see she doesn't look like she's dead. I want to people to see that embalming really does preserve a corpse.'

'Oh!' Tatty exclaimed, suddenly realising what was going on. 'You want photographs of your mother to advertise your embalming skills?'

'That's right.'

'Why didn't you just say that?'

'I did, didn't I?' Titus said, and walked out of the parlour.

Nellie and Tatty looked at each other for a moment.

Tatty said, 'Have you been crying?'

'Yes.'

'What's happened?'

Nellie sniffed, blew her nose then stuffed the handkerchief into the pocket of her dress. 'I'm sorry to be such a wet blanket.'

'You're not. Is it anything I can help you with?'

'I feel dreadful saying this but it's your husband.'

Tatty sighed. Rats. 'What's he done?'

'I had an appointment this evening to photograph a little deceased girl. She was the only girl in a family of seven boys and she died of quinsy and her loss is being felt dreadfully. The entire extended family are meeting at her home to be included in the occasion. Then Mr Crowe turned up at my house and demanded that I return here with him to photograph Mrs Crowe – immediately and at no cost to him or he'd —' Nellie didn't finish her sentence. 'I couldn't even get a message to the bereaved family. They'll think I'm so unreliable. And I am. I've let them down terribly.'

'Does he have something over you?'

'Pardon?'

'Is he blackmailing you?'

Nellie went bright red. 'I'm sorry, Tatty. I'd really rather not say. I *can't* say. I hope you don't mind.'

Tatty didn't: folk were entitled to their secrets. 'Shall I send Henry or Robert around to your bereaved family's house and let them know you've been delayed? Where do they live? Could you go after you've finished here? I'll ask Henry if he'll take you in the cart.'

Nellie's face lit up. 'Oh, would you? I would be so grateful. They live on Brickfield Hill. Except ...'

Tatty saw the uncertainty on Nellie's face. 'Except what?'

'Elias Nuttall's handling the funeral. I don't think Mr Crowe would appreciate his assistants conveying me to a job for his greatest rival.'

'Probably not,' Tatty said. 'So let's not tell him.'

Tatty thought Nellie looked as though she couldn't decide whether to gasp in shock or laugh. 'Well, I certainly won't.'

'And neither will I,' Tatty said. 'Now, I suggest we leave poor Lydia in her coffin. I think she's been pushed and prodded enough lately.'

*

Titus gave his mother the grandest funeral he could pull together, though he had to wait several days until everything and everyone was available. In the meantime, Lydia lay in state in the parlour in a very expensive mahogany coffin. He used the glass hearse and four Belgian Blacks – Spirit and Phantom, and two more Henry had named Spectre and Wraith that Titus had bought recently at auction, very satisfyingly bidding higher than Elias Nuttall, but as a result paying over the odds. There were also three mourners' coaches, each pulled by a pair of Belgians (hired) for family, Lydia's friends and important professional acquaintances; *four* mutes, two of whom spent four days standing outside Crowe Funeral Services, keeping ceremonial vigil outside the home of the deceased and trying not to look too bored; black-bordered funeral stationery on which he sent out invitations to the service at St Stephen's church at Newtown followed by the burial in adjacent Camperdown Cemetery; sugared funeral biscuits featuring two psalms on the wrapping;

and obituaries in multiple newspapers. Everything that could had *Crowe Funeral Services* printed on it and Cora said it was really clever of Lydia to do such a good job of promoting the business even when she was dead.

The weather on the morning of Lydia's funeral was overcast and it looked as though it might rain, which Tatty had long since discovered did actually happen in Sydney, and not infrequently. When it came time for the funeral procession to leave the house, Tatty, as the daughter-in-law, was allocated a seat in the front coach, but Cora found there wasn't room for her in either of the other two.

'Well, that's gratitude for you,' she said. 'I cleaned up her horrible messes for years.'

'Come in the front coach with me,' Tatty said. 'There'll be room. No one will care.'

'Oh yes they will. A housemaid in the same coach as the bereaved master of the house?'

'He's changed his mind. He's going with Henry on the hearse. Now shut up and get in.'

Cora did, ignoring looks from the three elderly women already ensconced in the coach.

As she and Cora sat down and made themselves comfortable, fluffing skirts and straightening hats, Tatty said, 'Good morning, ladies. This is Mrs Crowe's faithful attendant, Cora Billings. Cora took very good care of Mrs Crowe for some years. I don't know what Mr Crowe would have done without her help, I really don't.'

'And you are …?' one woman asked.

They all lurched as the coach moved off.

'Mrs Tatiana Crowe,' Tatty replied. 'Lydia's daughter-in-law.'

Another woman said, 'Didn't you die some years ago?'

'That was my husband's first wife.'

The third woman lifted a lorgnette and peered through the lenses. 'Oh, that's right, Titus married again. The housemaid, I believe?'

'No. I'm a bookkeeper and an assistant undertaker.'

Cora said, '*I'm* the housemaid.'

The first woman said. '*We* were Lydia's very good friends.'

'Were you?' Cora said. 'I didn't see you visiting her in all the time she was unwell, and that was for years.'

Tatty wondered if Cora had gone too far. If she annoyed these women enough they might bad-mouth the business.

'You'll have to forgive Cora,' she said. 'She's upset. She was very fond of Mrs Crowe.'

Someone made a disbelieving humphing noise.

'I must say Titus is putting on a splendid funeral for Lydia,' Lorgnette Lady said.

'Well, he should,' Woman Two replied. 'He owns a damn undertaking company.'

That was the last thing said on the journey to St Stephen's. To Tatty it seemed like an age and she could only imagine what it felt like to Cora, who often had trouble keeping her mouth closed.

The service at St Stephen's was very nice, not too long and with psalms chosen by Titus, who also spoke about his abiding love for his mother and the fact that his grief at losing her was tempered by the knowledge that she would shortly be joining his late father in heaven.

A gentle rain had started when it came time to bury Lydia and Tatty regretted not bringing an umbrella. Unlike when she'd buried her own mother, this time she wasn't consumed with grief, though she did very much regret that poor Lydia's last remaining years had been snatched away from her in the manner they had. She stood at the graveside as the vicar droned on and Lydia was finally lowered into her grave, the polished mahogany lid of her coffin glistening with a layer of raindrops like tiny jewels. A box of dirt was passed around and Tatty took a small handful and tossed it into the grave, wishing Lydia a peaceful eternity. Several feet away stood Titus, his hands clasped, his face set in a mask of resigned sadness.

Titus Crowe, the murderer.

Chapter Five

July 1866, Sydney

There was a lot less housework to do with Lydia gone: no preparation of special soft food, no time spent tending to her, and no laundering of soiled linen. Titus offered Tatty her room, but she didn't want to sleep where she was sure someone had been smothered to death, and she also didn't want to be that close to Titus. She liked her little room down the other end of the hallway.

It was lucky there was less domestic work because business was increasing: Titus said he sincerely hoped it was custom being lured away from Elias Nuttall. One morning a new widower, Mr Thorn, arrived at seven o'clock to purchase a coffin for his wife who had died in the night. He paid for it – a cheap but solidly made pine model – on the spot and took it away on his dray, depriving Titus of a delivery fee. Titus did, however, secure an appointment for the late afternoon at Mr Thorn's home to discuss funeral arrangements, so wasn't too sour.

Tatty went with him to the appointment. The house was on Albion Street in Surry Hills, and was a wooden shack with a verandah at the front and a dirt yard. In the single main room, where it seemed everyone slept, cooked and lived, Mrs Thorn was laid out in her coffin on the family dining table: a lace tablecloth had been draped over her body and a pillow placed beneath her head. She was dressed in what appeared to be a nightgown that had seen numerous washes, and she smelt not so much of decay but of serious illness including a hint of meat. Tatty knew that meant Mrs Thorn had likely died of cancer – possibly breast – and that she had an open wound.

There were eight children in the house ranging in age, Tatty estimated, from around two to perhaps sixteen. Mr Thorn had already mentioned he was a self-employed carter, so while he was out all day earning money, the older children would now have to care for their siblings. What an unfortunate situation.

The eldest girl, red-eyed and looking exhausted, offered tea as Tatty, Titus and Mr Thorn sat on chairs arranged away from the table.

'Thank you, love,' Tatty said. 'Would you like some help? Do you have water on the boil or can I fetch some for you? Is there a pump nearby?' If she'd known how poor the Thorns were she'd have brought some food – loaves and some butter and maybe some ham.

'We've got a pot on,' the girl said, indicating the sway suspended over the fireplace, 'but thank you.'

Titus withdrew his trusty notebook and Tatty thought, God, *please* don't bully Mr Thorn into accepting anything he can't afford.

But Titus tried, beginning his spiel with the need for the glass hearse and fancy horses with black velvet drapes and ostrich plumes to impress the neighbours, throwing in mutes, flowers, postmortem photography, mourning weeds for the children, and funeral biscuits for good measure.

Mr Thorn remained silent throughout. When Titus finally shut up he said, 'I doubt I can afford any of that. I could only just pay for the coffin. I have to feed my kids and I still owe the doctor for tending my wife. I dread to say this but I think I might have to bury her on the parish.'

Mr Thorn's daughter offered cups of tea on a tray: he and Tatty accepted, Titus didn't.

'No, you won't have to do that, Mr Thorn,' Tatty said. 'You don't need a hearse: you can take Mrs Thorn to the church and cemetery on your dray and mourners can walk behind. You also don't need mutes. Mr Crowe or perhaps our assistant Robert can walk ahead of you.' She glanced at Titus who glared back at her. 'Flowers aren't essential either and neither are photographs and biscuits. For mourning wear, go to Rodney Burton's emporium and buy a roll of cheap black ribbon and make armbands for yourself and the children.' That was as much as Tatty could think of to help Mr Thorn, though she couldn't assist with burial and gravediggers' fees.

Titus cleared his throat to speak but Mr Thorn beat him to it. 'I'd not thought of using my own dray. I could, couldn't I? If I did buy some of that black ribbon I could tie a bit to the horse's bridle and on the dray. There's nothing stopping me doing that, is there?'

'Nothing at all, Mr Thorn,' Tatty said. 'There's no shame in a homemade funeral.'

Mr Thorn looked much happier now. 'No, there isn't. Just about everything else we've ever had is homemade. But will you still oversee the proceedings and walk at the head of the procession, Mr Crowe? I'd like that at least.'

'For a fee,' Titus snapped, a vein in his temple throbbing like a fat worm.

A fee was agreed – hardly anything compared to what Titus usually made from a funeral – then he and Tatty took their leave.

Titus was silent on the journey home. Tatty knew him well enough by now to recognise that he was in a very bad mood.

'Are you upset?' she asked.

'What do you think?'

His tone of voice was enough to tell Tatty that no matter what answer she gave it would be the wrong one, so she kept quiet.

Arriving home, Titus bellowed for Henry, who came out of the stables and caught the reins as Titus threw them at him and climbed down from the dog-cart. Then he marched around to Tatty's side, took her hand and hauled her down, almost pulling her off her feet. Both frightened and angry, she regained her balance, yanked her hand out of Titus's grip and hurried into the house. Behind her she heard Henry say something curt to Titus, and her husband tell Henry to keep his nose out of it.

Inside she headed for the stairs to go to her room, but suddenly Titus was behind her, grasping her shoulder and steering her into the office. He shut the door after them.

'Let me out, please,' Tatty said, her heart racing and her legs suddenly wobbly. 'I'd like to go upstairs.'

Titus's face was red and his nostrils flared in and out like a horse's after a gallop. 'What do you think you were doing, talking that Thorn fellow out of more or less a whole funeral? I'm going to make less than two pounds on the whole ruddy thing! He isn't even in the burial club!'

Tatty decided to say exactly what she was thinking. 'He couldn't *afford* a funeral, Titus. Couldn't you see that?'

Titus moved closer. 'I don't care about what he can't afford, you stupid woman. He could have borrowed money but no, you had to interfere, didn't you? You had to meddle!'

'I was doing what I thought was best for the family!'

Tatty didn't even have time to duck: Titus's fist came out of the blue and hit her in the face. She fell to the floor instantly, face down. A second later she felt a hand grip her arm and another grab the back of her dress. Titus lifted her up, then slammed her down again, completely knocking the breath out of her. Finally, he kicked her in the side, hard, causing excruciating pain as his boot connected with her hip. She curled up, closed her eyes and lay there, too terrified to move until she heard Titus open the door and leave. And still she couldn't stir other than to draw in hesitant, pained breaths.

And then she realised the door was still open and someone might see her like this, and carefully sat up. She touched her face and her fingers came away bloody. Her nose? She thought she still had all her teeth, thank God. She crawled to the door to close it, but too late.

Cora was in the hall. She shook her head. 'God, girl. Did Titus do that? Henry sent me to find you. He was worried.'

Tatty nodded and winced: her face hurt and so did her hip.

'What a bastard,' Cora said. 'Come in the kitchen and I'll sort you out. We'll have to say you walked into something and banged your face, but Henry will tell Robert it was Titus, and if he doesn't I bloody will.'

'I know,' Tatty said.

Cora helped Tatty to her feet and to the kitchen where she sat her down and cleaned the blood off her face with warm water and dabbed witch hazel cream around her left eye, which was already sporting a spectacular bruise. Then she gave the jar to Tatty for her hip.

'You know, after this I'm thinking he really might have killed Maria.'

Tatty said, 'So am I.'

She also now thought that Titus actually *might* kill her.

*

Tatty's swollen and bruised face healed, although it took several weeks. She was sure people must have known how she'd received the injury but were too polite – or embarrassed – to comment. Titus never mentioned once what he'd done, and Tatty didn't raise the matter with him: she didn't think there was any point. She flinched every time he touched her, which he continued to do in his quest to conceive a son, but gradually she steeled herself to accept his advances without wincing, trusting that he probably wasn't going to punch her for absolutely no reason at all.

Lydia's will, apparently made before she'd lost her mind, was read in July, several months after her death, as it transpired that Titus hadn't believed she would have anything of real value to disburse – to him at least. While he was out seeing his solicitor,

Mr Stanley Parrish, Tatty went through his bedroom from floor to ceiling looking for anything she might find useful. In the inside pocket of a navy-blue grosgrain vest laid out beneath other clothing in a clothespress she found a small cache of high-quality jewellery – rings and ear-rings that had obviously belonged to Lydia – which she left in place. Then, standing on a chair, she discovered a square leather hat box pushed right to the back of the top of an armoire: that looked promising. She lifted it down and opened it: inside was not a hat but a ledger of financial records. She quickly read back through the most recent entries, which appeared to be payments from various people in the funeral industry, some of whom Tatty personally knew quite well by now. Obviously they were a record of commissions paid to Titus, though some were considerably larger than others. She turned to the front of the ledger, looking for further information, but found only columns of previous payments dating back years.

She checked the hat box again and this time noticed a discreet compartment, slipped her hand inside and found a small, leather-bound journal. Sitting down, she began to read and was immediately shocked. Apparently, Louis Coverdale the jeweller had a predilection for taking his pleasure with very young girls. Oh, that was horrible! How had Titus discovered that? Was it even true? If it was, Mr Coverdale would be considered a pariah if it ever became common knowledge. No wonder he continued to pay Titus, even if it wasn't true. Mrs Arnold the shroud-maker was an ex-convict but Tatty already knew that, and Titus had crossed out her entry, no doubt when she'd told him she would no longer pay him a commission. Mr Crumb the baker's entry similarly had a line through it. It seemed he had unwisely borrowed money from Titus but must have managed to repay the debt as he, too, had refused to work with Titus any longer. Rodney Burton the haberdasher allegedly was an invert, a word which Tatty had learnt described men who preferred men rather than women, and vice versa. But again, how did Titus really know his allegation was accurate? Where was his proof? There were additional entries, too, relating to Eliza McBride (allegedly she and her son were cursed!) and others Tatty knew, but not one for Nellie Harvey. Tatty wondered why not: she knew Titus very much took advantage of her, as did Elias Nuttall. In fact, Nuttall was probably also extorting money from everyone on Titus's list. It was a wonder anyone made a living at all.

She slid the journal back into the compartment, and lay the ledger in the bottom of the hat box, closed it, then carefully placed it at the top of the armoire, exactly how she'd found it. At least she knew now: Titus was not only a murderer, he was also a blackmailer, a cheat and without doubt a liar.

She couldn't have married anyone more despicable if she'd tried.

Titus came home from the solicitor in a bad mood. Lydia had left her jewellery to *my daughter-in-law, Maria Crowe*, and three hundred and sixty-five pounds to Titus, which Tatty thought was a very useful sum. As Maria had been dead for some years, Titus also by default received the jewellery.

Tatty said, 'Well, that's certainly a welcome windfall. Were you expecting that?'

'No, I wasn't. How long she was sitting on that I've no idea, the miserly old bat.'

Miserly? Tatty thought it was proof that Lydia had been very shrewd by holding on to some personal funds. It was just a shame she'd become so ill and hadn't been in a position to spend them.

She said, 'My mother could have done with a bequest like that when my father died. He was a lovely man but not the most reliable. We were left with the most complicated legal arrangement – it was intended to provide us with a home and income, but it all fell apart. It was very difficult to cobble together any sort of livelihood, and I believe it ultimately caused the death of my mother. In the end the government got everything – my father's lucrative business, our house, everything. I would *hate* to be left in that position again, of watching the government take all we had.'

She watched Titus's face closely. She'd lied about the fate of Hector's business (Selwyn Boyd had bankrupted that) and the family home — she'd walked out of that the day she'd left for Graves End to embark for Sydney, philosophical by then about the bank repossessing it — but New South Wales was a British colony and therefore operated under the English legal system. She was betting that Titus wasn't an expert on inheritance law, and she was certain he'd have no intention of giving anything to the government, or anyone else.

She was right. He looked outraged by the very idea, going red in the face, clutching his stomach and grimacing.

Tatty observed him for a moment. 'Are you quite well?'

'Dyspepsia.'

'Can I get you anything?'

'No. Stop fussing. Everything I own will be inherited by my sons. The business, this property, any funds in the bank, everything. That's already stipulated in my will. This government won't be getting its hands on anything *I've* worked for. To hell with that.'

Tatty blinked. 'Do you mean you've already made a will bequeathing everything you own to a son we don't have yet?'

Titus nodded, then let out an enormous burp redolent of the cup of tea he'd just finished.

Tatty couldn't quite understand what she was hearing. 'Have you considered what would happen if you were to be struck down before we *do* have a son? That would leave you, in effect, intestate, wouldn't it? Who would inherit the business then?'

'Well, not you.'

'I am aware of that. So what *would* happen?'

'I am not going to be "struck down", and you are going to damn well hurry up and produce a male child.'

It was clear to Tatty that Titus was in a particularly foul mood. 'May I ask, Titus, what is upsetting you?'

And off Titus went. Why hadn't his mother given him the three hundred and sixty-five pounds sooner, when he'd had bills to pay and purchases to make for the business? Why had she sat and watched him worry about things and work his fingers to the bone day after day knowing she could have helped him, but she hadn't? Why had she let him suffer, when she could so easily have eased his burden?

Possibly because she didn't like you, Tatty thought.

Titus stewed over his conviction that Lydia had deliberately withheld his inheritance money to such an extent that after several days he made himself physically sick, and Tatty had to visit the chemist to buy several one-ounce bottles of Dr Collis Browne's Chlorodyne to settle his stomach.

She emptied half of one bottle into a medicine glass and took it into the parlour where Titus was resting. Cora said he'd dashed to the privy twice while Tatty was up the street, but unsuccessfully as both times he'd puked in the yard.

'Here you are,' Tatty said. 'The chemist said this will fix virtually anything. Dysentery, hysteria, cholera, nerves, sick stomach, anything.'

'I don't have hysteria or dysentery and obviously I don't have cholera,' Titus grumbled.

'Would you like some lemonade to drink afterwards? I've just bought some lovely big lemons.'

'Tea.' Titus knocked back the chlorodyne in one swallow, and shuddered.

'Perhaps you should see a doctor,' Tatty suggested.

'No.'

'Do you *have* a physician?'

'A fellow used to come and see my mother, before it became obvious nothing was going to do anything to improve her lunatic behaviour. I saw him myself once or twice. Pickett? Pollock? No, definitely Pickett. But I'm not sick so what's the point? It's just dyspepsia. Cora's cooking, probably.'

'Well, it is something to think about, a doctor.'

'Tea?' Titus prompted. 'Then I have to deliver a coffin to Pitt Street, near the brickworks, and I want you to come. It's for a baby.'

'An infant or a toddler?' Tatty asked.

'Infant, so get the smallest size and put it in the dog-cart. I'll be with you when I've had my tea. Get Cora to make it.'

'You know, I could always deliver the coffin myself.'

'No!' Titus said, sounding alarmed. 'No. I don't want you working on your own. It would look ... It isn't appropriate. And you'll just go giving them discounts or free damn funerals.'

Cora was busy so Tatty made Titus his tea then selected a coffin, which was barely two feet long. She wrapped it in a blanket, stowed it under the dog-cart's seat and asked Henry to harness Shadow.

Poor Titus, he was in such a state. And tonight was a 'matrimonial relations' night, as she'd come to think of them. He seemed to have chosen Tuesdays and Fridays, and a note requesting her presence in his bedroom never failed to appear under her door on those evenings, except when he knew she was having her courses. He *could* ask her when she delivered his tea but he never did – it was always via a note, as though he couldn't make his request face to face, just as he couldn't take off his nightgown, only raise it to his waist. And at the end of the proceedings he would thank her and say, without fail, that he hoped there would be news of a pregnancy soon. He'd been saying it for almost five months now and was clearly becoming irate because she'd had nothing positive to tell him. Tonight, though, if he didn't feel better there would be no matrimonial relations, and for her that would be a relief: she could leave her sea sponge in its hiding place.

Soon Titus emerged from the house looking more or less recovered though heavy-lidded and moving rather slowly, and they set off up George Street, then turned left onto Liverpool, then right onto Pitt Street, Titus condescending to allow Tatty to drive the cart.

The baby had died of water on the brain and looked very odd with such a grotesquely swollen cranium above a tiny, sweet, almost transparent face. Tatty wondered if she had been in pain before she'd died, and feared she had. The mother and father certainly seemed as though they were suffering, and were exhausted. They were also extremely poor. They had three other children under the age of seven and were all living in one room in a rundown house they shared with two other impoverished families.

On the way back to George Street, Tatty said to Titus, 'What have they chosen for the funeral? Can they afford it?'

'They're getting the wooden hearse, two horses and Henry, nothing else. I believe they're borrowing the money for that. They're skint.'

Irritation washed over Tatty. '*Honestly*, Titus, where's your compassion? Couldn't you just *once* waive your fees for a family like that, or at least reduce them?'

'No, I could not,' Titus said. 'You *know* that. Have you not learnt your lesson? If I did it once they'd all want free funerals.'

Tatty had learnt a lesson and that was not to suggest cheaper options and discounts directly to bereaved families because she most certainly didn't want to be punched and kicked by Titus again, but she hadn't given up suggesting that he consider offering the bereaved some financial relief.

'But would they?' she said. 'I think it's a matter of pride for people to be able to pay for funerals if they can. You've seen how dreadful they feel when they can't.'

'No,' Titus said. 'It's out of the question.'

And that was that.

The following day she located Dr Pickett, who was younger than Tatty had been expecting and who had rooms in York Street near the corner of King Street, and asked him to visit Titus at home that evening. Titus wasn't thrilled at being ambushed but he agreed to answer questions about his stomach pain.

'Have you been generally well?' Dr Pickett asked.

Titus said, 'As a rule. You saw me last when I had the skin complaint, but I've had no recurrence.'

'Your wife tells me your mother died recently. Please accept my condolences. I hope her passing was peaceful.'

'She had an apoplectic stroke so possibly not as peaceful as it could have been, but quick, I believe.'

Dr Pickett nodded. 'That's a mercy, at least. How long have you been experiencing this discomfort relating to your stomach?'

'I've only really been bothered by it since my mother died. Well, no, since I discovered she left me some money. That was quite recently. I found that to be upsetting.'

Dr Pickett looked at Titus, then at Tatty, then back at Titus, his expression suggesting he didn't know quite what to say. What he came out with was: 'Is there anything else besides the pain?'

'I've been sick half a dozen times at least, and I've had flux.'

'Diarrhoea?'

Titus nodded.

'May I examine your abdominal area?' Dr Pickett asked.

Titus grudgingly reclined on the parlour couch while the doctor gently poked around his belly. Tatty could see that the prodding was uncomfortable for Titus.

Dr Pickett said, 'Thank you. Please sit up. I believe you have developed a stomach ulcer. These can occur from an excess of bile. For a long time an excess of bile was believed to be the result of the patient naturally possessing a choleric nature, but modern medical thinking now considers too much anxiety and worry to be at fault, and possibly even an over-indulgence in cheap red wine. Do you drink red wine, Mr Crowe?'

'No, I do not.'

'Then you need to do something to reduce the extent to which you worry. Your mother's illness must have been of great concern. Also, perhaps you fret too much about your business. You don't want to worry yourself into the grave, though if you did you could pre-organise yourself the most marvellous send-off, couldn't you? Ha ha!'

Tatty suppressed a smile. Titus remained stony-faced.

'Are you taking anything for your discomfort?'

'Dr Collis Browne's Chlorodyne,' Tatty answered.

The doctor nodded. 'That should help. It contains morphia and chloroform, which will slow the diarrhoea. I'm also going to recommend laudanum, also for the stomach pain. I could bleed you a little while I'm here? That sometimes helps.'

Titus said no.

'As you wish. Overall, however, a stomach ulcer won't heal unless you stop worrying. You should find yourself a pastime of some sort.'

'I'm too busy for a pastime.'

'And therein lies the problem, I'm afraid,' Dr Pickett said. 'You should also avoid citrus fruits.'

'It's not fatal, is it?' Titus asked. 'A stomach ulcer?'

'They can be, but in my experience usually not,' Dr Pickett said. 'Stick to a bland diet, use the laudanum regularly, find a relaxing hobby, don't over-tax yourself regarding your daily work, and you should soon be on the mend.'

*

September 1866, Sydney

Tatty stood outside the Observer Tavern at The Rocks end of George Street, steadying herself before she went in. She knew it was a rough pub, and that it wasn't a place for women such as herself. Also, she really didn't want to be recognised, and to that end she was wearing, as well as her usual black dress, a small bonnet and a short black veil of double tulle that concealed her face. People would definitely stare at the woman daring to enter a licensed hotel while in a state of deep mourning, but so what, if they couldn't identify her? And perhaps they wouldn't care anyway, if what she'd heard about the type of clientele who favoured the Observer Tavern was accurate.

As she entered through the double wooden doors, the level of conversation did subside a little, but not for long. The tavern's patrons gave her a quick look, then ignored her. She thought they were probably sailors as they were of all races and colours with a scattering of dock workers already drinking at ten in the morning, accompanied by a handful of prostitutes. She wasn't interested in the sailors and she definitely wasn't interested in the girls.

She made her way through the light haze of pipe smoke to the bar where a man stood drying tankards, his gut hanging over an apron (which surely must have been clean once?) tied around his middle.

'Lost your funeral procession, have you?'

Tatty ignored the man's sarcasm. 'I'm looking for Mr Samuel Tetley. I've been told to enquire here. Is that correct?'

'Who's asking?'

'I am.'

The barman continued to thoroughly dry his tankard – inside, outside and around the handle. Tatty could see he was deliberating.

Eventually he put the tankard aside and tucked his cloth into his apron. 'Follow me.'

He emerged from behind the bar and proceeded through a doorway and up some narrow stairs, farting with every step he took. Grateful she was wearing a veil, Tatty thought, God, even Shadow has better manners than that.

At the top of the stairs he led her along a short, dimly lit hallway to another door.

He knocked and shouted, 'Visitor!' then, retracing his steps, left her.

'Who is it?' a voice called.

I'm not falling into that trap, Tatty thought. 'Someone to see you, Mr Tetley. May I please come in?'

Nothing happened for well over a minute, then the door was opened by an elderly man not much taller or wider than her, with white hair, pale and softly lined skin, and small eyes magnified by very thick spectacles.

'Yes?'

'Mr Tetley?'

'Yes. Who are you?'

'Someone in need of assistance.'

Mr Tetley regarded her, then sighed and ushered her into his room. 'Please sit down,' he said, indicating a pair of chairs on either side of a table at a window. 'Don't tell me, someone recommended me to you?'

'Yes.'

Cora had, after asking her father, Thomas the ex-convict, for advice, without mentioning anything to do with Tatty, which had been difficult as Thomas was naturally nosy. According to Thomas, Samuel Tetley – barrister, master forger and ex-convict – was the man to see, since the infamous Avery Bannerman had been killed over a dozen years previously. Now, Tatty sincerely hoped Thomas knew what he was talking about.

'Sadly, I've retired,' Mr Tetley said.

Tatty ignored that. 'I have a problem.'

'Yes. Everyone who comes to see me does.'

'I'm willing to offer you a generous fee.'

'What magnitude of generous?'

'Ten pounds,' Tatty replied. It would make a hole in her secret nest-egg, but it would be worth it.

Mr Tetley looked out the window. 'Tell me your problem.'

'I'm married to a businessman who refuses to make provision for me of any sort in his will.'

'So he isn't dead yet?'

'No.'

'Legally he doesn't have to, you know.'

'Yes, I know that. But I want the business when he dies.'

'Is that likely to be soon? Because if it isn't, what sort of businesswoman will you be when you're eighty-five years old?'

'I won't be that old. I'm more than twenty years younger than he is. As to when he might die, I've no idea, but he isn't a well man at the moment.'

Mr Tetley sighed. 'So you want a will in your favour to produce when he does die?'

'Yes and no,' Tatty said. 'I want some sort of document that gives me full control of the business to the extent that it might as well be mine.'

'Let me think for a moment,' Mr Tetley said.

It was Tatty's turn to look out the window. She watched the traffic go by on the street below, and wondered what Titus was doing. She'd told him she was only popping out for half an hour.

Finally Mr Tetley said, 'Obviously, if you wish to engage my services, you're going to have to tell me who you are.'

Tatty took off the veil and bonnet. 'My name is Tatiana Crowe. I'm married to Titus Crowe. Titus owns Crowe Funeral Services.'

'I have heard of the business. Not a particularly popular man according to some, your husband.'

'Undertakers aren't.'

'No. Well, I suggest a will declaring that at some time in the past your husband put the business in your name, even though to all intents and purposes he has been running it. I can prepare a document specifically verifying that.'

'I have worked in the business since January, 1865,' Tatty said. 'I am the bookkeeper and an assistant undertaker.'

Mr Tetley said, 'Yes, I'm aware of that. You've made your mark. If it appears that your husband has transferred the business to you, then you already legally own it and there is no need for you to inherit it. As a widow you become a *feme sole*, meaning you have the same status as a single woman, and therefore the right to own property or a business in your own name. What you do with that property or business, and any income arising from it, is up to you.'

That sounded to be exactly what Tatty was hoping for.

She said, 'I should perhaps tell you that in the will he has now, Titus has stated he intends to leave the business to his sons. Or so he says. I haven't actually seen the will.'

'Hmm, that could be a complication. How many sons does he have?'

'None. He's expecting me to produce at least one.'

Mr Tetley frowned. 'And will you?'

'I don't intend to.'

'Yet he's written this into his will?'

'So he says.' Tatty handed Mr Tetley some folded papers. 'These are samples of Titus's writing.'

'Thank you. Your documents should be ready to pick up in three days.'

'Do I pay you now?'

'That's up to you.'

Tatty gave him the money.

'You must understand that if your subterfuge is discovered,' Mr Tetley said, 'you can never divulge who provided the forgeries. I do not relish spending the rest of my life in Darlinghurst Gaol, or hanging by my neck in the yard there.'

'I understand that, Mr Tetley,' Tatty said, getting to her feet. 'And I do appreciate it. Thank you very much for your help.'

Part Three

1867

*Because I could not stop for death,
He kindly stopped for me*

Emily Dickinson, 1890

Chapter Six

July 1867, Sydney

Titus soldiered on over the next nine or ten months but his health didn't improve. It seemed he'd been unwell almost since his mother had died. As well as the ongoing stomach pain and intermittent vomiting and diarrhoea, he also lost weight, which his already thin frame couldn't afford, he complained about tingling sensations in his hands and feet, and he found himself unable to perform sexually (much to Tatty's relief). He was constantly tired and even more short-tempered than usual, to the point that Tatty felt compelled to ask Dr Pickett to call at the house regularly every month to see him.

Dr Pickett continued to advocate liberal doses of laudanum and Dr Collis Browne's Chlorodyne, added pure morphine tablets for extreme pain to Titus's medicinal regime, recommended Orange Quinine Wine for good measure, and suggested plenty of bone marrow broth at mealtimes.

Titus didn't bother with the wine and actually quite enjoyed the broth, which Tatty and Cora made between them, but found after a month or so that he could barely function in the mornings until he'd had a good swig of the laudanum and several morphine tablets. After that, he told Tatty, his pain seemed to fade into the background (until the medication wore off), and even though he felt a little light-headed, he could see no reason why he shouldn't work as usual.

Tatty could – Titus just wasn't pulling his weight. Before he'd become ill he'd been adept at managing several funerals at the same time and had always known what was going on, who wanted what and where everything needed to be and when, but that was beyond him now. Tatty suggested to him that while he was ill he step back and allow Robert, or even her, to take on more of the work, but he'd been adamant: *he* was the undertaker and *he* would oversee the funerals. So she worked around him and quietly did more of the organising and decision-making and by mid-year he seemed to have very grudgingly accepted the situation – as long as, Tatty realised, it looked to all outward appearances as though he were still in charge of Crowe Funeral Services. She was happy with that.

Robert began to blossom. One April afternoon he'd returned in a glum mood from a visit with his fiancée, Julia, announcing at the supper table that their betrothal had finally crumbled under the pressure of her disapproval of his choice of vocation.

'Oh dear, I am sorry about that, Robert,' Tatty had said, though actually she wasn't. They'd all met Julia and none of them had liked her much, thinking her overbearing, and extremely opinionated about the profession of undertaking. They thought Robert deserved better.

'Thank you,' Robert said. 'It was a bit awkward. She was really angry and finally gave me an ultimatum and said I had to choose between her or … what did she say? "Those damn dead bodies."'

An anticipatory silence fell across the table, which Henry broke by laughing. 'You chose the dead bodies, didn't you?'

Robert nodded.

Cora gave one of her shrieks of laughter and slapped the table.

'I just got sick of lying to her,' Robert said. 'I like this job. I do. And now that Titus is so unwell …'

He paused and glanced over his shoulder at the doorway into the hall, as though expecting to see Titus hovering there. He wasn't and Tatty knew he wouldn't be. He was upstairs, resting and eating his supper off a tray. 'Now Titus is unwell and we're all more involved in the business,' Robert continued, 'I think things are even better. The work's really satisfying ...' Another quick backwards glance. 'At least, *I* think it is, especially now there's a lot less bullying and cheating of customers going on.'

'Hear, hear,' Henry said. 'It really galled me, all that fearmongering and underhandedness. It was just so ... shoddy.'

Tatty blinked. Henry had never previously mentioned anything about Titus's dishonesty. 'You're talking about Titus?'

'Of course he is,' Cora said. 'Who else?'

Tatty said, 'I didn't realise you felt so strongly about his —'

'Shitty behaviour,' Cora interjected.

Tatty said, 'Henry? You should have said something.'

'Who to?' Henry replied. 'Talking to Titus would have been a waste of time. He doesn't listen to anyone.'

'Why haven't you left then, if you really don't like the way he operates?' Cora asked.

'I'm not leaving my horses.'

Cora smirked. 'And?'

'And *what*?' Henry said, sounding irritated.

That caused an awkward silence, though Tatty wasn't sure why. She said to Robert, 'Will you remain friends with Julia?'

'I don't think so. Her mother told me this afternoon I was never to darken their doorway again.'

Tatty said, 'Oh.' That did sound final.

'You're not heartbroken, though, are you?' Cora asked. 'About your romance turning to crap?'

'*Cora*,' Tatty said.

Robert said, 'Well, we *were* courting for over two years, but it wasn't always the best of times. I expect I probably will overcome my disappointment.' He reached for the salt shaker in the cruet set. 'Is this chicken?'

'No, it's broiled fish,' Cora said. 'With curry sauce.'

Tatty sighed. The supper was awful, which meant Titus probably wouldn't have eaten it. She'd take him up some bread and butter with his cup of tea.

*

In July an event occurred that shook Titus out of his drug-induced lethargy and at least temporarily took his mind off his illness: a vast new cemetery of two hundred acres for burials of all faiths was consecrated out west at Haslam's Creek. Named Haslam's Creek Cemetery, it was intended to replace Devonshire Street public cemetery in town, which had been growing increasingly crowded and objectionable over the years and had just been closed. Haslam's Creek Cemetery could be reached by railway, a spur that split off from the Parramatta line that departed from Redfern Railway Station in the city. It cost a shilling per mourner to travel in a specially designated funeral train – coffins went free in the hearse van – which made the return trip out to the cemetery twice a day. Within the new cemetery grounds, mourners disembarked at a new mortuary station and coffins were unloaded and transported to waiting gravesites.

Titus stewed mightily about this new situation reducing the amounts he could charge for distances travelled, if most funeral processions would only be travelling to Redfern Station because everyone would be getting on the train. He fretted and griped to such an extent that Tatty thought she might lose her mind, so she thought about the matter then suggested to him that he raise his prices very slightly across the board to compensate, which cheered him up. And then when she had the idea of sending attendants (some combination of Titus, herself and Robert) out to Haslam's Creek with funeral parties to 'ensure smooth execution of proceedings' and charging for that, he was absolutely thrilled and went immediately to tell Robert about his new idea. When the other funeral companies, including Elias

Nuttall's, realised what Crowe Funeral Services were doing, they very soon followed suit.

In August, only a month after the new cemetery had opened, Crowe Funeral Services organised a burial that turned out to be enormous. The deceased was named Patrick Byrne, a furnaceman who'd been scalded to death at his place of work, and it seemed that almost every Irish Catholic in Sydney had turned out to farewell him. The Byrne family had hired the glass hearse with four horses with all the accessories, and *six* mourners' carriages, and what a scramble it had been to hire enough because apparently there was another big funeral on at the same time. Dozens of carts, drays and a handful of buggies and hired cabs, all packed with mourners, joined the procession, so that by the time it left the Byrne home on Campbell Street and headed for Redfern Station via Crown Street it was half a mile long and the mean little streets of Surry Hills were jammed with traffic.

'This might be the biggest funeral we've ever done,' Tatty said to the coachman beside her, whose name was Charlie and who normally worked for T Bragg, Undertakers.

She was riding with him on a mourners' carriage, Robert was with the carriage behind them, and Titus was with Henry on the hearse.

'It's big all right,' Charlie said, reining in his horses to avoid a hansom cab rudely barging through the procession at an intersection ahead. He trapped the reins between his knees and closed the upper buttons of his topcoat. It was starting to rain. 'At this rate we'll be lucky if everyone gets to the station before the train leaves. It's an Irish funeral, isn't it?'

Tatty nodded.

'Catholic or Protestant?'

'Catholic.'

The procession moved off and Charlie took up the reins again. 'Are you and Mr Crowe going to the cemetery?'

Tatty nodded. 'And Robert.'

Charlie said, 'Well, you should be in for an interesting morning.'

Tatty looked at him. 'Should we? Why?'

'I heard there's another Irish funeral on the train same time as you, except they're Protestants. Name of Walsh, I think.'

Her moderately good mood evaporating, Tatty said, 'Is it a big party, do you know?' Though she knew it probably would be – Irish burials usually were well attended.

'Nuttall Undertakers are doing the funeral,' Charlie said. 'A friend of mine works for them, and he said they're expecting a couple of hundred in the procession.'

Tatty expected Titus was going to be riled when he heard that. 'Will there be enough room on the train?'

Charlie shrugged. 'I expect they won't all go out.'

Tatty hoped not. She had, of course, been involved with Irish wakes and funerals previously, and knew that a good deal of alcohol was likely to be consumed. She'd never, however, been in the middle of two factions who were grieving, possibly drunk, and who also vehemently opposed each other on religious grounds. Her mother had warned her about the Irish. In Betsy's opinion the odd Irish person was perfectly decent, but in general they were lazy, rowdy, criminal and violent, and if you got a crowd of them divided along religious lines and threw alcohol into the mix, there would always be hell to pay. Which, Tatty had thought at the time, had been a tiny bit hypocritical given her mother's own social background.

Strictly speaking, Crowe Funeral Services only had to see that Patrick Byrne's body was taken off the train, safely transported to the Catholic section of the cemetery, and buried in the correct plot. Whatever happened beyond that was none of their business, as no undertaker was liable for the behaviour of mourners either on the train or at the cemetery, but she felt some responsibility for Mrs Byrne and her eight children, who she was sure wouldn't want the day of Patrick Byrne's burial ruined by a riot with mourners from another funeral party.

The situation didn't appear any less ominous when the procession reached Cleveland Paddock, the site of the corrugated tin shed that was Redfern Station, also known rather grandly as Sydney Railway Terminus. The building was one hundred feet long and thirty feet wide with a single low wooden platform, and horribly hot in the summer, especially when the train was inside it, waiting for passengers to board.

Parked outside now were a hearse and four black coaches – presumably the funeral vehicles supplied by Nuttall Undertakers – and a considerable collection of other assorted conveyances. In fact, almost a mirror image of the Byrne funeral procession.

Tatty checked her pocket watch and noted that the train was due to leave in fifteen minutes. They were running rather late. She could hear the engine hissing away inside the shed and see and smell its oily steam. She climbed down from her seat on the carriage and hurried across to the hearse to speak to Titus, who was knocking back a swig of laudanum.

'Did you know there's another funeral party on the train this mor—'

'I can see that,' Titus snapped, cutting her off.

'Also Irish, but Protestant,' Tatty said, trying not to snap back. 'And Elias Nuttall's attending.'

Titus stifled a burp, winced, pressed the heel of his hand below his sternum, then got down from the hearse. 'So?'

'Catholics and Protestants?' Tatty said. 'There could be trouble.'

'There could, and if some stupid Micks want to beat the life out of one another, what's that got to do with me? Or bloody Elias Nuttall, for that matter, may he rot in hell.' Titus turned away and said to Henry, 'Grab Robert, will you, and we'll move the coffin to the train.'

'Are you well?' Tatty asked. 'Perhaps you should stay here in town?'

Frankly, she thought at this point that everything would go much more smoothly during funerals if Titus wasn't staggering about looking and feeling so ill. She, Robert and Henry knew their jobs thoroughly so there was no need at all for him to attend, but he could not relinquish control. She expected he thought that if he appeared as usual people would assume he remained in charge of the business, but surely they must have noticed he was sick. On her part she was dismayed that he seemed stuck in a limbo of ill health, neither recovering nor growing mortally worse. She hoped the situation changed for him soon.

Titus completely ignored her suggestion and she watched as Patrick Byrne's coffin was taken from the hearse and transferred, flowers and all, to the hearse van at the rear of the funeral train waiting alongside the platform. Henry and the hearse then departed, as did the hired mourners' coaches and private transport, followed only minutes later by the funeral vehicles and other transport associated with the Walsh party, leaving Cleveland Paddock suddenly almost empty. Tatty hurried along the platform, peering through the carriage windows, hoping for a glimpse of Mrs Byrne and looking for somewhere to sit. She couldn't see the new widow and the carriages seemed moderately full, though she did spot three vacant seats together in the carriage immediately behind the engine. She beckoned to Robert and Titus farther along the platform, stepped into the carriage and secured the three seats. As soon as Titus sat down he swilled more laudanum, and the train, which had been building up steam, pulled slowly out of the station.

'Are you in pain?' Tatty asked Titus.

'What do you think?'

'Can I do anything to help you?'

'No.'

'Perhaps you *should* have gone home with Henry,' Tatty said again.

'No!' Titus tugged at his collar and looked out the window, avoiding her gaze. 'No. I've got work to do.'

He laced his fingers protectively over his belly, and allowed his head to fall against the back of the seat. His eyes closed.

Tatty expected him to fall asleep soon, in spite of the noise in the carriage, after all the medicine he'd swallowed that morning.

She looked across the aisle at a group of people sharing food from a basket, and a bottle of whiskey. The train hadn't even left the city yet. A man with the whiskey raised a hand in greeting.

'Good morning,' Tatty said. 'Are you with the Byrne funeral party?'

'No, love,' the man replied. 'We're here for Aidan Walsh, exceptional man that he was. Knew him yourselves, did you?'

'Er, no. We're here for the widow and family of the late Patrick Byrne.'

The man's face hardened and his companions all turned to stare. 'I heard tell he was one of them new Fenians,' he said. 'Would you be one of them as well, then?'

Tatty said, 'No, we're undertakers. Please accept our condolences regarding the death of Mr Walsh.'

'Oh, well. Right,' the man said, visibly mollified. 'Thank you.'

After a while Tatty said to Robert, 'The train really is quite full, isn't it? I'd say they'll have to add more carriages before long. Imagine if there wasn't enough room for all the mourners. I mean, when you think that clergy have to be booked and graves dug out at the cemetery, you can't expect families to turn around and take the bodies of their loved ones back home just because they can't get on the train.'

She was wittering and she knew it.

Robert half turned in his seat to face her. 'Do you mind if I ask, what is it you're really worried about?'

Tatty opened her reticule, looked in it for nothing in particular while she thought, then closed it again. He could be quite perceptive, Robert. 'I don't want there to be any trouble. Between, you know –' she tilted her head at Mr Whiskey across the aisle '– them and our mourners. People should be able to bury their dead in peace.'

'And I'm sure Mrs Byrne and her family will,' Robert said. 'And so will the other lot. Don't worry, you'll see.'

Tatty didn't reply, and hoped he was right.

The trip out to Haslam's Creek Cemetery was reasonably uneventful, Titus managing to doze through most of it. The train stopped twice to pick up more funeral parties: after the second stop there was barely even standing room in Tatty's carriage. Mr Whiskey and his group became progressively inebriated but not offensively so, evidently preferring to sing rather than pick fights. There was a lot of sloppy toasting to the late Aidan Walsh, which, together with the rocking and rattling of the train, meant the smell of liquor in the carriage was quite overpowering. At one point Tatty opened the window and stuck her head out for some fresh air, almost immediately getting a smut in her eye. Someone gave her Coca Eye Drops that were so effective that not only did the pain stop within a minute, she discovered she couldn't blink or move her eyeball for several hours. Rats.

When he awoke Titus didn't notice her eye was paralysed, though Tatty thought *his* discomfort seemed to have eased.

'Are you feeling improved?' she asked.

Titus just grunted. 'Where are we?' he said, looking out the window.

'Almost there. Perhaps another five minutes to Haslam's Creek Station,' Tatty said. Then another ten or so to the railway station within the cemetery, which wouldn't be a minute too soon as she could really use a privy.

The train changed engines so it could double back onto the dedicated rail spur at Haslam's Creek Station and in a few minutes it arrived at Mortuary Station inside the cemetery, steam spewing and brakes shrieking as it pulled up alongside the platform. Tatty thought the station was beautiful with its sandstone arches and carvings of angels and cherubs, flowers and fruits. She especially liked the ornate tower topped with a cross, which housed a bell that rang just before the train was about to depart. Too bad if you were a long way away into the cemetery when you heard it toll. You would either have to run like the wind or be prepared to walk into Haslam's Creek village and wait for the next train.

As soon as the train came to a halt at the station the carriage doors opened and people poured out, some the worse for wear, suggesting that Tatty's carriage-mates weren't the only ones who'd been refreshing themselves on the trip out. One man slipped and became wedged between his carriage and the platform and had to be hauled out by his companions, leaving his boots behind on the railway track beneath the carriage.

The guard opened the hearse van and four coffins were unloaded – the two Irishmen and the two further deceased persons picked up along the way – inciting a mad dash for the wheeled litters lined up along the wall of the station, though Tatty had already sent Robert to collect one for the body of Patrick Byrne. Titus had gone off somewhere saying he wasn't feeling well again. Tatty spotted the short, slightly stocky, impeccably dressed (in black) figure of Elias Nuttall, gave a polite but neutral wave, then asked Robert to organise lifting Patrick Byrne's coffin onto the litter – quite a task as he'd been a big man. She quickly used the privy designated to ladies (thank God the door had a lock on it) then, feeling much relieved, set off to find Mrs Byrne and her family among the crowd.

Eventually, everyone in the Byrne party separated themselves from the melee and gathered outside the station, ready to walk to the Catholic section of the cemetery.

And then it started to rain again.

'For God's sake,' Titus said, appearing at Tatty's elbow and dabbing at his mouth with a handkerchief. 'Could this day get any worse?'

Tatty could see he wasn't going to be much help with the grieving Byrne family, or anything else, and silently cursed him for not going home with Henry. She asked Robert to rally half a dozen burly men to take charge of the litter, as the ground was bumpy in places and the grass beyond the few carriageways a little long, and off they went. She and Robert led the procession, followed by the men pushing the wheeled litter, then Patrick Byrne's immediate family, then the large group of mourners, which had now been joined by a priest in a white cassock and purple stole.

At the gravesite, the coffin was lifted off the litter and carefully settled onto planks above it. The priest – the sexton holding a black umbrella over his head – intoned some long passages from the bible while everyone else endured the rain, responding where appropriate to the priest's supplications. Then finally the last blessing was read, the Pater Noster said, the planks were removed and Patrick Byrne's body was lowered into the earth. Tatty eyed Mrs Byrne, who stood motionless, holding the hands of two of her youngest children and staring sightlessly ahead as her husband's coffin disappeared into the ground, and wondered what she was contemplating. Was she thinking about how she was going to feed her kids now that the family breadwinner had gone? Or perhaps how she might keep a roof over their heads? Or simply, how was she going to go on without her man? All questions Betsy had asked after Hector had died, and the same dilemmas, Tatty knew, that sat heavily in the hearts and heads of most new widows.

On the other hand, if Titus died and *she* ended up with nothing – except for the money she had hidden in her trunk – would that really be so bad? She didn't have children to feed, clothe and house: she didn't have anyone else dependent on her. It would be so much worse if she did, just as it was going to be so much worse for Mrs Byrne.

Someone passed around a bucket of dry soil and mourners took a small handful each and threw it onto the coffin. Then everyone stood and watched while the gravediggers filled in the grave. Tatty understood why. They wanted to make sure Patrick Byrne was properly buried, and where he should be, before they left him for the last time.

She surreptitiously looked at her watch. The train wouldn't be leaving for thirty-five minutes and already people were drinking again, many from bottles tucked under their coats. She didn't blame them. It was cold and wet. If they had any sense, and she was sure they did, they'd soon move to the shelter of Mortuary Station and no doubt the Walsh party would too, if they weren't already there. Unease prickled her scalp as she imagined the clash that might ensue between the two groups. She hoped Robert was right. She hoped all her worries were for nothing and she was just being silly.

And where on earth was Titus?

She walked back to the station through the ankle-length grass with Mrs Byrne, chatting with her about her children and what sort of help she might expect from friends and family, and by the time they arrived she was satisfied she'd done what she could for the new widow. Behind them straggled mourners from the Byrne funeral party – dripping wet, many in various states of drunkenness, and all grieving for Patrick Byrne and his immediate family.

Tatty saw two things as they reached the station platform. One was Titus sitting on a bench, looking reasonably dry but miserable and bad-tempered. Clearly he wasn't any better. Tatty wasn't feeling that sprightly herself: she was cold and wet through to her underclothes, and her eye still felt extremely odd. She was also angry at Titus: yes, he was ill, but today he'd been absolutely no help at all.

The other thing she noticed, because it was unmissable, was the Walsh party trudging towards the station from the direction of the vast Anglican section of the cemetery, looking like a procession of drowned rats. Someone in the group hurled an empty bottle; it tumbled for some distance through the rain and hit one of the few mature trees on the lawn marked out for future graves, to the rousing cheers of the Walsh party.

Tatty didn't think that boded well at all.

Then someone else, a man from the Byrne party, shouted, 'Pick that up, you fucking Proddie. Have you no respect?'

He was backed up by shouts and jeers from his fellow mourners, who veered raggedly away from the direction of Mortuary Station and headed directly for the Walsh group.

Oh no, Tatty thought. Oh hell.

The women and children in both parties quickly separated themselves from the men, voices were raised, insults were traded, and the first punch was thrown. Within seconds a vigorous brawl was underway, with shouting and swearing, fists flying, hats sent spinning, clothes tearing, women screaming and children crying.

'Oh Christ!' Mrs Byrne cried. 'Can you not do something to stop them, Mrs Crowe? Please! This is my husband's *wake*!'

Tatty spotted Robert, beckoned to him, then marched over to Titus, still sitting on the bench, his handkerchief to his mouth. 'For God's sake, you and Robert go and find Nuttall, will you? Get him to make his crowd behave.'

'Where is he?' Titus said, his voice muffled.

Tatty peered out into the rain. There were bodies everywhere — men still throwing punches and others sitting on the wet grass dabbing at bloodied faces. She spied Nuttall and his assistant — whose name Tatty thought might be Benjamin — huddling beneath the tree at which that first bottle had been thrown.

'He's under that tree. Go and talk to him, Titus. Please.'

And to Titus's credit, he shoved his handkerchief into his pocket, downed a hearty swig of laudanum, and walked out into the rain, Robert beside him. Tatty followed: she'd seen familiar faces in the Walsh and Byrne parties, women she'd met while working at previous funerals, and she had an idea.

It didn't take her long. She quickly approached each woman and asked her to tell every man she knew to please stop fighting, for the sake of Mrs Byrne, Mrs Walsh and their children. And they all did, with the exception of one woman who told her that all Protestants had the right to fight for religious freedom, so bugger off.

Quite quickly the fighting ceased, leaving both groups standing sheepishly about in the rain, straightening coats, looking for dislodged hats, and feeling for wobbly teeth.

Except for one pair of men, still furiously swinging at each other as though prepared to fight to the death.

Stunned, Tatty saw that it was Titus and Elias Nuttall.

How could Titus be engaged in a violent round of fisticuffs when he couldn't stay awake on the train out, and was so ill he'd been next to useless during Patrick Byrne's actual burial?

And why were they fighting?

She trotted over to the crowd that was now forming a large circle around her husband and his arch-enemy and squeezed in next to Robert.

'What's happened?' she said. 'My God, Titus will get beaten to a pulp.'

Titus might seem to have an advantage over Nuttall because of his height, but Nuttall was a solid, powerful man and presumably in good health.

Robert said, 'Titus told Nuttall to get his mourners under control. Nuttall accused Titus of setting the Byrne mourners onto the Walsh mourners. Titus said he didn't. Nuttall said he did. Titus called Nuttall a second-rate little blackmaster and Nuttall called Titus a lying, swindling death-hunter. Titus threw a punch and, well ...'

He gestured at the fighting men. As Titus and Nuttall moved here and there, their wild swings causing them to stagger across the grass, the circle of onlookers followed, expanding and contracting like an elastic band.

Tatty heard the train pull into Mortuary Station, carrying mourning parties for that afternoon's funerals. God, this had turned into a nightmare.

'Stop them, Robert, for God's sake.'

At that moment, Titus and Nuttall, clutching each other's coats, reeled a good yard towards one side of the circle, which broke open, leaving Nuttall teetering on the edge of a gaping, newly dug grave. Titus promptly gave him a hard shove, and Nuttall went down with a shout and a splash into the mud- and water-filled hole. Most of the crowd cheered – including Titus – then immediately lost interest and headed back to Mortuary Station.

Tatty couldn't resist: she approached the grave and looked into it, where Nuttall stood ankle-deep in filthy water, his face, hair and clothing covered with mud, shaking a fist up at her. He looked to her like some awful little troll that might have been conjured by the Grimm brothers.

She couldn't help it. She laughed.

'Get me out of here *now*!' he bellowed.

Tatty couldn't see why she should: she didn't work for Elias Nuttall. She wasn't married to him, either.

She said to Robert, 'Where's Benjamin? It is Benjamin, isn't it?'

Robert nodded and waved out to Nuttall's assistant, still standing unhappily under the tree. Benjamin trotted over and peered down into the grave.

'*Get me out of here!*'

'God, there'll be hell to pay for the next week,' Benjamin said under his breath. 'Can I come and work for you?'

The bell in Mortuary Station's tower tolled.

'Quickly,' Tatty said. 'The train's leaving in a matter of minutes.'

Robert helped Benjamin to position a couple of planks against the side of the grave so Nuttall could inch his way up and out of it. Tatty stood and waited for Robert, although she wondered if Nuttall thought she was lingering just to enjoy his humiliation. She very much wasn't: as soon as he was out of the grave, she grabbed Robert's muddy hand and ran with him to Mortuary Station where the train had almost built up a full head of steam. They threw themselves into the nearest carriage regardless of whether there were seats or not, the guard closed the door and the train pulled away from the platform.

Tatty looked out the window but there was no sign of Benjamin and a muddy Nuttall.

Oh well.

*

September 1867, Sydney

Spring was showing signs of arriving, but Cora was still serving hearty fare at mealtimes. That day's dinner was fish pie with a mashed potato top, which Tatty was looking forward to, with braised cabbage and glazed carrots, except Cora had overcooked the glaze and had to gouge the carrots out of the pan with a fish slice. So mashed carrots, basically.

'Nice pie,' Henry said. 'What's the fish?'

'Mullet,' Cora said. 'I bought it at the market this morning so it's fresh.'

'It *is* very good,' Tatty agreed, quite surprised.

Robert said nothing, too busy stuffing his face.

Tatty passed Titus the bowl of carrots. 'Would you like some of these? Are you enjoying the pie?'

Titus leant back in his chair. 'I'm not particularly hungry. I thought I was but I'm not.'

'Is it your stomach?' Tatty said. She knew without doubt it would be.

'Fetch my laudanum, will you? There's some in the parlour. And get some of my tablets, too.'

Tatty knew there was laudanum in the parlour. There were also several bottles in Titus's bedroom, another in his office, and one each in the dog-cart and both hearses. She was forever replacing them, and was a familiar face now, she knew, at the chemist.

Titus took his usual decent swallow when she handed him the laudanum. In fact he used it to wash down the morphine tablets. His health hadn't improved in spite of Dr Pickett's visits, the medicine he was taking, and the fact that of all the staff at Crowe Funeral Services he was doing the least work. He had been chronically ill now for fourteen months, and it seemed he might never get better. He was extremely thin, his hair was starting to fall out, and Tatty thought he looked dreadful: a living caricature, in fact, like the undertakers lampooned by cartoonists in the papers.

'Would you prefer just a slice of bread and butter for now?' she asked him. 'Or perhaps a cup of tea? You could have some of the pie when the laudanum and the morphine's taken effect. If Robert's left any, that is.'

Titus shook his head.

Tatty frowned. He was looking at her oddly, as though he were about to say something but couldn't remember what.

Then he leant suddenly to his right and vomited a huge gout of blood. It splattered across the floor in all directions, making Cora shriek and Henry jump out of the way, fork still in hand.

Titus lurched to his feet, vomited again, this time down his front and across the table, collapsed back onto his chair then fell to the floor.

Tatty darted around the table and pulled him onto his side in case he vomited again, which he did – a fat, blackberry-coloured snake of congealing blood that truly shocked her before it settled and widened into a pool on the floorboards around his head.

'Fucking hell,' Henry said.

Robert just stared.

'Don't just stand there!' Tatty barked. 'Run and get Dr Pickett! *Now!*'

As Henry took off Tatty turned back to Titus, but she already knew Dr Pickett would be too late. It was probably too late now.

She pressed her fingertips against the bloodied skin over Titus's carotid artery, feeling for a pulse. She was no doctor but she definitely knew where that should be. She felt the weakest of flutters.

'Titus? Titus!'

His mouth opened but nothing came out.

'*Titus!*'

The life beneath Tatty's fingers gave one more faint beat, then ceased.

She waited, just to be sure, but there was nothing else.

Titus was dead.

'Has he gone?' Robert asked.

Tatty nodded and stood up, wiping her bloody hands on a table napkin.

'Fuck me,' Cora said. 'That was the most disgusting thing I've ever seen in my life. I thought a lizard or something was coming out of his mouth. *I* nearly threw up! Bloody hell!'

'Be quiet, Cora,' Tatty said. 'My husband is dead.'

Cora said, 'Sorry, I wasn't thinking. Robert, don't just stand there like a lummox, fill a couple of buckets with water – cold, mind – and we'll start mopping. God, what a mess.'

Robert said, 'But we've got a funeral party we have to get on the three o'clock train.'

Tatty was aware of that. They would have to do it without Titus, obviously. That would be the easy bit. But before that there was a lot of other work to do.

By the time Henry arrived back with Dr Pickett, Titus had been carried up to his bedroom, hastily washed down by Tatty and Cora to get rid of the worst of the blood, dressed in a clean nightgown and laid out on his bed. Robert suggested putting him in a coffin in the parlour, but Tatty said no: she had plans for her husband.

After hearing what had happened at the dinner table, Dr Pickett certified that Titus had died from one or more perforated stomach ulcers. Tatty could have gone to the Office of Births, Deaths and Marriages – where she and Titus had been married – and certified the same thing, as certification of death by a doctor wasn't a legal requirement. She only had to register the death within thirty days to make the notification legal. But Dr Pickett had treated Titus, and he'd now seen his recently deceased body, so it seemed fitting.

'Please accept my condolences, Mrs Crowe,' Dr Pickett said. 'And I realise this won't be much consolation, but exsanguination is perhaps one of the most gentle and least painful ways to expire. One just ... loses consciousness and then the spark goes out.'

'The way he was vomiting didn't look very gentle,' Tatty said.

'Mmm, perhaps not,' Dr Pickett agreed.

As soon as she'd paid the doctor and he'd left, Tatty called a meeting.

'We're going to be one short this afternoon. Henry, I want you to start getting the horses ready, please. Robert, I'd like you to go around to the other undertakers and ask if we can borrow someone. Tell them we'll pay. But *don't* ask Elias Nuttall, obviously.'

'He'll be cock-a-hoop when he hears Titus has kicked the bucket,' Henry said. 'With all due respect.'

Robert found an extra pair of hands and the funeral procession to Redfern Station went ahead as scheduled. He and Tatty had been intending to continue to the cemetery, but due to the changed circumstances only Robert accompanied the mourners on the train. Tatty returned home with Henry.

She went upstairs to check on Titus. He was still dead – she would have been very surprised if he wasn't – and had stiffened around the jaw, hands and feet. As she stood looking down at his thin, pale corpse laid out on the bed, she searched deep in her heart for any sensation of grief, or guilt, but found nothing. She wondered if Titus had encountered the same lack of feeling after he'd killed Lydia – and probably Maria. It was time to embalm him, but first she had a certain matter to address.

From the trunk in her room she collected a small bottle she'd hidden there, and slipped it into the pocket of her dress. Then she went downstairs to the kitchen, on the lookout for Cora, whom she noted was outside gossiping to Henry as he unharnessed the horses.

Confident she wouldn't be interrupted, Tatty retrieved another little bottle concealed at the very back of the pantry and pocketed that as well. She paused, wondering if she should replace it with a similar bottle containing something harmless, then decided she wouldn't: Cora was unlikely to have noticed it. Then she made her way to the embalming room, emptied the contents of both bottles into the large medicine jar on the shelf marked *Arsenic*, and placed the empties into a bucket to be washed out later.

Once Henry had finished with the horses, he helped Tatty carry Titus down to the embalming room, lie him on the table and undress him. Titus might have lost a lot of weight over the past year but he was still too heavy for one smallish person to move.

'Do you want to watch?' Tatty asked. 'Or you can help, if you'd like to learn how.'

Henry shuddered. 'No, thank you. I think it's disgusting, fiddling about with bodies after they're dead. It's not natural.'

Tatty shrugged. 'Times are changing, Henry.'

'Not for me, they're not,' Henry said. Then he gave a reluctant sigh. 'All right, I'll help if you want me to. Do you know what you're doing? Titus said it takes a lot of expertise to embalm a body.' He hesitated, then said, 'Will you be all right? I mean, he definitely had his faults but he *was* your husband. Are you bearing up?'

Tatty thought that was a very considerate thing for Henry to ask. 'Thank you, Henry. I'm fine. Really, you don't have to help if you don't like the idea. I'll come and get you when it's time to put him in his coffin.'

Tatty began the embalming process by emptying Titus's body of blood, which took very little time because most of it had ended up on the dining-room floor, then pumped in the embalming fluid, pleased to see some colour return to his milk-white complexion, even if it was artificial. Then she stitched the cuts closed in his neck and moved down to his abdomen. Here, she would have to be a lot more specific about what she was doing.

Taking the trocar she drove through the skin above his navel and angled upwards, going through the small intestine in several places, piercing the kidneys and the heart, and stabbing the stomach to release gas and fluids. Once in the area of the stomach, she had a really good rummage about, making sure she made plenty of holes. On the way out with the trocar she deliberately pierced the liver in several places, and had a few jabs at the large intestine to minimise expansion due to decomposition. Using the trocar actually wasn't as easy as suggested in the brochure that had come with Titus's case of embalming instruments, but neither was it as difficult as he'd made it look. She then injected the embalming fluid, pumping slowly to avoid overfilling the abdominal cavity. When she thought she'd added the right amount she stitched closed the trocar holes, watched for a minute as they leaked a little embalming fluid, then added an extra stitch to each wound.

Next she tightly packed Titus's mouth, nostrils and anus with muslin, shaved his face, sewed his jaw closed, and very carefully stitched his eyelids shut with a fine needle and thread. He'd never done that to the corpses he'd embalmed, with the result that several had apparently opened their eyes during visitations as rigor had worn off, but Tatty had already thought about how that unfortunate experience could be avoided.

When she'd finished she put the tools she'd used in the bucket with the small bottles, fetched hot water from the kitchen, washed and dried everything, then went in search of Henry.

*

Tatty sat in the office of Titus's solicitor, Mr Parrish, thinking here she was again, contending with someone's last will. Last time she'd only been sixteen and the will had been her father's: now she was just twenty, but years older, she felt, when it came to understanding the ways of the world.

Mr Parrish said, 'Please accept my condolences regarding your bereavement, Mrs Crowe. What a tragedy, following so soon after the death of your mother-in-law.'

'Thank you,' Tatty said. 'Yes, it has been a time of great sorrow. And I realise that my visit to you might seem somewhat hasty given my husband is yet to be buried, but Crowe Funeral

Services is a very busy company. I feel that it's important we establish legal ownership as soon as possible.'

'Quite right, Mrs Crowe. So, to your late husband's will, which I have on hand. Are you aware of his wishes regarding Crowe Funeral Services? I have to say they are a little, well, confusing. Unless of course I have not been privy to certain aspects of his personal life, which I admit is possible.'

'That depends. I'm not sure which will you have.'

'Oh. Oh dear. Are there multiple versions?' Mr Parrish pinched the bridge of his nose with finger and thumb and squeezed his eyes closed. Tatty thought it looked like he was already having quite a bad day. He opened his eyes again. 'The will I have states he wished to leave the business to his sons. Forgive me, Mrs Crowe, but you and Mr Crowe don't have any sons, do you?'

'No.'

'And did Mr Crowe have any sons, perhaps from an earlier marriage, or – forgive me – a clandestine or illegitimate liaison?'

'Not to my knowledge.' Tatty opened her reticule. 'Titus had this agreement drawn up after we married. We discussed the matter at the time and he said he would lodge the papers with you, but obviously he didn't because I discovered them when I was going through things in his private office last night. I'm the bookkeeper for the business.' She passed a document to Mr Parrish.

He sighed. 'People do this all the time, you know, make new wills and things and don't lodge them with their solicitors. It really can make life difficult. Or death, I should say.'

Tatty said, 'Obviously the business can't be inherited by Titus's sons because he didn't have any. I don't know when he wrote the will you have, but he was very worried for some time about the business, and working extremely hard. The worry was the cause of his chronic stomach ulcer, or ulcers, which his physician, Dr Pickett, has certified was the cause of his death. I was worried myself about his state of mind, and I believe the will referring to sons confirms that I was right to be worried. As you say, it's rather, er, perplexing. In light of what I've just given you, what is your interpretation of the situation?'

Mr Parrish took some time to examine the document. Then he said, 'As far as I can interpret, Titus Crowe, your late husband, signed ownership of his company, that is, Crowe Funeral Services, over to you seven months after you and he were married, with the strict and clear understanding that you could not manage it, lease it to any other party, sell it, control it, or make money from it without his consent. He clearly specified that he did not, and would never, give consent to you to pursue any of those options, and that he would continue to manage the business.' He cleared his throat. 'And your husband did this specifically so that he could not be held liable for any criminal or civil claims against himself via the company for fraud, bribery, blackmail and what have you.' Mr Parrish looked at her. 'As the owner of the company, Mrs Crowe, you would be responsible for those liabilities. And you were at ease with that arrangement?'

'I was, yes. I thought my husband was an honest man and I considered it very unlikely any claims would arise against him. I still do.'

'Yet you say you were his bookkeeper?'

'Yes, I was. And an assistant undertaker.'

'And you were privy to his financial dealings?'

'To a great extent, I was. I didn't have access to everything. Titus managed some accounts himself.'

'Yes, well.' Mr Parrish cleared his throat again. 'With regard to the will your husband lodged with me, we have established that he had no sons, so in effect his last wishes regarding the business going to them are null and void.' He tapped the document Tatty had given him. 'This therefore supersedes that will, and I believe possibly would have anyway, had there been a son or sons in the picture. So, when a woman is unfortunately widowed she becomes a single woman again in the eyes of the law, and therefore is not subject to the laws of coverture. What this means, Mrs Crowe, is that you now own a business and you may operate it and profit from it as you please. But if I can offer some friendly advice? Being a businesswoman in this town, and particularly in your industry, will not be without its challenges. And you will be the only female undertaker in Sydney. To my knowledge there are seven other local undertaking firms apart from yours, all chasing the same profit to be made from funerals. Be prepared.'

Chapter Seven

Tatty gave Titus the grandest funeral she could arrange – more extravagant even than Lydia's – and had Henry guide the multi-coach procession out from Crowe Funeral Services along King Street, then up Elizabeth, down Pitt, up George Street, then finally along Devonshire Street past the old cemetery to Redfern Station to meet the three o'clock funeral train, all so as many people as possible could appreciate the splendour of Titus's last journey. She wasn't having anyone saying she hadn't respected and honoured her husband. The funeral party disembarked, however, at Newtown Station and travelled the very short distance to Camperdown Cemetery, Titus's expensive, flower-bedecked coffin transported on the shoulders of six hired bearers. At the cemetery Lydia's grave was opened and Titus's coffin was placed on top of hers so that they could spend eternity together.

Tatty was surprised by the number of people who came to the public reception after the burial, held at civic rooms on Elizabeth Street that evening. Some, she suspected, might have come to gloat and share stories of how they'd been cheated or exploited by Titus, while others were simply paying their respects. Based on outward appearances he had been a reasonably well-known and successful businessman after all, albeit an undertaker. Some may just have attended for the gossip about what might be happening with the business now Titus was dead. That was definitely the case with the six male undertakers who one by one approached Tatty, informed her that their private carriages had been part of the procession to Redfern Station but of course they hadn't attended the burial themselves due to professional obligations. Tatty understood. So, had the will been read? It had? And what was to be the fate of Crowe Funeral Services?

When Tatty told them they were agog. A woman – a mere *girl* – doing all the work of an undertaker and actually managing an undertaking business? It was unheard of! No, no, in fact three could make her a much better offer than that on the spot. Why not sell the company for a very tidy profit and retire, leaving nothing to vex her mind or interfere with her leisure?

Tatty said a polite 'no thank you' to all three.

Elias Nuttall was particularly insistent.

Standing before her, a plate of smoked fish and dill puffs in one hand and a large glass of port in the other, the macassar oil gleam in his hair matching the sheen on his black silk jacquard waistcoat, he said, 'Whatever any of the others has offered you, I'll beat it.'

Tatty said, 'No thank you, Mr Nuttall. Crowe Funeral Services isn't on the market.'

'Name your price, then. Go on.'

Annoyed, Tatty said again, 'No. The business isn't for sale.'

'You'll change your mind. Undertaking isn't a job for a woman.'

'I *have* been working with Titus for over two and a half years.'

Elias bit into his puff, spilling crumbs down his front. 'You mean you've been trotting along behind him, doing all the easy jobs.'

Really irritated now because she'd been doing everything Titus and Robert had, bar lifting the very heaviest of corpses, Tatty said, 'I'm so glad you could come this evening, Mr Nuttall, and thank you for your condolences, but I really must mingle. Good evening.'

'Think about my offer!' he called after her.

Tatty didn't. As she said in the letter she wrote to Mrs Seddon and Lorna the following evening to tell them she was now a widow, selling Crowe Funeral Services was the last thing she was likely to waste her time and energy thinking about, though she *was* going to make some big changes. Owning a business of her own had been her ultimate goal ever since she'd left England, and now she'd achieved it.

Tatty immediately made what she thought were some significant improvements. First she changed the name from Crowe Funeral Services to Crowe Funerals, to reflect the fact that she would no longer be providing the bereaved with every single imaginable service and commodity required for a funeral. Then she visited every business and artisan from whom Titus had been taking a cut and advised them that those days had ended: if they were interested in working with her she would still refer customers to them, but with no strings attached and commission-free. Then she revised Titus's schedule of fees downwards, so that even the poorest families could afford to bury their dead. In the case of an infant's funeral where a hearse wasn't needed because the baby's coffin could be carried in the arms of a family member, she got the fee down to only one pound five shillings. Otherwise, a very respectable funeral could be had for anything between four and seven pounds.

She also went through the burial club ledger and noted which members had already paid in enough money for a decent funeral. Very soon she would inform them personally that they could either keep paying towards a grander funeral, or stop paying and wait until their club money was needed.

Crowe Funerals was officially a staff member short now that Titus was in his own grave. Tatty thought about hiring another man to work beside her, then reconsidered. Why should she do that, when someone in the house already knew quite a lot about the undertaking trade, was bright, physically strong, got along with Henry and Robert, and wasn't overly squeamish?

'But I don't know the first thing about dead bodies,' Cora said as she served the midday meal two weeks after Titus's funeral. 'Sorry about the burnt bits on the onions. I forgot about them.'

Robert poked what looked like a lumpy pancake on his plate. 'What's this, can I ask?'

'Whiting fritters. Out of Mrs Beeton's book.'

'You do so know about dead bodies,' Tatty said. 'You know all about laying out —'

'But who doesn't?' Cora interrupted.

'You know all the new prices,' Tatty went on, 'and you know about the coffins in the showroom. I can show you how to line and trim them; it's easy enough. And I can teach you what to say to families.'

'And what *not* to say,' Henry said. 'You'd have to watch your mouth.'

'And the pay would be more than what you're getting now,' Tatty said. She hesitated, wondering whether she should mention the matter of all their pay now. No, she'd wait until Cora had made her decision.

'Would I have to wear black all the time like you lot?' Cora asked.

Tatty said, 'Yes. It shows respect for the bereaved. You can't arrive at a grieving household wearing yellow or pink or green.'

'I only wear black when I'm driving the hearse,' Henry pointed out.

Cora said, 'I don't mind black but I don't have anything suitable. I'd have to organise something.' She ate a string of scorched onion and scowled. 'All right, I'll have a go. I'll be your assistant undertaker.'

Tatty said, 'Lovely! Thank you, Cora. Thank you, all of you. I think we'll make a great crew.'

'Crew?' Henry said. 'Like a band of pickpockets?'

'It was one of my mother's words,' Tatty said. 'She had a colourful life.'

Henry's eyebrows went up. 'Is that so? Then how is it you're so educated and genteel?'

Tatty said, 'It's a mystery, isn't it?' She cleared her throat. 'I mentioned pay before. My salary wasn't increased at all, until it stopped completely when I married Titus, and I don't think any of you have had an increase either, have you?'

Cora, Robert and Henry shook their heads.

'Then it's time you did,' Tatty said. 'I haven't noticed the price of anything getting cheaper since I came to Sydney so I'm increasing your salaries. You deserve it. You work extremely hard. I thought twenty per cent. Is that reasonable?'

'Hell yes,' Henry said. 'Thank you, Tatty.'

Robert said, 'I'll say! Thank you!'

Cora hugged Tatty, almost squeezing the breath out of her. 'Titus'll be turning in his grave!' Then she said, 'Oh, but my new job. Who'll do the housework and the cooking? Will I still have to do that?'

'Can we get someone else for the cooking?' Robert said quickly.

Tatty nodded. 'I was thinking we'll need a new housekeeper. Cora can't do both jobs.'

Cora said, 'My stepmother's a good cook. She's not working at the moment. Shall I ask her?'

Tatty hesitated. 'I don't mean to be rude, but didn't you say that she drinks? Because we'd need someone reliable.'

'Only when she's around my father,' Cora said, 'and he wouldn't be anywhere near this house. I wouldn't let him. She's fine on her own. Truly.'

'Well, she's welcome to have a trial for a few weeks, breakfast, dinner and supper, with light housework duties and laundry on Mondays. But it won't be a live-in position.'

'I'll see what she says,' Cora said.

Henry got to his feet, fritter in hand, and said to Robert, 'Come on, I've got to clean the wooden hearse before half past one and I'll need your help. I'm only harnessing Spectre and Wraith today, though.'

Robert nodded, piled blackened onions onto his fritter, folded it in half and shoved as much as he could into his mouth, then said something completely unintelligible.

When they'd gone, Cora sat looking at Tatty across the table. 'I suppose I'd better clean up.'

'I'll give you a hand.'

'It'll be strange having a new job. Thank you. I've only ever been a housemaid and a cook.'

'I'm sure you'll make an excellent undertaker's assistant,' Tatty said. 'As Henry said, though, you will have to be careful about your language. Mind you, half of the families we go to speak the same way, but we are supposed to be professionals. We can't forget that.'

'Titus's behaviour wasn't very professional,' Cora said. 'Robert said if there was a way to rob the poor buggers, he found it.'

'Well, Titus has gone now,' Tatty said. 'And things have changed. At Crowe Funerals we're not going to behave like that.'

Cora said, 'You're managing very well without him, aren't you?'

'Life goes on.'

Looking down at her hands Cora spent a few moments picking at a cuticle. Tatty thought if she wasn't careful she'd make it bleed.

'That little bottle in the pantry,' Cora said, staring straight at her now, 'the one right at the back that disappeared the day he died, what was in it?'

Tatty sat very still, her heart pounding, her gaze locked onto Cora's. 'Why? What does it matter?'

'Well, I saw it there one day a few months ago and I didn't know what it was, so I had a tiny taste —'

'Cora!'

'— and I still couldn't tell, so I just left it. And now it's disappeared.'

Tatty said nothing.

Cora asked, 'Was it yours?'

Again Tatty kept quiet.

'I think it might have been yours,' Cora said. 'I'm the only one who uses that pantry, and occasionally you. Robert and Henry don't, and Titus would never have gone near it, not even with a barge pole. Too much like women's work. So what was in it, I wonder?'

Tatty said finally, 'What do you think was in it?'

Cora pressed a finger against her lips and looked thoughtful. 'Well, if it was *my* bottle, and *my* husband had just died and he'd been a bastard and probably a murderer and I hadn't been that fond of him, I'd have to say it might have contained poison.'

Tatty said, 'You do have a vivid imagination, Cora.'

'But you wouldn't do a thing like that, would you?'

'Like what?' Tatty said.

'Poison Titus.'

'Of course not.'

'Even though you were looking for someone who could forge a will?'

'Not a will,' Tatty said. 'A Deed of Ownership, which is completely different.'

Cora nodded and said, 'Oh, well, that's all right then. Let's get this table cleared, shall we?'

*

Cora was happily settled in and working as an assistant undertaker by the time Elias Nuttall came to Tatty with another offer late in November. Agnes Billings, Cora's stepmother, had impressed during her two-week trial and Tatty had hired her on a month-by-month basis, and now they were all enjoying well-cooked and tasty meals three times a day and not missing Cora's efforts at all.

On the evening that Elias Nuttall made an appearance, Tatty

was reading the paper. He arrived at exactly eight o'clock. Cora let him in and showed him into the parlour.

'Mr Nuttall has come calling,' she announced.

'I hear you're working as an undertaker too, now,' Nuttall said to Cora. 'That's a good gimmick.'

'It's not a gimmick,' Cora replied. 'It's a proper job.'

'If you say so,' Nuttall said, removing his hat. 'Run along now. I need to talk to your mistress. And I'd rather have whiskey than tea.'

'I don't think we have any whiskey,' Cora said and departed, shutting the door behind her.

'How can I help you, Mr Nuttall?' Tatty asked, fully aware there was a brand-new bottle of whiskey in the pantry.

Nuttall sat down without being invited. 'Titus has been in his grave for some weeks. You must really be feeling his absence and struggling to manage everything yourself by now. Running a business isn't easy, is it? Have you given my offer any thought?'

'I'm sorry, what offer was that?'

Annoyance flashed across Nuttall's face. 'My offer to buy you out. I made it very clear the day you buried Titus that I'm interested in purchasing Crowe Funeral Services.'

'It's just Crowe Funerals now, and I'm still not interested in selling. You're wasting your time, Mr Nuttall.'

'I'm prepared to offer you four hundred and fifty pounds. That should cover the chattels Titus accumulated, including the horses and the two hearses and what have you, plus the name and the goodwill. Not that he generated much of that, according to what I hear.'

It was definitely a lot of money, but Tatty knew the first two horses alone had cost Titus almost that much including shipping fees to Sydney, and the glass hearse had also been very expensive. And she didn't want just money: she wanted the business so she could continue to be financially independent and make a difference to people's lives, or rather their deaths, so that those who survived them could carry on knowing they'd done their best to farewell their dead without having to beggar themselves to pay for it – her experience regarding both her parents. She could only make that difference if she kept Crowe Funerals. And Elias Nuttall had a damned cheek talking about goodwill: he was as unpopular as Titus had been.

'I have to agree with you about the goodwill, unfortunately,' Tatty said. 'However, I've made changes and I think we're seeing a difference already. So, no thank you, Mr Nuttall. Four hundred and fifty pounds is a very reasonable offer, but not one that tempts me.'

'It's a *fortune*!' Nuttall exclaimed. 'Who else is going to offer you money like that?'

'I'll admit it is the best one I've had so far,' Tatty said. Then she leant forward slightly in her armchair and enunciated very carefully as though she were speaking to someone either hard of hearing or a bit stupid. 'But I'll say it again. I am not interested. I do not want to sell. Do you understand?'

She watched as Nuttall's face went an interesting shade of fuchsia.

'It's *you* who doesn't understand!' he fired back. 'You're a *female*. Women don't work in the undertaking industry. Undertaking's *always* been a man's business. Only a man has the dignity and credibility to lead a funeral and Titus was a bloody fool for ever taking you on. Women belong at home or in a whore-house, not interfering with the business of burying the dead. It's an abomination!'

'Why is it?' Tatty asked.

Nuttall stared at her. 'Why? Because it goes against nature, that's why. Men have been undertakers for hundreds of years. Not women, men. You don't belong.'

'I think I do,' Tatty said, 'and I haven't had any complaints. No, Mr Nuttall, I know the business and now I own one.'

'Then sell it to me. You don't know what you're doing.'

'No.'

Nuttall launched himself to his feet and jammed his hat on his head. 'You'll regret this. You'll not get a better offer, you know. You'll ... Jesus, you stupid bloody woman!' He thrust out a quivering arm and pointed at her. 'Don't come crawling to me when you change your mind! It'll be too late then!'

Tatty said, 'Shall I see you out?'

'No, I'll do it myself.'

'Good night, Mr Nuttall.'

Tatty waited until she heard the front door slam, then let out her breath. That had been horrible. He was such a nasty little bully but she'd been determined to stand up to him. She'd risked so much to get where she was: selling Crowe Funerals to Nuttall, or anyone, was the last thing she'd do.

Cora reappeared. 'What an arsehole.'

'Yes, he is.'

'I couldn't quite hear all of that. I shouldn't have shut the parlour door.'

'He made another offer for the business. Four hundred and fifty pounds.'

'Bloody hell, that's a lot! Did you accept it?'

'No, I did not accept it. I'm not selling, Cora!'

Cora looked contrite. 'No, I know you're not. It's just, you know, four hundred and fifty quid. You could do a lot with that.'

'We can do a lot with Crowe Funerals.'

Cora nodded.

Tatty looked at her and bit her lip. 'Do you think I *should* sell?'

'No. No, I really don't. You've worked hard to learn all the ins and outs of undertaking. I bet no one else in Sydney knows how to embalm a body. Henry says business really has picked up since Titus died, and that must be down to you and all the changes you've made, so you'd be stupid to sell it, don't you think?'

'That is what I think, Cora. Thank you. I wish my father were still alive, though. It would be nice to have his opinion, even though I already know what he'd say.'

'And what's that?'
'Don't sell.'

*

Tatty paused outside the doors of the Rose of Australia Inn on George Street north and read the notice advertising the presentation that evening by the celebrated spiritualist Edith Drinkwater, direct from feted international appearances. For someone who wasn't convinced that people went anywhere at all after they died, she knew she was asking a lot to expect messages from them years later. It had been Cora's idea. Cora was a follower of spiritualism and had seen demonstrations by over a dozen different clairvoyants, both local and international; however, she was too busy (probably with a fellow) to come to the Rose of Australia that evening. She did warn, though, that Tatty might encounter Elias Nuttall: evidently he was also an avid supporter of the spiritualist movement.

Also, her mother, Betsy, had for a while gone to spiritualist meetings in London after Hector had died. Tatty had accompanied her and twice they had received 'messages' informing them that their 'loved one' had crossed to the other side, was content, and wished for them only to be happy. Betsy had been comforted but Tatty thought that such generic messages could have applied to anyone.

But she supposed the demonstration with Edith Drinkwater was worth a try, or would at least do no harm. She knew spiritualism was very popular and that even Queen Victoria attended seances – in an attempt to contact Prince Albert, no doubt. There were always advertisements in the papers for public spiritualist meetings, private seances, and gatherings of societies founded to further knowledge concerning clairvoyance, crystal-gazing, thought-reading, spiritualism and what have you. And she knew, of course, that a number of the recently bereaved she encountered via her work attended spiritualist sessions in the hope of receiving messages from deceased loved ones. But she personally had doubts about how the essence of a person could continue to survive after death, and where exactly it would exist if it could, just as she had fundamental misgivings now about the existence of God.

Inside the venue she found herself in a noisy, smoky bar room filled with drinking men, but soon spotted another sign indicating that she should go upstairs. She did, and encountered quite a large, well-lit and rather pleasant room furnished with rows of chairs, most of which were already occupied even though Mrs Drinkwater was not due to appear for another twenty minutes. Tatty took one of the few remaining seats towards the back of the room, had a thorough look around for Elias Nuttall and noted his absence with relief. She also had a good stare at the sorts of people who evidently came to see mediums. She had thought that in general they would be lonely old widows desperate for a few words from deceased husbands, which would have been sad enough, but apparently she was mistaken. There were young women – well over half of them wearing black – and young men, and old men, and children and middle-aged people (and one small dog). In short, every sort of person was represented. It wasn't what she'd been expecting.

At the front of the room was a dais on which sat a comfortable-looking armchair, for Mrs Drinkwater no doubt. Beside that was an ordinary ladder-backed chair Tatty assumed would be for her assistant, if she had one.

They all sat and waited ... and waited. The noise from the audience increased as people grumbled and several got up and left. Tatty took the opportunity to grab a vacated seat closer to the front.

Finally, nearly twenty minutes after the advertised start time, a man (possibly the Rose of Australia's proprietor) appeared through a door to the right of the dais and announced theatrically, 'Ladies and gentlemen, all the way from sell-out appearances on foreign shores, the amazing, the transcendental, the most mysterial Mrs Edith *Drinkwaaateer*!'

Grumbles forgotten, the audience burst into enthusiastic applause and the lady herself appeared through the door, drifted to the dais waving regally and sat in the armchair, taking a few moments to arrange herself.

Tatty was impressed: Edith Drinkwater did look spectacular. She was a moderately heavy woman, a fact that was obvious even though her corsets must have been laced tightly. She wore a black moire silk skirt with a modest crinoline and a panelled black bodice with a high neck and fitted sleeves. Over that she'd layered five or six voluminous silk scarves in colours such as emerald green and sapphire blue and royal purple, and on top of the scarves she'd added long ropes of amber and turquoise and jet beads. She looked like a large raven sporting a very bright jacket. Her pudgy fingers were crowded with glittering rings, turquoise-and-gold pendants hung from her ears, and on her feet she wore fashionable mid-heeled, elastic-sided boots. Tatty had several pairs herself and wore them frequently. She hoped hers didn't make her feet look like pig trotters, because Edith Drinkwater's did. Edith's brunette hair was plaited and arranged on top of her head, and her face, somewhat heavily made up with rouge and powder, was still strikingly handsome in middle age.

Tatty was so intent on looking at the spiritualist that at first she hardly noticed when someone else stepped unannounced on to the dais and sat down. She was a slender blonde girl of perhaps twenty, wearing an unadorned pale-grey dress, little round spectacles, and no visible jewellery. Something in the set of the girl's features made Tatty think she might be the spiritualist's daughter, or at least a relative.

Neither woman on the dais said anything, and gradually the whispers and rustlings from the audience died away to absolute silence until the tension became uncomfortable.

'*Ah!*' Edith Drinkwater suddenly cried.

Tatty, along with probably everyone else, jumped in her seat. She pressed a hand against her chest over her thumping heart.

'I feel a presence!' the spiritualist called out. 'Someone is with us. But the light. The light is too bright! He can't bear the light!'

The blonde girl left her seat and went around the room turning down most of the wall lamps, leaving the audience sitting in a cosy dimness. Or disconcerting gloom, Tatty thought, if the idea of talking to dead people frightened you. The audience began to whisper and mutter again, and the girl took her time returning to her seat, walking between rows, touching a shoulder here, smiling at someone there, reassuring that everything would be all right.

Edith Drinkwater dug her beringed fingers into her temples as though in pain and squinted out at the audience. 'Is there anyone here tonight who has lost someone who had trouble with light? Someone who suffered with cephalalgia, perhaps? Or meningitis?'

The blonde girl, back in her seat now, whispered something to Edith, who nodded sagely.

'My assistant says I should explain that cephalalgia simply means headache,' she said. 'And you will know meningitis as brain fever. I do apologise. I frequently forget that I have such an extensive knowledge of medical matters.'

Several hands rose in the audience.

Edith pointed. 'Yes, madam? Yes, you in the paisley shawl.'

Everyone turned and looked as the woman said, 'My husband passed away five years ago. He suffered from terrible headaches. In fact he probably died from them. Could it be ... Could it be *him* here now?'

Edith touched her temples and closed her eyes as though concentrating. 'Is his name ...?' Her eyes flew open and she shot out a hand, palm facing the audience. 'No, don't tell me. Is it ... Robert?'

Every gaze in the audience swivelled back to the woman, whose face had sagged with disappointment.

'Er ...'

'No!' Edith exclaimed. 'No, it's Rupert, isn't it!'

'Yes, it is!' The woman now looked delighted. 'It *is* Rupert!' She clutched her hands together at her throat, tilted her head back and closed her eyes in elation.

Good guess, Tatty thought.

The woman went on. 'What does he say, Mrs Drinkwater? Does he have a message? Does he have anything to say to me?'

Edith nodded. 'He says he loves you and misses you terribly even though it's been five years now since he crossed over, and you are not to continue to grieve for him.' She cocked her head as though listening, then went on. 'He also says that should the opportunity present itself, you should marry again and find it within your heart to be happy.'

'Oh, no, I couldn't do that!' the woman said. 'But just to know he'd condone it if I did, that's typical of Rupert. Oh, thank you, Mrs Drinkwater. You don't know how much this means to me.'

Edith bowed her head regally. Then she jabbed her temples again and screwed up her eyes. 'Someone else is here. A man in a tall hat?'

Tatty did think that one was a bit vague: almost every gentleman in Sydney — perhaps the western world — wore a tall hat.

'Between forty and fifty?' Edith said. 'I'm sensing that he died of debility, or flux of humour, or perhaps he was even hypertrophic?'

The girl leant over again and whispered for several seconds.

'There I go again with my medical terms,' Edith said. 'My apologies. His name, I believe, could be Leonard? Does that have an association for anyone?'

A gasp from a woman wearing an outfit of deep mourning. She stood and said, 'That's my husband. He died eight months ago of an enlarged heart and general weakness. I want to know, can you ask him, is he ... is he happy?'

A short pause while Edith consulted with Leonard in the spirit world.

'He says he is and he dearly hopes you are, too.'

The woman burst into tears and sat down.

'I can —' Edith began, but then she was interrupted by a woman sitting in the same row as Tatty. She was probably somewhere in her early fifties, Tatty thought, pleasant-looking and smartly dressed though not in black.

'Excuse me,' the woman said.

Edith glared at her. 'Actually it can be very dangerous to interrupt a medium when she's mid-connection with a visitor from the other side. It distorts the spiritual energy waves rather badly and could result in someone getting hurt in the astral realm, and sometimes even our plane of existence.'

'Oh, I *am* sorry,' the woman said. 'It's just that I'm hoping to communicate with a friend. Normally I'm in touch with her regularly but I haven't heard from her in months and I'm worried. Her name is Rachel Winter. I wonder if you could contact her for me, please?'

Edith said, 'Well, no, it doesn't work like that. I don't have a list of everyone who now resides in the spirit world, you know.'

'No, I know, but I thought you could at least try. Please?'

Edith wriggled around in her seat, frowned slightly, then said. 'When did she die, your friend?'

'In 1829. She was sixteen.'

'Eighteen twenty-nine!' Edith exclaimed. 'That was, what, thirty-eight years ago! And you've been seeing this ... apparition since then?'

'Well, yes, except not lately,' the woman said, 'and I'm worried something's happened to her. And please don't call her an apparition.'

Tatty stared at her. So did a lot of other people.

Edith shrugged, closed her eyes and pressed her temples. Beside her the assistant focused on her hands clasped in her lap.

After a minute Edith said, 'No, nothing, I'm sorry. Your friend must be busy. Or perhaps she's finally moved on.'

The woman looked extremely disappointed, but all she did was nod and thank the spiritualist. Tatty wondered if she were mad, though she didn't sound unhinged despite the oddness of her request.

Over the next forty minutes Edith passed on more messages to people in the audience, many of them apparently moderately accurate, some of them missing the mark completely, then announced she was exhausted.

Tatty jumped in. 'Mrs Drinkwater, I desperately need some advice. I own a business and I have received an offer from someone who wishes to buy it. I would like to hear from my late father regarding what he thinks I should do. Can you help me, please?'

Edith stared at her for a moment, then spoke to her assistant behind her hand. Then she straightened up.

After a period of what appeared to be very intense concentration, she said, 'There is someone here, but I can't quite catch his name. Is it … J-something? James or John?'

Tatty didn't respond.

'William, perhaps? No, actually, I'm sensing George.'

'None of those.' If she'd also said Charles, she would have listed the five most popular male names Tatty could think of.

'No matter,' Edith said, flapping a sparkling hand. 'Perhaps he doesn't want to use his name. I'm fairly sure it's your father, though, and I *can* tell you he's telling me you should take the offer, but that you should ask for more money. The price is too low.'

'Really?' She was obviously guessing, Tatty thought.

'Yes. Your father says to get someone with a really good grasp of money to negotiate for you. Do you understand what that means?'

Tatty did. It meant Edith Drinkwater was a charlatan and making things up because her father had known she was perfectly competent with numbers and money. He should – he'd taught her himself.

'Thank you,' she said.

Edith's assistant helped her off the dais and out of the room, then reappeared almost immediately with a basket asking for donations from the audience before they dispersed, even though everyone had already paid a shilling and ninepence for a ticket to get in.

As she (somewhat reluctantly) dropped a shilling in the basket, Tatty asked, 'Are you Mrs Drinkwater's daughter?'

The girl hesitated briefly then nodded.

'What's your name?' Tatty asked.

'Hannah Drinkwater.'

Tatty said, 'I don't mean to be rude, but what your mother does is mostly clever guesswork, isn't it?'

Hannah held her gaze and something passed between them: for a second Tatty thought that Hannah had *almost* been about to agree.

Then she said quickly, 'My mother definitely has her talents,' and hurried off with her basket.

Outside on the street Tatty literally bumped into the woman who had been hoping to contact her dead friend.

'I'm sorry you didn't get what you were looking for tonight,' Tatty said.

'You did, though, didn't you?' the woman replied.

'Not really. I'm Tatty Crowe, by the way. Missus but I'm widowed.'

'Oh, how dreadful for you. I am sorry. Recently, too, was it?' the woman asked, indicating Tatty's black dress.

'Thank you. It was, quite. I'm managing.'

'I'm Harriet Downey, Harrie to my friends. Missus and not widowed, thank God. I just don't know what I'd do without my lovely husband, I really don't. Mind you I have lots of children, I'm sure they'd be an *enormous* help. Do you have children, Mrs Crowe?'

'It's Tatty and no, I don't. It just … no, I don't.'

185

'That's a shame. Children are lovely. Have some one day, you'll see. So, do you think you will sell your business?'

'No, I think I will not. I think Mrs Drinkwater ... well, I don't think she really was in communication with my late father. I'm not sure she's quite on the square, that woman.'

Harrie Downey smiled. 'My friend Friday says that: "on the square".'

'Is she dead too?' Tatty asked without thinking. So much for being tactful with the bereaved!

But Harrie only laughed, 'No, she's actually alive, not like poor Rachel.'

'Have you really been in contact with her for all that time?'

'Oh yes, just not lately.'

'And you talk to her and she talks back?'

Harrie nodded. 'Oh yes. We have really quite a close friendship. I raised her daughter, Charlotte. Rachel died giving birth to her, you see, so it's only natural Rachel likes to keep in touch. What sort of business are you in?'

'I'm an undertaker.'

Tatty thought Harrie looked fascinated.

'Is that so? You're *actually* an undertaker?'

'I have several excellent male employees who assist when it comes to carrying coffins and working with the horses and what have you, and a young woman I'm also training to assist me, but yes, I'm an undertaker.'

'How marvellous! Wait till I tell James. My husband, I mean. In fact, why don't you come for supper one night?' Harrie ferreted in her purse then handed Tatty a visiting card. 'He'd love to meet you.'

When Tatty saw Harrie's surname in writing something occurred to her. 'Is your husband James Downey, the surgeon?'

'Yes – how did you know that?'

'I've met him through work, but I doubt if he'd remember me. He does the occasional postmortem for the coroner. I sometimes deal with the bodies.'

'Oh. Yes, right. You would.'

Tatty thought Harrie looked a little queasy at talk of postmortems and corpses, which was somewhat odd for someone who had cheerfully been having a friendship with a ghost for nearly forty years. If Harriet Downey was a mad woman, she was quite a personable and unobtrusive one.

'Well, it was very nice to meet you, Mrs Downey.'

'Call me Harrie. And you too, Mrs Crowe.'

'Tatty.'

'Yes. Let's hope we meet again. Though not in a professional capacity, if you don't mind.'

Tatty laughed. 'Everyone says that.'

Chapter Eight

Tatty sat beside Henry in the dog-cart, heading south up Pitt Street on her way to the Benevolent Asylum to attend to a matter she'd been meaning to address ever since Titus had died. Summer was very much on its way and the weather was pleasantly warm, but not yet as enervatingly hot as it would be in late January and February.

'I shouldn't be too long,' she said as Henry halted Shadow inside the asylum gates. The building itself was quite unlovely – large, square-shaped, and two-storeyed with thirteen windows on the front face and an entrance door without a portico. Chimneys sprouted across the roof.

Henry didn't look happy, probably because there weren't any decent trees he and Shadow could wait beneath.

'I'll go around the back,' he said. 'There must be stables.'

'There are,' Tatty said. 'By the morgue. I'll come and find you.'

Tatty climbed down, straightened her hat and entered the asylum through the front door. She was aware that the asylum was administered by the New South Wales Benevolent Society and cared for pregnant women, married and unmarried, during their confinements, unlike in the past when males were also treated at the facility. These days the only male patients accepted were male babies and small boys. Before long she was sitting in the office of the superintendent, Dr Arthur Renwick.

'Thank you for visiting us today, Mrs Crowe,' Dr Renwick said after sipping his tea. 'I have to say, however, your letter wasn't at all clear. You said you're interested in making a non-pecuniary contribution to the asylum but, and please do forgive me, am I correct in understanding that you're in the business of undertaking?'

Tatty suppressed a scowl: he knew she was. He'd been present several times when she and Titus had collected corpses for inquests from the asylum's morgue. 'I am, yes.'

'Yes, I thought so. In that case I can't imagine what you might contribute.'

Why are you being so obtuse, Tatty thought. 'I don't have money to spare at the moment,' she said. 'I'm expanding my business. But I can still help you. I know that, sadly, women and children do die here. If any of those unfortunates don't have family, and I'm aware some probably don't, I'm offering to give them respectable funerals free of charge so they don't have to be buried on the parish. Would a service like that be of use to you?'

Dr Renwick's demeanour changed markedly. 'It most certainly would, Mrs Crowe. How extraordinarily generous of you! Really, I hadn't remotely thought something like *that* might be what you had in mind!'

He seemed so pleased Tatty wondered if the asylum had to pay something towards burying its dead, even to the parish. She was only making her offer because she couldn't stand the idea of all those dead babies lying cold and alone in mass graves: the thought made her think of Lorna all by herself behind the privy in the snow. And also because it was something she knew Titus would never ever do, but now he was dead and she could do whatever she liked.

'Well, that's agreed then,' she said. 'Whenever you need us just send someone and we'll come. You know where we are? George Street?'

Dr Renwick nodded. 'You know, you're nothing like I was led to believe. I was categorically told —'

He stopped talking.

Tatty waited.

Dr Renwick turned pink.

'You were told …?' Tatty prompted, suspecting she might know what and by whom.

'Forgive me, but an acquaintance told me you're a very difficult woman to deal with. However, I can see for myself that you're not.'

'Would that acquaintance be Mr Elias Nuttall?'

'Actually, yes, it was. May I give you some advice, Mrs Crowe?'

'You may,' Tatty said. She didn't have to take heed if she didn't like it.

'I don't believe he has your best interests at heart so be very careful when it comes to your dealings with him.'

Tatty laughed. 'Oh, I know *that*!'

*

Tatty was used to bad language – Betsy had been a champion swearer and Cora wasn't far behind – but Agnes Billings was unequalled when the mood was upon her. It was today and Tatty, working in her office, could hear her belting out the most colourful swear words. People going past on George Street could probably hear her. She went out to the kitchen to see what was wrong.

Agnes was a solid woman, more muscle than fat, several inches taller than Tatty, and physically very capable. Her mouse-brown hair was greying and she kept it tucked under a cap when she worked, and refused to wear 'any of them silly fashions in the kitchen because I don't want to turn into a human torch', which Tatty thought was more than reasonable. Agnes was forty-nine years old and semi-literate and she worked hard.

Unfortunately she'd just dropped a pot of cooked stew on the kitchen floor, splattering it far and wide.

'Get a spoon because that's your dinner,' she said as Tatty appeared in the doorway. 'This sodding kitchen's far too small. How I'm supposed to bloody well cook in it without spilling everything all over the bloody place I'm buggered if I know.'

Cora managed, Tatty thought. But then Cora hadn't cooked particularly nice food. Agnes did. The stew smelt delicious.

'Do you need help cleaning up?' Tatty asked.

'I'll get Cora.' Agnes went to the kitchen door and shouted for her stepdaughter, almost deafening Tatty. 'You'll all have to wait now for your dinner.'

'We've got a busy afternoon.'

'Then I'll do something quick. Omelettes, maybe. I've got a bit of ham.'

'Very nice,' Tatty said, and returned to her office.

Agnes was right to complain – the kitchen was small. The whole house was on the cramped side and the layout of the rooms downstairs didn't really work for an undertaking business. A customer, come to look at the coffin showroom, could just as easily inadvertently find themselves in Tatty's parlour, or worse, the embalming room with its shelf full of poisons and jars and rubber tubes. And upstairs she and Cora still occupied the two small bedrooms, because neither wanted to move into either Titus's old room or the room in which they both knew Lydia had been murdered. Outside the stables were all full now as were both carriage houses, and the dog-cart had to be parked in the yard and covered with a tarpaulin when it rained. The yard itself wasn't quite big enough, especially when Henry had to harness four horses to a hearse. They got grumpy standing in the confined space during the time it took to buckle them all in and arrange their feathers and drapes, and frequently kicked and bit one another, unsettling themselves for the procession to come. Tatty had thought for some time, even before Titus had died, that they needed bigger premises, and now perhaps the time had come to find somewhere more suitable. Also, George Street was rented: Tatty wanted to buy a property. Except she didn't have the money. Crowe Funerals was reasonably comfortably in the black, and she still had much of her nest-egg, but there wouldn't be enough money to purchase the large house plus stables she thought the business would require if it were to expand.

The following week she made an appointment at the Bank of New South Wales where Titus kept his accounts: it was time she had the name on them changed to Tatiana Crowe. She also wanted to discuss a loan.

Transferring the accounts to her name wasn't the performance it could have been, especially after she produced the documents proving Titus had conveyed ownership of Crowe Funeral Services to her after they married, but the loan was a different matter. The bank manager proved, in Tatty's opinion, to be particularly difficult and refused to concede that she was capable of running a successful business, in particular a funeral company, and therefore wasn't prepared to risk the bank's money by lending it to her. Tatty had always understood that bank loans consisted of money belonging to the bank's customers, not the bank itself, but assumed that pointing this out would be a waste of breath. Hers, of course. Instead she said she'd take her custom elsewhere, whereupon the bank manager wished her luck as no bank he knew of was likely to lend a female undertaker three hundred and sixty pounds to buy new business premises. Tatty thanked him and took her leave.

She brooded about that for a day, then paid Samuel Tetley another visit.

'Very nice to see you again, Mrs Crowe,' he said. 'How did your venture with your new documents conclude? I saw that Mr Crowe died recently. My condolences. Unexpected, was it?'

'Not particularly,' Tatty said. 'He'd been ill for a long time but absolutely refused to take care of himself.' She handed Mr Tetley the package of biscuits she'd bought for him at the bakery.

'Thank you. Mmm, ginger, very nice.'

'Your document was exactly what I needed, thank you. I now have my own undertaking business.'

'Excellent. And what brings you here today?'

'I need money and I can't borrow it from the bank.'

'I forge documents, Mrs Crowe. I don't counterfeit money.' Mr Tetley bit into a ginger biscuit, then offered the package to Tatty.

She shook her head. 'I thought, travelling in the circles you do, you might know of someone prepared to lend me money at a reasonable rate.'

Mr Tetley gestured with his biscuit. 'You see, it's the last part of that sentence most likely to cause a problem.'

Tatty was already aware of that, and suppressed a sigh.

'There are plenty in Sydney who will lend you money,' Mr Tetley said, 'but only with exorbitant interest rates attached and you don't want to be paying those. How much were you looking to borrow?'

'Three hundred and sixty pounds.'

Mr Tetley winced. 'No, you really need to keep rates down on a sum like that or you'll never pay it back.' He finished his biscuit and cleaned around his teeth with his tongue. 'I do know of someone who *might* be interested, but only because you're a woman in business and so is she. She's a little, ah, shall we say, hard-shelled, but I understand she has integrity. It might be worth a try.'

'What's her name? I might even know her.'

'Friday Woolfe. She owns the Siren's Arms hotel on the corner of Harrington and Argyle streets just up the hill here.'

Tatty didn't know her, but the name 'Friday' was vaguely familiar. Where had she heard it?

'Well, I'll think about it,' she said. 'It's awkward.'

'Borrowing money always is.'

'Thank you for your advice.'

'You're welcome. Thank you for the biscuits. It's been a very long time since anyone brought me a gift of any sort.'

'My pleasure.'

And it really was, Tatty thought as she walked home. She liked Samuel Tetley. He was pleasant, interesting, easy to talk to, and useful. And in some ways he reminded her of her father, and that made her both happy and sad.

It wasn't until she reached the intersection of George and King streets that she remembered where she'd heard the name Friday. She was the friend Harriet Downey had said used the expression 'on the square', like Betsy did. She must be: surely there weren't two women in Sydney with that name. Tatty looked in her reticule for Mrs Downey's visiting card, hoping she hadn't lost it. She knew she wouldn't have thrown it away. But there it was, at the bottom, hiding beneath a handkerchief, several folded papers covered in jotted notes, a lip balm, a clean menstrual rag wrapped in paper in case she was caught short, a package of lemon drops, two pairs of gloves, several other visiting cards, her purse containing four pounds in cash, a silver vinaigrette filled with very concentrated perfume for use around extremely smelly corpses, and a bottle of smelling salts.

Perhaps she would pay Mrs Downey a visit and ask her to arrange a meeting with this Friday Woolfe, which would probably be a smarter approach than turning up at the Siren's Arms, leaning on the bar and asking to speak to her out of the blue.

*

And that's exactly how Tatty came to be at the Siren's Arms on a rainy but muggy late January mid-morning. She'd debated whether to take Cora with her and had decided in the end she wouldn't – not to an initial meeting. Harrie Downey's instructions had been to go to the back door of the pub via the stable yard, and someone would let her in.

A housemaid answered her knock, then led her to a private room that was already quite crowded. Harrie was there, and so were three other women. She thought immediately she'd never seen such an exotic-looking gathering.

Harrie came forward to meet her. 'Sorry about the rain! I hope you didn't get too wet. Did you get a cab?'

'A colleague dropped me off,' Tatty said.

'Oh good. Well, everyone, this is Mrs Tatiana Crowe. Mrs Crowe, these are my friends, Mrs Sarah Green, Miss Friday Woolfe, and her business partner, Miss Aria Te Kainga-Mataa.'

Tatty said hello while she tried not to stare, though Sarah Green looked conventional enough, if not very happy to be at the meeting. Tatty wondered why she actually was.

'I expect you're wondering why I'm here?' Mrs Green said.

She was perhaps the same age as Harrie Downey, small and slim, dark-haired, and slightly sharp-featured though not unattractive, and her midnight blue dress was fashionable, beautifully cut and obviously expensive. She wore tasteful ear-rings — sapphires, Tatty wondered? — and a ring featuring substantial diamonds on her wedding finger.

Slightly shocked by Mrs Green's clairvoyant abilities, Tatty said, 'Yes, actually, I am.'

'Your husband didn't like me and I didn't like him. The last time I spoke to him he called me a fishwife and slammed the door to my shop so hard a display of pearl necklaces in the window collapsed.'

Tatty suddenly understood. 'You're not the jeweller, are you?'

Sarah Green nodded. 'I wanted to meet the woman who was foolish enough to marry Titus Crowe. You're not what I expected. Though I am sorry for your loss,' she said, not sounding sorry at all.

'He did talk about you,' Tatty said. 'I'm afraid he wasn't very kind. In fact he was quite rude.'

Harrie said, 'Oh, do tell.'

Tatty winced. 'Forgive me, Mrs Green, but he said you can't hold your tongue and you're a troublemaker.'

Friday Woolfe laughed and Harrie said, 'Yes, that's Sarah.'

Sarah Green shrugged and it appeared to Tatty that she truly didn't care. 'He suggested I pay him a commission if he sent customers my way. Well, I wasn't likely to do that, was I? We get more than enough customers as it is. Then when he dared to say he'd blackmail me I said do your best, dig your dirt, everyone knows I'm an ex-convict and I'm not ashamed of it, and he'd damn well rue the day if he did try a caper like that. He must have got my message because he never came back. Fool.'

'Well, whatever my husband thought,' Tatty said, 'it's very nice to meet you, Mrs Green.'

She turned to Friday Woolfe, easily the most colourful woman in the room, literally. Possibly in all of Sydney. Her hair — hennaed a vibrant copper, the colour it probably had been when she was younger — was semi-bound in a bun at the nape of her neck with curly lengths escaping energetically all around her face, and her pale, freckled complexion accentuated her hazel eyes. She had a very voluptuous figure emphasised by a tight corset, and she wore a silk dress in a truly vivid cobalt blue, but the most striking thing about her were her tattoos. She was tattooed on her upper chest, parts of her neck, her forearms, and even on her calves and shins, which Tatty glimpsed when she sat back on the couch and crossed her legs. Was she tattooed *everywhere*? How absolutely extraordinary. Perhaps she should have brought Cora after all. She would have been fascinated.

Swallowing her thumping heart and hoping her nerves weren't visible to anyone else, Tatty said, 'Miss Woolfe, thank you for meeting with me today. As I know Mrs Downey has discussed with you, I need to borrow some money. I'd like to buy a property suitable to house my funeral business. I'm renting at the moment and that property is too small. I have multiple horses, several hearses, carts, a large range of coffins, considerable other apparatus, and an expanding staff to accommodate. I'm looking to borrow three hundred and sixty pounds to add to my own financial contribution. Are you able to help me, please?'

'Well, first off, it's Friday, not Miss Woolfe, all right? You're making me sound like a shrivelled-up old schoolteacher.'

Tatty bowed her head slightly in acknowledgement. 'And please call me Tatty, not Mrs Crowe.'

'Ha! Tatty Crowe!' Friday exclaimed, looking at the woman named Aria sitting opposite. 'Did you hear that? Crowe? She's a *Tatty* Crowe?'

'Do not be so rude, Friday,' the woman said. Then she gave Tatty a pained, slightly apologetic look. 'You must forgive her. Sometimes she has the sense of humour of a child.'

Aria Te Kainga-Mataa was a very handsome woman, also, like Friday, probably somewhere in her fifties. She was dark-skinned with long, black, slightly wavy hair, and a tattoo of her own in dark blue/green ink on her lips and chin. Tatty suspected she was a native of New Zealand. She wore a beautifully cut and fitted dress in bronze silk, a colour that showed off her dark, wide-set eyes, and gold pendants in her ears. None of the women in the room was short of money, that was clear. Except herself.

'Well, sometimes I do lend money, but only to women,' Friday said. 'I charge interest though. I don't give it away. Fuck that.'

'I wouldn't expect anything else,' Tatty replied, suspecting Friday was looking for a reaction to her obscenity. But she didn't know Tatty was Betsy Caldwell's daughter. 'The terms would have to be reasonable, however. I'm not committing myself to penury over a bad and never-ending loan. And I do know what bad terms are.'

Sarah Green and Aria both laughed, and Sarah said, 'Well, she's not just a pretty face, Friday. You'd better watch your step or you might end up owing *her* money one day.'

'Oh, shut up,' Friday said. Then she gave Tatty a big, genuine smile, revealing gaps where back teeth had once been. 'Have you tried at the banks?'

'Yes, the Bank of New South Wales. What a waste of my time.'

'They don't lend to women. Don't think any of the banks do. And you don't have any rich friends?'

'I emigrated here three years ago and went to work for Titus Crowe as housemaid, bookkeeper and assistant undertaker, and then I married him. I haven't had time to make friends, never mind rich ones.'

'I'm surprised you haven't had offers from other undertakers to buy you out,' Sarah Green said.

'I have.'

'Any that looked tempting?'

'One, but I'm not interested in selling. My plan is to expand. I'm looking to spend around five hundred altogether on a new property.'

'Well, good for you,' Friday said. 'So, what do we think?' she asked, looking around the room at her friends.

Tatty had the clear impression they were communicating without speaking, and perhaps they were, if they'd been firm friends for as long as Harrie Downey had suggested.

Sarah Green nodded.

'I am happy with the proposition,' Aria Te Kainga-Mataa said.

'And so am I,' Friday said.

Harrie clapped her hands. 'Good, that's settled then. Friday, you'll have your legal person write something up, just to keep everything neat and tidy?'

Friday said yes.

'And Tatty can have the money when?'

'Now, if she wants it. There's probably that much next door. I haven't done the banking for a couple of days.'

Tatty thought three hundred and sixty pounds was a hell of a lot of cash to leave behind the bar of a hotel. 'You keep that much money here?'

Harrie shook her head. 'No, not in the hotel. Friday and Aria own a brothel. It's right next door on Argyle Street. It does very well and makes a *lot* of money.'

Tatty looked at Friday and Aria. Then, echoing Friday's earlier comment, she said, 'Well, good for *you*.'

Sarah Green let out another laugh. 'Oh, I'm glad I came. This has ended up being quite entertaining.'

'I'll get that money,' Friday said, unfolding herself from the couch and getting to her feet. 'Anyone coming for a walk?'

Tatty did quite want to have a look inside a brothel, but felt it would be vulgar to say so, and stayed behind with Harrie and Sarah.

'Will they just walk in the front door?' she asked, trying not to sound nosy.

'Of the brothel?' Sarah said. 'There's an alleyway that goes from the yard of the Siren's Arms to the back door. It's about a two-minute walk. Very handy.'

'Oh,' Tatty said. Then, in an attempt to pre-empt an awkward silence, she asked Harrie, 'Has your friend reappeared? The, er, the one who died?'

Sarah rolled her eyes.

Harrie's face fell. 'Not yet. But I'm sure she will.'

'You'd know, wouldn't you?' Sarah said to Tatty.

Tatty looked at her. 'I'm sorry?'

'Being an undertaker. You'd know whether there's life after death. Spirits, ghosts, that sort of thing.'

'I look after the deceased before they're buried,' Tatty said. 'What happens to the soul or whatever you want to call it after that isn't my domain at all. I have no idea.'

'You do rather sound as if you don't believe.'

'It doesn't matter what I believe, does it?'

'You did say you thought Edith Drinkwater was a charlatan,' Harrie said.

Tatty nodded. 'So I did.'

Friday and Aria returned then, and handed Tatty the money wrapped in a cloth bag.

'You can count it if you like,' Friday offered.

'No, thank you very much: I'm sure it's all in order. Will you send the loan papers around when they're ready? Here's my card.'

'We will,' Friday said. 'Happy property hunting!'

March 1868, Sydney

Tatty looked at three or four properties before settling on a large, three-storey, six-bedroom, sandstone house on Pitt Street near the corner of Hunter Street. It had multiple reception rooms downstairs, its own water pump, a spacious yard at the rear with stables for ten horses, two large carriage houses (with accommodation above) and covered parking for three smaller vehicles. It hadn't sold at auction, at which the reserve had been six hundred pounds, so Tatty negotiated later with the vendor's agent, offering four hundred and sixty, which was declined, but five hundred and ten wasn't and the sale went through.

She also hired another assistant undertaker – Benjamin Everitt, who had previously worked for Elias Nuttall.

She'd placed an advertisement in the *Sydney Morning Herald*, and when Benjamin arrived for an interview, she'd asked him, 'Is Mr Nuttall aware that you're applying for a job here?'

'No. He'd stop me from coming if he knew,' Benjamin said. 'He'd *hate* anyone leaving Nuttall Undertakers to come and work for you. Sorry, Mrs Crowe. No offence intended.'

'None taken,' Tatty said. 'What will you do if I don't give you the job and he finds out you were here and fires you?'

Benjamin crossed his arms. Tatty thought he looked very confident for someone who was only twenty-one and whose curly copper hair and cheerful, boyish face made him look like a cherub in a painting. 'Then I'll have to find work somewhere else, won't I? Although I'd prefer to stay in the undertaking business if I can.'

'How long have you been working for Mr Nuttall?' Tatty asked.

'Four years.'

'And why do you want to work for Crowe Funerals now?'

'Elias Nuttall cheats his customers. I don't like that. So did Mr Crowe, I believe, if you don't mind me saying so. But Robert says things have changed here now you're in charge, and I've been hearing people saying lately they wished they'd chosen Crowe Funerals over Nuttall's. I want to work for a crew that makes people feel they've been respected and treated well when someone's died.'

Tatty liked the sound of that and thought Benjamin would fit in quite nicely. He was already friends with Robert, which was a little surprising as Robert was normally more reserved in character than Benjamin seemed to be, but evidently they got on well. On the other hand if Benjamin turned out to be *too* confident, meaning cheeky, he'd hear about it from Cora and probably also Henry. But as long as he behaved appropriately at work, which obviously he had for years at Nuttall Undertakers, he should be an asset to Crowe Funerals.

She had been *very* tempted to employ another young woman rather than a male, but Sydney, she decided, probably wasn't ready for a funeral company staffed predominantly by females. And someone had to lift the really heavy coffins. She offered Benjamin the job and he accepted.

She heard via undertaker gossip that Elias Nuttall was indeed furious when Benjamin left.

Tatty offered both him and Robert rooms in the new house, which they accepted. Henry, however, chose to sleep above the carriage houses to be nearer his beloved horses in case trouble arose during the night.

Crowe Funerals moved from George Street to Pitt Street on the first day of March 1868; Tatty placed notices in the papers advertising the changed address, and hung a freshly painted shingle above the new front door.

Elias Nuttall must have been watching it all bitterly. Just when Tatty had everything organised in the new premises, and business was picking up after the move, he called again.

It was before supper one evening halfway through March; Robert and Cora had only just arrived back on the train from a burial at Haslam's Creek, and Agnes was getting ready to serve the meal, so Tatty answered the front door when the bell rang. People came by at all times of the day and into the evening, so it wasn't unusual for someone to be at the door at suppertime. This time, Tatty's heart sank when she saw who it was.

'Mr Nuttall.'

'Mrs Crowe! What a lovely new house you have!'

'What do you want?'

'Don't be like that. Invite me in, go on. I've got a proposition for you. I promise you'll be interested.'

Instinct told Tatty to keep Elias Nuttall out of the house, but she stood aside and let him in. Perhaps she should at least listen to what he had to say.

She ushered him into her office and closed the door, wanting their conversation to remain private. Sitting at her desk she indicated the chair opposite. Elias sat and removed his hat.

'A little bird told me —'

'Oh, can we please not play games?' Tatty interrupted.

Elias shrugged. 'As you wish. I know you poisoned Titus and that's what put him in his grave.'

Tatty felt suddenly dizzy, as though she'd lost her balance, but forced herself to remain relaxed and her expression neutral. 'You're mistaken. He died from perforated stomach ulcers. Dr Pickett confirmed it on the death certificate.'

'He very well might have, but I *know* you poisoned your husband and I intend to inform the police of that and have them order a coroner's inquest. I have *witnesses*.'

Witnesses? Tatty thought. What witnesses? 'You'll be wasting your time, and you know as well as I do the coroner doesn't like to exhume bodies. Titus has been in the ground for six months. Mr Shiell will say no.'

'Mr Shiell will order bodies exhumed whenever he has to, *you* know *that*,' Elias countered. He held up a finger. 'Unless, of course, you sell me Crowe Funerals. Then I guarantee you'll have my absolute silence.' He looked around the office. 'I must say it's an even tastier prize now you've bought this property. But

I'm afraid my offer's dropped to three hundred pounds, and I'd expect you to go back to England immediately. I'm sick of the sight of you. You're about as welcome in this town as these foul Antipodean cockroaches, and I hope you know that's the general consensus among the Sydney undertaking fraternity.'

Tatty ignored that – for now – and continued to hold his nasty, arrogant gaze as she hurriedly considered the situation – and tried to slow down her galloping heart. What witnesses *could* there be? There just weren't any. She'd been so careful. No, Nuttall was bluffing.

'Go on, then,' she said. 'Feel free to inform the police and push them for an inquest.'

Elias looked taken aback. 'What?'

'Tell the police. I have nothing to hide. Now, get out of my house.' Tatty went to the window and opened it. '*Henry!* Your help, please!'

But she didn't need Henry: Elias headed out under his own steam.

At the front door, he said, 'You're going to be extremely sorry you ever met me, Tatiana Crowe. *Extremely* sorry.'

'I already am,' Tatty said and shut the door in his face.

She immediately went in search of Cora, who she found in the washhouse sponging a mess off the skirt of her dress.

'Look at this!' Cora protested. 'Some drunken bloody pig threw up on me on the train coming home. Bloody mourners: why can't they do their spewing at the cemetery or out the train window? Filthy bastards. I'm travelling in the hearse van from now on.'

'No, you're not,' Tatty said. 'You're supposed to be offering comfort and direction to bereaved families, not hiding from them.'

'Well, I don't think everyone wants that. I think some people really do just want to get pissed at a funeral.'

Tatty poked her head out of the washhouse to make sure no one was listening. 'I just had Elias Nuttall here.'

'That arsehole. What did he want?'

'He says he has evidence Titus was poisoned.'

Cora stopped what she was doing.

Tatty said, 'The only people who know anything about that are you and me, and I certainly haven't said anything to anyone. Have you?'

'Of course I bloody well haven't! Jesus Christ, Tatty!'

Tatty believed her. 'Then how did he find out?'

'How should I know?' Cora threw her bucket of dirty water out into the yard. '*Has* he found out, or is he bluffing? *Did* you poison Titus?'

Tatty hesitated. Titus had beaten her badly causing her to fear for her life, and had murdered his own mother and probably his first wife. He'd also routinely cheated his vulnerable customers and his colleagues, and it had become obvious he was never going to share the undertaking business with her. Her response had been to get rid of him. She'd come to terms with what she'd done but this would be the first time she'd openly admitted it. She took a deep breath in, and then out.

'Look, you know I did.'

'How?'

'I put arsenic in his tea. Just a little bit at a time, but every day for months and months.'

Cora said, 'You shouldn't have lied to me. I thought we were friends.'

'We *are* friends,' Tatty said. 'And I'm sorry, I really am. But wouldn't you have lied?'

Cora blew out her cheeks. 'Maybe. Probably.'

'So don't tell me off for doing it,' Tatty said. 'And you did know, really, didn't you?'

'I had a good idea.'

Tatty nodded, then said, 'I think Nuttall might be bluffing, but he says he has witnesses.'

Cora stared. 'Witnesses? Someone who saw you poisoning Titus? Well, that could only be Robert or Henry, because there was no one else around except me, and I'm sure they didn't see anything.' She shook her head. 'No, there's no witnesses. He's making that up.'

Tatty didn't feel any less uneasy. 'But what if he *does* really know Titus was poisoned? How can I find out who told him?' She pressed her hands against the sides of her head, which made her feel like Edith Drinkwater, so she took them away. 'This is making my head spin, Cora. I mean it, how can I find out?'

'Ask around on the quiet, find out who he's been talking to. Or better yet, get someone to do it for you.'

'Who?'

'I could ask my father,' Cora said. 'He's bound to know who's been gossiping to who. He's always sniffing out the latest dirt.'

Tatty thought about that. 'Not this time. I might try Friday Woolfe. She'll know and I think she'll be discreet, no offence meant to your father.'

'None taken.'

Friday Woolfe, who as predicted didn't pry, put Tatty in touch with someone named simply 'Luther', who made his living poking around and finding things out. Luther came back to Tatty after a week with a polite request for seven pounds in exchange for some very definite news.

'But I won't be disclosing it,' he said, 'until you've paid my fee.'

Tatty frowned but gave the man his money. 'It had better be good. Seven pounds is rather a lot.'

'I think you'll be satisfied,' Luther said, pocketing the cash then adjusting his eye patch. 'Right, it's a well-known fact that William Pickett's a sly drunk so I went round a few —'

'Is he? Willim Pickett the doctor? A drinker?'

Luther nodded. 'So I went round a few of the drinking establishments near his rooms, and there's a lot of them, and I asked does he come in, and got told yes he does, now and then, but I was more likely to find him in the Duke of Wellington. So I went there and sure enough that's his favourite watering hole, not that he drinks water by all accounts, but who does in this town? Rum's his tipple. So my mole at the Duke tells me he was there one night recently, pissed as a fart, when Elias Nuttall comes in and spends about half an hour and six shillings on him, then leaves looking as happy as a sand boy. Now, Nuttall can't keep his own mouth shut, especially when he thinks he's got one over on someone, and at the moment he thinks he does and unfortunately that's you. He's also cheap and underpays his staff and it didn't take much, and by that I mean a couple of shillings, to acquire knowledge of several remarks he let slip to his employees.' He held up a hand, made a fist then stuck up a single finger. 'The first is he's sure he'll soon be buying your business at a knock-down rate; the second is ...' up went another finger '... when that happens you'll either be back in England or here in Sydney in gaol; and third ...' and up went a third finger '... a member of your own household told him you poisoned your husband, and that person is prepared to testify against you in the coroner's court, at the very least.' Luther shrugged. 'I'd be looking at my employees if I were you. Don't bother with William Pickett. I doubt he'd even remember what he said to Elias Nuttall in the Duke.'

So Tatty was back to Cora. Obviously she'd lied about talking to Nuttall. As for Cora testifying against her in *any* court – she couldn't understand why she would. She just couldn't believe it. The sense of betrayal was enormous: it actually physically hurt.

She confronted Cora again, this time while she was in the coffin showroom carefully adding the padding, satin lining and ribbon trim to a coffin they would be delivering to a family that afternoon.

Tatty marched straight into the room. 'I've just talked to Luther.'

'Who's Luther?'

'The man I paid to do some asking around. *Your* suggestion, remember?'

'Ooh, that was quick. What did he find out?'

Tatty thought Cora sounded excited.

'That someone on my staff told Nuttall I poisoned Titus. Cora, you *swore* to me you didn't but it must have been you. It *can't* have been anyone else! Why would you do that? *Why?*'

Cora's demeanour changed instantly. 'But I *didn't*, Tatty, I didn't tell anyone! I promise! I just —' And then she froze, her mouth open, her face slowly draining of colour.

'What?' Tatty said, her furiously racing heartbeat now growing sluggish with dread. 'What have you remembered? What have you *done?*'

'I did say ... Oh, *bloody* hell.' Cora's hands came up to her mouth, as though she wanted to stop her words from coming out. 'Agnes was asking me one day what Titus had been like to work for, cos she'd never really asked me that in all the time I've been here, and I said he was sometimes quite a bastard, and he'd been horrible to his mother. And you sometimes. And I said after he got the stomach ulcers he was always whining on about it and making everyone's lives a misery, and she said that sounded terrible and it must have been a lot for you to put up with, being his wife and that. And I did say, I might have said ... Christ, I'm so sorry, Tatty, I said he was such a shit no one could blame you if you had hurried things along with a bit of poison. But I didn't know for sure. I only thought you might have. Well, probably had. I don't even know why I said it to her. She was just being so ... kindly, and listening to me, and she doesn't do that very often.'

Tatty *really* wanted to slap Cora: she lifted her hand, then lowered it. 'Honestly, Cora, how could you be so dense? Nuttall must have come sniffing and asked Agnes to keep her ears open for anything useful to him.'

Cora looked horror-struck. 'But why would she do that?'

'Money, you stupid girl. He would have paid her. Where is she now?'

'I don't know. Up the street?'

There was a funeral to conduct that afternoon: Tatty told Henry, Robert and Ben they might have to do it without her if

Agnes didn't return home soon. She sent Cora in the dog-cart with the dressed coffin to the newly bereaved family to keep her out of the way.

Agnes appeared within the hour, sweaty and red-faced, her shopping basket filled with vegetables and fruit from the market. Early morning was the best time to buy meat, fish and poultry; a bit later was better for fruit, vegetables and other foods.

Tatty watched her from an upstairs window as she trudged down the street, then disappeared around the back of the house and presumably into the kitchen. She hurried down the stairs and made her own way to the kitchen. She said, 'Agnes, I need to speak to you.' Did her voice sound calm? She didn't feel calm. Her armpits were damp and her heart was racing yet again.

Agnes turned, eyebrows raised.

'Did you tell Elias Nuttall I poisoned my husband?'

Agnes's eyes moved very slightly from side to side, but otherwise she stood steady. 'I don't know any Elias Nuttall.'

'He would have come here to the house when everyone else was out. Except for you, Agnes. He would have come when only you were here. Medium height, slightly heavy, clean-shaven, dark hair brushed straight back? And he would have had money. You took it, didn't you?'

'No.'

'Yes, you did,' Tatty said. 'He asked you to find out anything you could about the death of my husband, and he offered to pay you for it, didn't he?'

'No.'

'Yes. So you tricked Cora, your own stepdaughter, into saying to you that I may have poisoned my husband.'

'May have!' Agnes exclaimed, suddenly becoming animated. 'She said you definitely did because he was such a bastard.'

Tatty took a deep breath in through her mouth, and let it out through her nose. 'Why are you doing Nuttall's dirty work? What have I ever done to you?'

'You wouldn't hire me for more than a month at a time. Why not?' Agnes demanded. 'Am I not good enough for the likes of you?'

Tatty was absolutely gobsmacked. Of all the reasons for Agnes Billings to hold a grudge against her! 'It's not that at all. I told you your employment here would only be temporary.'

'I was trying to put a bit of money aside, but you can't do that if you don't know whether you'll still have a job in four weeks. I have to get away from Cora's father. If I don't, he'll be the death of me with his drinking and his fists and his boots. I need the money to go somewhere hundreds of miles from here, somewhere like Melbourne. He won't find me there. And now, thanks to Elias Nuttall, I *am* going, very soon.'

Tatty couldn't believe what she was hearing. 'Why do *I* have to suffer because *you* married the wrong man?'

'Well, you married the wrong man, too, and you murdered yours. I got transported all the way to this shitty bloody country for seven years just because I did a bit of shoplifting, so why should *you* get away with murder? Why should there be two sets of rules, one for me and one for you, just because your voice sounds fancy? Bugger that: that's not fair.'

Tatty said, 'Life isn't fair, Agnes. Cora was wrong. I didn't poison my husband. And you're fired so get out of my house *now.*'

Chapter Nine

April 1868, Sydney

Cora was so angry with her stepmother for tricking her and for taking money from Elias Nuttall to spy on the Crowe Funerals crew that she told her father what Agnes had done, though she didn't tell Thomas what it was she'd been duped into telling Agnes. Thomas, in the Walter Scott Inn at ten in the morning and drunk as usual, had been enraged – not because Agnes had been fired from her temporary job or because she'd been devious, but because she'd been paid money for it and hadn't given it to him. He'd immediately insisted that Cora accompany him to look for Agnes, whom he hadn't seen for twenty-four hours, but she'd declined as she had to work and also he was deeply unpleasant to be around when he was drunk. She did hope, though, that Agnes would get into trouble if he did find her, which had been the point of telling him. And then she'd started to worry that instead of just a beating, Thomas might do something much worse to Agnes, and it would be her fault.

But when Cora saw her father several days later, he told her he'd looked for Agnes all over Sydney but hadn't been able to find her anywhere.

Cora told Tatty what she'd done. 'I do wonder if he did find her,' she said, 'and he's done away with her. I wouldn't put it past him.'

Tatty thought Cora looked uneasy. 'Do you really think he would? Just for the money Nuttall paid her?'

'No, because she tried to run away from him.'

'Well, she probably has,' Tatty said. 'She's probably miles away in Melbourne by now.'

So Cora went back to hastily preparing the meals (and Henry and Robert to complaining about them – Ben was too new to criticise out loud though the faces he made let everyone know what he was thinking), and the whereabouts of Agnes Billings became yesterday's news.

The following week, Tatty received a visit from the police. She was in her office when Cora showed the officer in, and saw the barely concealed fear in Cora's eyes, but she felt quite calm herself. She had expected they would turn up eventually because she knew in her heart Elias Nuttall was never going to let the matter go. She thought that, for him, it had gone well past just a chance to acquire a new business. He wanted to ruin her, and now he thought his opportunity had arrived. It wasn't just that she was making a success of managing Crowe Funerals, but that she was a woman working in a man's industry and Nuttall, she suspected, very much did not like women. Well, perhaps his opportunity had arrived and perhaps it hadn't.

'Good morning,' she said to the policeman, wondering whether this would be the last day she spent in her new house. 'How may I help you?'

'Good morning, madam,' the policeman said. 'Sergeant Grieves from the Hunter Street watch house.' He took out a notebook and flipped a few pages until he found what he wanted. 'I have to advise you that —'

'Please, do have a seat.'

'Thank you, no.'

So Tatty stood up herself and faced him, though she was a good ten inches shorter than the sergeant.

He started again: 'I have to advise you that a complaint has been lodged with the Sydney constabulary that you did poison your husband, Titus Crowe, to death on or about the twenty-fourth day of September 1867. No evidence has been provided with this complaint except hearsay, but the matter has been referred to the coroner, Mr Henry Shiell, who has declared that an inquest is in order. This will require exhumation of your late husband's body to assist in either confirmation of the originally certified cause of death, or establishment of an alternative cause. At this point this is not a police matter and you are not under suspicion of committing a crime, though that may change in accordance with the coronial jury's verdict and Coroner Shiell's recommendations. Do you have any questions?'

'Yes. Who laid the complaint against me?'

Sergeant Grieves consulted his notes. 'Mr Elias Nuttall.'

'Thank you. Is there anything else I need to know?'

Another look at the notebook. 'The exhumation will take place tomorrow, and the inquest will start the day after.' The sergeant looked up. 'Anything else?'

'Thank you, no.'

Tatty saw the sergeant out, and closed the door softly behind him. She'd known there would have to be an inquest if Nuttall went to the police. She felt immediately better now the day had finally arrived, and immensely relieved that she hadn't been arrested for murdering Titus. She was also reassured that Nuttall didn't have any evidence except for Dr Pickett's drunken ramblings and Agnes's gossip from Cora, and now Agnes was nowhere to be found. And that left Nuttall with nothing but a handful of scuttlebutt.

But what would the surgeon who did the postmortem on Titus find?

*

The inquest was held at the Printer's Arms on Liverpool Street, Darlinghurst. The room was packed with spectators come to see the drama play out. Tatty was pleased to see customers whose deceased relatives she'd organised funerals for, signalling to her their support, but it was humiliating all the same to know that potentially the whole of Sydney knew her dead husband had been winkled out of his grave because someone had accused her of murdering him. She fervently hoped the matter wasn't going to cause too much damage to her business. Of course, there would be no business at all if Henry Shiell found that Titus *had* been murdered, and the matter went to the criminal court and she was convicted for it and hanged.

Among the audience were several members of the town's undertaking fraternity who, while she knew they didn't despise her regardless of what Nuttall had said, would probably be quite happy if she and her business both disappeared. She knew she was taking custom from other undertakers with her cheaper funeral prices and less aggressive sales techniques, but they were free to lower their fees, too. She saw plenty of other faces she recognised, including the draper Rodney Burton, who waved out energetically, Mrs Arnold the shroud-maker, photographer Nellie Harvey, and Edith and Hannah Drinkwater, whom she didn't personally know, so she was intrigued as to why they were attending. Nosiness, perhaps? Several rows ahead of her sat Dr Pickett, looking miserable, and there was Nuttall, seated deliberately near the front, no doubt so he could dash up when the time came to deliver his 'evidence' against her. She caught him turning to look at her, and, despite her own awful nerves, gave him a jolly little wave just to annoy him.

Beside her Cora said, 'Arsehole.'

'Calling him that every time you see him or hear his name isn't going to change the fact,' Tatty said. 'Unfortunately.'

'No, but it makes me feel better. Look, there's the boys.'

Henry, Robert and Ben stood together against the wall at the side of the room. Tatty waved out: Ben and Robert waved vigorously back and Henry gave a thumbs-up.

A disturbance caused almost everyone to turn towards the entrance doors in time to see Friday Woolfe sail in accompanied by Aria Te Kainga-Mataa, Sarah Green and Harrie Downey. Utterly unmissable in a crimson gown with a fashionable bustle, a scoop neck and elbow-length sleeves revealing her tattoos, and a small velvet hat perched on her brick-red locks, Friday stopped, looked around until she spotted Tatty, waved, then headed for the last remaining seats at the very back of the room. Beside her Aria was equally striking, in burgundy and a black hat with an ornament of bird feathers, though considerably more understated, as were Sarah and Harrie. Tatty suspected Friday was one of those women who couldn't dress down even if she tried. Everyone in the room stared at the little group and the buzz of chatter went up a level.

At the last second Harrie swerved and headed for Tatty and Cora, taking the empty seat beside Tatty. Good wishes aside, it seemed no one else had wanted to sit beside the widow who had allegedly poisoned her husband.

'Very best of luck for today,' Harrie said, squeezing Tatty's arm. 'Everything will work out, you'll see.'

'Thank you,' Tatty replied. 'And thank you for coming, all of you.'

'It was Aria's idea. She might seem like a grumpy old trout but she isn't really. And I would have come anyway.'

'That's nice of you.'

'Friday would have, too. And Sarah. We're all quite nice, really.'

'I'm absolutely sure you are.'

Harrie leant towards Tatty and cupped her hand around her mouth. 'So, *did* you poison him?'

Tatty blinked. 'I beg your pardon?'

'Your husband. Did you poison him? It's all right if you did. I won't tell anyone. Well, only Sarah and Friday and Aria, and they can keep a secret because we've got one just like yours. Me and Friday and Sarah killed someone once, too.'

Tatty stared at her, not entirely sure of what she'd just heard. 'No, I didn't poison him,' she said. Was poor Harrie having some sort of nervous episode?

Sarah Green appeared. 'I hope Harrie hasn't been bothering you. You must be a little anxious about the proceedings today.'

'Er, well, I've just been informed that she, along with you and Friday, at some point killed someone.'

Sarah sighed and tapped her head. 'Harrie has some trouble up here sometimes.'

'Don't be so rude, Sarah,' Harrie said.

'Come and sit with us, love,' Sarah said. 'Tatty has lots to think about.'

Harrie got up and marched off, skirts swishing, clearly offended by Sarah's comments.

'Whoops,' Cora said.

'This is Cora Billings,' Tatty said. 'She's my assistant at Crowe Funerals. Cora, this is Mrs Sarah Green, an associate of Miss Woolfe's.'

Sarah and Cora nodded at each other.

'Good luck today,' Sarah said. 'I know you're not on trial but obviously the outcome is going to matter. And by the way, Friday, Harrie and I did not kill anyone.' She held Tatty's gaze for a long moment.

Tatty stared back just as intently. 'And neither did I.'

Feeling oddly calmer now, although she wasn't quite sure why, Tatty sat with her gloved hands clasped loosely in her lap, waiting. There was nothing she could do to change things now.

By the time Coroner Shiell took his seat behind his table and began proceedings there was truly standing room only in the Printer's Arms. A jury of twelve men was chosen from the available pool and sworn in, then Mr Shiell explained that a complaint had been made suggesting that the death of Mr Titus Crowe on the twenty-fourth of September 1867 might not have been from natural causes as first assumed and certified by Dr William Pickett. To that end, Mr Crowe's body had been exhumed from Camperdown Cemetery and subjected to a postmortem carried out by senior surgeon Mr George Montague from Sydney Infirmary.

At that point Titus's corpse was brought into the room on a wheeled litter in the coffin in which he'd been buried. The solid mahogany had barely lost its sheen, and Tatty couldn't help feeling pleased: it proved you got what you paid for. The fact that he was there at all and not confined to the morgue for viewing by the jury only also augured well for her embalming skills: he'd been dead for seven months and should have been decomposing badly by now. The jury and then the public were given half an hour to file past the corpse and satisfy their curiosity, and when Tatty took her turn, letting out a few discreet sniffles behind a hanky to demonstrate her ongoing grief, she noted there was an obvious smell of decay, but definitely nothing like there should have been. The skin on Titus's face, now a dark mottled grey, had collapsed against his skull, and was almost completely covered in black mould, and much of his hair had parted company with his scalp and lay inside the coffin. He now had a ring of black stitches presumably all the way around his head just above his ears, no doubt from the postmortem. His eyes and mouth were still sewn shut. It also seemed that for the postmortem Titus's burial clothing had been discarded, as he was now wrapped in a shroud – the sort that would once have been called a winding sheet. Perhaps the garments had been too badly affected by mould.

Once everyone had had a good stare and Titus had been returned to the Benevolent Asylum's morgue, and all the doors and windows had been thrown open to disperse the smell, and everyone had finished scraping their chairs and stools on the wooden floor and had settled themselves again, Mr Montague presented himself at the front of the room to deliver his medical report.

Despite the noise of traffic passing on Liverpool Street outside, you could have heard a mouse sigh in the bar of the Printer's Arms.

'I am Mr George Montague,' the surgeon said, tugging lightly at his silk cravat, 'senior surgeon at Sydney Infirmary and fellow at the University of Sydney School of Medicine. At four o'clock on the afternoon of the fourteenth of April 1868 I performed a postmortem on the body of Titus Bartholomew Crowe, aged forty-five, who died on the twenty-fourth of September 1867. The death certificate, completed by Dr William Pickett, who examined the deceased soon after expiration, states that cause of death was due to perforated stomach ulcers. Coroner Shiell decreed that the body of Mr Crowe be exhumed from Camperdown Cemetery, and this occurred yesterday morning, also the fourteenth of April. I noted at the outset of the postmortem that Mr Crowe had been embalmed, a procedure performed after death that is intended to slow the natural processes of decomposition. It is my understanding that Mrs Tatiana Crowe, the deceased's wife, herself an undertaker of some experience, performed the embalming procedure. The process involves replacing the deceased's blood with various fluids to preserve the tissues and organs, and therefore the corpse, for a period of time.'

A wave of chatter rippled through the room at this before a hush descended once more.

'To my limited knowledge, based on experience, and I would have to say the experience of most surgeons,' Mr Montague went on, 'embalming does impede the execution of a postmortem examination, but not, I feel, to any great extent.' He consulted his notes. 'These, therefore, are my findings. It was far too late to consider any of the states of mortis, and decomposition had set in to some extent despite the embalming process, so I limited my examination to what was left of the deceased's internal organs. I found the deceased's brain on removal to be normal, no larger or smaller than what is to be expected. The heart also appeared normal, as were the liver and lungs. The kidneys were not symmetrical – one was noticeably smaller than the other – but I do not consider this had any bearing on Mr Crowe's death, nor in fact on his health in general. The liver, kidneys and heart had been perforated several times with a dedicated instrument, which I understand to be part of the embalming process. This is to let out gas caused by the early stages of decomposition and to allow embalming fluid to seep into the organs to preserve them.' Dr Montague paused and took a sip from a flask in his coat pocket.

'Booze, do you think?' Cora whispered to Tatty.

'It could be cordial.'

'And I'm Jesus's mother.'

The surgeon continued. 'I also checked the bowels, small and large. These were also perforated, and quite advanced in their decomposition, but still I did not find any obvious anomalies. And finally, we come to the stomach.'

Tatty tensed to the point that she almost cramped across her shoulders. This was where she could be caught out. This was where everything could all come tumbling down. Slowly she forced herself to relax, muscle by muscle, so that her apprehension wouldn't be obvious to anyone watching her. And many would be: she was well aware of that.

On and on went Mr Montague. 'As mentioned, the death certificate states that the deceased died from perforated stomach ulcers. The exact wording is: *exsanguination due to ruptured stomach ulcers*. So naturally I expected to see at least one breach of the stomach wall contiguous with an ulcerous mass.'

Tatty held her breath.

'And that is exactly what I did see,' Dr Montague said.

For a second Tatty felt distinctly light-headed with relief, which, she reminded herself, could well be premature.

Dr Montague continued. 'In fact, I saw many breaches, though it was difficult to tell which were organic in nature and which may have occurred during the embalming process, and even during decomposition. I do have to say that the stomach was in an utterly ragged state, and there is no doubt that catastrophic disruption occurred to that organ both before and after death.'

Coroner Shiell spoke up. 'Thank you, Mr Montague. And your findings regarding the toxicology test?'

'I used the Marsh test to look for arsenic as specified prior to the postmortem, as I believe there was an accusation of that chemical having been used as a poisoning agent? And there clearly was arsenic in the stomach tissue tested, but I consider the deceased to be an unsuitable candidate for the test.'

'And why is that?'

'Two reasons. Firstly, Mr Crowe was embalmed, a process that deliberately uses arsenic among other chemicals, therefore the Marsh test was highly likely to detect arsenic in his body. Secondly, he was an undertaker. He himself embalmed deceased persons. Probably not many, but even so it is quite possible he'd absorbed a considerable amount of arsenic during the course of his work.'

Coroner Shiell said, 'Thank you for your findings, Mr Montague. Is it your opinion then, as a senior medical professional, that Mr Crowe died as a result of perforated stomach ulcers or from deliberate arsenic poisoning?'

Tatty held her breath, blood pounding in her ears.

'On balance, based on my postmortem, I would have to say that exsanguination from perforated stomach ulcers was the immediate cause of death.'

Tatty felt her shoulders drop at least six inches, although it was probably only one inch, and she allowed herself a moment of relief. Mr Montague's professional opinion carried a lot of weight. It still wasn't anywhere near over, however.

Next, Mr Shiell called Elias Nuttall.

'Mr Nuttall, would you please recount the complaint you lodged with the Sydney constabulary, and the evidence you have to support it.'

Nuttall practically galloped up to the front of the room, then fussed about with his coat tails as he settled into the witness chair. 'It first came to my attention —'

'Please identify yourself,' Mr Shiell said.

'Elias Nuttall, undertaker, owner of Nuttall Undertakers, Sydney. It first came to my attention that Mrs Tatiana Crowe murdered her husband when I was in the —'

Cora shot out of her seat. 'Hey! That's a lie! That's slander!'

Mr Shiell said, 'That *is* slander, Mr Nuttall. Can you please keep your comments to allegation? And could you please return to your seat, madam?' he added, pointing at Cora.

Cora sat down.

Nuttall scowled. 'It came to my attention that Tatiana Crowe *might* have murdered her husband. I was in the Duke of Wellington not long ago when I ran into Dr William Pickett, who's sitting there,' he said, and indicated the physician. Everyone turned and looked at William Pickett. 'We got talking and the doctor told me that although he'd said on Titus Crowe's death certificate that the cause of death was stomach ulcers, in retrospect he realised the man could well have been poisoned to death.'

Dr Pickett stood up this time. 'Here, I say, I don't remember saying that!'

Mr Shiell raised his hand. 'Please be seated, Dr Pickett. You'll have your opportunity to speak shortly.'

'So I thought to myself,' Nuttall said, 'that sounds like a rum deal for a fellow undertaker and I vowed to do something about it. I went to Mrs Crowe's house – a big, fancy place – and asked around on the quiet, and one of her employees, Mrs Agnes Billings, told me in confidence that yes, Mrs Crowe had indeed poisoned her husband. My informant, that teller of the truth, that decent upholder of integrity, promised to appear here today, not to mention at the Central Criminal Court if necessary, but she's mysteriously disappeared and yes, I *do* fear for her safety, I truly do.'

'She's buggered off to Melbourne!' Cora shouted.

That elicited a burst of laughter, especially from the back of the room.

Nuttall ignored it. 'I reported my newfound knowledge to the police, but they in their wisdom chose not to arrest Mrs Crowe, an "alleged" murderer now walking among us, and passed the matter to yourself, Mr Shiell. I only hope you can see your way to making the right decision.'

'I'd rather you didn't tell me how to do my job, Mr Nuttall,' Mr Shiell said. 'So, in summary, Dr Pickett told you one night in the Duke of Wellington that although he'd said on the death certificate that stomach ulcers had killed Titus Crowe, looking back he thought the deceased may have been poisoned.'

'Could *well* have been poisoned.'

'And this encounter you had with Dr Pickett in the Duke of Wellington was purely serendipitous?'

'Completely.'

The coroner stroked his beard thoughtfully. 'And Dr Pickett was sober when he told you this?'

Elias looked very much like he wanted to lie. Tatty thought he really should get himself a mirror and practise looking impassive.

Mr Shiell said, 'This is not a criminal court, but you must still tell the truth, Mr Nuttall.'

'Not entirely sober, no.'

'Thank you, Mr Nuttall,' Mr Shiell said. 'You may step down.'

William Pickett was next. 'Dr William Pickett, general physician, Sydney,' he said.

'Had you attended Mr Crowe regularly before he died?' Mr Shiell asked.

'Not until he became ill,' Dr Pickett replied. 'I'd seen him regarding minor concerns over the years. In the main I attended his mother, who was a very unwell woman and bedridden for some time before she died, although I hadn't seen her for a while, either. And then Mr Crowe developed the ailment with his stomach and after that I saw him monthly for over a year during consultations his wife unfailingly arranged.'

'Can you describe this ailment?'

'I diagnosed stomach ulcers. It was quite obvious. He had ongoing stomach pain, vomiting with some blood, diarrhoea, fatigue and weakness. In my mind he was suffering from the stresses of his mother being ill and dying recently, and also overwork.'

'What did you prescribe?'

'He was already taking Dr Collis Browne's Chlorodyne, and I suggested adding regular doses of laudanum to that regimen, and then morphine tablets, which he did. I also raised the possibility of bleeding as a treatment, which Mr Crowe declined, plus the notion that he take up a pastime for relaxation, which he also failed to pursue.'

'So after Mr Crowe's death, and on examination at that time, you were satisfied that it had been ruptured ulcers that had killed him?'

'Yes, I was. He was extremely underweight and showing other signs of ongoing physical distress, and was virtually exsanguinated. This all tallied with witness accounts of the catastrophic episode that killed him, and, frankly, the residue of the blood he vomited, which his wife and colleagues hadn't had time to adequately clean up by the time I arrived. The scene really was somewhat gruesome.'

Mr Shiell looked at his notes. 'So can you explain to me then, why did you tell Mr Nuttall recently in the Duke of Wellington that you thought Mr Crowe, and I quote, "could well have" been poisoned to death?'

Dr Pickett said, 'I ... I don't think I did. At least, I can't remember telling him that.'

A round of animated muttering from the spectators, quelled by a strong look from Henry Shiell.

'Is it possible you were in your cups, Doctor?'

William Pickett sighed. 'It's highly likely, yes.'

'So you can't remember what you said at all?'

'I may have ... I *do* remember ...' Dr Pickett hesitated, then frowned. 'I *may* have said something about this new art of embalming and Mr Crowe possibly accidentally ingesting arsenic.' He shook his head. 'Or perhaps I only read about such a thing in *The Lancet*. No, I'm sorry, I really can't recall.'

'Thank you, Dr Pickett. You may step down.'

Tatty knew any decent person would feel at least a hint of sympathy for William Pickett. He'd been badly humiliated, even if Nuttall had completely made up what the doctor had allegedly said about Titus being poisoned. And without saying so directly he'd testified in her favour. Yes, he'd as much as admitted he was a drinker, but there had never been a single indication he'd taken alcohol on the many occasions he'd attended Titus. She thought he was a good doctor and would continue to engage him, and she was going to tell everyone else that, too.

Then the coroner called Thomas Billings, who strode from the back of the room to the front, leaving a waft of alcohol fumes in his wake.

'Thomas Billings, unemployed, Sydney.'

'And you are the husband of Agnes Billings?' Mr Shiell asked.

'That's right. Common law. Sixteen years.'

'Common law!' Cora said in a loud whisper. 'I thought they were properly married!'

Mr Shiell said, 'And when was the last time you saw Mrs Billings?'

The lines on Thomas's forehead deepened as he concentrated. Finally he said carefully, 'The day before the day she disappeared.'

'Where do you think she is now?'

'I'm fucked if I know.'

More laughter.

'Is she a reliable woman, your wife?' Mr Shiell asked. 'Is she honest? Would she make up a story just so Mr Nuttall would pay her?'

'No, no, and hell yes,' Thomas said.

'What a charming man your father is,' Tatty whispered to Cora.

'I told you they were always at each other's throats. And he's still angry she got one over on him,' Cora whispered back. 'That's if she did and she's not dead in a ditch somewhere.'

Tatty thought Thomas Billings's bitterness towards his wife was probably working in her favour today.

'Thank you, Mr Billings,' Mr Shiell said. 'You may step down.'

Thomas did, and walked right out of the Printer's Arms.

Tatty was called next. She swallowed her fear as she made her way to the front of the room and sat down, her crinoline worn specially for the occasion subsiding around her.

'Mrs Tatiana Crowe, undertaker, Sydney,' she said.

The coroner said, 'I remind you, Mrs Crowe, that this is not a criminal court and you are not on trial. We are here today to establish an accurate cause of death regarding your late husband. Could you please describe for the jury the course of his illness up until the day he died?'

Tatty cleared her throat. 'My husband first became ill in the stomach not long after his mother died in April of 1866. Initially he treated himself with Dr Collis Browne's Chlorodyne, but his pain and other symptoms worsened and we had to request a visit from Dr Pickett. He has already testified that laudanum and morphine were prescribed. My husband took more and more of these medications as the months passed so he could continue to work. To him the idea of not working was untenable. Towards the end of his life he needed the laudanum and the morphine before he attempted virtually anything including rising from his bed, the pain in his stomach was that severe and constant.' She wondered if she should get out her hanky and dab at her eyes. No, that would be as gratuitously theatrical as Nuttall describing her as a murderer wandering the streets. 'Then in September last year, on the twenty-fourth, at dinner my husband had a terrible episode where he suddenly just vomited and vomited all this blood. It was absolutely horrific. I've never seen anything like it. We sent for Dr Pickett but it was too late. My husband died almost immediately.'

'And that was when Dr Pickett stated on the death certificate Mr Crowe had expired from perforated stomach ulcers?' Mr Shiell asked.

'That's correct.'

'And there were witnesses present at this unfortunate event?'

'Yes, my staff: Miss Cora Billings, Mr Robert Edmonds and Mr Henry Dodds.'

Mr Shiell nodded. 'Do you feel that your husband did work too hard, Mrs Crowe?'

'I do, but there was nothing to be said or done that would encourage him to slow down. I certainly tried, but he was dedicated to his business.'

'And do you believe he took the death of Mrs Crowe senior badly? Did that grief, as suggested by Dr Pickett, perhaps have a physical bearing on Mr Crowe?'

'Every man suffers with the passing of his mother, doesn't he?' Tatty said. 'My husband had a unique bond with Mrs Crowe senior, and I believe he felt particularly responsible for her death.'

Coroner Shiell made a few notes then thanked and dismissed Tatty. She returned to the back of the room on legs she prayed wouldn't collapse before she reached her seat. Why she'd been so nervous she didn't know: as the coroner had pointed out she wasn't on trial today and she'd told the truth about the progression of Titus's illness. Next, Henry and Robert were called to testify regarding the tone of Titus and Tatty's relationship. Tatty hoped neither would paint Titus in such a bad light that he sounded eminently murderable, and they didn't, though they couldn't completely whitewash his character and behaviour, as some of the spectators in the room today must surely have been exploited or fleeced by him. They did make her sound like some sort of saint in comparison, which was gratifying, if inappropriate.

After that five people came forward to comment in favour of Tatty's good character. Sarah Green was the first, followed by Rodney Burton, Ruth Arnold, and representatives of two families for whom Tatty had organised funerals, including Mrs Byrne, whose husband Patrick's funeral had turned into such a circus, thanks to religion, alcohol, Titus and Elias Nuttall. She'd had no idea any of them had planned to do so, and was startled and really quite touched. She did wonder why the coroner considered the character references to be relevant, but they'd all been positive which would only work in her favour.

The jury then retired to a back room to consider all the evidence and make their decision. The owner of the Printer's Arms was pressed to open the bar during the interim but refused. Regardless, no one left, except Mr Montague, who had duties to attend to at Sydney Infirmary.

Tatty individually thanked everyone who had spoken on her behalf.

Rodney Burton, wearing a peach satin coat over a mint-green waistcoat with a mauve cravat of silk moire, said, 'Thank you, dear. Really, though, why on earth would anyone accuse you of poisoning Titus? He was such an utterly delightful man!'

'Morning, Rodney,' Friday interrupted. 'Christ, here you are again looking prettier than me, you old mollycoddle. Sod off, will you? I want to talk to Tatty.'

'Sod off yourself, you carrot-haired old barrack hack.'

Friday laughed and whacked Mr Burton on the backside. He smirked and trotted off, waving out to someone across the room.

'Sorry I couldn't get up and speak for you,' Friday said. 'I would have, but Aria says I'm one of those people you either like or you hate. Be a shame if today the jury all decided they hated me. And Aria, well, people don't know how to take her, being Maori, and arrogant as well. Poor old Harrie's a bit under the weather at the moment so we thought Sarah would come across best.'

'You don't need to apologise,' Tatty said. 'Sarah was wonderful, especially as she doesn't know me at all well.'

Friday raised her artfully plucked brows. 'I've an idea we know you better than you think.'

Tatty hoped not. 'Well, thank you very much for your support.'

The jury reappeared and there was a noisy scuffle as everyone returned to their seats. Gradually the hubbub died down and an expectant hush fell across the room.

A wave of prickly heat passed through Tatty and her skin turned clammy, convincing her she was going to be sick. She set her reticule on her lap, opened it just in case and swallowed back a rush of excess saliva.

'Are you all right?' Cora asked.

Tatty shook her head.

Coroner Shiell said, 'Mr Foreman, how has the jury decided?'

The nausea passed. From her reticule Tatty took a handbill for the latest play at the Royal Victoria Theatre and discreetly fanned her face with it, feeling her heartbeat begin to slow down again. No, she wasn't going to vomit into her purse from nerves or fall off her chair or burst into tears. She was stronger than that. She would sit here and listen to the jury's decision, and *then* decide what to do.

The foreman of the jury stood and declared, 'We the jury have considered all the evidence put before us today. This has included Mr Elias Nuttall's allegation that Titus Crowe was poisoned to death; the findings of the postmortem carried out by Mr Montague with the inclusion of the Marsh test for the presence of arsenic; the testimony, or lack thereof, given by the deceased's physician Dr William Pickett; and the various character references for Mrs Crowe. In conclusion, it is the jury's opinion that Titus Crowe did in fact die as a result of exsanguination due to ruptured stomach ulcers on the twenty-fourth day of September 1867.'

A ripple of hesitant applause went through the room.

Coroner Shiell raised his hand for silence. 'The jury has decided. Consequently, there will be no further referral of this matter to any other court, including the Central Criminal Court. The proceedings are complete.'

Louder applause this time and everyone rose, including Tatty, though she wasn't entirely sure her legs would hold her. She leant on a chair and waited for her heartbeat to return to normal.

'I knew everything would be all right,' Cora said. 'Nuttall looks quite pissed off. Good job.'

Tatty, feeling stronger, peered through the crowd and spotted Nuttall staring at her. He looked more than quite pissed off: he looked livid.

The only way to stop him from ruining her now, Tatty knew, was to ruin him first.

*

May 1868, Sydney

By the time Tatty and Ben arrived home late one cool and windy autumn afternoon after overseeing a funeral at Camperdown Cemetery, it was getting dark. It had been a long afternoon, and Tatty was tired. The service at St Stephen's church had gone on for a bit and both she and Ben had sat unobtrusively through it at the back – mostly to get out of the weather. Then the vicar read the burial rites over the grave for a further ten minutes while Tatty developed an earache from the wind. She was more than ready to go home by then, but kept a professionally neutral expression on her face and made sure the widower was satisfied with the day's proceedings.

Henry collected her and Ben from Redfern Station and as they pulled up in the stable yard Tatty could smell something nice cooking.

'Is that coming from our kitchen?'

Henry nodded. 'Robert and Cora. Steak and kidney pie, from Mrs Beeton's book.'

'Ambitious,' Tatty said.

Her crew were all mucking in with meals where they could now (Henry himself demonstrating a previously hidden talent for making Welsh rarebit, bubble-and-squeak and scones), and were grumpy because she wouldn't hire another cook and housekeeper, but their predicament would be solved soon, she was sure of it.

She was so tired she barely had the energy to wash her hands and face, tidy her wind-blown hair, change her boots, and sit down at the dining table. The pie actually was very nice – savoury and succulent and perfectly baked. That, Tatty thought, was probably due to Robert's involvement. He was meticulous and measured in most things he did, whereas Cora believed close enough was good enough when it came to many of her endeavours. Except, that was, when she dealt with the bereaved: she seemed to have a knack for comforting those in mourning, and for knowing what to say to them. Her bad language did in fact recede (usually), and she listened, which, Tatty thought, perhaps provided the greatest comfort of all.

'That,' Ben said as he sat back in his chair, 'was the best pie I've ever eaten. Well done, Robert.'

Tatty sighed and waited for the explosion.

'Excuse me,' Cora said, 'I helped make that pie. I bawled my bloody eyes out chopping onions *and* I rolled out the pastry and browned off the kidneys. I don't even like kidneys.'

'You did all that very well, too,' Robert said, ever the peacemaker.

'I just meant —' Ben began.

Cora said, 'I know what you meant. You meant Robert can cook better than I can, and you're right, he can. I fucking hate cooking so from now on I'm on strike. I'll do housework, but I'm not cooking.'

Nobody argued with her.

'Really, Cora, I'm sorry,' Ben said. 'I just meant Robert made a good pie and I didn't think he had it in him. You *always* serve us something filling, even if it hasn't quite turned out the way it was supposed to, and I've never left this table hungry. I appreciate what you do for us. We all do.'

Murmurs of agreement from Robert and Henry.

'Ben's right,' Tatty said. 'We really do.'

'I'm still not cooking any more,' Cora said. 'You can do my turn as well as yours, Ben.'

'That's fair, don't you think?' Tatty said, looking at Ben. His apology had been lovely but he wouldn't have had to make it if he'd thought before he'd opened his mouth. And hopefully he wouldn't be spending time in the kitchen for much longer.

Henry and Ben volunteered to attack the dishes, so Tatty made a pot of tea, excused herself, and went upstairs to bed, hoping to read for a while before she slept.

But her tea went cold on the nightstand, and her book lay page-down on her chest as she fell asleep in less than fifteen minutes. And she would possibly have slept like that all night if a noise hadn't woken her some hours later.

She sat straight up, her book falling to the floor, and stared around her room. What had made that noise? The lamp was still burning, though the wick was flickering erratically: her clock read two o'clock.

She threw back the covers and climbed out of bed, took the lamp and opened her bedroom door.

Cora was in the hallway, in her nightdress, holding a candle. 'Did you hear that?' she asked.

'I heard something,' Tatty said. 'I'm not sure what it was.'

'I think it was breaking glass.'

Someone came pounding up the stairs. It was Robert – bare feet, trousers on under his nightshirt, hair sticking up. With him came the smells of kerosene and something burning. 'The house is on fire!' he shouted. 'We have to get out!'

Tatty couldn't quite believe what he was saying. 'What?'

Robert grabbed her arm and steered her to the head of the stairs. 'The house is on fire! Get out *now*!'

All three hurried down the stairs. At the bottom Tatty could really smell burning now, but she couldn't see anything alight.

'Where is it?' she cried. 'Where's the fire?'

She was terrified and panicking, but also angry. Her beautiful house and business on fire, and she hadn't even paid for it yet! But it was insured, thank God.

'In the parlour. Henry's trying to put it out.' Robert turned Cora around and gave her a shove towards the back door. 'Go out to the yard. Get ready to let the horses out if we need to. You too, Tatty.'

Tatty said, 'No!' and ducked around him and ran down the hall to the parlour doorway.

At least half the carpet in the parlour was alight; so were a sofa and an armchair; one wall was partially scorched; flames were beginning to climb up the drapes at the smashed window overlooking Pitt Street; and smoke billowed to the ceiling. The stink of kerosene was eye-watering.

Henry and Ben were using blankets in an attempt to extinguish the flames. 'Are they outside?' Henry shouted without turning around. 'Get us some more blankets, will you?'

Tatty assumed he thought he was talking to Robert. She raced upstairs and grabbed as many blankets from the blanket box as she could carry, then, downstairs again, she hurled them through the parlour door – to find Robert had obviously informed Henry that she wasn't out in the stable yard.

Henry's face was bright red as he roared at her: 'Get the hell outside, Tatty! *Go and save my horses! Now!*'

Tatty went.

Cora was in the stables. She'd lit the lamp in the tack room, unlatched the stable doors but left them closed, and was now slipping a halter onto each horse in case they had to be led out. The horses were agitated: Tatty thought they could smell the smoke. She also thought Cora was very brave going into the stalls with nothing on her feet – and then she saw she had on Henry's large, leather blacksmithing boots, which looked ridiculous sticking out beneath her nightdress.

'Is the fire out?' Cora asked. 'Where is it?'

Tatty said, 'It's in the parlour, and no.'

'Bloody hell. Will the boys be able to put it out?'

Tatty ignored the snorts and whinnies of the horses and tried to suppress her own panic. There was a volunteer fire company with an engine housed on Pitt Street but that was at Haymarket. By the time someone rode or drove down there and the engine arrived, the house could have burnt down. But would it? She forced herself to be rational. The external walls of the house were all made of sandstone, as were many of the internal walls. The ceilings were of wood and so were about half the floors – the rest were stone. The roof was terracotta tiles. Now she thought about it, the whole building was unlikely to be razed to the ground if the fire couldn't be put out. She could lose the contents of the house, which would include everyone's possessions, except perhaps Henry's, and her business records, and her coffins, but as long as no one was hurt, including the horses, and they saved the hearses and the harnesses and stopped the fire spreading to any other properties, things wouldn't be too catastrophic.

No, she thought after a minute of standing on cold cobbles, her feet freezing, shivering in the night breeze, it *would* actually be catastrophic.

It seemed as though she and Cora waited in readiness with the horses for an age, but no one came to tell them to lead them out onto the street.

When someone finally did come, it was Ben. Soot was smudged across his face and all over his hands and nightshirt. 'It's out,' he said, wiping his mouth with the back of his hand, then spitting. 'But the parlour's a mess. I think you're going to need new drapes.'

Tatty stared at him, then burst out laughing.

Henry appeared then, equally filthy. He held up a chipped and battered demijohn. 'It looks like someone chucked this through the window. It stinks of kerosene. I'll wager it had a bit of cloth in it for a wick.' He looked grim. 'Someone's tried to burn down your house.'

Tatty took the heavy spirit jar from him and sniffed at the narrow neck. She knew exactly who would have thrown a flaming stoneware jar filled with a gallon of kerosene through her window at two o'clock in the morning.

Chapter Ten

Tatty and Robert had just spent an hour with a family who had suffered the deaths of their two youngest children, aged seven and five. They'd been playing outside in the yard near a rubbish fire when the youngest child had fallen into the flames. The older child had pulled his sister out but his clothes had also ignited, and both were badly burnt. A doctor was summoned, but by the following day the brother and sister had died.

The family were poor. Tatty didn't charge the parents for the coffins, and gave them a steep discount on other services they requested: the glass hearse – in which both small coffins would travel – two horses, and one mourning coach.

Tatty had almost cried when the parents gently laid the two burnt little bodies in their coffins. Robert did cry, on the way home in the dog-cart.

'Sorry,' he said, blowing his nose loudly. 'Normally I'm all right, but this one's just so unfair.'

'It is,' Tatty agreed. 'Perhaps we'll ask Henry to harness all four horses, with all the accessories.'

'Free?'

'Of course free.'

Nearing home, Shadow pricked up his ears and slowed, then turned without being asked into the carriageway at the side of the house, letting out an enthusiastic whinny to his friends as he reached the stables.

Henry appeared, took hold of Shadow's bridle and stroked the horse's velvety nose. 'You've got visitors,' he said to Tatty.

Her heart plummeted. 'Oh God, not Nuttall?'

'No, a couple of ladies.'

Smiling widely now, Tatty climbed down from the dog-cart. Then she told herself not to count her chickens. If her visitors didn't turn out to be who she thought they were, she was going to be very disappointed.

In the kitchen, Ben was cutting up turnips, whacking at them with a carving knife, presumably for their supper. Tatty didn't like turnips.

'Watch your fingers,' she said.

Ben said, 'You've got some visitors. They're in the parlour. They said they were happy to wait. I've given them a pot of tea and a plate of Garibaldi biscuits.'

'From the bakery?'

Ben nodded.

Oh dear, Tatty thought. They were stale.

She hurried down the hall and almost ran into the parlour. 'I thought you'd *never* get here,' she exclaimed as she threw herself into Mrs Seddon's open arms.

'So did we, believe me,' Maggie Seddon said, adjusting the spectacles Tatty had almost knocked off her face. 'So did we.'

Tatty gave Mrs Seddon a kiss on the cheek and then hugged Lorna. 'Oh, I've missed you both so much. I'm *so* pleased you're here.'

'I'm never going on another ship again,' Lorna said.

Tatty said, 'No, neither am I.'

Lorna made a face. 'I was sick the *whole* way.'

'Not the whole way,' Maggie Seddon said. 'Only for the first few weeks.'

'Have you just arrived?' Tatty asked. 'Where are your trunks?'

'We did, very late last night, but the captain insisted we sit out at anchor beyond the mouth of the harbour until daylight. Daylight! We didn't dock until after ten o'clock, then it took us forever to disembark, and *then* we had to wait for our trunks to be brought up from the hold and off-loaded. As they're far too unwieldy for me and Lorna to manage, they're currently in a shed near the wharf waiting to be collected.' Maggie leant forward. 'Did you know, Tatty, there's a young man chopping vegetables in your kitchen? What on earth is going on here?'

'Ben? The one who gave you tea?'

'And some rather disappointing biscuits.'

Tatty said, 'We haven't had a cook for a couple of months. It used to be Cora, who you'll meet. I think she's out shopping. Then when she became my assistant I took on someone else temporarily, but she left and I didn't replace her because I was hoping you and Lorna would take up my offer. We've all been taking turns to cook and do the laundry.'

'Men as well as ladies?' Lorna said. 'Men *cooking*?'

Tatty nodded. 'Henry makes a very good bubble-and-squeak.'

Lorna gasped and shot a scandalised glance at Maggie, who said, 'I told you things would be upside down here.'

'So why did you decide to come?' Tatty said. 'I really didn't know if you would. And did I send you enough money to cover all your costs?'

'Have you not had a letter from me recently?' Maggie said.

Tatty said she hadn't.

'You should have. I sent one about three weeks before we set sail. How annoying. I wonder where it is?' Maggie polished the lenses of her spectacles on a corner of her shawl. 'It was all in that letter. We didn't like where we were working, did we love?' she said to Lorna. 'The lady of the house was nice enough but the gentleman, well, he didn't deserve the title, not by a long shot. Mind you, I think we were spoilt from working for your mother and father. They were so lovely to us. They treated us like family.'

Tatty found herself having to blink back sudden tears. 'You *are* family, both of you. You're *my* family.'

'You're a good girl, Tatty,' Maggie said. 'You always were.'

I'm not, Tatty thought, a sharp little pang of guilt stabbing her just under the ribs. Not any more.

'So when you asked us to come and work with you, I decided we might as well,' Maggie continued. 'I decided that if you could learn to live with monstrous insects and freakish animals and ex-convicts and people with no refinement, then so could Lorna and I. But we had to work out our month's notice, then wait more than a fortnight until the ship was ready to sail, all of which means we've arrived later than I expected.'

'Really, it doesn't matter,' Tatty said. 'You're here now.'

Maggie said, 'And how are *you*? A widow at twenty, you poor thing. You must have been broken-hearted, after not even two years of marriage.'

'I have friends around me,' Tatty said. 'Cora and everyone else I work with. And Titus signed over the business to me when we married, so I wasn't left without an income.'

Maggie's eyes opened comically wide behind her spectacles. 'He signed over his business? How did you get him to do that?'

Tatty gave a small shrug. 'It was his decision.'

She felt rather awful lying to Maggie Seddon. She'd not told her about Titus's repugnant behaviour in her letters because she hadn't wanted her to worry, and she'd certainly said nothing about arsenic. She'd tell her the truth one day, but not now. Not on her very first day in New South Wales. And she would have to tell Cora to keep quiet about all of that, too.

'Well I never,' Maggie said. 'He sounds like he was a treasure. What a shame he died.'

'Isn't it?' Tatty agreed.

'But you're managing? Because it's only been, what, eight months since he passed, hasn't it?'

Tatty said, 'I'm fine: I work with a great crew, and the business is doing better and better every month.'

'When you say crew, dear,' Maggie said, 'do you mean like a band of brigands?'

Tatty laughed. 'Not quite. There are five of us – myself, Cora, Benjamin, Robert and Henry. Everyone is in their early twenties except for Henry, who is our old man at thirty-four.'

'Early twenties?' Maggie repeated. 'Isn't that a little young to be organising other people's funerals?'

Tatty said, 'Is it? We seem to be doing quite well.'

'In London, undertakers all seem to be middle-aged men, if not elderly. You know that. And are there lots of lady undertakers here in Sydney?'

'No. Just me.'

'Oh well,' Maggie said. 'I suppose you know what you're doing. You usually do. So, we're cooking and cleaning for five? And everyone lives in?'

'They do, and there's accommodation on the top floor for you and Lorna, a room each. Or there are a couple of spare rooms above the carriage houses. You can have those if you'd prefer them, although Henry sleeps over there to be near the horses.'

'We'll take the rooms upstairs in the house, thank you,' Maggie said. She wrinkled her nose. 'Have you had a fire in here? It smells as though something's been burnt.'

Tatty said, 'Yes, a few weeks ago. I've had to replace some of the floorboards, paint and paper the whole room, and replace all of the soft furnishings and most of the furniture. It was quite a shock.'

'I'm sure it was.'

Cora arrived home then, grumbling about how cabbage, carrots and parsnips got heavier the farther you had to carry them.

Tatty called everyone together – Henry, Robert, Cora and Ben (who was fed up with peeling and slicing turnips and had just dumped them in the pot) – and formally introduced Maggie and Lorna.

'This is why I haven't taken anyone else on,' she explained. 'I've been waiting for Mrs Seddon and Lorna to arrive.'

'Well, it's lovely to meet you,' Cora said, 'but I hope you realise we've been eating a lot of pretty disappointing meals because of you, most of them cooked by me, I admit.'

Tatty saw that Lorna thought she was being blamed for something, and was blinking back tears. She said, 'What Cora's saying is she's very glad you're here now, aren't you, Cora?'

A look of understanding crossed Cora's face. 'Oh, definitely. We all are.'

Tatty was extremely grateful her friend hadn't made a spectacle of Lorna's lack of sophistication.

Maggie added, 'Lorna helps me in the kitchen but she's more of a housemaid. She's very good with cleaning and laundry and taking care of clothing and the like.'

Henry said, 'Can you make a good fish pie, Mrs Seddon?'

Maggie said, 'I like to think so.'

'Then I'm a happy man. Custard tarts?'

'With one hand tied behind my back. What's on the menu for today?'

Ben said, 'Reheated boiled mutton, mashed turnips and silver beet.'

Maggie looked at him over her spectacles, then said, 'I'd better get to work, then, hadn't I?'

Lorna and Maggie settled in over the next few weeks, though Tatty had no doubt they found Sydney as strange as she had when she'd first arrived. For a start they'd left London at the end of winter, and now here they were going into another cold season, though it would be nothing like as harsh as the winters to which they were accustomed. Poor Lorna had a terrifying encounter with a Huntsman spider that sent her running from the washhouse screaming her head off, which Tatty was convinced must be a rite of passage for new immigrants to New South Wales. Maggie, however, cornered the beast and bashed the life out of it with a broom, earning copious praise from Robert, who also feared them.

Over those weeks, Tatty told Maggie about the problems she was having with Elias Nuttall. She described how he'd been

Titus's arch-rival before Titus had died and since then had been obsessed with first taking over her business and now destroying her; that he'd publicly accused her of poisoning Titus, resulting in an inquest that had proved she hadn't; that he was maligning her to anyone who would listen, which she didn't think would be the people she worked with but might be a few of the town's more affluent society types, though she could ignore supercilious looks from them; and that when her house was set alight she'd strongly suspected Nuttall was responsible.

Maggie was appalled. 'Did you go to the police?'

'I couldn't. I can't prove it was him.'

'Well, you're going to have to do something,' Maggie said. 'The man sounds unhinged. What will it be next? Firing a pistol at you in the street?'

Tatty didn't think Nuttall would ever be that brazen – or demented – but Maggie was right. The time had come for her to do something.

*

First, she visited her friend and colleague, the photographer Nellie Harvey.

'I really have had enough,' she said as Nellie poured tea into fine china teacups. 'We could have died, all of us.'

'Why don't you tell the police?' Nellie asked.

'Because I can't prove it was Nuttall.'

Nellie said, 'No, that's the problem with all of this, isn't it? You can't prove he tried to burn your house down and we can't prove he's threatening to blackmail us. Or actually *is*. Cinnamon biscuit? I baked them last night. Would you like to take some home with you? Somehow I made around five dozen and there's only me to eat them.'

'Thank you.' Tatty took one and bit into it. It was sweet and crisp. 'Mmm, lovely. It annoys me that he picks on single women.'

'So did your late husband.'

'I know,' Tatty said. 'And I'm sorry.'

'I think that's probably what they prefer, bullies like Elias and Titus,' Nellie said. 'I expect they think we're weak and helpless because we're women, and perhaps we are. But it's not just women, is it? What about Mr Crumb, the baker? And Rodney Burton? And the jeweller, Mr Coverdale? And what's the name of the man who does the mourning stationery?'

'Joseph Todd. Mr Crumb told Titus what to do with his commissions, though, and so did Mrs Arnold,' Tatty said. 'She's not still paying a commission to Nuttall, is she?'

'I don't know,' Nellie said. 'She might be. Elias Nuttall's always been nastier than your husband was. I don't see Mrs Arnold very often, and when I do it's not the sort of question one asks out of the blue, is it?'

'Not really.' Tatty finished her biscuit. 'Anyway, what I'm here for is to discuss my plan. In confidence, please, Nell.' She knew she could trust Nellie. Anyone who cared so much about providing bereaved families with photographic memories of their deceased loved ones, as Nellie had with the family of the little girl who'd died of quinsy, was more than likely to be dependable. She wouldn't be talking to Nellie if she thought otherwise and she knew her quite well now. 'I'd like to try to derail Nuttall to the point that he can't interfere in our businesses. At first I thought I'd try to do that by myself, but I realise now I probably can't. Then I thought there're probably a good few people who'd like to see Nuttall's extortionate behaviour stopped, so I wondered – who might like to help? And of course I thought of you.'

Nellie took a biscuit but didn't bite into it. 'When you say derail and stopped, what exactly do you mean?'

'I'm not entirely sure yet. I wish there *was* an easy way to make him just stop what he's doing, but I'm not sure there is. I suppose I mean I'd like to put him out of business. Unless you can think of some other solution?'

Nellie frowned and ate her biscuit, chewing slowly and thoughtfully. Tatty waited, but after she swallowed all Nellie would say was, 'No, I can't.'

Rats. 'Well, I'd like to keep everything discreet,' Tatty said. 'I'm not intending to launch any sort of overt public crusade against Nuttall, and I don't even know if my plan will work, but I thought if I got a group of us together and we all did a little bit each, it might make a difference and slowly undermine him to the point that his business will suffer and hopefully fail.'

Nellie said, 'That sounds like the sort of unscrupulous thing Nuttall would do.'

'Well, you have to fight fire with fire,' Tatty said. 'And I'm the one whose parlour still stinks of smoke.'

'You do have a point.'

'So, are you interested?'

Nellie took another cinnamon biscuit. 'Yes. Yes, I am.'

'Excellent. I'm also going to talk to Eliza McBride. I assume Nuttall has his claws into her and her son because I know Titus certainly did, and I'm hoping she might refuse to sell Nuttall her beautiful coffins. And also Rodney Burton. He's the biggest supplier of mourning drapery and haberdashery in Sydney so he must be on Nuttall's list. So with those two and yourself, I think we'd be off to a good start, don't you?'

'And what will you be doing?' Nellie asked. 'Oh, I know. You could poach his customers. You know, families who have traditionally gone to Nuttall Funerals when someone's died. You could get in first.'

'They're changing to Crowe Funerals anyway,' Tatty said. 'No, I'm thinking Nuttall must have secrets. Most people do. It's just a matter of winkling them out. That's what I'll be doing.'

'Ew, I don't know if I want to know Nuttall's secrets,' Nellie said. 'May I suggest one other person for our group? Well, two, actually.'

Tatty raised her eyebrows.

'Edith Drinkwater and her daughter,' Nellie said. 'The clairvoyant?'

'Really? Why would we want her?'

'I was photographing the body of a deceased gentleman the other day when the widow told me she was desperate to know if her husband had gone straight to heaven after he'd died, and that Nuttall had arranged an appointment for her with Edith Drinkwater. I thought that was reasonable if she absolutely *had* to know, but he also told the poor woman that for a fee of ten pounds – *ten* pounds! – Edith would contact her husband directly and ask him if he was in heaven. And she paid the ten pounds to Nuttall, who said he'd pass it on to Mrs Drinkwater.' Nellie shook her head. 'That really sounded questionable to me so I asked another medium I know, Frederick Haseltine?'

Tatty nodded. She knew Mr Haseltine – another clairvoyant whose psychic abilities she doubted.

'I asked him if ten pounds was an excessive fee and he said most definitely,' Nellie continued. 'He said he never charged more than three pounds for a private session, and even that was on the high side and only when he knew the customer could afford it. But when I told him it was Edith Drinkwater charging the ten pounds – which I have to say made me feel like a gossipmonger, but I'll just have to pray extra rigorously for absolution next time I'm at church – he said, "Oh, well, that explains it." When I said, "Explains what?" he told me that according to the scuttlebutt Edith Drinkwater owes Nuttall quite a lot of money and is at his bidding until she repays it. Which she can't.' Nellie sat back in her seat. 'So that's why I think she'd be a good person to have in our group. I expect she'd be quite motivated to see Nuttall put out of action.' She frowned. 'What *is* her daughter's name?'

'Hannah.'

That same afternoon, Tatty called on Eliza McBride, who lived with her son, Carl, in a tenement at the north end of George Street right near the waters of Sydney Cove. Her house was poky and two-storeyed and Carl couldn't easily negotiate the stairs – Tatty understood he slept in one of the two downstairs rooms – but Eliza did have a big backyard. Not far away at all were the Government Wharf and Campbell's Wharf where ships unloaded imported timbers, and beautiful timber felled from Tasmania and the New South Wales coast. So the location of the house was ideal for their work.

Tatty knocked on the front door but no one answered. It wasn't locked so she pushed it open and heard hammering sounds coming from the rear of the property. Ignoring propriety, though she didn't think Eliza would mind as they'd known each other for over three years, she walked through the house and out to the backyard, where Eliza was busy building a coffin.

She was a slender woman in early middle age, and her dark hair was tied back beneath a large kerchief. She wore a plain brown dress with patched elbows, and a well-worn leather apron covering her from her chest to her knees. Sweat stains spread out from her armpits, even though the day wasn't warm.

The workspace was under a roof of corrugated iron with makeshift walls on two sides, and the yard also contained several small wooden sheds, a privy and a clothesline.

Tatty hailed Eliza from the back steps, off which a ramp also descended to the cobbled ground.

'Hello! I did knock. The door was open. I hope you don't mind.'

Eliza waved. 'No, no, come through; I didn't hear you. I'm glad you're here. I could do with a cup of tea.'

During their shared pot of tea, Tatty explained her plans for Elias Nuttall. She'd hardly finished speaking before Eliza said, 'Yes, please, I'll join your group. And would you like to have our first meeting here?'

'Here?' Tatty echoed, then realised she might have sounded a little rude.

'Yes. If Nuttall is becoming as unpredictable as you think he is, he could be watching your house. Or paying someone else to watch it. What's he going to think if we all turn up there? That could really upset the bats in his belfry, don't you think?'

Tatty hadn't thought of that. 'That's true. Thank you, Eliza. How clever of you. I'll have to let Nellie know.'

When Tatty called briefly at Edith and Hannah Drinkwater's house, Edith was nowhere to be seen but Hannah accepted her invitation to attend the meeting at Eliza's, and said they would think about joining Tatty's group. She, Hannah, wanted to know more about it before they made a commitment. That was understandable, Tatty thought as she made her way to Burton's emporium on George Street.

Rodney Burton seemed, as always, pleased to see her. His very large store was busy as autumn was slipping into winter and women were shopping for fabrics and accessories more suited to the coming season.

'Can we go somewhere a little more private?' Tatty asked. 'Do you have an office?' She presumed there must be somewhere he kept his accounts and correspondence.

'I do, dear, but it's so boring,' Rodney said. 'I much prefer to be out here among all my beautiful fabrics and laces and ribbons.' He looked around, fingers pressed over his mouth. 'Private, private. I know! The footwear aisle. That's hardly ever busy because shoes and boots are so expensive. I import most of mine, you know. Perhaps I shouldn't.'

He took Tatty's hand and led her to a section of the store where a considerable range of both men's and women's footwear was on display. He was right, Tatty thought: it wasn't busy at all.

They sat on the chairs provided for those trying on footwear. It was actually a loveseat – two chairs facing in opposite directions but sharing the same curved back – upholstered in silk velvet the colour of wisteria flowers.

'Did you choose this seat?' Tatty asked.

Rodney said, 'Yes, but I had to have it re-upholstered. It was the most revolting yellow-brown colour when I bought it. Now, what can I do for you?'

Tatty told him. At the end of her account he gave an enormous sigh.

'I would *love* to be part of your group, Tatty, I really would, but I just can't risk it. I have too much to lose. You mention that Elias Nuttall might have secrets? Well, he most definitely has *mine*, and I fear that if I were involved in provoking or persecuting him he wouldn't keep his mouth shut. I *know* he wouldn't. He'd tell the whole *world*, and while it's acceptable for me to flit about in my silks and satins because I own a drapery and haberdashery, it is *not* acceptable for any other reason.' Rodney swooped his arm in an expansive half-circle. 'If that other reason were to be exposed I'd lose all of this – my beautiful emporium, my reputation, my freedom, possibly even my life.'

Tatty understood then that what Titus had written in his poisonous little journal about Rodney was most definitely true.

'So I'm terribly sorry, dear,' he went on. 'Even though I'd dearly love to help ruin Nuttall and get him out of my life, and yours, I can't afford the risk.'

Tatty nodded. 'Thank you for explaining that, Rodney. And I understand, I really do.'

'Do you?' Rodney said. 'You understand everything?'

'I think so.'

'And we're still friends?'

'Of course we are!'

The look of relief on Rodney's face almost made Tatty cry.

*

There wasn't a lot of room in Eliza McBride's parlour. There was just enough space for a couch and two armchairs facing the fireplace, and on this suite sat Nellie Harvey, Tatty and Cora, Edith and Hannah Drinkwater, and Eliza, presiding over a tray containing a teapot, cups, saucers and plates and a sliced fruit loaf. The room was lit by three lamps. A fire burnt and a pile of small logs and dried branches sat beside it. Tatty watched as a mouse darted around the firewood, possibly scavenging for food crumbs.

'Did you see that?' Cora whispered to Tatty. 'Shall I give it a tiny little piece of cake?'

'No. Just ignore it.'

'Carl has gone out,' Eliza announced. 'To the pub, probably.'

Cora frowned. 'Do you mind if I ask how, if he can't walk?'

'Years ago he made a little cart with wheels on it. He sits in that and scoots himself along. If he goes anywhere with steps, and that's just about everywhere, people usually give him a hand and lift him up. He gets by.'

'Shall we start?' Tatty said. 'Thank you, Eliza, for hosting our little group here this evening. I might as well start with my story, which I think most of you know. Elias Nuttall very publicly accused me of poisoning my husband, and then he tried to burn down my house in the middle of the night. Obviously he's trying to ruin my business, and I suspect me personally, so I have an interest in getting rid of him, to put it bluntly.'

Then Nellie Harvey spoke up. 'I for one am tired of him recommending me to his customers, then charging them my fee, and only passing half of it on to me after I've done the work. It's bordering on theft. I can barely make a living from postmortem photography, which I prefer because I find it more rewarding than photographing living subjects. It means so much to the bereaved. But at this rate I'll be taking photographs of people's favourite cats and dogs and parrots soon, just to get by. What a ridiculous thought.'

'Why do you let Nuttall do it?' Tatty asked.

Nellie looked uncomfortable. 'I'm sorry, Tatty, I've never told you this, because of our friendship. And then when Titus died it just seemed, I don't know, irrelevant by then, but it started with him. When I was first establishing my photography business, which as a woman I have to say wasn't easy, he offered to help by referring customers to me, at least for the postmortem work. This was before he took you on as an assistant. I was grateful, as you can imagine, and at that point I didn't mind paying him a commission. In fact I thought it was reasonable. And then the amount he demanded increased and when I complained about that he threatened to let it be known publicly that a commission wasn't all he was getting from me, which was a flagrant and deeply offensive lie.'

'Oh, I'm so sorry,' Tatty said. 'I had no idea.' What an utterly nasty thing for Titus to do.

'So I'm afraid to say that when he died I wasn't exactly heartbroken. In fact, I thought all my troubles had come to an end. And then Nuttall came to see me and told me he was aware I'd been … having relations with Mr Crowe, and that if I didn't enter into the same commercial arrangement with him that I'd had with Titus, he'd make sure the entire town knew the truth about me.' Nellie blinked hard several times then retrieved a handkerchief from her reticule and blew her nose. 'It is *not* the truth. I am a single woman, I can't afford to have that sort of thing said about me while I'm trying to make a living, and I'd prefer it wasn't said at all. He's only doing it because I'm a woman and he thinks I can be bullied. And as it turns out, I can.'

'Elias Nuttall —' Cora began.

Tatty gave her a sharp look.

'Really does deserve his come-uppance,' Cora said.

'He does,' Tatty agreed. 'Mrs Drinkwater, would you like to tell us about your predicament?'

Edith Drinkwater wasn't dressed as flamboyantly as she had been on the night of her public seance, but there remained a hint of the exotic about her all the same. She wore a taffeta dress in dark maroon that wasn't quite fashionable, with very fitted three-quarter sleeves that made her arms look like sausages, a basque waist and a modest neckline corralling her full bust. Tatty thought the dress was either one for which she was getting too fat or bought second-hand and not a perfect fit. Mrs Drinkwater had accessorised with jet beads and ear-rings, multiple rings and an ornament pinned into her piled-up hair.

Edith heaved out an apparently heartfelt sigh. 'And what a predicament it is. It all started when Elias Nuttall offered to lend me money.'

'Mother,' Hannah Drinkwater said.

'Shush, dear, I'm talking.'

Hannah – who, compared to her mother, looked a lot like the little grey mouse bustling about in the firewood – gave Edith a very pointed look, but remained quiet.

Tatty was suspicious already. 'Have you known Elias Nuttall for some time?'

Edith said, 'Since we moved here from Tas— ... after our international engagements. So not long, no.'

'Mother!' Hannah exclaimed.

'What?' Edith snapped.

Hannah said, 'Really, if you don't tell the truth you're just going to get us into even more trouble.'

Tatty blinked. This wasn't the aloof and (almost) impassive girl she'd talked to either at the Rose of Australia Inn or when inviting her to this meeting.

'I *am* telling the truth,' Edith said, and took a hasty sip of her tea. '*Directly* before we came here, we actually were in Tasmania. Then when we arrived in Sydney ...' She stopped and looked at her daughter. 'When exactly was that, dear? I have so much going on in my mind I forget these things.'

'November,' Hannah said. 'November last year.'

'That's right. Well, Elias Nuttall got in touch with me and asked me to —'

Hannah interrupted: 'Oh, for God's sake. My mother approached Elias Nuttall, and also some of the other undertakers, and asked him if he'd be interested in referring the bereaved to her for private seances in exchange for a commission, and he agreed. She didn't ask you, Mrs Crowe, because she'd heard your husband had recently died and she didn't know what the situation was in terms of his business.'

'It's my business,' Tatty said. 'It has been since I married him.'

'I know it's yours *now*,' Edith said.

'And then she borrowed money off Elias Nuttall,' Hannah said. 'Quite a lot of money, and we can't pay it back.'

Tatty asked, 'Money for what, do you mind me asking? Are you in some sort of trouble?'

Hannah said, 'No. Mother wanted new furniture and a fancy phaeton and a pretty horse to pull it.'

'Business expenses!' Edith exclaimed. 'They're all business expenses! I hold private seances at our home and I can't have customers sitting on crates and barrels. I needed decent furnishings. And a person of my standing in the world of spiritualism can't be expected to arrive at public appearances on foot or, God forbid, the omnibus. I have a professional reputation to uphold.'

'Mother doesn't make enough money to repay Nuttall,' Hannah said. 'And the rate of interest, which is extremely high and which Mother happily accepted at the time ...' a glare at Edith '... is compounding every single day.'

'I do regret that,' Edith said. 'I admit I'm not very good with numbers.'

'While we're all being honest,' Tatty said, 'how genuine *are* your talents, Mrs Drinkwater? I attended one of your sessions and I rather thought you might have been reading the room and improvising. Quite cleverly, though, I must admit.'

Nellie Harvey gasped. Cora gave a muffled snort.

Hannah just sighed.

Tatty expected Edith to respond with real anger, but what she said was, 'How au fait are you with the world of spiritualism, Mrs Crowe?'

'I'm not, really.'

'Then perhaps you shouldn't comment on matters you don't understand.'

Hannah said, 'Look, whether my mother's a charlatan – whether we're both charlatans – isn't really the point at the moment.'

'No,' Edith agreed. 'What's more important is how we're going to get rid of Nuttall so I don't have to pay back what I owe him.'

'I think you *should* pay him back,' Tatty said.

Edith looked startled. 'What?'

'You borrowed money from him, and you spent it. All of it, I presume?'

'Yes.'

'So why shouldn't you pay it all back?'

'Because he's ...' Edith trailed off. Tatty could see her mentally putting thoughts into a sequence she thought would benefit her argument. 'Because he's greedy and he's taken advantage of us all because we're women and we're single and vulnerable and we don't have any means of fighting back.'

Tatty said, 'Yes, yes, all of that's true, but you willingly borrowed that money off him and you agreed to the high interest rate, whether you understood what you were doing or not, and now you don't want to pay the money back. I think you should.'

Edith reached for a slice of cake then changed her mind, crossed her arms and sighed. Tatty thought the sigh sounded like it was made up of anger, irritation and resignation, which was a lot of sentiment for one expelled breath.

'Yes, I know,' Edith said. 'But I can't. I don't have a hope in hell of paying it back. You might think the spiritualism business is a money-maker, but it really isn't. Not once you've paid for all your overheads and what have you.'

'But I saw how crowded your seances are. Do you really not make much money from them?' Tatty said.

'It's a living, barely, by the time I've forked out to rent the venue for the night. Room and chair hire's not cheap, you know, and it bloody well should be, the custom I bring into those places. And then there's the advertising in the papers, and the public notices, they cost a lot to have printed, and then I have to pay someone to go around town and post them. Hannah and I can't be seen doing that. Well, I certainly can't.'

Tatty thought for a minute. The mouse in the woodpile nibbled on a piece of bark then spat it out. 'Look, I'll take on your loan. I'll lend you what you need to repay Nuttall, at a fair rate of interest, as long as you clear your debt with him in full. How much is it?'

'It's two hundred and twenty-seven pounds now,' Hannah said. 'Why would you do that?'

Hell, Tatty thought. She'd have to see Friday Woolfe about borrowing more money. But that was all right. She thought Friday would probably be amenable to that.

She said, 'Because you can't disassociate yourself from Nuttall commercially if you owe him money, and that's what we're all going to have to do if we want to have an impact on his business. Well, Crowe Funerals don't have anything to do with him anyway, but you do, Mrs Drinkwater, and you'll have to as well, Eliza and Nellie.'

Eliza nodded. 'I can stop supplying him with coffins, which he won't like. We do make some of the best coffins in Sydney.'

'And if you do, what has he threatened to do?' Tatty asked, though she thought she had a good idea.

'He says he'll put it about that Carl is cursed, hence his useless legs, and that the curse can be passed on through whatever he touches, meaning of course the coffins he and I make.'

'Oh, how bloody ridiculous,' Cora said.

'I said that,' Eliza replied, 'but then Nuttall said how is it that everyone who ends up in one of Carl's coffins goes straight to the grave?'

Cora looked astonished. 'Because they're dead?'

'And that's exactly Nuttall's point,' Eliza said.

Tatty thought Nuttall's logic was so moronic it wasn't even funny. 'But would anyone really believe that, about a curse?'

'You'd be surprised how superstitious people can be,' Edith said. 'Especially – how shall I say it – folk from the lower rungs of society.'

'They're not going to buy your coffins anyway, are they?' Cora said to Eliza.

Eliza said, 'I don't know. We just make them, we don't sell them. But probably not.'

'But it's not *just* the hoi polloi who believe in curses and the like,' Edith said. 'Plenty of the more well-heeled will believe in absolutely anything of a similar nature.' And then she had the good grace to turn pink.

Tatty asked Eliza, 'If Nuttall does tell people that, how will Carl feel? And do you think your business will be affected because of it?'

'Carl knows he isn't cursed. He's learnt to live with the way he is. I don't know if our business will be affected. Possibly not but I worry it would be and I wouldn't be able to make enough money to keep a roof over our heads and take care of Carl. It's why I got caught up with Nuttall after your husband died. I should have put an end to it then, no matter the cost. I'm ready now, though. Carl and I both are.' Eliza turned to Nellie. 'Are you ready?'

'If you are, I am. I'll tell Nuttall there'll be no more referrals or commissions and no doubt he'll boycott me and slander my reputation and I'll just have …' Nellie stopped and reached for her handkerchief again and held it to her mouth, swallowing hard.

Tatty said, 'If it helps, Eliza and Nellie, I'll recommend your services to my customers as much as I can, and if you do find you're out of pocket, I'll reimburse you for any losses. This is my idea and I'll not see anyone suffer because of it.'

Eliza reached out and squeezed Tatty's hand in thanks, and Nellie blew her nose extra loudly and fanned the air in front of her face with one hand as though that would stop her tears. It didn't.

'That's generous of you,' Hannah said.

'Look,' Cora said. 'Everyone knows Elias Nuttall's a bastard. And after his performance at the inquest when he accused Tatty of poisoning Titus and he couldn't come up with any evidence, he just looked vindictive and unhinged. No one will take any notice of what he says, don't you think? They'll just say, there goes Nuttall, gobbing off again. If we can put him out of business, people will forget about him soon enough.'

'No,' Tatty said. 'I think you're underestimating him. The fire?'

Cora made a face. 'That's true.'

Nellie gave one last sniff and put away her handkerchief. 'Well then, I suppose I'll just have to hold my head up and carry on with my work until everything passes. If I still get work, that is. I'm sorry, I am *such* a wet blanket.'

'You are not and you will get work, don't worry about that,' Tatty said. 'Your photographs are wonderful.'

'Oh!' Nellie said suddenly. 'I keep meaning to tell you: a few months ago Nuttall had the body of that American Indian sailor Caleb Blackfeather at his house. He died in the Infirmary and Nuttall provided a funeral and buried him. It was in the papers. Did you see the article?'

Tatty had and had dismissed it as a scheme to drum up publicity and goodwill.

'Well,' Nellie continued, 'Nuttall wanted me to take a series of postmortem photographs of the body. Photos of Mr Blackfeather *naked*.'

'Why?' Tatty asked. How bizarre.

'I'm really not sure.'

'And did you?'

'Yes, although as usual he didn't pay me,' Nellie said. 'I did think it rather ... odd.'

The room was silent as everyone contemplated why Elias Nuttall might have wanted photographs of a naked dead American Indian seaman.

Eliza shuddered. 'Really, it doesn't bear thinking about.'

'Do you think we *can* put him out of business?' Hannah asked. 'I don't.'

'Maybe not,' Tatty said. 'But what we're planning is a start. And then there's your contribution, Mrs Drinkwater.'

'What would that be?' Edith sounded wary.

'During your public seances, you could relay messages from the spirit world to the effect that Elias Nuttall steals from dead people in their coffins, or some such dreadful behaviour that will make him look terrible and ruin his professional reputation. You don't have to name names. You didn't get many names right when I saw you perform and that didn't seem to make much difference to how the messages were received.'

Edith actually laughed. 'That sounds like fun. And he couldn't accuse me of libel because it's not me talking, it's coming from the spirit world!'

'Slander,' Tatty said. 'Libel is when it's written down; slander is when it's spoken.'

'If you say so. Yes, we could do that, Hannah, couldn't we?'

Tatty didn't think Hannah looked very happy with the prospect, but she nodded anyway.

'And your offer of a loan to pay Nuttall back?' Edith said. 'I'll accept that, thank you very much. I appreciate it.'

Tatty said, 'You don't even know what the interest rate is yet.'

'Talk to Hannah about that,' Edith said. 'She looks after the money side of things.'

'I do not,' Hannah said. 'If I did we wouldn't be sitting here tonight discussing our debts, watching that mouse poke around in the woodpile, waiting for some crumbs.'

'Oh damn, is there a mouse?' Eliza said. 'I thought I'd got rid of all of them. I'll have to put some arsenic down.' She darted a glance at Tatty. 'Oh, I'm so sorry.'

'It's all right,' Tatty said. 'If I'd known I'd have brought some. I've got lots at home.'

Part Four

1868

*One need not be a chamber – to be haunted
One need not be a house
The brain has corridors – surpassing
Material place*

Emily Dickinson, 1862

Chapter Eleven

June 1868, Sydney

Several days later, during a gap between funerals, one of which was a small private affair for a mother and infant who had sadly died during childbirth at the Benevolent Asylum, Tatty and Cora ducked around to the Siren's Arms to see Friday, only to be told she and Aria were out visiting Harrie Downey. Tatty thought perhaps she should have sent a card and made an appointment, but she was in too much of a hurry for that. So, having been given the address, they headed back the way they'd come, to Harrie's house on Hunter Street, off George Street – not, in fact, that far from the premises of Crowe Funerals.

Harrie answered the door herself and seemed pleased to see them, but Tatty suspected Harrie was the sort of woman who made everyone welcome at her home.

'What a lovely surprise!' she said. 'Friday and Aria are here. We're having tea on the back verandah. Come and join us, except we're not to make a lot of noise. James is home. He's writing one of his essays. It's to be published in some journal or other.'

'Your home is beautiful,' Cora said, having a good stare around as Harrie led them through a hallway of considerable length traversing the front of the house to the back. 'Have you lived here long?'

'Oh, forever, just about,' Harrie said.

Outside on the wide, shaded verandah, Friday and Aria sat at a wrought-iron table watching a cat in the garden stalking a bird.

'Visitors!' Harrie announced, and the bird flew away.

'Bugger,' Friday said. 'That just cost me a quid.'

'Did it?' Harrie said, squinting after the bird as though she might see the money disappearing with it.

'Friday bet a pound the cat would catch that bird,' Aria said. 'I bet that it would not.'

'Please, have a seat,' Harrie said to Tatty and Cora. 'I'll organise fresh tea. Help yourself to scones and cake. Or would you prefer shortbread? I think there's some —'

'Harrie, I don't think they've come round for a meal,' Friday said. 'You haven't, have you?'

'No,' Tatty said, pulling up a chair. Its iron feet made a horrible noise on the verandah boards. She winced. 'It's you I wanted to talk to, actually. And I do apologise but we are in a bit of a hurry. We have a funeral this afternoon. I hope you don't mind me interrupting your visit.'

Friday shrugged.

'You recall Elias Nuttall?'

'Who?'

'For God's sake,' Aria said. 'He is the one who alleged Tatty poisoned her husband. The inquest?'

'Oh, that's right. What about him?'

Tatty said, 'Well, he's not on the square at *all* and he's cheating people who work in the funeral industry, women in particular. A group of us have joined forces and, to be blunt, we're trying to put him out of business. One of our number owes him money she can't repay. I've offered to settle her debt, but I'll have to take on more debt myself. Would you be prepared to increase the amount of my loan by two hundred and thirty pounds so I can do that?'

Friday tapped her saucer with a cake fork, then crossed her arms. 'That's quite a bit more. You must really hate this Nuttall.'

'My business is doing well,' Tatty said. 'I can pay off extra debt. It's the principle of the thing, isn't it? I'm fairly sure he wouldn't be such a bully if it wasn't women he was intimidating and cheating. If, say, he were dealing with men in positions of authority who could publicly out him for his dishonesty, or even just big brawny fellows who'd give him a good punch in the face.'

'I'd give him a good punch in the face,' Friday said.

Aria said, 'Ever the lady.'

Friday leant over and kissed Aria on the lips. 'I love you, too.'

Tatty nearly fainted and shot a glance at Cora, whose eyebrows had almost disappeared, they'd risen so high. Rodney Burton had not been such a surprise but ... well!

Friday laughed. 'Aria's my partner when it comes to *everything*. Aren't you, love?' she said to Aria. 'So, shall we give Tatty more money? I say we do. I think our money's safe with her, don't you?'

'I believe so,' Aria said. 'And I am always pleased to hear of the ruin of a man who mistreats women, in whatever form that ruin may take.'

'And you're quite happy to pay off this woman's debt?' Friday asked. 'That's generous of you.'

'Our plan won't work if someone doesn't,' Tatty said. 'If I don't. And she will be paying me back, but over time and at a much more favourable interest rate.'

'It's the clairvoyant,' Cora said.

'Cora!' Tatty reprimanded. 'Some discretion, please.'

'What? I didn't say her name.'

'Which one?' Harrie asked. 'I bet it's Mrs Drinkwater.'

Cora nodded. 'She's going to say during her seances, you know, as if she's talking to a spirit from the other side, that Nuttall's been thieving off dead people in their coffins. That should put a few nails in his.'

Friday laughed merrily. 'I'd love to see that.'

Cora said, 'I reckon she should say he gets his leg across dead people in their coffins. That would *really* ruin his business.'

There was quite a long silence, then Friday started to giggle.

Aria belted her on the arm. 'That is not amusing.'

Tatty said, 'I can*not* believe you said that, Cora.'

'I only said what people are probably thinking.'

'I wasn't thinking that,' Harrie said.

'Neither was I,' Tatty said. 'It's disgusting.'

A man stepped out onto the verandah. 'What's disgusting?'

'Hello, dear,' Harrie said. 'We were just saying it's disgusting when tea sits in the pot for too long. James, this is Mrs Tatiana Crowe and her colleague Miss Cora Billings. I think you might have met Mrs Crowe in a professional capacity?'

James Downey was a pleasant-looking man with receding semi-grey hair that was otherwise mouse-coloured, and nice eyes.

'Good afternoon, ladies,' he said. 'Yes, Mrs Crowe and I have met and I think also Miss Billings more recently?' He turned to Harrie, pulled aside the hem of his jacket, pointed to a very black splodge near his hip and looked at her helplessly. 'I'm sorry to disturb your tea party, dear, but I've got Indian ink on my trousers. You did tell me to let you know straight away if I spilt any.'

Harrie jumped out of her chair and herded him back inside.

No one said anything for a minute, then Friday remarked, 'James doesn't normally behave like he's five.'

Tatty nodded. It was probably time to go anyway. She'd got what she'd come for. 'Shall I expect new papers for the loan? Oh, and will the interest rate remain the same?'

She was getting careless: she should have asked that well before now.

Friday and Aria shared a glance.

'I see no reason to raise it,' Aria said. 'And yes, you will receive new papers in due course.'

Tatty stood. 'Thank you very much once again, both of you. I really do appreciate your support, both financial and personal.'

'That's all right,' Friday said. 'We might need your help one day.'

Tatty said, 'I'm really not sure what I could possibly do for you.'

'You could bury us,' Friday said.

Well, that was true, Tatty thought as she and Cora saw themselves out. Harrie was nowhere to be seen and she didn't want to go nosing around the house looking for her. But just as they were leaving the property, James Downey hurried after them.

'Excuse me, Mrs Crowe!'

Tatty waited for him, noting he was now wearing different trousers.

'Harrie says she's very sorry she didn't say goodbye but she's in the washhouse with my trousers and the maid, trying to decide between rubbing alcohol and ammonia.'

'Thank you, but tell her not to worry about it, please,' Tatty said.

'I know. It's not that important,' James said. 'I'll use them for gardening trousers if the stain won't come out.'

Tatty opened her mouth then shut it again.

James went on: 'Harrie told me about this business with Elias Nuttall. I've met the man a few times professionally but I can't say I actually know him. As it happens, however, I did hear something interesting about him recently. Well, when I say interesting I don't mean titillating; I mean something that could be of possible interest to the police. Though also possibly not. You never know what the police are going to think is worth pursuing, do you?'

Tatty tried not to appear eager. 'No, you don't. So, what you heard …?'

'Did you read anything in the papers recently about the case of Caleb Blackfeather?' James looked thoughtful. 'Actually, no, I won't start there, I'll start with William Lanne. Have you read anything about him?'

'I can't say I have, no.'

She had, but wanted to hear James's version in case he had details that hadn't made it into the papers.

'Well,' James said, 'William Lanne, also known as King Billy, aged thirty-four and the last full-blooded Aboriginal man in Tasmania so they say, died recently from cholera. Dr William Crowther, a member of the Royal College of Surgeons of England, applied to the Tasmanian government to have Lanne's skeleton sent to the College's Hunterian Museum in London for their ethnographic collection. But his request was denied, so Crowther broke into Hobart Town General Hospital morgue where Lanne's corpse was being held, decapitated it and replaced the skull with one from a white man's corpse, then stole Lanne's skull.'

'Bloody hell!' Cora said.

'Indeed,' James agreed. 'And it gets worse. After that, Dr George Stokell and *his* colleagues from the Royal Society of Tasmania, who also wanted Lanne's remains, amputated Lanne's hands and feet to prevent them from also being stolen, or so they maintained. Poor William Lanne's body was buried minus his head, hands and feet, before Stokell and his friends dug the remains up – to prevent, they said, Crowther from doing it. It's the most appalling display of behaviour I've ever heard of, and from individuals who are supposed to be respectable and learned men of science.'

Tatty nodded. 'That *is* barbaric.'

'Yes,' James said, 'and I suspect the case of Caleb Blackfeather may evolve into something similar, though perhaps not as messy. He was a full-blooded American Indian seaman who broke both legs unloading cargo on Campbell's Wharf, and subsequently died in the Infirmary. I attended him there once and I can confirm the breaks were quite dreadful. Being a native of America and thus somewhat exotic here, there was a story about him in the *Sydney Morning Herald* even before he'd died.'

'I saw that,' Tatty said.

'By the time he did,' James continued, 'his ship had sailed and there was no one to stand up for him, meaning he was headed for a pauper's grave. At that point, Elias Nuttall philanthropically volunteered to give Caleb Blackfeather a decent funeral and a Christian burial at Haslam's Creek. Who knows if the man even was a Christian, but that's what he was given.'

'That really doesn't sound like Nuttall at all,' Tatty said.

'No, especially as what I'd heard about him, to get back to that, is that he could be, or intends to be, involved in supplying the skeletons of Chinese and Aborigines and Maoris and other non-Europeans to museums and universities in England, for anthropological and ethnographical research and for private collections. I do therefore wonder if he was in the market for an American Indian specimen.' He paused. 'Can you make use of that information?'

'I think perhaps I can,' Tatty said, her heartbeat thumping with excitement at the possibilities the information presented when considered alongside what Nellie Harvey had told her about Nuttall and the postmortem photographs of Caleb Blackfeather. 'May I ask, why can't *you* use it? What he's doing is illegal, isn't it? With your positions at the Infirmary and the School of Medicine you'd have access to all the right authorities, wouldn't you?'

'That's exactly the problem, Mrs Crowe. The majority of my colleagues here and my counterparts in England are happy to look the other way while types like Elias Nuttall provide a steady supply of anthropological specimens, as long as they get *their* skeleton to study or display, or just to quietly possess. It's all the fault of Charles Darwin and his theories of natural selection and favoured races. Now every so-called scientist and doctor wants examples of what we've apparently evolved from, and that is, allegedly, the less-civilised, darker-skinned ethnic peoples. It's almost become a craze. In my opinion the procurement of specimens would have to reach a point that utterly disgusts the public, such as it did with Burke and Hare with their murder of innocent people for the use of the anatomists, before anyone does anything about it.' He hesitated, then said, 'And I fear that may not ever happen with bodily remains that aren't European.'

Tatty said, 'So are you saying *you* won't do anything about it?' It came out more curtly than she'd intended, but she didn't apologise.

'I'm saying I don't think there is anything I *can* do, which is why I'm passing the information on to you. Harrie told me you have a vendetta against Elias Nuttall.'

Tatty opened her mouth to say she didn't, but actually she did. She must look like a fish by now.

'I thought you might have a different way of using the information,' James went on. 'I know you've formed an allegiance of sorts with Friday, Aria and Sarah. Harrie has spoken about you before now. She likes you. They're a remarkably talented and loyal little group and they've been friends for a very long time.'

'How long have you known them?' Cora asked.

Tatty stifled a sigh. Cora had been doing so well, staying mostly quiet in the background.

'We came out on the same ship.'

Cora said, 'Really? Were you married to Mrs Downey then?'

'No. I was the ship's surgeon. Harrie, Friday and Sarah were convicts. It was all a very long time ago.' James turned his attention back to Tatty. 'But if you do decide to do something and Friday and the others get involved, I'm asking you to please leave Harrie out of it. She's very fragile at the moment.'

Cora said, 'I think she's lovely even if she is cracked.'

Shocked, Tatty looked at James.

But he just laughed. 'No, Miss Billings is right. We all know what Harrie's like. Even Harrie knows what she's like. I just don't want her subjected to any distress or unpleasantness or trouble. It's far better for her to spend time with family and friends and potter about in the garden and bake cakes and get ink stains out of trousers and what have you. Do you understand?'

'Of course.'

'Good. Thank you. Friday and Aria and Sarah or some combination thereof, on the other hand, could be very useful to you. But I'll leave that up to them.'

Tatty turned to go, then had a thought. 'When was Caleb Blackfeather buried, do you know?'

'Some time in March, I believe. You'd have to check the newspaper article. Or the burial records at the cemetery, I suppose.'

Walking along the street Tatty thought she'd rather trust the burial records at Haslam's Creek Cemetery over what had been printed in the paper, though cemetery clerks only recorded what they were told had happened, not necessarily what had really occurred.

That was if Caleb Blackfeather had been buried at all.

*

A week later Tatty and Cora were delivering a coffin to a family who lived on Castlereagh Street. Their sixteen-year-old son had been killed the previous day when he was run over by a train coming into Redfern Station and both his legs were amputated at the upper thigh. He'd been bundled onto a cart to be taken to the Infirmary but had bled to death before he'd arrived. There was to be an inquest as the death was sudden and had involved public transport, and the family had asked Tatty if it was possible to provide a coffin that would conceal the body's very conspicuous disfigurement.

Tatty had talked to Eliza and Carl McBride, who overnight had used hinges to adapt a coffin so that the bottom half of the lid could remain closed over the body's severed limbs, while the top half opened to reveal the relatively unscathed torso, arms and head. At the inquest the entire coffin could be opened for the jury to inspect the body. The McBrides charged Tatty the absolute minimum for the extra work, which Tatty didn't pass on to the bereaved family, who weren't well off. The family were very pleased with the outcome, or as pleased as they could be given the circumstances.

Crowe Funerals were on duty for morgue service for inquests for the next five days, so Tatty and Cora helped the dead boy's mother and elder sister place him in his coffin wrapped in just a shroud at that point. He could be dressed in his burial clothes after the inquest. Tatty advised that she would come by early the next morning to collect the boy's body and take it to the morgue at the Benevolent Asylum, where it would wait until the inquest was convened later that day.

On the way home in the dog-cart Tatty said to Cora, 'I've been thinking. I have to dig up a grave and I might need some help.'

'You're talking about Caleb Blackfeather, aren't you?' Cora said.

Tatty nodded. 'Obviously I'll have to do it in the middle of the night. I *could* break into Nuttall's house —'

'How?' Cora said. 'You're not a burglar.'

'I don't know. I haven't thought about that yet. Anyway, I could break into his house and look for the remains there, but what if they aren't and Nuttall or someone catches me? I wouldn't be able to say Caleb Blackfeather's not in his grave so now I'm looking for him here, if he *is* actually in his grave. I need to look in the cemetery first, just in case Nuttall really did do the decent thing.'

'Do you think he did?' Cora asked.

'No.'

'Can you dig up a grave by yourself?'

'I don't know. That's why I'm asking you to help me.'

'Six feet of dirt, Tatty. That'll take us all night.'

'It won't, not with two of us. The soil will still be reasonably loose and knowing Nuttall he didn't pay the gravediggers enough to go down six feet. The coffin's probably only three or four feet under, and empty.'

'What if we're caught?' Cora said. 'We'll be accused of grave robbing. We'll be hung, won't we?'

'I don't know,' Tatty said again. 'Other people haven't been, have they? Those doctors in Tasmania weren't. And you can't be accused of robbing an empty grave.'

'That's true. When are you thinking of doing it?'

'Tomorrow night. There's a new moon.'

Cora said, 'Won't everything be pitch black?'

'We can use candles or a lamp.'

'They'll blow out and if they don't someone might see them. And if we're going to light candles we might as well wait until the moon's brighter.'

Tatty thought about that. 'All right then. The cemetery's miles away in the middle of nowhere and Caleb Blackfeather's grave will be somewhere in the middle of that. No one will see us in the small hours. We'll just have to make sure we know exactly where we're going before we get there. You know how big the place is.'

And that, perhaps, would be one of the problems with her plan – the vast size of the cemetery and its distance from town.

'Would we take the train out in the afternoon?' Cora said. 'And come back the next morning?'

'I don't know.' Tatty was getting sick of saying that. 'I haven't thought about that yet, either. We don't really need the dog-cart so we *could* take the train.' Then she realised something. 'Rats, we do need it. We can't travel all the way from town carrying grave-digging shovels over our shoulders, then get off the train at the cemetery. That would look a bit suspicious.' She thought for a moment. 'Unless we don't come back after one of our funerals and break into the gravediggers' hut, wait there until it gets dark, then use their shovels.'

'If we did that we'd have to walk all the way back to Haslam's Creek Station in the middle of the night after we've dug up the grave, and hang around till morning waiting for the first train back to town,' Cora said.

'I *know* that,' Tatty snapped. It was all starting to feel too difficult.

They were silent for a while.

Then Tatty said, 'Maybe I should just pay someone to do it.'

'Who?'

'I don't know, do I?'

'No need to bite my head off.'

'I'm sorry,' Tatty said. 'You're right, there isn't.'

'What about my father?'

'I don't trust your father, Cora.'

Cora said, 'No. I don't either.'

'I'll think about what to do for a few days. Paying someone else might be easier. Then again it might not. Speaking of your father, have you heard from Agnes at all?'

'No, nothing.'

Another silence. Shadow's iron-clad hooves clip-clopped on the street's paved surface, then became muffled as he moved onto stretches of crushed rock and sand.

Tatty said, 'Edith Drinkwater is giving one of her seance sessions tonight. I was thinking I might go along and see what her spirits say about Nuttall. I could do with being entertained.'

'Ooh, me too. Can I come as well?'

'Of course you can,' Tatty said. 'But *please* be careful of what you say. We don't want to give the game away, do we?'

'Are you saying I've got a big mouth?'

'No, I'm just saying you can be a bit enthusiastic sometimes.'

*

Edith's seance that evening was held in the large upstairs reception room of the Fountain of Friendship Inn on the corner of King and Kent streets, which was filling quickly before the scheduled start time. By eight o'clock there were no vacant seats, and Tatty was wondering why Edith hadn't in fact been able to repay her original loan to Nuttall, if all her performances were this well attended. She knew, though, that Edith had just given back every penny she owed him, plus the exorbitant interest that had accrued, with the money Friday Woolfe had advanced and was feeling considerably relieved. To show her appreciation, she and Hannah had visited and presented Tatty with a large bouquet of carnations, irises and sweat peas, and a selection of small fancy cakes from a George Street bakery, which Mrs Seddon said were all style over substance.

Tatty, Cora and Maggie Seddon had managed to grab seats halfway towards the front of the room, and Maggie especially was looking forward to Edith's demonstration. Tatty hadn't mentioned to her that she thought the Drinkwater women were frauds, or at least that Edith was, because Maggie was a great believer in all things supernatural. Whether it was spiritualism, thought-reading, fairies, ghosts, tarot cards, mesmerism, the Ouija board or crystal-gazing, over the past ten years Maggie had developed a fascination for it all. This had always surprised Tatty as in most other respects Maggie was probably the most sensible and practical person she knew. *And* she went to church every Sunday without fail, managing to align her belief in spiritualism very neatly with her strong Anglican faith. Lorna, on the other hand, was frightened by things she couldn't understand, and she definitely couldn't understand how a conversation could be had with a dead person, so she was at home, happily re-organising the downstairs linen press.

When Edith Drinkwater finally appeared – late – it was to a very enthusiastic round of applause. Hannah went around the room turning down the wall lights, taking her time, weaving in and out of rows of chairs: Tatty suspected she was once again eavesdropping on people talking to neighbours about who they hoped to hear from that evening, and what messages they would like to receive. If she was doing that it was a clever strategy, and Tatty thought it took a very smart and organised brain to hold on to all those titbits of information and feed them to Edith at just the right times.

Edith started off with a few messages from 'the other side' for various people in the audience that seemed to make them happy, or at least satisfied, concerning the welfare of the recently passed, several declarations of ongoing love, and in one case, the whereabouts of a lost set of keys. Then Cora put her hand up and Tatty thought, Oh no: she wasn't supposed to be asking questions.

'Yes, young lady?' Edith said, obviously recognising Cora and not appreciating being interrupted.

'I'm looking for someone. Can you ask your spirits if they've seen her? I want to know if she's alive or dead.'

'And who would that be, dear?' Edith said.

'My stepmother, Agnes Billings.'

Edith gave a really grumpy sigh, flapped her coloured scarves and shifted in her seat, pressed her fingers into her temples and screwed up her face in concentration. After a minute she said, 'Nope, no one there.'

'No spirits or no Agnes?' Cora called out.

'I don't know. Neither,' Edith said and closed her eyes. 'Now I'm sensing a woman who passed over perhaps a year ago? Yes, quite a wealthy woman too. And she's telling me ... Oh, no, that can't be right.'

'Why did you ask her that?' Tatty whispered to Cora. 'You know she's a charlatan.'

'*You* think she's a charlatan,' Cora whispered back. 'I haven't made up my mind yet.'

'Anyway, Agnes is in Melbourne,' Tatty said.

Cora said, 'We don't know that for a fact.'

They both shut up as Edith glared at them.

She held up her hand, her rings glittering in the half-light. 'Wait. No, that *is* what she's saying. How extraordinary. I almost can't bring myself to repeat that. In fact, *can* I repeat it, or will I be exposing myself to accusations of libel?'

Hannah leant towards her mother and whispered something.

'Slander,' Edith said. 'Accusations of slander. But wait! If someone from the spirit world is passing me this information and I'm simply sharing it with the living, I *can't* be accused of slander, can I?'

No one shouted out an answer to Edith's question, but Tatty wondered just how many solicitors or barristers familiar with the legality or otherwise of messages received from the spirit world were in the audience.

'Get on with it!' someone did shout.

Edith did. 'I have been informed by this particular spirit that while she lay at rest in her coffin, just before the lid was screwed down by a certain undertaker, her soul, on the verge of passing over, looked down from on high and witnessed the removal of a valuable ring and pair of ear-rings from her dead body.' She threw her hands up and shook her head in disbelief. 'That's right!' she shouted, making Tatty jump. 'This undertaker, the person we trust most at the close of our final hours and on whom our families rely for advice and support, *stole* from her while she was lying dead in her coffin! And that undertaker, ladies and gentlemen, is a man you may all know because he does business in this very town. He may well have buried your own kith and kin. He may well have *stolen* from your own kith and kin! His name, ladies and gentlemen, is ...' and here almost everyone in the upstairs reception room of the Fountain of Friendship Inn leant forward, even Tatty and Cora, who knew what was coming '... Elias Nuttall!'

A loud gasp resounded, as though the room itself had inhaled.

Well, that was satisfying, Tatty thought. Edith certainly had a talent for theatrics.

But that was it in terms of revelations about Elias Nuttall for the evening's seance, as she soon returned to relaying humdrum messages from loved ones, getting some right and just as many wrong. Tatty wondered what Hannah and her mother did at venues where the lighting consisted of one central candelabra or an oil chandelier.

Mingled first, perhaps?

*

Tatty decided she would open Caleb Blackfeather's grave herself. It had been tempting to pay someone else to do it, but ultimately too dangerous; the fewer people who were aware of what she was doing, the better. And she also decided not to involve Cora, in case she was caught. Although she was almost certain that the grave would be empty, and that digging up an empty grave wouldn't be considered a crime, the public censure for such a trespass would be severe. She would prefer to face that alone and not bring into disrepute any of her crew, who could continue to operate Crowe Funerals if she weren't able.

She planned the mission carefully, starting with what she would wear. Digging up a grave in a gown was not going to be practical, so off she went to see her friend Rodney Burton.

'Trousers? *You* want a pair of trousers?' he exclaimed. 'How ... Well, I have to say I had no idea.'

'I'm sorry?'

Rodney waved a hand that roughly outlined her from head to toe. 'Trousers. You know.'

Tatty was mystified. 'I have to do quite a mucky job and I really don't think I can do it in a gown. I think trousers would be far more practical.'

'Oh!' Rodney pressed his hands against suddenly pink cheeks. 'Oh, I completely misunderstood. I'm so sorry, dear. How terribly amusing!'

Tatty couldn't see why. 'I was hoping you might have some off the peg?'

'Honestly, dear, if the job is that horrible, get someone to do it for you.'

'No, I'd prefer to do it myself.'

'You're a stubborn little thing, aren't you?' Rodney said.

'Thank you.'

Rodney laughed. 'Well, it's hard to tell exactly what size you are under those skirts but I'd say there's not a lot to you, am I right? Mind you, it's still a revelation to me how some women can hide huge thighs and an elephantine derriere under a half-crinoline. I'm sure that's not you, though. We do have some trousers off the peg but everything will be far too big for you.'

Everything was.

'We could make you something,' Rodney offered.

'I'm in quite a hurry, but thank you,' Tatty said.

'We do have trousers for boys. Would you like to see those?'

Tatty would and took a punt on a dark grey pair made for older lads that looked like they would fit across her backside, although they were too long.

'I'll try them on at home,' she said.

'Of course. Bring them back if they're ridiculous and we'll try something else,' Rodney said.

Tatty said, 'Er, and I need a shirt and a coat as well. And a hat.' She frowned. 'Do I need a hat? Yes, and a hat, please.'

Rodney shook his head. 'I'd be lying if I told you I wasn't dying to know what you're up to, but I'm not going to ask. Everyone's entitled to their secrets. Of course, if one day you want to tell me …' He flicked through the clothing on several racks. 'Here you are, one shirt and one short coat, both for boys. I won't give you the waistcoat; you're the wrong shape for that. Do you want a flat cap, a boater or a bowler?'

'I don't know.'

Rodney gave her a flat cap. 'Most of your hair should fit under that if it's a disguise you're wanting.'

'I never said …'

'I know, and I didn't ask,' Rodney replied. 'Now off you go, and good luck and be careful.'

The clothing was all loose on her and the trousers needed a belt to hold them up, Tatty noted when she tried everything on at home, but it would do. She was only digging up a grave, not attending a gala performance at the Royal Victoria Theatre.

After much thought she decided to travel out to Haslam's Creek Cemetery in the dog-cart, and she chose the following night to do it. The trip out in the afternoon would take about two and a half hours, perhaps three, and a little longer coming back in the dark – a lot slower than the train but with her own transport she was in complete control of her mission, and it did solve the problem of shifting a shovel around. Also, Crowe Funerals didn't have a funeral booked for the next afternoon, which gave her free time. The dog-cart had two carriage lamps if she needed them, and she could always place a portable lamp in the grave if necessary as she dug down.

So the next day, around mid-afternoon, she surreptitiously packed the equipment she would need and the clothes Rodney had given her into the bottom compartment of the dog-cart, then asked Henry to harness Shadow.

'You're not delivering a coffin, are you?' he asked.

'No, I'm going visiting.'

'Visiting? With a …' He paused, then said, 'Never mind. Whereabouts?'

Tatty wondered why Henry was being so nosy. He wasn't usually. It was making her nervous and she wanted to tell him to mind his own business, but that would be just rude. She said, 'Out towards Parramatta. I might even stay overnight. I've told Mrs Seddon I may not be back until morning.'

'That's a long journey,' Henry said. 'Why don't you take the train?'

'I don't want to.'

'Fair enough,' Henry said, tightening a strap around Shadow's muscular neck. 'You should take some feed for him, if you might not be back until tomorrow.'

'Oh. That's a good idea,' Tatty said, feeling guilty because she'd forgotten all about what poor Shadow would need.

'I'll sort something out before you leave.'

'Thank you.'

'And you're going by yourself?'

'That's right.'

'You're sure you'll be all right?'

'Definitely.'

Henry sniffed the air. 'Not sure what the weather's going to do.'

'I know how to put the hood up on the cart, Henry.'

'Good.'

Cora gave her a bundle of warm scones wrapped in a tea towel and a bottle of cordial, both only just made by Maggie, and by half past four she was finally on her way.

The winter sun went down as she travelled, shining blindingly into her face every time the road pointed directly west. She tilted her bonnet so the brim would shield her eyes, but at times she felt that the glare might burn holes in her eyeballs, which of course it wouldn't, and she could feel a headache coming on. But soon enough the sun dipped behind the Blue Mountains, bringing her eyes relief, at least.

She stopped near Ashfield to relieve herself and have something to eat, and to let Shadow drink, eat and rest for twenty minutes. She also took a few sips of laudanum for her headache. She'd brought it along in case she strained a muscle digging, but there was no point starting off in pain, was there?

She reached Haslam's Creek Cemetery at a quarter to eight. It was dark and the entrance gates were closed, which didn't matter a whit because the cemetery hadn't yet been fully fenced. Tatty simply found a spot on the boundary that didn't look, in the light of the cart's lamps, too rugged and urged Shadow to cross into a field. The expansive area still hadn't been fully consecrated or landscaped so she drove on across the grass until she came to a gravel carriageway, then reined Shadow in. The silence was so complete it rang in her ears, as though absolutely nothing at all were alive in the cemetery. And then, gradually, she began to notice them – insects, night birds and other creatures, calling to one another, softly at first, then with more vigour. Perhaps it had been her that had silenced them. Or perhaps it was just the laudanum making her think strange thoughts.

She saw no other living person and heard none either. She saw no lights moving about, and heard no footsteps, or hooves, or wheels moving across gravel. She was certain she was by herself.

In a darkness punctuated by occasional patches of weak moonlight she recognised the distinctive shape of Mortuary Station, and realised where she was. She knew, too, roughly where Caleb Blackfeather's grave would probably be. Rather than arouse suspicion by quizzing the cemetery clerk about its location, she had gone to the offices of the *Sydney Morning Herald* and read that Blackfeather had been buried in the Anglican section of the cemetery, although the grave had not yet been furnished with a headstone.

She knew where that was, of course, and flicked the reins to urge Shadow on, followed the carriageway around to the sweeping Anglican burial ground, then guided him towards a stand of mature trees. They weren't part of the landscaping efforts to make Haslam's Creek a 'garden cemetery' and Tatty assumed they must have been growing there when the land was purchased. Their size was considerable, tonight creating a deeper darkness useful for concealing a horse and cart. Tatty climbed down, retrieved Shadow's nose-bag and slipped it over his head, leaving him to munch on chaff and oats.

She doused the carriage lamps and took off her dress, grateful she could slip it over her head by opening only half a dozen buttons at the back of her neck. Then she removed her stays, taking a few seconds to scratch where she'd sweated and her skin had become irritated. Next came her petticoats, which she folded with the dress and stays, then she put everything in the cart. That left her in her finely knitted knee-high stockings, her oldest boots, and her drawers and camisole. Quickly, even though she was surrounded by acres of emptiness, she pulled on her new trousers and shirt, and discovered that the trousers wouldn't go on over her boots, so she had to take her boots off first. Rats. It was cold but she didn't think she'd need the jacket once she started digging, so she left it in the cart.

Finally, she collected the shovel from its compartment, leather gloves and a single lamp, and headed off towards the gravesite.

After half an hour of walking up and down among the most recent graves and peering in the lamplight until her headache started to creep back, Tatty began to think she'd made a mistake – or that Nuttall had lied. There was no grave marked with Caleb Blackfeather's name. All new graves had to be identified in some way if they weren't to receive a headstone immediately, and often they didn't because the soil of a newly dug grave tended to sink and need topping up over the period of a year. Then, when the ground was stable, the headstone could be erected. Tatty stood still and concentrated: if she'd been Nuttall prising open his purse, which plot would she have purchased for Caleb Blackfeather? The cheapest one possible, without doubt.

She went back and examined the graves in all the poky little sites she was sure wouldn't have cost as much as the plots laid out in nice tidy rows, and there he was, Caleb Blackfeather, marked with a wooden cross that had already tilted to one side.

She set the lamp on the ground and stepped on the grave, testing the soil. It had sunk a little, even after only three months or so, but it was still soft, which was a relief: she'd been worried the late summer heat might have dried out and baked the ground. Grass and a few weeds had started to grow across the soil. She pulled on the gloves and started digging.

Her plan was to only remove the grave dirt at one end – just enough to allow her to look inside the coffin, which she would do by breaking the lid once she reached it. He would be in there or he wouldn't, and she was sure he wasn't, but she had to be *positive*. Once she'd had a look she would refill the grave to cover what she'd done, though someone might notice that part of the ground looked freshly dug again. But who *would* notice? And would anyone care? Caleb Blackfeather had no one in Sydney.

After an hour she'd dug a hole waist deep and about three feet long by two feet – any smaller and she wouldn't be able to use the shovel. She climbed out and returned to Shadow to remove his nose-bag, and to get herself a drink. He whickered when he saw her coming, which was gratifying because she was very much not enjoying what she was doing. She was sweating freely, her clothes were sticking to her skin, her sweat-soaked hair had fallen out of its bun and she was filthy.

'Another couple of hours should do it,' she said to Shadow. 'And then we can go home. That'll be good, won't it?'

Shadow whickered again.

'Are you sick of standing up? Do you want me to unharness you so you can lie down and have a rest?'

No reply this time, which was fortunate because she wasn't entirely sure she knew how to reharness him. She'd have to get Henry to show her how to do that one day.

Back she went to the grave, taking the bottle of cordial with her. In less than thirty minutes her shovel scraped the top of Caleb Blackfeather's coffin. She'd known she was getting close because the ground beneath her boots felt vaguely hollow. As she'd suspected the grave hadn't been dug the full six feet. She cleared the soil off the coffin, raised the shovel, and smashed a hole in the lid. Then she lifted the lamp and peered in.

Sandbags, but no corpse.

She'd been right.

'Can I give you a hand?'

Tatty's heart almost burst from her chest and she only just stopped herself from letting out a shriek.

She looked up out of the grave and stared wildly around, blinded by the absolute darkness.

'It's me, Henry.'

Tatty put the lamp down, leant her elbows on the dirt beside the grave and rested her head on her hands, almost crying. Her legs felt weak and she felt horribly faint. 'Jesus *Christ*, Henry, you gave me *such* a fright.'

'Sorry, but I'm trying to be quiet, just in case we're not the only people in the cemetery.'

Another burst of fear. 'Aren't we?'

Henry squatted at the end of the grave. 'I didn't say that. I said just in case we're not. What are you doing?'

Tatty was suddenly absolutely furious. 'What does it *look* like I'm doing, Henry?'

'Cora told me you're digging up a grave. Someone called Caleb Blackfeather?'

Could that girl not keep *anything* a secret? 'Yes, but he's not in it. Elias Nuttall's handiwork.'

Henry said, 'Cora said you thought he wouldn't be.'

Tatty said, 'I made her *swear* she wouldn't tell anyone.'

'Well, she told me,' Henry said. 'She was worried about you. Anyway I saw you putting the shovel in the dog-cart.'

'How did you get out here?'

'I caught the late afternoon train to Haslam's Creek and walked the rest of the way.'

'Why?'

'Why what?'

'Why did you follow me?'

'I thought you might need some help digging the grave. Whose trousers are you wearing?'

Tatty looked down at her trousers, now filthy. 'Mine.'

Henry extended his hand. 'Hop out. I'll fill it in if you like.'

'No. I started this and I'm going to finish it.'

'Don't be stupid. You look worn out. Have a rest. I'll do it.'

Tatty had actually underestimated the physical effort it would take to excavate the grave, even if she had only emptied half of it, and a quarter of a proper one. Her back and shoulders ached and so did her buttock muscles and her thighs. In fact there wasn't much of her that didn't.

She took off her gloves and extended a hand. Henry grabbed it and pulled her out of the grave.

'Go and sit in the cart. This shouldn't take me long. Then we'll head back home, all right?'

Tatty nodded, too tired – now she'd given in to her fatigue – to reply.

She trudged back to the dog-cart in the trees, felt around until she found the gallon jug of water she'd wedged under the seat, divested herself of her filthy shirt and trousers and had the best wash she could manage. If Henry appeared as she stood there in her under-garments, her glory highlighted by the intermittent moonlight, then so be it. She slipped her dress on over her head, wincing as she closed the buttons, and put on a clean pair of boots. Her stays and petticoats could remain where they were for the ride home. Then she popped the cork out of the laudanum bottle, took a couple of very hearty gulps, and lay down on the seat.

She woke when she heard Henry talking to Shadow. 'Oh God,' she said, struggling to sit up straight. 'What time is it?'

'Not sure,' Henry said. 'Last time I looked it was just after midnight. Then the lamp ran out.'

'You worked in the dark?'

Henry nodded. 'There was enough moonlight.'

'But you finished?'

'I did,' Henry said and lit the carriage lamps, almost blinding himself.

Tatty stifled a wild desire to giggle. 'You're hardly dirty at all.'

'That's because I was shovelling dirt into the hole, not standing in it shovelling dirt out, like you were,' Henry said.

This also struck Tatty as quite hilarious, and this time she did giggle, on and on, while Henry stood and watched her.

Finally she gained control of herself. 'I'm sorry, Henry. You're right, I am quite tired.' She also realised she'd possibly taken a little too much laudanum, which inexplicably made her do one of Cora's snotty, snorty laughs and set her off again. 'Oh, ew, excuse me,' she said, wiping her face on her sleeve.

'You're excused,' Henry said. 'I think it's time we got you home.'

'I'll drive, shall I?' Tatty suggested.

'No, you won't,' Henry said, swinging himself up onto the seat beside her and gathering the reins. 'Now for God's sake, hold on.'

Chapter Twelve

July 1868, Sydney

On the one hand Tatty was grateful to Henry for turning up at the cemetery to help her. On the other, she deeply resented his uninvited interference and the fact that he was now yet another person who knew she'd dug up Caleb Blackfeather's grave, even if it had been empty, and who now knew what else she planned to do. And that was her own fault because she had slightly lost her head on the journey home from Haslam's Creek – the result of fatigue, relief at not being caught, and too much laudanum – and babbled away to him about how she intended to break into Nuttall's premises and look for Blackfeather's remains. That he hadn't immediately volunteered to help with that as well had, at the time, been welcome, but, on reflection the following day, made Tatty realise how dangerous and probably foolhardy her plan was. In spite of regretting almost everything she'd told him, and also the way in which she'd allowed him to observe her during an episode of weakness (and silliness), she'd decided she would definitely pursue a suggestion he'd made.

'There's an art to house-breaking,' he'd said. 'It's not just a matter of hoping no one's home and climbing in a window.'

'How do you know? Are you a burglar?'

'No, I'm an ostler. Are *you* a house-breaker?'

'Of course not. I'm an undertaker.'

'Then you might need one, mightn't you?'

'But I don't know any.'

'I thought you did.'

'I don't think so.'

'That woman who stood up for you at Titus's inquest,' Henry said. 'The jeweller? Mrs Green?'

'Sarah Green, yes,' Tatty said. 'But I don't know her that well. And to be honest she doesn't really know me. She's not a house-breaker anyway, she's a jeweller. What *are* you talking about?'

'Well, don't quote me, but I have heard she's an ex-convict.'

'Yes, I know *that*.'

'I've also heard you'd have to go a long way to find a better burglar. Well, she used to be one of the best at any rate.'

Tatty thought about that. 'Really? She doesn't look like one.'

Henry shrugged. 'Well, that's what I heard.'

'You are such a gossip, Henry Dodds.'

'It's not gossip if it's true, is it?'

Tatty said, 'Plenty of gossip is true. So *is* it true?'

'I don't know. Go and ask her.'

And that was why Tatty was now standing outside Green's Fine Jewellery store, composing herself before she went in and asked Sarah Green if it was true that she broke into people's houses.

The door opened and a man popped his head out, giving Tatty a mild fright. 'Good morning. May I be of assistance?'

'Pardon me?'

'Can I help you? It's just that you've been out here for a while. I saw you through the display window.'

He was rather nice-looking, Tatty noticed, middle-aged with dark hair swept back from his forehead, equally dark eyes, and he was clean-shaven, despite the current fashion among older men for bushy facial hair.

'I was about to come in,' she said. 'I was hoping to speak to Mrs Green.'

'Well, then please do.' The man stood back to let her in. 'I can fetch her, if you like. I'll just be a trice.'

Tatty entered and the man disappeared through a door behind the counter, to be replaced moments later by Sarah Green. Tatty supposed it didn't pay to leave people standing around unattended in your jewellery shop.

'Good morning, Tatty,' Sarah said. 'My husband said you wanted to speak to me?'

'Good morning to you, too. Yes, I have two things I'd like to discuss, if you have the time,' Tatty said.

She took a velvet bag from her reticule and emptied the jewellery she'd found in Titus's room onto the counter. 'This jewellery belonged to my mother-in-law. Titus inherited it when she died, and now I've ended up with it. There are a couple of nice gems, I gather, these rings and the ear-rings and this brooch, but also some not so valuable costume pieces. I don't really care for any of it so I wonder, do you buy estate jewellery?' She was keeping her (or rather Lydia's) engagement and wedding rings, though, as she felt they granted her an air of respectability.

Sarah looked vaguely insulted and said, 'We don't deal in cast-off gewgaws. We're purveyors of *fine* jewellery.'

'I was referring to just the best pieces, obviously,' Tatty said.

Sarah raised the loupe hanging on a gold chain around her neck, then selected a ring and examined it. 'Hmm, not bad,' she said, and chose another one. 'Also acceptable. The emerald is quite nice.'

In the end she agreed to buy all three rings and the ear-rings but not the brooch, because in her opinion the gold was suspect.

'All the rest is rubbish. I don't want any of that. How much do you want for the rings and ear-rings?'

'As much as possible, please. The money's going to charity.'

Sarah's dark eyebrows went up. 'This is your jewellery. Don't you think you should profit from it?'

Tatty shook her head. 'I'm giving the money to the Benevolent Asylum. I'd rather it went towards helping women during childbirth, especially the unmarried ones. I'm tired of seeing what happens when they don't get help.'

Sarah stared at Tatty for so long she started to feel uncomfortable.

Then she said, 'I'll give you five pounds for each ring, and four for the ear-rings, and I will take the brooch. Three for that. The gold looks like pinchbeck but I can re-use the topaz in something else. It's a good big one with a nice cut.' She wrote something on a piece of paper and passed it to Tatty. 'Take everything else to this man on Pitt Street. He's an honest second-hand dealer, which I have to say you don't come across every day. He'll give you a good price.'

'Thank you,' Tatty said. 'I appreciate that.' And she did, though so far she'd only achieved half of what she'd come for.

Sarah opened the till, gave her fourteen pounds, said, 'Wait here, there's not enough in the till,' and disappeared out the back.

Tatty packed up what she hadn't sold. Sarah returned a minute later with another eight pounds. Tatty thanked her and put it in her purse.

'You said there were two things you wanted to talk about?' Sarah prompted.

Tatty nodded, her stomach fluttering with apprehension. Rats. She was just going to have to come out with it. She said, 'I've heard you used to be very good at breaking into houses.'

Another uncomfortably intense stare from Sarah. 'I used to be, yes. But that was a long time ago. Who told you that? Harrie, I suppose.'

'No, it wasn't Harrie.'

'Well, I don't do that sort of thing any more.'

'I need help getting into Elias Nuttall's business premises,' Tatty said. 'I'm sure he has the remains there of a man he told everyone he buried out at Haslam's Creek Cemetery. But he didn't.'

'How do you know he didn't?'

'I dug up the grave. There's a coffin in it but no body.'

An expression of admiration flitted across Sarah's face. 'And what does Nuttall want with someone's remains?'

'The dead man was an American Indian. I've been told Nuttall intends to export the skeleton to England, if he hasn't done so already, in which case I'll be too late. There's a swift trade in the remains of native people, like Aborigines and Maoris, to museums and private collections.'

'That's been going on for decades,' Sarah said. 'Forty years ago someone stole Aria's uncle's decapitated head from New Zealand and smuggled it off to England. That was made illegal then and it still is now. Surely exporting other body parts must be, too?'

'Not if you have friends in high places, it isn't.'

'Does Elias Nuttall?'

'I wouldn't think so.' Tatty frowned. 'But then undertakers do know how to handle dead bodies, and that's a vital part of this particular trade.'

'When did this American fellow die?' Sarah asked.

'Months ago. In March.'

Sarah screwed up her face. 'Wouldn't he be absolutely green by now? How *could* Nuttall hide a body in that state?'

'No, I'm sorry, I haven't been clear. He will have cut most of the flesh off the bones, and then boiled them to remove everything else. What he'd have left then is a nice clean disarticulated skeleton he'd need to dry out for a month or so, which he could then package up in a tidy wooden crate with straw and perhaps some naphthalene to kill any insects, and send back to England.'

'So that's what you'd be looking for, bones?' Sarah asked.

'I suspect so, at this stage. As you say, there'd be an almighty stink coming from his premises if he hasn't taken the flesh off yet. But then he is an undertaker, so maybe a bad smell at his workplace is to be expected.' Tatty thought for a moment. 'No, it isn't, actually. I'm the only undertaker in Sydney doing embalmings as far as I'm aware, so there'd be no reason for him to have a corpse at his premises. It would absolutely have attracted attention.'

'What will you do if the bones are there?'

'I'll leave them as I found them and go to the police.'

'But you just said that what Nuttall's doing isn't illegal.'

'No, I'm not entirely sure if exporting human remains is illegal, though I really do think it depends on who's accused of doing it. I am fairly certain that announcing in the newspapers that you've given someone a decent Christian burial when you haven't buried them at all, then hacking the flesh off their bones and then boiling those bones for hours and hours *is* illegal. I think that's called interfering with a corpse.'

Sarah said, 'Tell me, why are you doing this?'

'You heard Nuttall at the inquest. He accused me of poisoning my husband. He wants to ruin me. And he's coming close to ruining quite a few others in the funeral trade by extorting commissions from them using blackmail. All I'm doing is making sure I ruin him first.'

'What do you hope the police will do?'

'I hope they'll arrest him, and he'll be convicted of something and gaoled — exporting human remains or interfering with a corpse — either will do, I don't care. I don't think he'll be hanged, which is a shame.'

'Friday and Aria said you were quite a tough nut,' Sarah said. 'I wasn't so sure. But now …'

'No, it's not that,' Tatty said. 'I just like things to be neat and tidy. And I don't like unfair, underhanded treatment, especially against women.'

Sarah's fingernails beat out a tattoo on the glass of the display counter while she thought. Eventually she said, 'I will help you break into Elias Nuttall's house. Or is it his place of business? Or are the two combined? It's important to know.'

'Will you really?' Tatty was so relieved she forgot to say thank you.

'I'll have to speak to Adam first,' Sarah said. 'My husband. He doesn't like it when I backslide, as he calls it. He says my luck won't last forever. Well, it didn't, did it? It ran out when I was convicted for pickpocketing and transported here. On the other hand, look at me. Lovely husband, very profitable shop, wonderful loyal friends, so perhaps it *didn't* run out.'

Tatty frowned. 'Pickpocketing? I assumed you were transported for burglary.'

'No, I was never caught doing that and to tell the truth I've done more house-breaking here than I ever did in England.'

That surprised Tatty.

'So find out if he lives where he works,' Sarah went on, 'and when it's likely that the place will be empty, if it ever is. If someone's always there the job will be that much harder, but certainly not impossible.'

'I don't want him to know anyone's been inside his property,' Tatty said. 'He might move the remains.'

Sarah said, 'Don't worry, Tatty, *I'm* doing the breaking in – he'll have no idea anyone's been there. So, can I leave the snooping to you? You're the one with the undertaker contacts.'

Yes, Tatty thought, I am.

*

When Tatty arrived home, Maggie Seddon asked if she could speak to her in private, so they sat down in the parlour with the door shut.

'It's Henry,' Maggie said.

Tatty didn't understand. Henry was one of the most reliable, honest and decent people she knew. 'What's he done?'

'Oh, it's nothing he's done, it's what he'd like to do that might cause a problem,' Maggie said.

Tatty was still mystified. 'I'm sorry?'

'He came to me this morning while you were out and said that as I'd known you for such a long time, did I mind if he asked me some questions about you. I said yes I did mind, and if he really wanted to know something about you he should ask you himself. Then he informed me that the night you were supposed to be out visiting, he and you were at Haslam's Creek Cemetery digging up a grave. I told him not to be ridiculous – you wouldn't do a thing like that. I said you're an undertaker, you prepare folk for their graves, you wouldn't dig one up. And then he said it was the grave of an Indian fellow Elias Nuttall was supposed to have buried. So, I have to ask, did you dig up that grave?'

Tatty sighed. 'Yes, but it was empty. Caleb Blackfeather wasn't in it.'

'Tatiana! Imagine if you'd been caught!'

'Yes, I did imagine that,' Tatty said.

'Henry said he followed you out there.'

Tatty nodded. 'He turned up just when I was shovelling the dirt back in.'

'That's what he said. And do you know why he turned up?' Maggie asked. 'It's because he loves you.'

'I'm very fond of him, too,' Tatty said. 'We make a very good team. And Cora and Robert and Ben. We really do work well together.'

Maggie shook her head, the lenses in her spectacles glinting in the lamplight. 'No, you silly girl, that's not what I mean at all. I mean Henry's *in* love with you.'

Tatty felt her face burn as she realised exactly what Maggie was saying. Henry, *in love* with her? Surely she would have noticed? But she had, though, hadn't she? He'd been very grumpy when she'd married Titus – Cora had even teased him about the reason he wouldn't leave Crowe Funeral Services not really being the horses – and she knew he'd been disgusted at Titus for hitting her, and he *had* put himself at considerable risk following her to the cemetery.

'Oh, he is not,' she said, more to herself than Maggie.

'He is, and he told me the story about the grave to prove it. So I took pity and asked him what he wanted to know, as long as it wasn't too personal, of course. And his question was, did I think you'd want to marry again after your awful marriage to Titus? I couldn't answer that, of course, and I'm not sure you've told me quite how unpleasant that man was. I know you're holding something back but I expect you'll tell me when you're ready. Henry said Titus had been horrid – dishonest, greedy, and utterly without compassion. And then he asked, if you did remarry, did I think you would accept someone like, say, an ostler, and could it be someone you worked with day in and day out? So that's why I know he's in love with you. Anyway, you only have to watch him watching you to know how he feels. Cora's noticed it and Ben and Robert probably have, too.'

'Well, that's unfortunate,' Tatty said, 'because I'm not in love with him.'

She paused for a moment and let herself imagine what things would be like if she was. Henry was most definitely an attractive man and he had a good strong physique, and he was competent, kind and decent but he knew his own mind. They could marry – but then Crowe Funerals wouldn't be hers any more and she'd lose control of everything she had and all she hoped to achieve in future, and Henry might want children and she'd be back to where she was with Titus, only with a man who was nicer and better-looking. Of course, they need *not* marry: they could be lovers. The notion made the skin on her buttocks prickle with goosebumps and she dismissed the idea immediately before it could take root. She didn't have time for that sort of thing and neither did she feel her constitution could cope with even such an informal relationship, not after everything that had happened with Titus.

And then another realisation popped unbidden from the dark recesses of her mind: quite apart from the issue of property, she didn't want a husband or a lover she genuinely cared for because if she lost him she would end up alone and broken-hearted, just like her mother had.

'I don't want a husband and I don't want any children,' she went on. 'Titus *was* awful. He wasn't particularly nice when I came to work for him but I thought I could change him after we were married. I was wrong, though. He was even worse, especially to his poor mother. I don't know why I thought I was going to be able to make a difference. It was a shock when he died, but not really a tragedy. All I've really wanted is to be independent, to have some sort of business so I can make my own money and be useful to other people in some way. I've got that now and I'm not giving it up. I don't even want to share it. What did you tell Henry?'

Maggie said, 'I didn't tell Henry anything. He can either talk to you about it or you can talk to him. It's not my business.'

'I can't talk to a man about that sort of thing!' Tatty exclaimed.

'Well, someone has to tell Henry how the land lies and it isn't going to be me. And while I'm not interfering in your business,' Maggie added, 'I really don't know why you put up with Cora. Yes, I know you say she's good with your customers but she can be quite immature sometimes, and just when you think she's decided to behave, she's being silly and foul-mouthed again.'

Tatty said, 'Ma was foul-mouthed.'

'I know she was, but it's different coming from Cora.'

'No, it isn't,' Tatty said. 'It's just the way she is. You'd be foul-mouthed and a bit childish, too, sometimes, if your mother died when you were six and you'd been raised by a constantly drunk father and stepmother who belted you all the time and didn't look after you or your siblings.'

Maggie looked contrite. 'Well, how was I supposed to know that?'

'And she's loyal and honest and cheerful and hard-working. And don't forget that Lorna adores her. Already. Cora will settle down. She *is* settling down. And she really is wonderful with our customers.'

Maggie shrugged. 'Well, as long as you're happy with her.'

'I am, and you should be too. She thinks the world of you.'

'That's me told, isn't it?' Maggie said, crossing her arms.

'Oh, don't be silly,' Tatty said, and gave Maggie a kiss on the cheek. Then she said, 'Oh, hell. I will talk to Henry. I don't want to, but I will.'

Tatty found Henry outside the stables, working at his blacksmith's forge, which was just a small one as all he ever made were horseshoes, repairs to the harnesses, and the occasional basic item for the house. He stood with his back to her, wearing a leather apron and his smithy boots, with his shirtsleeves rolled to his elbows, hammering loudly at something on the anvil. She had to walk around him so he knew she was there. When he did he stopped hammering, left a new horseshoe hanging over the end of the anvil, and wiped his sweaty face with a large handkerchief.

'Did you go and talk to Sarah Green?' he asked.

'I did.'

'And will she have a look in Nuttall's house for you?'

'Yes, we've come to an arrangement,' Tatty said.

Henry nodded. 'I hope you're not going with her.'

'No, I'm not,' Tatty lied.

'Good.'

Tatty hesitated, wishing fervently that she didn't have to say what she was about to. 'I've been talking to Mrs Seddon.'

Henry said, 'Oh.'

Tatty felt her insides curl up. 'She seemed to think you might have hopes concerning ... us.'

It appeared that Henry was also deeply uncomfortable as he'd turned scarlet. 'I'd make you a far better husband than Titus ever did. I don't have money or a business to bring to the table, but I can contribute everything else a decent man should.'

Tatty swallowed, her mouth suddenly dry. 'The thing is, Henry, I don't want a husband. I'm happy the way I am now. I know you're a decent man and I'm very grateful that you're working here, but ... I just don't want a husband. And, well, I don't love you, not in a romantic sense.'

Henry looked at her, then at the ground, then at the fire in his forge. 'Well, thanks for telling me. At least I know now not to waste my time.'

'Oh, *please* don't be like that,' Tatty said.

'I'm not. I'm grateful, really,' Henry said. 'Can we still be friends? I mean, we still have to work together. Or are you firing me?'

'No, I'm *not* firing you.'

'Good. Thank you. Now if you don't mind I've got work to do,' Henry said, and went back to hammering the shit out of his horseshoe.

Tatty walked away but she knew she'd hurt his feelings, and probably his pride, really quite badly. She felt awful for him, and unexpectedly sad and lonely for herself, and only just made it inside the house before she started to cry.

*

'Has she gone?' Sarah said.

Tatty craned her neck, watching to make sure the housemaid didn't reappear. Nothing but weeds flourished on the vacant lot on the corner of Erskine and York streets, so it would be easy to see if the girl had turned back, but Tatty didn't think she would because she was heading towards the market with an empty shopping basket. Furthermore, Nuttall and his crew were out doing a funeral. Tatty knew this because Ben was still quietly in touch with his old mates, who weren't averse to sharing sensitive information in revenge for Nuttall's unpleasant behaviour and stingy pay. There was no Mrs Nuttall, so that meant the only people at the property were likely to be Nuttall's cook, Mrs Owens, and possibly the man who came regularly to collect the old hay and horseshit from the stables. Ben's mate had said he was due some time that day.

'It looks like it,' Tatty said.

'Right, then. Are you ready?' Sarah asked.

As she would ever be, Tatty thought. 'I think so.'

They sauntered away from the wall they'd been leaning against and wandered across Erskine Street, looking like two coves with nothing better to do than waste time dawdling on the streets. Both wore trousers, shirts and short coats (Tatty in her outfit from Rodney Burton's), boots, and hats covering their hair – a passable disguise from a distance, but one that wouldn't bear close scrutiny. They'd prevailed upon Cora to drive them the half-mile or so in the cart from Tatty's house and drop them off. She was at present slowly and repeatedly circling several blocks, waiting to collect them after their mission had been accomplished. Tatty had been worried Henry would spot her and Sarah heading off in their 'house-breaking outfits' and follow them, but that morning a message had arrived from the Benevolent Asylum advising that a baby had been stillborn so she'd sent him off to Devonshire Street in the old cart with a tiny coffin.

Tatty followed Sarah along the side of Nuttall's house to the rear of the property. The house was built on a slope. One side was two storeys high and the other three storeys, with the lower floor on the triple-storey side built into the hill. The house wasn't new, but it was solid. Behind it on a long strip of land were a cobbled yard, stables and a large carriage house. Currently, a horse eating from a nose-bag stood hitched to a wagon heaped high with used hay and horse droppings, a pitchfork jammed into the smelly pile.

Tatty hoped she and Sarah looked like a couple of young men going about the houses looking for work, which was to be their explanation if anyone approached them – preferably not too closely.

Suddenly Sarah stopped and raised her hand, then tapped her ear.

Tatty froze. What did that mean? She had forgotten Sarah's instructions already. Then Sarah touched a finger to her lips and moved closer to a partially open window. She had a sneaky look inside, then beckoned to Tatty.

Tatty was almost too scared to follow suit. She could hear voices now – a woman chatting away, punctuated by the odd male grunt of agreement. And she could smell pipe smoke. Finally she did look, very furtively.

The room was a kitchen and in it a middle-aged woman sat with her booted feet up on the table, smoking a pipe and pouring something the colour of amber from a decanter into a tumbler. A man also sat at the table with a tumbler of his own, energetically tucking into some sort of pie. Tatty could smell it. Smoked fish? Neither was facing the window.

Tatty stepped away. Sarah pointed back the way they'd come.

At the front of the house again, Tatty said, 'That must be the cook, Mrs Owens. Presumably her friend is the horseshit man.'

Sarah said, 'With a bit of luck they'll be busy drinking Nuttall's brandy or whatever it is for a while. We'll go round to the other side of the house and climb in a window.'

'What if they're all closed?' Tatty said.

'Don't worry about that. Just concentrate on not making a noise.'

They found an open window. Sarah looked inside to make sure the room was empty.

'Just a cat,' she said over her shoulder. 'Give me a leg up, will you? I'm not as young as I used to be.'

Tatty did and Sarah vaulted up onto the windowsill and climbed inside. Tatty followed her without too much effort.

The room appeared to be some sort of combination office and library. A tabby cat lay curled in an armchair, eyeing them suspiciously. It stood, stretched and jumped to the floor. Sarah trod lightly across the carpet in an effort to avoid any creaking floorboards, and peeked out into the hallway through the half-closed door. The cat trotted along after her.

'No one's about. Where should we be looking?' she whispered.

'Follow your nose,' Tatty said.

Sarah sniffed. 'Boiled cabbage?'

'No, underneath that.'

Concentrating, Sarah sniffed again, then made a face. 'Rotten meat? Rotten eggs? Shit?'

Tatty nodded. 'All of those. That's decomposition.' She'd noticed the faint smell of decay the moment they'd climbed through the window. 'From outside it looks like there might be a basement, so look for stairs.'

The cat sat down in the doorway.

Sarah had another look. 'I think there might be a flight of stairs at the far end of the hall.'

She lifted her finger to her lips again. In the kitchen at the rear of the house the man and woman were having a good old laugh together.

Tatty looked out into the hall at the stairs, balancing with one hand on the hinge edge of the door, which at that moment Sarah closed slightly, squashing Tatty's index finger between the door and the doorjamb. She let out a short, high-pitched yelp of pain.

The laughter coming from the kitchen stopped: chair-legs scraped across a flag floor.

Tatty and Sarah stared at each other, frozen with fear.

Sarah snatched up the cat, gave its tail a really hard yank so it let out a blood-curdling yowl, and hurled it down the hallway towards the kitchen. It shot off, claws scrabbling on the wooden floor, and out through the open back door. Tatty and Sarah ducked back into the library cum office.

A moment later they heard Mrs Owens calling, 'Puss! *Puss!*' followed by inaudible muttering, then, 'I don't know what's got into him.' Then the chair-legs scraping again.

Tatty and Sarah waited for close to ten minutes until they were sure everything had settled down, Tatty with her wounded finger in her mouth. She was going to have quite a bad bruise by the end of the day.

When they could hear Mrs Owens and the man yapping away again and were sure it was safe for them to move, they crept out of the office and along the hallway to the stairs, which did appear to lead down to a basement.

However, there was a door at the bottom of the stairs, and it was locked.

'Rats,' Tatty whispered.

Sarah said, 'I wouldn't be surprised.'

She bent and squinted at the keyhole, barely visible in the muted light of the stairwell, then retrieved a cloth package from inside her jacket, laid it on a step and unrolled it, revealing a set of long, very thin tools.

Tatty said, 'What are they?'

'Lock picks.'

Sarah took two, inserted them together into the keyhole, jiggled them gently then turned them to the right until there was a dull clicking noise, and opened the door.

Tatty was very impressed. She waited a few seconds while Sarah repacked her tools, then led the way into the basement.

There were three rooms behind the locked door. One was full of rubbish – broken bits and pieces and old newspapers – the other seemed to be a storage room for surplus furniture, and the third was locked, so Sarah repeated her trick with the lock picks.

The third room, which was windowless, contained a stained wooden table, a bench along one wall, several tin tubs and buckets, and half a dozen wooden packing crates, one on the bench and the remainder beneath it. The room was the source of the smell, which was foul the moment they opened the door, though Tatty couldn't immediately see what was causing it.

'For God's *sake*,' Sarah said, her hand over her nose and mouth. 'Is the body in here somewhere?'

'Not the whole body, I wouldn't think. Not now,' Tatty said.

She crossed to the packing case on the bench and lifted the lid, unsurprised by what she found. She beckoned to Sarah.

'Is that him? Caleb Blackfeather?' Sarah asked, looking down at the collection of clean, off-white bones.

'I'd say so. I'd look to see if the thigh bones are broken but I don't want to touch them in case Nuttall can tell someone's been poking around. He must be quite close to sending these away.' Tatty set the lid back on the box. 'I'll have to go to the police as soon as possible.'

'Are we done here?' Sarah asked.

'Yes.'

'Then we should go.'

Sarah relocked both basement doors, and they left the way they'd gone in, through the office window.

'That was easier than I expected,' she said as they took their places on the wall down the street to wait for Cora. 'We could almost have worn our ordinary clothes. Mind you, as soon as you do, you have to jump out a second-storey window, slide down a drainpipe, run a mile and climb five fences.' She lifted her jacket and pressed her face against it. 'God, my clothes stink of that bloody basement. How do you put up with it?'

Tatty said, 'I don't notice it any more.'

'How's your finger?' Sarah asked. 'I'm very sorry about that.'

So was Tatty: it looked like a blackberry already. 'Sore. That poor cat.'

Sarah laughed. 'That was a bit mean of me. He saved our bacon, though, didn't he?'

'I hope my fingernail doesn't fall off.'

'If it does I'm sure it'll grow back. Where was the rest of him?'

'Caleb Blackfeather?' Tatty said.

Sarah nodded.

'Probably carted out of that room by Nuttall in those tubs and either burnt or dumped in the harbour or a drain somewhere. The mess would have gone everywhere when he defleshed him, and he won't have been able to clean up properly while trying to keep what he was doing secret – there'll still be bits and pieces in that room and that's what we could smell. That stink will be there for quite a while even if he scrubs and scrubs, I can assure you.'

'There were half a dozen of those packing cases down there. Is he going to do it again, do you think?'

'I don't know.'

Sarah said, 'I wonder if anyone else in his house knows what he's done?'

'I bet he thinks they don't,' Tatty said and waved out to Cora as she appeared around the corner. 'We'll drop you off at your house, then I'm going home to get changed and have a nice cup of tea. Thank you very much for coming with me, Sarah. I probably wouldn't have had the guts to do it by myself, and if you hadn't unlocked those doors I wouldn't have any evidence to prove what he's done.'

'I quite enjoyed myself, actually,' Sarah said. 'It's been a while since I've had the lock-picking tools out. I have to say, though, I don't envy you your job, putting up with that smell day and night. It's enough to make you spew.'

'You *do* get used to it.' Tatty laughed at the look of disbelief on Sarah's face. 'No, you really do. Now and then I still come across one that really affects me, but otherwise it's like noise in the background. I just ignore it.'

'Are you still talking about the smell,' Sarah said, 'or the fact that you work every day with grief and misery and people in pain?'

Tatty looked at her. 'The smell. I'm talking about the smell.'

*

The next morning Tatty told Cora she hoped she wouldn't be long and to wait for her outside the Central Police Station on George Street in the dog-cart, and went in through the gate in the tall iron-rail fence. Inside she told a policeman she wished to make a complaint.

'And what would that be, ma'am?' the policeman said after he'd taken her name and address. He was portly, grey-haired and looked close to the retirement end of his career with the New South Wales constabulary. An embroidered name tag above his right breast pocket stated that he was *Sergeant S Copeland*.

'I have recently seen evidence that Elias Nuttall, who is a Sydney undertaker and who has premises on Erskine Street, is preparing to send the skeleton of a deceased American Indian seaman named Caleb Blackfeather to England, after having publicly announced that he paid to bury Mr Blackfeather out at

Haslam's Creek Cemetery. I also strongly suspect that Mr Nuttall grossly interfered with Mr Blackfeather's corpse to prepare it for shipment overseas.'

Tatty could see that the man didn't know whether to believe her. 'And what is this evidence you've seen?'

'Caleb Blackfeather's bones in a packing case in the basement of Elias Nuttall's house.'

'And when was this?'

'Yesterday morning.'

'Did you confront Mr Nuttall about the matter?'

'He wasn't present.'

'Was anyone?'

To lie or not to lie? 'I didn't see anyone.'

'Then how did you get in?'

'The back door was open.'

'How do you know the bones belong to this Indian fellow?'

'Let's call it a very educated guess,' Tatty said. 'You need to arrest Nuttall. Caleb Blackfeather should be in a grave, not a packing case with all his flesh stripped off him, awaiting shipment to some anatomist's or scientist's collection in England.'

Sergeant Copeland tapped the end of his nose with his pencil. 'You're that lady undertaker, aren't you?'

'Yes.'

'Are you sure this isn't just a professional spat?'

Tatty stared him down. 'May I speak to the superintendent, please?'

The sergeant sighed. 'I'll get someone to go and have a look.'

'Well, hurry up, please. Those bones were just about ready to be sealed and sent off. Nuttall won't keep them much longer. And I want to go with your constables. Elias Nuttall will lie through his teeth.'

'I think not.'

'I think so. Can your men tell the difference between fresh bones that have been stripped of flesh and boiled clean, and bones that have come out of a grave and been scrubbed and bleached?'

'I wouldn't think so.'

'Neither would I. Nuttall could say he's just repatriating old remains to England at the request of family.'

'Yes, he could, I suppose.'

'So I need to be there to tell your men what they're looking at.'

'No you don't: they'll uplift the bones regardless of what Nuttall says and bring them back here.'

'Oh.' Tatty hadn't expected the sergeant to be so practical.

'Where you can give us the benefit of your extensive knowledge, and your theories regarding what this Nuttall's been up to,' Sergeant Copeland continued. 'But you're not accompanying my men.'

Tatty couldn't tell if the sergeant was being sarcastic or not, so she assumed he was. 'When will you send someone to get them?'

'Now, if it's as urgent as you seem to think it is.'

'The bones are in the basement,' Tatty said. 'It may be locked.'

'Was it locked when you were there yesterday morning?'

'Er, no.'

Sergeant Copeland gave her a suspicious look.

'May I wait here, please?' Tatty asked.

She could see the sergeant wanted to say no, but couldn't think of a good reason to decline her request.

'You may.'

'Thank you.'

Tatty ducked outside to tell Cora she was going to be a while, and to go home and get ready to lead that afternoon's funeral in the event that she still wasn't back by then. Then she returned to the police station and sat down in the foyer to wait.

An hour later, just when she was running out of patience, a young policeman arrived carrying the packing case she'd seen in Nuttall's basement.

'Got it, Sarge,' he said to Sergeant Copeland.

'No trouble?'

'No. It was just the cook and the housemaid home.'

Sergeant Copeland gestured at a room off the foyer. Tatty followed the policeman, whose name tag declared him to be *Police Constable G Aston*, as he set the packing case on a scratched wooden table in the centre of the room, which needed a good paint from floor to ceiling and smelt as though someone had recently pissed in it. There was one small, high, unglazed window, with bars on it a cat probably couldn't squeeze through. The sergeant joined them, leaving the door open, for which Tatty was grateful. The stink of decomposition she didn't mind — having to smell other people's piss, she did.

Constable Aston lifted the lid off the packing case and set it aside, revealing the same white bones she and Sarah had seen the previous day.

Sergeant Copeland stared into the case. 'So how do you know it's this Indian fellow?'

It didn't matter now how much she disturbed the bones, so Tatty had a good rummage and extracted several broken pieces of femur. 'These are his thigh bones. He had an accident on the wharf and broke both of them badly, and died from that in the Infirmary.'

She stuck her hand back in the case and had another good feel, this time under all the wood shavings at the bottom, hoping that what she was looking for would be there. She pulled out a flat package wrapped in soft fabric and tapped the wood dust off it, then opened it. Inside were several photographs of an obviously dead male. Two were forward-facing images of his head taken from the shoulders up, depicting skin that clearly wasn't white, a high-bridged nose, pronounced cheekbones and very long dark hair; two were of his head taken in profile; and two each were of his entire naked body front and back, showing a well-developed physique. The deformities caused by the broken thigh bones were quite visible.

Tatty noted that Constable Aston's face had turned a dusky red. Because the photographs showed Caleb Blackfeather completely naked, she wondered, or because she was looking at them? How silly. As an undertaker she'd seen dozens of naked dead male bodies, plus she was a widow.

'How do you know those photographs match these bones?' Sergeant Copeland asked.

'Because they're in the same box,' Tatty said. Honestly, what was wrong with the man? 'Also you can see in the photographs that the thigh bones are broken. That's a significant clue.'

'And what do you say Elias Nuttall has done?'

Tatty suppressed a sigh. 'When Caleb Blackfeather died, Elias Nuttall gave him a free funeral and buried him at Haslam's Creek, stating in the newspapers that it was his philanthropic duty. However, I was reliably informed that Caleb Blackfeather hadn't actually been buried, just an empty coffin, and that Nuttall is either sending, or plans to send, ethnological specimens to collectors in England for profit. So I visited Nuttall's premises, where I found these remains, packed up and almost ready to ship. It's obvious they belong to Caleb Blackfeather and that Nuttall has stripped them of flesh and reduced them to bone, which I believe is illegal. Consequently I reported the situation to you. You could always dig up Mr Blackfeather's coffin. I'm sure you'll find it's empty.'

And smashed, but she wouldn't have to explain why – she hoped.

The sergeant took one last look into the packing case, made an expression of distaste, then said to Constable Aston, 'Get Dunstan and Slee, find this Nuttall fellow and arrest him. Where did you say he is?' he asked Tatty.

'I didn't, but he's probably overseeing a funeral. If it was at Haslam's Creek he'll be back on the funeral train early this afternoon. If it wasn't at Haslam's Creek, or he's busy doing something else, I've no idea where he'll be, I'm sorry.'

*

Tatty hurried home, which was only a few blocks away, occasionally breaking into a run, her skirts and the ribbons on her hat flying. She told herself she hoped to get back in time to help with that afternoon's funeral, but in her heart she knew that what she really wanted was to be at Redfern Station to watch Nuttall get arrested when he got off the train, if he had in fact been out to Haslam's Creek.

Arriving home she ran into the carriageway, her boots crunching on the gravel, only to almost be knocked over by Henry driving out of it in the hearse. Phantom and Wraith, the lead horses, baulked slightly as she skidded to a halt in front of them.

'Sorry!' she said to Henry. He seemed to have recovered from their recent talk and was back to his normal cheerful self, and for that she was profoundly grateful.

'You would have been if they hadn't stopped. Why the hurry?'

'Sorry, Phantom and Wraith,' Tatty said, patting their noses and getting suspicious looks from them for her trouble. 'I'm supposed to be leading the funeral this afternoon.'

'Cora said she was because you were busy.'

'Well, I'm not now, but that's all right. Cora can lead it. I'll just tag along. Where is she?'

'Here,' Cora said, appearing from behind the hearse, Ben beside her. 'I thought you were going to be busy?'

'I'm not so I'm coming, but you can lead. I'll just need five minutes to change my jacket and hat.'

'We have to pick up the mourners' coach at twelve o'clock,' Henry said. 'It's nearly that now.'

'Five minutes!' Tatty said as she hurried off down the carriageway.

In the house, Maggie came out of the kitchen after her as she shot past. 'Have you had any dinner, young lady?'

'I'll have something later,' Tatty called over her shoulder.

'You will not!'

'I'm *busy*!' Tatty shouted as she thumped up the stairs.

She'd buttoned her fitted silk jacket with the high neck, the grosgrain braid and the jet buttons, tidied her hair and was just putting on her hat when Maggie appeared.

'You *have* to eat, Tatty. Here, I'll put these jam tarts in your reticule. I've wrapped them so they don't make a mess.'

'Oh, thank you, Maggie, that's lovely,' Tatty said, knowing she probably wouldn't eat them.

She, Henry, Cora and Ben rode together on the hearse to the firm that was renting them the mourners' coach and horses, then Henry and Cora, followed by Ben driving the coach with Tatty beside him, proceeded to the home of the deceased. The dead man's coffin was loaded into the hearse and the small procession travelled slowly to the family's church for a service, then continued to Cleveland Paddock to await the departure from Redfern Station of the afternoon funeral train out to Haslam's Creek.

It wouldn't be leaving just yet though, Tatty thought, because it hadn't returned from the morning run, and if Nuttall wasn't on it, she could very well die from disappointment. She knew it was mean and petty of her to want to see him get what he deserved, but she did.

The Sydney police's Black Maria drove across the paddock and pulled up near the station building. Constable Aston was the driver and beside him sat two other policemen. Everyone stared at them. Tatty wondered if they knew with certainty now that Nuttall would be on the train.

To pass the time she unwrapped Maggie's jam tarts. They looked really quite delicious but she definitely couldn't eat them. The gulls might, though. As usual there were about a dozen hovering about, resting on the wind.

'What are you going to do with those?' Henry said.

'Feed them to the birds.'

'Give them here; I'll eat them.'

Tatty did. Henry ate them whole, one at a time.

'Gannet guts,' Tatty said.

'I'll tell Mrs Seddon you were going to throw her tarts away.'

Tatty knew he was only teasing her, but she still felt guilty. 'No, don't. Tell her I ate them. All of them.'

'I won't tell on you,' Henry said. 'Here comes the train.'

Tatty could see and hear the train herself now as it slowed down and steamed noisily into the railway shed.

Constable Aston and his colleagues climbed down from the Black Maria and strode over to the station platform, disappearing into a billow of steam. By the time it had dissipated, people were disembarking from the train. Henry signalled to Ben and Cora for their assistance, jumped down from the hearse's driver's seat, and opened the rear doors in preparation for removing the coffin and loading it onto the train.

Tatty stayed where she was, sitting high up on the hearse, a perch from which she had a good view of the station platform.

Elias Nuttall appeared at the door of a train carriage, settled his black top hat on his head, and stepped across the gap onto the platform. Constables Aston, Dunstan and Slee immediately moved forward and surrounded him, Constable Aston gripping him by the arm. Nuttall said something Tatty couldn't hear, but she thought he looked very discomposed and more than a little alarmed. Then Constable Aston said something to him; he tried to pull away and was immediately hand-cuffed.

Between them, the three police constables bundled Nuttall off the platform and across the paddock to the Black Maria, leaving dozens of mourners disembarking from the train and others waiting to get on staring after them. Within a few seconds he'd been pushed into the back of it, but not before he'd caught sight of Tatty and their gazes met for a fierce second, then the Black Maria doors slammed and locked, and the police were away, presumably to the police station.

Tatty watched the Black Maria as it left Cleveland Paddock. It had been gratifying to see Nuttall arrested, but she had thought it would be a lot more satisfying than it was. And what if he went to court and was acquitted, or his treatment of Caleb

Blackfeather wasn't considered a crime and he didn't even get to court?

He'd be walking around a free man in no time.

*

October 1868, Sydney

One Sunday morning when everyone else was out and Tatty was enjoying a nice quiet house, Friday and Aria came to visit.

'Would you like tea?' she asked.

'No thanks, we can't stay long,' Friday said. 'We've just popped in to pass on some scuttlebutt you might find interesting about Elias Nuttall. Interesting or useful.'

'But he's on remand in gaol,' Tatty said.

Friday nodded. 'We know. One of our girls next door —'

'Working in the brothel,' Aria clarified.

'Who's telling this story?' Friday said. 'Anyway this girl's brother is a gaoler at Darlinghurst and he says Nuttall's been given a cell to himself because he's caused a ruckus going barmy thinking he's being haunted by the ghost of that Indian cove he killed.'

'He didn't kill him,' Aria said. 'The man died and Nuttall mutilated his body.'

Friday said, 'Well, whatever it was he did. I thought, So what if he's got rats in the garret, but then Aria said maybe he's only bluffing so he doesn't have to go to trial.'

Tatty's heart gave a savage thump of panic as she envisioned Nuttall avoiding going to court, spending perhaps a year in an insane asylum pretending to be unhinged then quietly slipping away from Sydney and starting his life again, blighting people's lives somewhere else. No, she wasn't going to let that happen, she thought, as she thanked Friday and Aria very much for their information.

Nuttall did go to trial only a week or so later, at the Central Criminal Court on George Street, accused of the crime of interfering with a corpse. The charge sounded repugnant and was considered scandalous, and as a result the courtroom was uncomfortably crowded.

The judge was His Honour, Justice Joshua Tait, a man of considerable experience and little patience, and the crown prosecutor was Mr Cecil Fletcher, QC, known for his competence and steely intelligence. Nuttall's barrister was the loud and theatrical Mr Herbert Seymour, who charged the earth for his considerable skills. The jury of twelve men had already been selected.

Tatty, Cora and Maggie sat squeezed into the public gallery, cooling themselves with makeshift handkerchief fans. It was spring and not yet properly hot but there were so many people in the courtroom the air was nevertheless close and stale. Cora had bought herself a warm baked potato topped with cheese and wasn't the only person in the gallery with food – every second person seemed to have brought along a snack.

The conversation died down as Nuttall was led into the courtroom and escorted to the dock, where he sat staring at his hands. Tatty thought he looked half the man he'd been: his hair didn't appear to have been cut for months and was greasy and lank, he'd lost weight and his clothes were hanging off him, and he seemed dejected and spiritless. Also, uncharacteristically, he wore a large cross on a chain around his neck and carried a bible.

The court clerk announced, 'All rise!'

The entire courtroom stood as Justice Tait sailed in, black robes flapping behind him, and settled himself on his throne.

'You may be seated,' the clerk said.

Everyone sat. Justice Tait fiddled about with some papers, adjusted his wig slightly, then his spectacles, then said to the clerk, 'You may proceed.'

The clerk stood and read out the charge against Elias Nuttall, and stated that he pleaded not guilty.

And then the drama began. First the crown prosecutor, Cecil Fletcher, rose and described, in minute and revolting detail, exactly what Nuttall was alleged to have done, from hoodwinking the public regarding his so-called philanthropy, to reducing Caleb Blackfeather to mere bones packed in a box. Each new revelation was met with boos or gasps of horror, and a warning from Justice Tait that the next significant outburst would see the public banned from the courtroom. Then Mr Fletcher read out his list of who he'd be calling to provide testimony against Nuttall. Tatty's name was near the top of the list so she knew she wouldn't have to wait long.

Mr Seymour then stood and delivered his introduction, striding energetically about, his robes lifting around him and giving him the appearance of a bat, an effect Tatty was sure he'd been cultivating for years. In Mr Seymour's version of events, Elias Nuttall had most definitely buried Caleb Blackfeather; then someone else had removed the body from the grave and rendered it a skeleton. Subsequently Nuttall had done nothing but very temporarily keep Caleb Blackfeather's remains at his house at the behest of an acquaintance, who would at this point remain anonymous due to his standing in the community. No other accusation was in any way provable. And then Mr Seymour read out his own list of witnesses.

Tatty thought Mr Seymour sounded very confident but she knew the accusations made against Nuttall were actually provable. However, she remembered her father saying once that justice in the courts wasn't about truth — it was about who had the cleverest barrister, and she couldn't tell yet who was more likely to convince the jury: Mr Fletcher or Mr Seymour.

Justice Tait called a recess and Tatty made her way down from the public gallery and out through the doors of the courtroom to the waiting area, where she saw familiar faces — witnesses who would also be called to testify later — including James Downey and Edith Drinkwater. She had expected James would be called but not Edith, and especially not by Cecil Fletcher. She couldn't imagine what testimony from a clairvoyant the crown prosecutor could hope would be useful.

She waved at James and sat down next to Edith, who, true to character, had dressed moderately inappropriately for a court appearance. Her purple taffeta dress was almost acceptable, but the ropes of beads, bangles, rings, and the large feather ornament pinned at the back of her head were ostentatious.

Tatty asked her, 'Do you know why you're being called?'

'Not a clue,' Edith said. 'I was only told yesterday afternoon.'

'And you know you're being called by Mr Fletcher, the crown prosecutor?'

Edith closed one hand around her throat. 'Yes, I do know. But I don't like courts. They make me nervous.'

'Well, when Mr Fletcher's questioning you, do you think you could look at it as an opportunity to hammer another nail into Nuttall's coffin?'

'I could, but do I need to? Surely he'll go to gaol for what he did to that Indian fellow?'

'That's not guaranteed, though, is it?' Tatty said. 'I think we should fire every bit of ammunition we have. Perhaps you could use your clairvoyant skills and summon Caleb Blackfeather. I'm sure Nuttall would love to hear from him. Just a thought. Is Hannah not with you today?'

'We're doing a seance tonight, upstairs at the Walter Scott Inn. She's having a look around there now, making sure everything's the way I like it.'

After the recess, Tatty was called to the witness box by Mr Fletcher. She told him exactly the same story she'd told Sergeant Copeland at the police station, and then it was Herbert Seymour's turn to interrogate her. He was a proper bulldog, in Tatty's opinion, tugging at as many potentially loose threads in her story as he could.

'Who told you Caleb Blackfeather's grave was empty?' he demanded.

'I don't recall.'

'Come on, Mrs Crowe, it wasn't that long ago, surely?'

'No, but unfortunately I don't recall.'

'It was you who dug up the grave, wasn't it?'

'No.'

'Then who was it?'

'I don't know.'

'So who told you it was empty?'

'I don't recall.'

'Then why did you go to Mr Nuttall's premises on the day you saw the packing case allegedly containing Caleb Blackfeather's bones?'

'I wanted to speak to him.'

'To Mr Nuttall?'

'Yes.'

'About what?'

'About the whereabouts of Mr Blackfeather's remains.'

Mr Seymour said, 'We've just heard testimony from Mrs Owens, Mr Nuttall's cook. She said she was alone in the house at Mr Nuttall's premises on the morning you claim to have seen Caleb Blackfeather's remains. She has stated under oath that she did not see you at Mr Nuttall's. How do you account for that?'

'I expect she just didn't see me, just as I didn't see her,' Tatty said. 'The door was open so I simply walked in, looking for Mr Nuttall.'

A ripple of laughter ran through the public gallery.

'Order!' exclaimed Justice Tait.

'And did you find Mr Nuttall?' Mr Seymour asked.

'No.'

'So what did you do next?'

'I found myself in the basement and almost immediately discovered Caleb Blackfeather's remains.'

Mr Seymour said, 'How did you get into the basement? Mrs Owens just testified that to access the room in question, two doors must be unlocked.'

'They weren't locked the day I was there.'

Mr Seymour stepped close to the witness box and stared at Tatty. She stared defiantly back. She could see he was perfectly aware that there was nothing at all wrong with her memory, and also that he knew she wasn't telling the truth.

'I have no more questions, Your Honour,' Seymour said and stalked off with a swish of his robes.

Tatty stepped down and made her way back to the public gallery, relieved her ordeal was over. She suspected Mr Seymour knew Nuttall was guilty. She wondered if he would get Nuttall to testify. He didn't look very well at all, hunched in the dock, his face pale and his expression slack, clutching his bible as though he'd fallen overboard and it was the only thing keeping him afloat. He hadn't even bothered to look at her in all the time that Mr Fletcher and Mr Seymour had questioned her.

James Downey went next, and the now famous packing case was brought into the courtroom on the bottom tier of a wooden trolley. The top tier contained Caleb Blackfeather's bones arranged in a tidy pile, together with the postmortem photographs.

Mr Fletcher asked James a series of questions, including whether he'd attended Caleb Blackfeather in the Sydney Infirmary – yes, he had – then asked him to confirm that the man in the photographs was Mr Blackfeather. James looked at the images and said it was. Mr Fletcher then asked James whether, in his opinion, there were any other objects on the trolley that might also identify Mr Blackfeather. James stepped out of the witness box, considered, then selected several pieces of broken bone, aligning them so that they appeared to be whole.

'I believe these to be Mr Blackfeather's femurs, or thigh bones. They're broken more or less in the same places that I recall his to have been broken.' James selected a full-body photograph. 'And see here, on this image, the malformation of the upper thighs? They correspond with the breaks in these bones. To me there is little doubt that these are Caleb Blackfeather's remains.'

James returned to the witness box.

'And how does one reduce a body to this state, Dr Downey?' Mr Fletcher asked as he gestured at the bones.

'By slicing off as much of the flesh as possible —'

A groan from the gallery.

'Quiet!' Justice Tait barked.

'Which is a not inconsiderable job, especially with regard to a man the size of Mr Blackfeather,' James continued. 'A surgeon would be best placed to do it, followed by a butcher, but anyone with a rudimentary knowledge of anatomy could manage. Of course, the less adroit the man wielding the knife, the bigger the mess.'

'And in your opinion was the man who cut the flesh from Mr Blackfeather clumsy?'

'I can't say because the bones also appear to have been boiled. This would have been to remove the marrow and the smaller pieces of flesh, which is standard practice when cleaning a skeleton.'

Another groan of disgust rose and fell, followed by a lively murmur of conversation.

Justice Tait leant forward, forearms on his bench. 'This is your last warning! I will not have animal noises in my courtroom!'

Mr Fletcher waited until everyone had settled, then asked, 'How *would* you be able to tell whether a skilled or an unskilled person removed the flesh from Mr Blackfeather's skeleton?'

'As I said, an unskilled person would have made a mess. He would have spread fat and skin and a certain amount of blood about – although not much of the latter as blood will barely ooze from a corpse in which the heart has stopped beating – and these traces are always hard to clean up, especially under duress. One would expect, therefore, an ongoing smell of decomposition at the site of the defleshing, due to those remaining traces of flesh and body fluids.'

'Thank you, Dr Downey,' Mr Fletcher said. 'Does my learned friend have any questions for the witness?'

Mr Seymour didn't.

Mr Fletcher said, 'You may step down, Dr Downey, and I now call Police Constable Gilbert Aston for the prosecution.'

Constable Aston made his way to the witness stand.

'Police Constable Aston, can you describe the room at Mr Nuttall's premises from which you uplifted the packing crate containing Mr Blackfeather's bones?'

'It was a basement room. The door was locked and I had to ask the cook, Mrs Owens, to unlock it for us.'

'Who was "us"?'

'Myself and Police Constables Dunstan and Slee.'

'Thank you. Go on.'

'So she did and upon going in we saw a table in the middle of the room, and a bench, and buckets and some packing crates, one of which contained wood shavings and human bones. We uplifted this and took it back to Central Police Station.'

'And what was the atmosphere like in that room, Constable?'

'Atmosphere?'

'The air,' Mr Fletcher said. 'Was there a smell?'

'Oh, it smelt all right. It stank of dead body. Nowhere near as bad as I have smelt, but bad enough.'

'And could you see a cause for that smell?'

'Not really. The bones in the packing case were as clean as a whistle. But the flag floor was damp and the stains on the table might have been blood.'

'But you're surmising that?'

'Er, yes, sir.'

'Thank you, Constable Aston,' Mr Fletcher said. 'Does my learned friend have any questions?'

Mr Seymour stood. 'Constable Aston, how long have you been a police constable?'

'About four years.'

'And how many dead bodies have you encountered?'

Constable Aston remained silent.

Mr Seymour said, 'Shall I repeat the question?'

'No, sir, I'm counting. Probably around three hundred and fifty.'

Tatty could see Mr Seymour knew he was beaten, but he struggled bravely on.

'And what percentage of those would have been in a state of discernible decomposition?'

'Maybe a hundred?' Constable Aston said. 'Anyway, once you smell a decomposing corpse you never forget it. Everyone knows that.'

'No more questions,' Mr Seymour said. 'Thank you, Constable Aston, you may step down.'

And then Mr Fletcher stood. 'I call Mrs Edith Drinkwater for the prosecution.'

Edith made a meal out of making her way from her seat in the public gallery, rattling her bangles and standing tall and proud once she arrived in the witness stand. To Tatty it didn't *look* as though she were averse to being in court, but then Edith Drinkwater was an entertainer and perhaps she was just making the best of hiding it.

'Mrs Drinkwater, you are a clairvoyant of some talent and reputation, are you not?' Mr Fletcher began.

'Yes, I am,' Edith replied.

'And is it a fact that you've been presenting a series of public seances in Sydney over the past ten months or so?'

'Yes, it is.'

'And very popular they've been too, I'm led to understand.'

'I believe so.'

Justice Tait interrupted. 'Where are you going with this chit-chat, Mr Fletcher?'

'If Your Honour will grant me leave, you will soon see.'

'I hope so,' Justice Tait said.

Mr Fletcher bowed to the bench, then turned back to Edith. 'I understand that in June of this year, during a public seance, you were contacted by entities in the spirit world and informed that Elias Nuttall robbed the dead in their coffins. Is that correct?'

A roar went up from the public gallery and Justice Tait rose to his feet. 'Order! *Order!* This is your absolute last warning! I will *not* have my courtroom treated like the most raucous of public houses!' He sat down and straightened his wig. 'Mr Fletcher, I fail to understand the point of these questions, and indeed ...' he flapped his hand at Edith '... this witness.'

'Spiritualism could very well be relevant to this trial, Your Honour,' Mr Fletcher said. 'It does, after all, concern someone who has died. And far be it from me to disparage a practice so close to the heart of Queen Victoria.'

Tatty was too far away to hear precisely what Justice Tait said under his breath, but she thought it could have been, 'Bah!'

'Order!' called the clerk to settle everyone once again. 'Order, please.'

When there was a semblance of quiet, Mr Fletcher said, 'To return to my question, did that in fact occur during at least one of your seances?'

'Irrelevant!' Mr Seymour interrupted.

'Overruled,' Justice Tait said. 'Get on with it.'

'Of course it occurred,' Edith said. 'And everyone there saw it.'

Don't overdo it, Tatty thought. You'll trip yourself up.

'Mrs Drinkwater, could you explain to us how you receive these messages from the spirit world?' Mr Fletcher asked.

'Why?' Justice Tait said. 'Is it relevant to today's trial?'

'I believe it demonstrates the absolute perfidy of Elias Nuttall,' Mr Fletcher said. 'And *that* is what is on trial today.'

Justice Tait heaved out such a big sigh the papers in front of him fluttered. 'Then please keep it brief.'

'I will. Mrs Drinkwater?' Mr Fletcher prompted.

But Edith said nothing.

'Mrs Drinkwater?'

Again Edith stayed silent, although she slowly lifted her arms then firmly gripped the rail along the top of the witness stand, her arms rigid. She tilted her head back so that she was looking down her nose slightly, then calmly surveyed the courtroom from left to right. Her gaze settled on Justice Tait for a few moments, then moved on. And then her eyes rolled back in her head and she spoke in a deep, gravelly, masculine voice that bore only a hint of similarity to the one she'd used a minute previously.

'Where is the man who harmed me?'

Oh, well done, Edith, Tatty thought. Risky but very well played, and surprisingly realistic.

Mr Fletcher, standing directly in front of the witness box, stared at Edith, then took three hasty steps backwards.

Several screams came from the public gallery, but none were louder than the shriek of terror from Elias Nuttall in the dock. Tatty shifted her gaze just in time to see him slide off his chair and crumple in a heap on the floor.

Then Edith herself cried out, starting with a low moan that rose to a distinctly feminine-sounding scream, and fell over backwards, her head bouncing audibly off the wooden floor. Tatty winced.

'We'd better go and see if she's all right,' Cora said. 'Bloody hell, I haven't had this much fun in ages.'

The clerk of the court beat Tatty and Cora to it, kneeling beside Edith and gently patting her face in an attempt to bring her round.

'Slap her, go on,' Cora said.

'You slap her,' the clerk replied. 'Do you know her?'

'We do, yes,' Tatty said, and crouched beside Edith. 'Wake up! Edith, wake up!'

Edith did, blinking and coughing. She sat up and pressed her hand against the back of her head. 'Ow, that hurts. What happened?'

Tatty asked, 'Have you hurt yourself?'

Edith checked her fingers for blood. 'No, I think my feather fancy cushioned me. Why is everyone looking?'

'You went into a trance.' Tatty bent close to her ear and whispered, 'Well done, you were very convincing.'

Cora and Tatty helped Edith to stand. Cora said, 'Nuttall shat himself and fainted dead away.'

'Has the trial finished?' Edith asked, looking blearily about.

'No, but I think we might be having a recess,' Tatty said.

In the end Justice Tait declared the trial adjourned.

When the trial reconvened the following day, Justice Tait closed the public gallery: he'd had enough of unruly spectators. Mr Fletcher retained all witnesses already called in case further testimony was needed, and called others to support the crown's case against Elias Nuttall. Mr Seymour, however, was reduced to cross-examining those witnesses rather than presenting new attestants of his own. It seemed that since all the publicity regarding the fate of Caleb Blackfeather's corpse, any authority or social standing Nuttall had once enjoyed in the town had more or less evaporated and he therefore lacked friends in high places on whom he could call for support. The fact that it was rumoured he'd lost his mind also wasn't helping his case.

Mr Seymour did, however, unexpectedly request that one person take the stand, and that was when Tatty realised he – they – must be getting desperate.

'I call Elias Nuttall to the witness stand for the defence.'

'This should be interesting,' Edith said, sitting next to Tatty.

Tatty replied, 'It depends how they're going to play it and if he's genuinely unhinged. But yes, interesting I'm sure.'

The gallery, nowhere near empty due to the number of witnesses held over, fell as silent as the grave as a gaoler opened the gate to the prisoner's dock, took Nuttall by the arm and led him to the witness stand. Nuttall immediately sat down.

'Will the prisoner please stand,' the clerk said.

Nuttall pulled himself up. He was wearing his cross again and Tatty thought he looked very wobbly and pale.

'Mr Nuttall,' Mr Seymour began, 'at the commencement of this trial I outlined what are clearly the basic facts in this case. As an act of pure philanthropy you undertook to bury the remains of Mr Caleb Blackfeather at Haslam's Creek Cemetery. At some later point those remains were disinterred and processed so as to reduce them to a disarticulated skeleton. That had nothing to do with you, although someone of your acquaintance did deliver Mr Blackfeather's bones to you for safekeeping before, I believe, they were to be sent to England. As I said previously, that person cannot be named. Your only crime, Mr Nuttall, if philanthropy can ever be considered a crime, is burying the body of a man who had the misfortune of dying far from home and without friends and family. You are, I submit, an innocent man.' He shot his cuffs and brushed a speck of something off his gown. 'I believe the jury would benefit from hearing your version of those events. So, if you will?'

Elias Nuttall opened his mouth, and then closed it.

'Mr Nuttall? Could you perhaps start at the beginning?' Mr Seymour prompted.

'The beginning?' Nuttall said, as though he hadn't heard a word that had been said.

'Yes, when you first became aware of Mr Blackfeather's plight.'

Nuttall rubbed his bottom lip with a shaking hand. 'He was a seaman. He'd broken both his legs unloading cargo from his ship and he was in the Infirmary. And then he died. I was at the morgue there when they brought his body in. I thought ...' he paused, swallowed then swallowed again, 'I thought it wretched he had no one to bury him and I took it upon myself, upon Nuttall Undertakers, to provide him with a funeral and see him properly buried.' Another pause during which he wiped his brow with a kerchief, leant both hands on the stand and hung his head for a few seconds. 'It was some time after that, a matter of months I believe, that an acquaintance, a person with far more social and political authority than I have, arrived at my house and asked me to take possession of a box of human bones until it was time ...' He stopped again.

To Tatty it looked as though he'd forgotten what he was saying.

Mr Seymour flapped up to the witness stand. 'You took possession of a box of bones until it was time to ... what?'

Tatty thought it sounded like a prompt, as though Nuttall had been coached, but not quite well enough.

Nuttall frowned, then said, 'Time to send them to a collector in England. I'm an undertaker and it's my job to oversee the final delivery of human remains.' He frowned again, as though wondering whether what he'd said was correct.

'And then what happened?' Mr Seymour asked.

'I opened the box.' Nuttall swallowed once more then pulled at his collar. 'I was appalled to find that the bones belonged to Caleb Blackfeather.'

'And how did you know that?'

'There were postmortem photographs of him also in the box.'

'But you had nothing to do with Mr Blackfeather's exhumation or anything that was done to his body after that?'

'No.'

'Do you think this acquaintance of yours is responsible for that?'

'I don't know.'

Mr Seymour said, 'And then you came home one day to find the box of bones had been stolen from your house?'

'Objection!' Mr Fletcher exclaimed. 'The police uplifted those bones.'

Judge Tait said, 'Sustained.'

'Yes,' Nuttall said, 'and then I was arrested and charged with interfering with a corpse and sent to gaol and then *he* started appearing in my cell at all hours of the day and night, accusing me of —'

'Thank you, Mr Nuttall,' Mr Seymour interrupted. 'You may step down.'

Tatty was confused now: was the defence not going to use the justification of insanity to try and mitigate what Nuttall had done or perhaps even acquit him altogether? He'd sounded for a moment as though he was about to go off on a bit of a deranged tirade, but Mr Seymour had stopped him. Or was Mr Seymour worried that if Nuttall sounded too unhinged the jury might not believe anything he said at all, including that he hadn't interfered with Caleb Blackfeather's corpse?

Mr Fletcher leapt to his feet. 'I'd like to cross-examine the witness, if my learned friend has no objections.'

Tatty thought Mr Seymour looked like he had plenty of objections but she didn't think he could stop Mr Fletcher.

'Mr Nuttall,' Mr Fletcher said, standing squarely in front of the witness stand, 'I put it to you that you didn't bury Caleb Blackfeather at all and that his coffin was empty and the whole funeral business was a charade.'

'No!' Nuttall said, his hands flying up. He managed to stop them just before they covered his ears.

'Objection!' Mr Seymour barked. 'These are statements, not questions.'

Judge Tait said, 'Overruled. Carry on.'

Mr Fletcher did. 'I say instead that you, Mr Nuttall, retained Mr Blackfeather's corpse, reduced it to skeletal form and were preparing to send it to England to be added to some institution or private collector's collection – all for a handsome payment to you, no doubt.'

'*No!*'

'I say yes, Mr Nuttall. I say you deprived a man of a decent Christian burial and desecrated his dead body most horribly all because you were offered money to deliver his remains to anatomists or phrenologists or whoever it was who felt the need to own the bones of an American Indian.'

'*No!!*' This time Nuttall almost screamed it. The jury stared at him in shock and so did almost everyone else in the courtroom.

Mr Fletcher stuck his hands in his coat pockets beneath his robe and began to slowly pace. 'Do you feel guilty for what you did to Caleb Blackfeather, Mr Nuttall? Is that why you're seeing things? Is that why you think you're being haunted?'

'I *am*,' Nuttall said. 'I *am* being haunted and it's a nightmare! You don't *know*!'

'For something you say you didn't do?' Mr Fletcher said. 'That isn't fair, is it?'

'But I ...' Nuttall covered his face with his hands. 'I did do it.'

'Objection!' Mr Seymour bellowed.

'Overruled!' Judge Tait shot back.

Mr Fletcher stopped pacing. 'You did what, Mr Nuttall? Tell me what you did.'

'I don't know what I did.' Nuttall looked confused and as though he might cry. 'I'm being haunted and I'm in hell.'

'By *who*?' Mr Fletcher said. 'By Caleb Blackfeather? Because of what happened to his corpse? Because of what you did? What did you do, Mr Nuttall?'

Mr Seymour stood up. 'Objection, Your Honour. Mr Fletcher is harassing the defendant with this haunting business. He knows very well how the defendant reacted yesterday when that tea-leaf reader faked being a voice from the beyond.'

In the gallery Edith said, 'Tea-leaf reader? How rude.'

'Sustained,' Judge Tait said. 'Mr Fletcher, you *are* browbeating the defendant. Either desist or stand him down.'

'I have just one further question for Mr Nuttall, Your Honour,' Mr Fletcher said. 'Will you provide the name of this alleged acquaintance who you say gave you the box containing Mr Blackfeather's bones?'

Nuttall pressed his lips together in a small grimace and shook his head.

'Not even to save yourself from a gaol sentence of some years?' Mr Fletcher asked.

Mr Seymour bounced out of his seat again.

'Mr Fletcher,' Judge Tait warned.

'That will be all, thank you, Mr Nuttall,' Mr Fletcher said. 'You may step down.'

As Nuttall was escorted back to the prisoner's dock Tatty caught his eye: he returned her gaze but she suspected he didn't even recognise her. He was shut back into the enclosure and sat with his head in his hands. Tatty had no idea what Mr Seymour had hoped to achieve by putting him on the stand, or what Mr Fletcher had by questioning him, for that matter. Her suspicion that Nuttall was faking insanity had faded to nothing: clearly he was deranged, at least temporarily, and she wasn't at all sure how she felt about that.

It was nearly three o'clock by then and Judge Tait spent some time directing the jury on how to go about making a decision, then declared the court in recess until the jury was ready to deliver their verdict. He also stated that at that point the court would be reopened to the public.

Tatty went home, assuming that the jury wasn't likely to make a decision in the next couple of hours.

The next day she, Cora and Maggie, and, it seemed, half of Sydney, returned to the Criminal Court. They'd left home early, too, hoping to beat the crowds.

'Oh hell, we'll never get a seat,' Cora grumbled as they were almost crushed to death in the wide but utterly packed main hallway of the courthouse. They couldn't move forward and now neither could they move backwards. They were stuck.

From where she stood, jammed behind a woman wearing a full crinoline that should have been permanently abandoned for the sake of fashion several years ago, Tatty had a view into the courtroom. In the gallery she noticed the unmistakable figure of Edith Drinkwater furiously waving a lime green handkerchief, her bangles and rings glittering in the lamplight.

'*Tatty!* Over here! Hurry up. I've saved seats!' she shrieked in a voice a fishwife would be proud of.

That's easy for you to say, Tatty thought, though she was profoundly grateful to Edith for thinking of them.

'Edith's saved us seats in the gallery,' she said to Maggie. 'We just have to get to them.'

'Watch this,' Cora said. She started moaning, quietly at first then louder and louder, then clapped a hand over her mouth and cried, 'Oh God, I'm going to spew!'

Immediately a space opened up around her, allowing her,

Tatty and Maggie to squeeze through the courtroom door and up into the gallery where they claimed their seats.

'Thank you,' Tatty said to Edith, noting Hannah was with her mother this time. 'That was kind, saving us seats.'

'Well, I knew you'd want to see what the jury decides,' Edith said.

Tatty sat down, hoping the jury wasn't going to take all day. They could, of course: they could take several days. However, she couldn't justify wasting that much time at court doing nothing. She had work to do.

It was a relief then when the officers of the court filed in at just before eleven o'clock, Nuttall was brought in, everyone rose for Judge Tait, and then the jury returned. Tatty didn't think the defence had made a very good case for Nuttall and believed he would probably be found guilty, but that's what she wanted so she was biased. However, the jury might have decided otherwise and, now, the fear that they had was making her feel ill.

The clerk stood. 'Silence in the court.'

That was just about impossible with the number of people squashed into the gallery and out in the hallway: feet shuffled, noses sniffed, floorboards creaked, but no one spoke.

'Has the jury made a decision?' the clerk asked.

The jury foreman stood. 'We have.'

'And do you find Elias Alfred Nuttall guilty or not guilty of the crime of interfering with a corpse?'

'Guilty.'

The crowd burst into cheers and applause. Tatty didn't know why: none of them would have known Caleb Blackfeather but she supposed everyone liked to see a villain get their just deserts. She looked at Nuttall standing in the prisoner's box, where he was staring straight ahead as though he hadn't even heard the verdict.

'Order!' Justice Tait shouted over the hubbub. '*Order!*'

The noise subsided to some extent until Judge Tait announced that he refused to pass sentence unless he had complete silence, then it faded away completely. He sat on his elevated and elaborately carved chair staring out over his courtroom, silently challenging anyone to make a single peep. No one did.

'I sentence the prisoner to three years of hard labour in Darlinghurst Gaol, less time already spent on remand,' he said. 'Take him down.'

Nuttall was led away.

Tatty sat back and relaxed her neck and shoulders, waggling her head from side to side until her neck bones clicked. There, it was done now: Nuttall was gone and she had stopped him. They all had. She felt … curiously flat, just as she had when he'd been arrested. Perhaps the feeling of revenge wasn't actually as satisfying as people made it out to be. But she wouldn't have to worry about jars of burning kerosene flying through her windows now – well, not for several years at least – and her friends and colleagues could conduct their businesses without being blackmailed. So it had all been worthwhile. No, it had been essential. Nuttall had been an albatross around many necks.

Three days after his conviction, Tatty arranged a private funeral for Caleb Blackfeather and his remains were buried in a new grave at Haslam's Creek Cemetery. Her crew attended, and so did James Downey and Constable Gilbert Aston.

Nuttall's business had already been placed into a state of hiatus when he'd been remanded, and his horses and equipment rented out to other undertakers, but after his conviction the liquidators moved in and sold everything including his house.

He had been ruined.

Tatty thought he had no one to blame but himself.

Chapter Thirteen

November 1868, Sydney

Tatty and Ben were delivering a coffin on a late spring afternoon to a new widow who lived on Elizabeth Street. Her husband had been drinking in a pub near the waterfront the previous evening, staggered out in a state of inebriation, evidently lost his bearings and fallen off the Government Wharf and drowned. His body had been retrieved that morning, with no other apparent injuries. Tatty was relieved he hadn't been in the water long as corpses that had could be rather grotesque – bloated, skin sliding off, and fish- and crab-nibbled – and physically difficult to manage.

Nellie Harvey was also at the widow's home.

'Oh good,' she said. 'Mrs Finch was hoping you'd arrive soon. She'd like some photographs of her husband in his coffin. I've already taken some of him upstairs on their bed.'

Mrs Finch was a small woman with nut-brown hair pulled back in a tight bun, darting little eyes red from crying, and bony hands. She looked like her surname.

'Is it time for Mr Finch to be placed in his coffin?' Tatty asked.

Mrs Finch nodded. 'I can't do it by myself, though. I couldn't get him up the stairs, either. I had to get next door over to help.'

Tatty said, 'Of course you can't. We'll help you, and so will Nellie. And don't worry, we'll carry him downstairs, too, if that's what you'd like?'

'Oh, yes please. It's so much easier when people come to visit, to have everything in the front room. Thank you.'

Tatty and Ben carried the coffin up the narrow stairway, avoiding banging it against the wall. Mr Finch was on the marital bed in one of two bedrooms, dressed in what appeared to be his good suit. That was fine – there would be no inquest, as the reason for his death had been obvious to all. His face was the colour of parchment, his jaw was tied and his lips and fingernails had turned blue. He was a big man – tall and very well built.

Ben swore under his breath.

Tatty assumed that Mr Finch was coming out of rigor – it was hard to say with him having been in the water overnight – but he was easy enough to manoeuvre into the coffin, though he really was very heavy. Then came the fraught job of getting him down the stairs without dropping him and upsetting Mrs Finch further. Where are her friends and family? Tatty wondered as she sweated away at the feet end of the coffin, backing carefully down the stairs alongside Nellie, while Ben took the head end.

On the other hand, she decided as she strained, her job was to be of help to the bereaved, and she loved it, so she should stop moaning, even if it was only to herself. If she'd known what a big man Mr Finch was, she'd have brought Robert along as well, but she hadn't thought to ask when Mrs Finch had come by this morning to request a coffin. And that was her fault.

Finally they got Mr Finch in his coffin into the front room and settled him on the floor before the fireplace, the head end propped up on a footstool so his dead, opaque eyes weren't staring at the ceiling.

Tatty thought Mrs Finch didn't look entirely happy. 'Is there something wrong?'

'Oh, no, not at all.' Mrs Finch swept a non-existent strand of hair off her forehead. 'Well, it's just a little thing. It's his eyes. They don't look right open like that and all milky and I couldn't make them stay closed when I laid him out. He doesn't look at peace.'

Tatty said, 'I could fix that for you with just a couple of tiny little stitches. You won't even notice them.'

Mrs Finch looked doubtful.

'You don't have to watch. It should only take me ten minutes or so. And it won't cost you anything,' Tatty said.

'Yes, please, could you do that?' Mrs Finch said. 'Would anyone like cordial?' And she darted off, presumably to the kitchen.

'Lord, I thought I was going to drop him coming down the stairs, I really did,' Nellie said, wiping sweat off her forehead.

'So did I,' Tatty said.

Nellie began to set up her photographic equipment. Then she said, 'Do you want to fix his eyes first? He does look like something's scared the living daylights out of him with them wide open like that. It doesn't look very natural, does it?'

Tatty asked Ben to fetch her kit from the dog-cart. One day, she thought, I won't be at all surprised if Shadow gets bored waiting and goes home without us. Her kit contained everything she needed for corpse touch-ups – rouge, face powder in three different colours, lip salve, combs and a hairbrush and pins, muslin for leaking orifices, a sewing kit (eyes and jaws), and phials containing pure essence of jasmine and of rose to mask smells. She also carried a bottle of juice made from native limes and a jar of ordinary salt, which, when mixed together, killed maggots almost immediately.

She threaded her needle with fine oatmeal-coloured cotton and got on with sewing Mr Finch's eyelids shut.

Ben was fascinated, and even Nellie moved closer to watch. 'You're very good at that. I really can't see where the stitches are. Mrs Finch should be very happy.'

Tatty put two final stitches into the right eyelids, then snipped the thread. 'There we are. He looks like he's sleeping now. More or less.'

'It's a pity there aren't any flowers,' Nellie said. 'People usually like flowers in their photographs, especially with the coffin. Perhaps I should ask Mrs Finch if she's ordered any. I can always come back and take a few more photographs later.'

Tatty said, 'Better you than me. If I ask her, she'll think I'm being a pushy undertaker.'

'Oh, I'm sure she wouldn't,' Nellie said. 'Not after you've just fixed Mr Finch's eyes and not charged her for it. That reminds me, though, have you heard about Elias Nuttall?'

'No.'

'He's not in Darlinghurst Gaol any more.'

Tatty felt an immediate stab of unease 'Why not? Have they let him out?'

'Yes and no,' Nellie said as she settled her camera on its tripod and adjusted the angle so it pointed down at Mr Finch. 'Apparently he's *completely* lost his mind now and been sent to the lunatic asylum out at Gladesville.'

'Has he really?' Tatty didn't know whether this was good news or bad.

'So they say.'

Ben said, 'I heard something about that.'

Tatty stared at him. 'And you didn't tell me?'

Mrs Finch reappeared with a jug and tumblers and slices of cake on a tray.

'I'll tell you later,' Ben said.

He and Tatty stayed with Mrs Finch until relatives finally arrived, then left with Nellie, who had finished taking her photographs.

Tatty offered Nellie a ride home. After they'd dropped her off, she said to Ben, 'So tell me about Nuttall.'

'Well, this is according to what Evan told me.'

Tatty nodded – Evan was Ben's friend who had remained working for Nuttall until his business had collapsed.

Ben said, 'Apparently Evan went to see Nuttall in gaol because he owed him some wages. This was straight after he was sent down and Evan said he was unhinged then. He said being haunted by Caleb Blackfeather's ghost was all Nuttall would talk about. On and on and on. So he gave up and left and forgot about getting his money. Nuttall must have got even worse if they've sent him to Tarban Creek.'

'It's called Gladesville Hospital for the Insane now,' Tatty said.

'Same difference,' Ben said. 'I'd say you'd have to be pretty cracked to be shifted out of gaol to the lunatic asylum, wouldn't you?'

Tatty said, 'Why didn't you tell me this when Evan told you?'

Ben shrugged. 'I thought you might have had enough of Elias Nuttall. I know the rest of us have.'

Tatty had thought she had, too. But maybe she hadn't.

*

Gladesville Hospital for the Insane was situated on the northern banks of the Parramatta River, an area whose farms and dairies had supplied Sydney for over seventy years. Tatty caught the ferry upriver and disembarked at Abbotsford wharf on the left bank, took the punt across the river to Bedlam Point, then walked the rest of the way to the hospital, which wasn't far. She hadn't written in advance for an appointment, and hoped the person she had come to see would be available.

The hospital was a collection of buildings, many built of pale sandstone, with, in her inexpert opinion, little architectural merit except for a fancy clock tower stuck incongruously on top of an otherwise bland and impersonal two-storey building. She thought the gardens, however, had a lot of potential, and significant headway had already been made with landscaping.

Inside what she assumed was the main building, Tatty looked around for someone to ask for directions, but saw no one. So she sat on a chair in a row set against a bare white wall, and prepared to wait for as long as it took.

After ten minutes or so, a woman perhaps in her forties hurried out of a corridor and into the foyer, almost skidding to a halt in her solid black shoes when she saw Tatty. She wore a plain black dress with no crinoline or any other adornment, a long white apron, white cuffs and a white gathered cap.

'Oh. How long have you been sitting there?'

'Not long,' Tatty said. 'Are you a nurse?'

'Yes. I'm afraid visiting hours aren't until this afternoon.'

'I'm not really a visitor, Sister, er …'

'Nurse Radley.'

'Nurse Radley. I was hoping to speak to the medical superintendent. I believe that to be Dr Frederic Manning?'

'That's correct. Is he expecting you?'

'No.'

Nurse Radley made a rueful face. 'Oh dear. I'm sorry but you'll have to make an appointment and come back then.'

'Is he here today, though?' Tatty asked.

'Yes, but you'll have to make an appointment if you want to see him.'

'That's unfortunate. I've come all the way out from Sydney town just to speak to him. And it is about a patient here, a colleague of mine. It *is* quite important.'

'Which patient?'

'Mr Elias Nuttall.'

'Oh yes. No, I'm sorry, you'll still have to make an appointment.'

'Why?' Tatty asked.

Nurse Radley's lips tightened into a straight and unattractive line. 'Because Dr Manning is an important man and he's busy.'

Tatty gave a radiant smile. 'Right now? Do you know that for a fact?'

Nurse Radley's face flushed. 'You are being somewhat rude! I really would prefer you to leave and come back when you have an appointment!'

Tatty didn't think she was being rude but she stood up anyway. 'As you wish,' she said, and walked out the front door.

Five minutes later she returned, checked to see that Nurse Radley had departed and stepped into the long corridor from which the nurse had originally appeared. Halfway down she came to an office with a nameplate on the door announcing *Dr FN Manning*.

She knocked.

'Enter,' came a disembodied voice.

In she went.

Frederic Manning had a longish face with eyes that turned down at the outer edges, giving him a vaguely doleful but not unpleasant look, like a breed of some faithful sort of hound.

'May I be of assistance?' he asked.

'Yes, I think so,' Tatty said. 'My name is Mrs Tatiana Crowe, and I've come out from town today specifically to talk to you about one of your patients, Elias Nuttall.'

'Ah,' Dr Manning said.

Tatty wondered what that particular 'ah' meant. She also wondered where to start because she still hadn't quite worked out why she was at Gladesville. 'Elias Nuttall is an undertaker by profession and so am I,' she said. 'Though I should say, he *was* one. He doesn't have a business any more. It closed down after he was sent to gaol.'

Dr Manning said, 'You're an undertaker yourself?'

Tatty nodded.

'An assistant?'

'No. I operate my own company. I *have* assistants.'

'How interesting,' Dr Manning said.

'You will be aware of why Elias Nuttall was gaoled?' Tatty said.

'Of course. Are you?'

'Yes. He reduced the corpse of a man named Caleb Blackfeather to bones in order to ship them to England. I reported him to the police before he could send them.'

Dr Manning's eyebrows went up. 'Oh. That was you, was it?'

'Yes. He boasted in the newspaper about having given Mr Blackfeather a decent Christian burial, but the coffin was empty when he buried it. I thought that was unacceptable and I searched his house and found what remained of Mr Blackfeather there. What I need to know, Dr Manning, is am I responsible for Elias Nuttall's insanity?'

Dr Manning sat back in his chair, loosely crossed his arms and made a thoughtful face. 'Now that's a question I've never been asked before. How could you be responsible?'

'I went to the police about the bones. I testified against him in court. If I hadn't done those things, would he be here today, in this hospital?'

'Are you looking for some sort of redemption, Mrs Crowe?'

Tatty thought about that for quite some time. 'I don't think so, no. I think I'm just hoping to better understand what happened to him.'

Dr Manning made a steeple of his fingers and touched them to his lips. 'You told the police about the bones, and Mr Nuttall was duly arrested, yes?'

Tatty nodded.

'But had Mr Nuttall not desecrated Mr Blackfeather's corpse, there would have been nothing to arrest him for. Therefore, it very much seems he was the author of his own fate.'

Tatty came clean. 'I did everything I could to make sure he was arrested. Prior to that he was a thorn in my side. In fact he was more than that. He was a festering wound.'

'As I said, he was responsible for his actions, not you,' Dr Manning said. 'And it is *not* you who crowds his nightmares and torments him during most of his waking hours. It is the spectre of Caleb Blackfeather, who he believes is hounding him in revenge for what he did. The haunting, as he refers to it, began even before he entered Darlinghurst Gaol and since then has grown increasingly real to him. When he was transferred here I received a letter from the superintendent stating that his warders could no longer be responsible for Mr Nuttall's care as they feared he might attempt to take his own life, and they were right to send him on to us. A prison is not the right place for a man suffering such severe delusions.'

'Will he ever get better?' she asked.

'I don't know.'

'Shouldn't he be in a facility for the criminally insane?'

'Oh dear me, no,' Dr Manning said. 'Don't wish that on him. The man's in hell already. All he did was interfere with a corpse. He didn't kill Caleb Blackfeather, after all. He's a mere petty criminal in the eyes of the law, although, as it has transpired, his actions were such that he personally has been driven past the very limits of his own sanity.'

Tatty thought interfering with a corpse wasn't particularly petty, but she kept her mouth shut.

'Would you like to visit him?' Dr Manning said.

'I'm not sure he'll want to see me.'

'You don't know that. He hasn't had many visitors while he's been here. In fact, he hasn't had any.'

'All right, but I hope we don't see your Nurse Radley. She told me visiting hours weren't until later, and that you were too busy to speak to me.'

Dr Manning smiled. 'Yes, she can be a little proprietorial.' He rose from his chair. 'Come with me. I'll take you to Mr Nuttall's accommodation.'

Tatty had imagined Elias Nuttall chained to the wall in a cold bare cell, wearing rags, frothing at the mouth and spouting gibberish, but his circumstances were nothing like that. He was housed in a single room with a bed made up with a mattress and comfortable linen, and a chair and a chest of drawers and a rug on the floor. The window was barred but glazed and hung with drapes.

Elias sat on the chair fully dressed and with leather slippers on his feet. Someone had cut his hair and if he hadn't lost so much weight he might have looked like the Elias Nuttall of old. Except that he rocked backwards and forwards constantly, his hands clutched together in his lap, muttering to himself, and didn't look up when Dr Manning knocked on his open door.

'Mr Nuttall, you have a visitor.'

No response.

'Mr Nuttall! A visitor!'

Gradually, the muttering got louder. Tatty realised Nuttall was praying.

'*Yea, though I walk through the valley of the shadow of death, I will fear no evil: for thou art with me: thy rod and thy staff they comfort me. Thou preparest a table before me in the presence of mine enemies: thou anointest my head with oil: my cup runneth over.*'

Tatty said, 'Mr Nuttall, it's Tatiana Crowe. I've come to visit you.'

Finally he looked up. At first his face was blank and there was no indication at all that he recognised her. Then, slowly, his expression changed to one of awareness and he raised an arm and pointed at her, all the while still rocking on the chair.

'You're dead,' he said.

A chill crept up the back of Tatty's neck. 'I can assure you I'm not, Mr Nuttall.'

'You are. You were hanged. You were hanged for poisoning your husband. I was there, I saw you on the gallows.'

Tatty glanced at Dr Manning, who gave the smallest of shrugs. It was clear to Tatty he was accustomed to hearing this sort of talk. She didn't know what to say next to Nuttall, but as it happened she didn't have to say anything because off he went.

'We're all dead,' he said. 'You are, I am.'

'You are not dead, Mr Nuttall,' Dr Manning said. 'You're safe and sound with us in the land of the living.'

'Oh no I'm not. He wants me to be dead, therefore I am. He comes to me and tells me I owe him a resting place. He tells me I have harmed him and that he will walk forever because he has nowhere to lie. He tells me he will never feel his essence seeping into the earth from his flesh or the soil staining his bones or his soul lifting free and rising to the sky, because of me. He tells me he will *never* let me rest because *he* can't rest, and he's here in this room now watching me and no matter what I do I can't get away from his eyes and they're so *very* full of hate.'

Tatty couldn't help it: she looked around but there were only three people present – a doctor, a madman and someone who wished now she'd left well enough alone.

'He tells me I owe him a resting place,' Nuttall said again. 'And I know what he means. He wants me to die so he can use my grave, but I'm already dead and I don't know how long I can go on pretending I'm not. God has forsaken me for my sins and I'm dead.'

It seemed to Tatty that Nuttall was completely mad and Dr Manning was right: it wasn't her fault. Nuttall was paying for his own sins.

'Caleb Blackfeather does have a resting place now,' she said. 'His bones have been given a proper burial and I believe he's at peace as much as he can be, but that's no thanks to you.' Tatty turned to Dr Manning. 'I'd like to go now, please.'

'Of course.'

As she and the doctor left Nuttall's room, he called after them, 'I'm glad you're dead, Tatiana Crowe. I hope you rot in hell.'

Dr Manning flinched. 'I'm terribly sorry. He can be very unpredictable.'

'Please don't apologise,' Tatty said. 'Frankly, I heard worse from Mr Nuttall before he lost his mind.'

Now Dr Manning looked shocked. 'Really? That is unfortunate.'

In the foyer, Tatty said, 'Thank you very much for your time and assistance, Dr Manning.'

The doctor replied, 'You're welcome, Mrs Crowe. It was very nice talking with you and I hope you achieved what you came for. Will we be seeing you again?'

'I wouldn't think so.' Tatty retrieved her purse from her reticule and handed the doctor fifty pounds in bank notes. 'This is a donation to go towards the welfare of the patients here. I had initially intended it for Mr Nuttall, to offset my guilt, I suppose, but I've changed my mind. I've realised I don't actually feel guilty about him after all. So use it how you think best.'

Dr Manning looked at the money in his hand. 'Well, thank you very much, that's certainly a very generous gift, Mrs Crowe. Do enjoy your trip back to Sydney.'

'I will,' Tatty said, and she walked off down the carriageway towards Bedlam Point to wait for the punt to take her back across the river.

*

February 1869, Sydney

Another year had passed and a new year had begun. Towards the end of February Tatty received a letter from Dr Manning at Gladesville Hospital. It read:

> *Dear Mrs Crowe,*
> *Re: Elias Nuttall*
> *As you were the only visitor Mr Nuttall ever had here at Gladesville, I write to inform you of the sad news that he died by his own hand two days previously. As required by law there will be a coronial inquest, after which Mr Nuttall's remains will be buried in Gladesville Hospital's private cemetery. May he rest in peace.*
> *Yours sincerely,*
> *Dr FN Manning*

He was gone for good now. Tatty folded the letter, slid it back into its envelope and waited to feel something, but nothing happened. No glee, no satisfaction, and certainly no sadness or regret.

She had been living in Australia for four years and in that time she'd been married and widowed, and now had her own very successful undertaking company, and she was still not quite twenty-two. She had a home, friends, cultural interests, rewarding charitable commitments, and financial security – everything she thought she needed to make her happy, and if anyone had asked her if she was, she would have said most definitely.

As far as she could see there was only one small sandfly in the Bates' Salve – Agnes Billings. Cora believed her stepmother was probably dead but Tatty didn't necessarily think she was, and Agnes knew she'd poisoned Titus. Agnes, though, had been gone a year now.

No, the future looked bright and Tatty didn't regret her decision to emigrate to Sydney, or to invite Maggie Seddon and Lorna to follow her: they'd settled into the household beautifully. She had plans to expand Crowe Funerals by taking on more young men and women, and perhaps at some point she might even open a branch or two in other towns.

She had hopes for her romantic life, too. As much as she insisted that she didn't want another husband, she did feel lonely at times and often thought wistfully about the loving relationship her mother and father had shared. Once she wouldn't even have considered such a possibility for herself, not after Titus and not while the law around property remained as it was, but times were changing. Australian suffragists were agitating to improve the lives of women in all sorts of areas, including the law, and Tatty could see herself making her own contribution to their efforts.

The future looked bright indeed.

Author Notes

I always enjoy writing the author notes, so I hope you enjoy reading them. I do quite a lot of research for my books and it feels like such a waste not to present at least some of it, just in case someone's interested. I can't include everything in the actual story because then I'd be guilty of the dreaded 'info dump', which really would slow the pace of the narrative, so some of it's here instead.

When I was researching and writing this book I couldn't go anywhere, mostly because of Covid. Instead, I relied on my own ever-expanding reference library, a couple of specifically purchased second-hand titles and an absolute gem of a book called *Murder, Misadventure and Miserable Ends: tales from a colonial coroner's court* by Catie Gilchrist, very kindly contributed by my publisher, HarperCollins Australia. It's a fantastic read and I couldn't have written this story without it.

And, also the internet. Gasp! But that's not a reliable source of historical information! Well, it can be, providing facts are double- and even triple-checked. Sometimes, though, numerous checks do just lead to multiple answers, which can be frustrating, but that is the nature of the internet, and perhaps of historical research itself. You shouldn't automatically believe what you read in books, either. Just because something's printed on paper doesn't mean it's more likely to represent the truth than any other medium.

So, to the background information I wanted to share with you. On one level this story is about what happened when women were widowed in 1860s England and New South Wales. The situation was more or less the same in both places because New South Wales was a British colony and operated under similar laws to England.

From the 1200s to 1870, under English common law, single or widowed women were considered to be *femes sole* (feme sole is the singular, meaning woman alone) and had the right to own property in their own names, earn money and keep it. If, however, a woman married, by law she became a *feme covert* (a protected woman, covered by marriage – this was called coverture) and had to give up the rights to the use and control of all of her personal property – money, furniture, livestock, land, stocks (with the exception of a dowry) – to her husband, who could do whatever he liked with it, even though technically she still owned it. Even when she died, the husband continued to control all her property unless she stipulated otherwise. In that way the woman's identity became completely absorbed into that of her husband. And people wondered why so many husbands were poisoned to death. If a woman's husband did die (by fair means or foul), his eldest son would automatically inherit his real (physical) property, while daughters would receive the rats and mice, i.e. furniture, jewellery, etc. If there was plenty of money, presumably the widow would be set up in accommodation with a yearly income via some sort of trust arrangement, in the manner of Violet Crawley, the Dowager Countess of Grantham, in *Downton Abbey*. This is what Hector Caldwell tried to do for Betsy and Tatty, except Selwyn Boyd ruined the arrangement by mismanaging Hector's accounting business.

Not unsurprisingly, by the mid-1800s women had had a gutful of being treated as chattels and began to campaign for the law to be changed – the beginning of the movement for the enfranchisement of white women. In 1868 a Married Women's Property Bill, proposing that married women should have the same property rights as unmarried women, was introduced into the English parliament. After a long campaign by women's groups, supported by some men, the *Married Women's Property Act* was passed in 1870, allowing that any property and money a wife inherited or earnt herself would be regarded as her own. The *Married Women's Property Act 1882* extended this principle to all property regardless of its source or when it was obtained. In New South Wales, the *Married Women's Property Act* was passed in 1879 and also enabled married women to hold property of their own.

This legislation released married women from coverture and allowed them to support their children and live away from their husbands, a huge step forward for women previously trapped in marriages that had been loveless and/or abusive. But it only helped women who had the means to escape such marriages – and many didn't.

Now, on to undertakers. The most straightforward summary I've seen of how the profession of undertaking might have come about appears in *Australian Ways of Death: a social and cultural history 1840–1918* by Pat Jalland (p. 109), and here it is:

> *The undertaking trade may have started in England as far back as 1689 when coffin maker William Russell obtained the blessing of the College of Arms to provide clients with all the heraldic ritual and accoutrements for a funeral. In the next two centuries, undertakers increasingly seized control of funerals from executors and families, centralising the labour of the various artisans previously involved. Trades such as carpentry, wreath making, metal working and drapery all specialised in the production of funeral commodities and were gradually taken over by the 'expert' undertakers.*

By the early 1840s in England, funeral expenses for a deceased person from an aristocratic family could range from five hundred to fifteen hundred pounds (which today is approximately NZD124,031 to NZD372,093, but please don't quote me because I do words not numbers, or go here if you want to work it out yourself: https://www.officialdata.org/uk/inflation/1840?amount=20), while a middle-class funeral could cost between fifty (~NZD12,403) and seventy pounds (~NZD17,364). Undertakers, who clearly made considerable money from funerals, were not popular. They were seen as greedy and guilty of exploiting the bereaved, especially the poor and low-income working-class folk who absolutely dreaded the shame of a pauper's funeral, also known as being buried on the parish, i.e. interment at the public's expense in a mass grave with no headstone. In 1843 English social reformer Edwin Chadwick released a milestone report that heralded a move among the middle and upper classes to more modest private funerals. As a consequence, undertakers were obliged to offer their services at cheaper prices or risk not being hired. By the 1870s London undertaking firms were advertising a range of funerals from three pounds and five shillings to fifty-three pounds. By 1894 you could bury your loved one perfectly respectably for ten to fifteen pounds.

In Sydney in 1844, the family of a deceased merchant paid sixty-one pounds and four shillings for his clearly rather flash funeral with fully outfitted horses, porters and mutes etc., but by the 1850s you could get a decent funeral for four pounds and ten shillings, or something even smarter for around ten pounds. In 1859 there were eight full-time undertaking firms operating in central Sydney, which had a population of approximately ninety thousand (Jalland, *Australian Ways of Death*).

What *was* a funeral mute? Generally they were ordinary men who could be hired for several days and nights to stand outside your front door dressed in black in silent vigil (they weren't truly unable to speak; they just kept their mouths shut for the duration) and look mournful while your dead loved one lay in state prior to burial. When the funeral procession set off for the church and/or the cemetery, the mutes would walk at the front, staves held high (Jalland, *Australian Ways of Death*).

When I looked into the difference between funeral mutes and professional mourners, I note that these days the two have been confused and even conflated. They were definitely not the same thing. Professional mourners (or moirologists), which you could also hire, walked alongside the hearse crying and wailing, giving the impression that the death of your loved one was having a far more catastrophic impact than perhaps it actually was.

Slightly off topic: for an interesting read, have a look at Jessica Mitford's *The American Way of Death*, published in 1963, which is a blistering (as they say) exposé of abuses in the American funeral home industry. And yes, she was one of *those* Mitfords.

So if there were undertakers in the 1700s, obviously funeral and mourning traditions didn't start with Queen Victoria's response to the death of her beloved Prince Albert in 1861, as is sometimes assumed. Funerals were originally for royals and aristocrats only, but by the 1800s the trend for fancy and expensive funerals had inevitably filtered down to the middle class, eager to show they'd 'arrived' by staging flashy funerals for their own dead. Soon the idea of skimping on funeral and mourning costs came to be seen as a lack of respect for the deceased, not to mention a thumbed nose at the proper way of doing things. By then funerals for 'ordinary' people had lost most of the heraldic elements associated with royal funerals, although some vestiges remained, including the public procession, the funeral mutes representing castle porters, and the black feathers worn by horses signifying heraldic shields. But it's possible that by Victorian times people had forgotten what those symbols meant: they were 'customary' and thus necessary to make a 'good' funeral.

A word about horses: the supreme funeral horse has traditionally been the Belgian Black, or Friesian. These are light draught horses originating from Friesland in the northern Netherlands. The breed is usually black, though there are occasionally chestnuts and bays, they stand between 14.2 hands at the withers (which is only pony-sized) and 17 hands (definitely not pony-sized). They have long, full tails and manes, compact muscular bodies, and really are beautiful animals. If you google *Belgian Black horse*, you'll see plenty of them prancing around looking fabulous, and in harness to amazing antique and vintage hearses.

At some Victorian funerals, definitely in the UK and in Australia, guests were given funeral biscuits to take home. Similar to shortbread they were either plain or stamped with a motif such as a cross before baking. Afterwards they were wrapped in paper, which was frequently black-edged and printed with either bible verses or psalms or an obituary of the deceased, and fastened with black ribbon or black sealing wax. Sort of a little funeral goody bag. I can't find any evidence online of funeral biscuits in New Zealand. If I google it I get either 'Anzac biscuits' or 'are Afghan biscuits racist?'.

At home, before the funeral and while the body was lying in state, superstition could be rife. Curtains were closed and mirrors covered with black fabric so that the deceased's image wouldn't get trapped in the reflective surfaces. I'm not sure how this could happen while the dead person was lying in their coffin, but anyway ... To prevent bad luck, all clocks had to be stopped at the time of death. Family photographs were turned face-down to protect family and friends from possession by the spirit of the dead person, who had to be carried out of the home feet first so he or she couldn't look back and call someone else to follow them. Flowers around the body at home were very popular, but not just because they were pretty – they also helped to conceal the smell of decay. White arum lilies in particular have become associated with funerals, and traditionalists and floriographists and florists have attributed all sorts of symbolism and special meanings to them, but I grew up knowing them as death lilies, and I'm sure I'm not alone.

The extended process of mourning in Victorian times was a complex social ritual, and just as important as the funeral. Mourning clothes during that period were intended to be the outer reflection of the wearer's grief and sorrow. I should point out here that I'm mostly talking about the middle class (represented by educated professionals) and to some extent the working class (dominated by those with little to no education), but not the underclass (the very poor). They, and even a lot of working-class people, wouldn't have been able to afford special black mourning clothes. It cost a lot of money to drift about for eighteen months to two years dressed head to toe in black, advertising your grief to the world.

The most commonly used fabrics for women's mourning costumes were coloured black, obviously, and dull in texture. Perhaps the most popular material was crape. This was actually crepe, a matte silk common today, crimped with heated rollers and known as crape when specifically used to make mourning gowns. Between the 'matteness' of the fabric and the crimping process there was no chance of the silk producing an attractive or showy lustre and it was therefore the perfect textile to use during deep mourning, i.e. the first twelve months after a significant bereavement. Other popular fabrics were: bombazine; cashmere; silk bengaline (a heavy corded fabric containing more cotton than silk); and taffeta.

Women who couldn't afford to go out and purchase whole new wardrobes of black dresses, jackets, hats, gloves, veils, bags and shoes etc. would dye clothing and accessories they already owned. By the 1860s it was possible to buy dyes, including a good, true black that wouldn't quickly fade to blue or brown. Dresses were generally sponged and dusted rather than washed: boiling a dress in the copper would most definitely have destroyed it.

I've read a number of Victorian-era accounts of how long women should stay in mourning and what they should wear while they did, and they all differ to some extent. In general, I think it's safe to say that bereaved women were expected to mourn

Black Silk and Sympathy

the loss of a husband for between eighteen months and two years. (This was unless you were Queen Victoria, who remained in mourning for Prince Albert until she died, forty years later.) For the first year women wore deep, relatively unadorned black clothing with no jewellery, and thereafter they could wear black gowns made of more luxuriant fabrics, or trimmed with white, or in colours of mauve or grey. Jet and black enamel mourning jewellery was also allowed.

The following website lists how long mourning should be for every dead relative you can think of, and also what should be worn during that period of mourning. The instructions are taken from *Manners and Rules of Good Society, Or, Solecisms to be Avoided by a Member of the Aristocracy*, London, Frederick Warne, 1888 (https://victorianweb.org/history/mourning/6.html).

I read the relevant section of that publication (which you can access here on Project Gutenberg: https://www.gutenberg.org/files/33716/33716-h/33716-h.htm) and thought, Surely not? What a lot of faffing about. But it was written by 'a member of the aristocracy' so they should know.

While freshly bereaved women were running around buying new wardrobes or dyeing old ones black, men were expected to wear a dark suit and a black arm or hat band, and perhaps black gloves, for up to two years. That's it.

Did children wear mourning clothes? They did, but the 'rules' seem to be inconsistent – every source I looked at said something different so maybe they were flexible. Some said children wore black for six months, others said twelve months, still others said children wore white. Google has photos of children in mourning wearing both black and white. Children's coffins, though, seem to have been uniformly white.

To mourning jewellery, which I find fascinating. Mourning rings were very popular during the 1800s. Usually made of gold, they could be enamelled in black with the deceased's name and date of death in gold script on the outside of the band, or engraved inside, or the top of the ring might feature hair from the deceased under a tiny rock crystal dome surrounded by natural seed pearls. Sometimes the hair was tightly plaited and set within the gold band of the ring, which would be engraved inside with the deceased's details. Black onyx was also used in rings, but enamel was probably more versatile and easier to work with. For those with plenty of money to spend, amethysts, pearls, garnets, rubies and opaline could also feature in mourning rings.

Mourning jewellery made using hair was extremely popular and came in a wide range of styles – not just rings but brooches with the hair set under rock crystal, lockets and pendants, bangles, ear-rings, necklaces, and watch chains. If you had the time you could do your own 'hair work' at home. You could buy patterns and instructions on how to construct a braiding frame (very simply, apparently) and make your own basket-weave-style jewellery out of a dead family member's hair at leisure in your lamplit parlour. That must have been hard on the eyes.

Jet was the favourite gemstone used for mourning jewellery. It's actually lignite, the crappiest type of coal you can get, formed from wood compressed over millions of years. It can be carved (carefully) and polished and makes very beautiful, glittery black jewellery. It will also smell like coal and crack if you heat it, so don't. The best jet comes from the Whitby Mudstone Formation at, yes, Whitby in the UK, but it's also found in Dorset, and in France, Spain, the US, Poland and Turkey. Queen Victoria loved it and wore it constantly after Albert died.

Bog oak was used as a jet substitute. It's the timber of oak and other forest trees, which has sunk into peat bog and been preserved and stained almost black by tannins in the acidic water. Eventually it turns into coal. It's traditionally associated with Ireland, where it was popularly used for mourning jewellery in the 1800s, but is also found in Scotland and England.

Gutta-percha and vulcanite were also used to make mourning jewellery and were considered the poor man's jet – or more accurately the poor woman's jet. Gutta-percha is a form of dark latex that comes from the sap of the Palaquium tree, indigenous to today's South-East Asia. It is thermoplastic, which means it becomes plastic when heated and solid when cooled. The Victorians made all sorts of things with it, not just mourning jewellery, though apparently it did get a bit brittle when exposed to air so not many examples have survived. You knew you had a genuine gutta-percha product because it tasted salty if you licked it.

Vulcanite, also known as ebonite, was discovered in 1839 by Charles Goodyear when he mixed rubber with sulphur, the result being anything between flexible or hard depending on the amount of sulphur added. Like gutta-percha it could be moulded, but it lasted longer. As well as jewellery it was also used to make items such as pipe stems, buttons, combs, vesta (match) cases, and fountain pens (in later years). It was also widely used as an electrical insulator when this became a necessity.

In the story, Louis Coverdale the jeweller sneers at pinchbeck, which is a form of brass, an alloy of copper and zinc, that resembles gold. It was invented by clockmaker Christopher Pinchbeck (1670–1732) and was used in watchmaking and to make cheap jewellery. You could tell you'd bought pinchbeck jewellery because it gave off a coppery glow in natural light and bits tended to flake away and it could tarnish and turn green. Rich Georgians wore a lot of well-made pinchbeck pieces, especially when travelling, as a way of safeguarding their real jewels by leaving them securely locked up at home. In the 1800s when some unscrupulous jewellers started to sell pinchbeck as genuine gold, it attracted a bad reputation and was relegated to the status of costume jewellery.

Cemeteries – another favourite subject of mine. Fun fact: if, like me, you have an interest in cemeteries and funeral customs, you are what's known as a 'taphophile': 'taphos' is ancient Greek for funeral rites, tomb, etc., and 'phile' means friend – so, 'friend of cemeteries'.

Sydney's first cemetery was known as the Old Sydney Burial Ground, and later George Street Burial Ground, and, retrospectively, Town Hall Cemetery. The site was chosen in 1792 because it was some distance from the original settlement so wouldn't affect the health of the living and could remain a place of quiet seclusion. Convicts and free people alike were buried there but by 1820 when Sydney town had grown around it, the cemetery was so full of bodies it had become disgustingly unsanitary and had to be closed. A new four-acre location was chosen farther south on Brickfield Hill (where bricks were made), and the new Devonshire Street Cemetery opened when the Old Sydney Burial Ground closed. By the 1840s even Devonshire Street was getting a bit full, even though eight more acres had been added.

So, in the early 1860s, another site was chosen. The fashion by this time was for garden cemeteries located beyond city centres, and as the railway line from Sydney out to Parramatta in the west had been completed, that's where the New South Wales government looked, settling on around two hundred acres purchased privately at Haslam's Creek (sometimes referred to as Haslem's Creek). This was unimaginatively named Haslam's Creek Cemetery, which is the name I'll use here because it's the one I used in the story. The land was divided into areas for burials of different denominations, i.e. the Catholics got thirty-four acres, the Anglicans got fifty-two, and fifty-seven acres went to burials of other or no denomination (the proportions being based on a recent census). No, it doesn't add up to two hundred. I assume the rest was for roads, gardens, etc.

The burial sites were consecrated in July 1867, when the first burials took place, although the cemetery wasn't officially opened until the *Necropolis Act* came into force on 1 January 1868. In the meantime, Devonshire Street Cemetery was closed to all new public burials and later became the site of the new Central Railway Station in 1901. *Most* of the occupants of the Devonshire Street graves were moved to other cemeteries, primarily Haslam's Creek Cemetery. A further five hundred and seventy-five acres were purchased to extend Haslam's

Creek Cemetery in 1879, and areas for Presbyterian, Wesleyan, Independent (Congregational), Jewish, Lutheran and Methodist burials laid out and consecrated.

A rail spur coming off the Sydney to Parramatta line at today's Lidcombe Station had been providing access to Haslam's Creek Cemetery since 1865. When Lidcombe Station opened in 1859 it was originally called Haslam's Creek Station, and it serviced the tiny settlement of Haslam's Creek. At some time in the 1870s the station and the growing suburb were renamed Rookwood because residents didn't want to be associated with the cemetery, but almost every source I found gives a different specific date for that change, and I'm not listing them all here. Over time the cemetery also took on the name Rookwood, and in response in 1914 the suburb was yet again renamed – as Lidcombe, serviced by Lidcombe Station.

In April 1867, work was completed on a very elegant, Gothic-styled train station situated within the cemetery grounds, which was named Mortuary Station No. 1, ready to receive the first burial parties to arrive by train in July. Three further stations were built when the line was later extended inside the cemetery, and were named – yes, that's right – Mortuary Stations No. 2–4, though they weren't as grand as No. 1, and more akin to open-air platforms. From these, coffins were transported by wheeled litters to gravesites. At some later point the names were changed from 'Mortuary Station' to the far more interesting 'Cemetery Station'.

The Cemetery Stations opened between July 1867 and June 1908. New South Wales Rail states that they all (including Station No. 1) closed on 29 December 1948, which was when the rail line into the cemetery also closed (https://www.nswrail.net/lines/show.php?name=NSW:rookwood_cemetery). Stations No. 2, 3 and 4 were demolished, and Station No. 1 was sold to All Saints Church of England in Canberra for one hundred pounds (courtesy of the All Saints Ladies Auxiliary), dismantled, transported, then reassembled at Ainslie. I'm not sure when.

Once again I found a range of dates, although there does seem to be a consensus around 1958–1959.

The funeral train departed from Sydney town from Mortuary Station, also known as Funeral Station, located on Regent Street, Chippendale, which opened in April 1869. It's still there. You see it on your left every time you arrive overground by train at Central Station from the south, and you can walk right up to it from Regent Street. Trains left twice a day at 9.30 am and 3.00 pm, stopping at pre-arranged stations on the way out to Haslam's Creek Cemetery to pick up other mourners and coffins. The funeral trains laid on for mourners used cars known intriguingly as 'unimproved Redferns', according to the Transport Heritage NSW website. Unfortunately I haven't been able to find out exactly what an unimproved Redfern is. It cost a shilling per person for the return trip, though the dead travelled free in the hearse van at the rear of the train. There were two types of hearse van: one that took ten coffins and another that accommodated thirty. Both handily opened along one side onto the platform for easy loading (https://sustainabilitysoapbox.com/2014/04/25/the-end-of-the-line-sydneys-mortuary-train-stations/).

By the time the funeral train service from the city and the rail line from Lidcombe Station to the cemetery both closed by December 1948, road travel was well established and motor hearses frequently drove out to the cemetery, thereby ending what must have been a truly memorable era in Sydney's history. If you *are* a taphophile you really should visit Rookwood Necropolis. But be warned, it's absolutely huge and takes days to see completely. But it's *so* worth it (https://rookwoodnecropolistrust.com.au/history/ and https://www.rookwoodcemetery.com.au/blog/mortuary-station-no-1).

And now to a really jolly subject – body-snatching. Although the illegal removal of corpses from graves or morgues to supply medical schools had been pretty well eradicated in the UK by the 1830s, the horror of the dark deeds of the body-snatchers, or resurrection men, remained fresh in the public mind for decades afterwards. The reason body-snatching so horrified folk had to do with religious convictions. Belief in resurrection of the body after death was still commonplace, so to interfere with its peaceful interment was an extremely serious matter. If you had no body you couldn't be resurrected when the time came – a truly ghastly prospect.

In actual fact, chopping up dead bodies to advance anatomical study had been legal for a long time. In 1506, Scotland's James IV ruled that members of the Edinburgh College of Surgeons and Barbers were allowed to dissect the corpses of some executed criminals. England followed in 1540 when Henry VIII granted anatomists (surgeons) the right to dissect four hanged felons each per year – in public. Charles II later increased that number to six.

Unfortunately, there evidently weren't enough legal corpses to go around so surgeons adapted, robbing graves, or getting their pupils to do their dirty work. By the 1720s a body-snatching industry had been established: professional resurrectionists were stealing corpses mostly from the graves of the poor and selling them to medical schools. In 1752 an Act was passed allowing *all* those executed by hanging to be dissected for medical purposes, which did increase the supply of bodies, but fresh cadavers were still in great demand, rather than corpses that had been left hanging off gallows for days, teaching the public a lesson.

An interesting diversion: Scottish brothers William (the elder) and John Hunter, leading anatomists in the mid-1700s, ran a private anatomy school in London, at which each student had access to their 'own corpse', so they used quite a lot of them. John sourced the bodies for the school, allegedly sometimes digging them up himself. The Hunters also collected for and operated a museum of human and comparative anatomy, known as the Hunterian. When William died in 1783 he bequeathed his enormous personal anatomy collection to the University of Glasgow, where it reopened in a custom-made building in 1807.

This is where it gets a bit confusing. John Hunter died in 1793, and in 1799, the English government purchased *his* enormous anatomy collection, the remainder of the original Hunterian museum, and presented it to the Royal College of Surgeons of England, which is located at Lincoln's Inn Fields in London. So essentially, after 1807, there were, and still are, two Hunterian Museums, one in London and one in Glasgow.

In the London Hunterian, until very recently, hung the skeleton of Charles Byrne, a seven-foot-seven Irish giant who desperately wanted to be buried at sea when he died in 1783 aged twenty-two, to avoid the clutches of anatomists. But John Hunter allegedly paid a five-hundred-pound bribe (a *huge* amount, if this is true) to Byrne's friends or perhaps the undertaker, and Byrne's grieving family unknowingly transported a coffin filled with rocks to the coast, and Hunter got his prized specimen of a giant for his museum. Charles Byrne's skeleton was finally removed from public display in 2023, two hundred and forty years after his death. The museum still has possession of the skeleton, however: Charles Byrne has not been returned to his family for burial.

John Hunter Hospital in Newcastle, New South Wales, Australia, is allegedly named after three John Hunters: one a former New South Wales state governor (1795–1800); one an Australian anatomist who died in 1924 aged twenty-six and who was the youngest-ever professor of anatomy at the University of Sydney; and the third the corpse-grabbing John Hunter discussed above. But I did get that from a Wikipedia article.

Back to the history of body-snatching. By the end of the eighteenth century the practice was rampant. The crisis reached its peak in 1828 with the horrible events involving William Burke and William Hare. Burke and Hare, both Irish, lived in Edinburgh. Hare kept a lodging house where Burke stayed. When an old man died in the house owing four pounds, Hare stole the corpse from its coffin and sold it to Robert Knox at Knox's school of anatomy for seven pounds and ten shillings.

Thrilled with the profit, Hare – and Burke and their common-law wives – lured at least fifteen people to the lodging house, smothered them to death, and sold the bodies to Knox. They were arrested when neighbours discovered the death of a local woman in October 1828. Hare turned King's evidence and, with his wife, testified against Burke and *his* wife. Burke was hanged, his body made available for medical dissection, and, bizarrely, his skin was used to make a pocketbook. You can view his skeleton in the anatomical museum at the University of Edinburgh, if you really want to. Hare was imprisoned but eventually released. Burke's wife was released from gaol after charges against her were 'not proven'. Robert Knox, who had knowingly purchased the murder victims, was not tried for his involvement in the crime but his reputation was ruined and he moved to Hackney in London, where he continued to work as a doctor and wrote several books. Hare's wife apparently emigrated to Ireland.

In London in November 1831, James May and John Bishop were arrested by police for delivering the suspiciously fresh corpse of a boy to the dissecting room at King's College. After searching May and Bishop's lodgings in the East End, where they found property indicating multiple murders, police also arrested residents Michael Shields and Thomas Williams. This group came to be known as the London Burkers (after William Burke). Questioning revealed that a woman and another boy had also been murdered, though only by Bishop and Williams, who were found guilty at trial. They were both hanged – allegedly before an enthralled crowd of thirty thousand – and their bodies made available for medical dissection.

Obviously, something really had to be done, and in 1832 the *Anatomy Act* was passed allowing surgeons/anatomists to take for dissection the unclaimed dead from hospitals and asylums, and prisons and poorhouses, which did seem to go a long way towards solving the problem of illegal body-snatching and murder for supply to the anatomists.

There is a true account mentioned in this story concerning the body of William Lanne, also known as King Billy, who was said at the time to be the last 'full-blooded' Tasmanian Aboriginal man, which made Lanne's remains a real prize for anatomists, ethnologists and phrenologists. Lanne died in March 1869, aged approximately thirty-four, from dysentery and cholera. Note that in this story I have brought William Lanne's death, and all the horror that came with it, forward a year to 1868. Basically I've chopped up his history, which is nearly as bad as chopping up his body and I'm not at all sure that's ethically right. In this story's original timeline William Lanne died when he actually did, but then I changed things so I had to bring his story forward a year to include it. And I really did want to include it because I want readers to know what happened to him. Anyway, after his death in 1869 there was a disgraceful squabble for his body between the Royal College of Surgeons of England, represented by member Dr William Crowther, and the Royal Society of Tasmania, represented by Dr George Stokell. Crowther, who for ages had been dying to send a quality Aboriginal skeleton to the Royal College's Hunterian Museum in London, applied to the Tasmanian government to send them William Lanne's. After the application was declined, Crowther broke into the Hobart Town General Hospital's morgue, decapitated Lanne, degloved the skin from his head and removed his skull, substituted it with one from a deceased white man, then made off with Lanne's skull.

When Stokell and the Royal Society crowd discovered what had happened, they amputated Lanne's hands and feet and hid them (allegedly in the Royal Society museum) so no one else could take them as 'samples'. Lanne was buried in that state – with someone else's skull in his unattached head, and handless and footless – after a funeral paid for by the captain of the *Runnymede*, the whaling ship on which he'd been employed before he'd died. Stokell and his colleagues then robbed Lanne's grave of everything but the replacement skull. Infuriated,

Crowther and friends (who had also gone to the cemetery to rob Lanne's grave) tracked Stokell to the General Hospital, where they battered their way into the morgue, but too late. Piles of decomposing flesh and fat lay about but Lanne's skeleton was nowhere to be seen.

As for what happened to William Lanne's skull, this is a quote from the City of Hobart website:

Tasmanian Aboriginal people fought a long battle to have Lanne's skull returned from the UK and buried in accordance with cultural practice. This happened in 1991, over 120 years after Lanne's death. (https:// yoursay.hobartcity.com.au/crowther/widgets/336275/ faqs)

Although Stokell admitted to cutting the hands and feet off Lanne's corpse, he wasn't convicted of any crime, allegedly because there wasn't enough evidence. Crowther's honorary appointment as surgeon at the General Hospital was terminated and he was suspended from the medical profession for his part in the debacle. However, the following year the Royal College of Surgeons gave him a gold medal and the first Fellowship the College ever awarded to an Australian. Crowther later became Premier of Tasmania, albeit for less than a year, and a bronze statue of him was erected in Franklin Square, Hobart, in January 1889. In August 2022, one hundred and thirty-three years later, the Hobart City Council voted seven to four in favour of removing the statue as an act of reconciliation, although no action was taken. A year later in August 2023, the Council voted again, eight to two in favour of removing the statue; however, the plinth is to remain as an 'interpretive piece' telling the story of Crowther, Lanne and society at the time, and the statue will be conserved elsewhere.

This story is set in the 1860s, the dawn of modern embalming. The Egyptians did it BC and so did a few other cultures, and although early Christians generally saw embalming (and cremation) as pagan mutilations of the corpse, they did embalm some important dead people as a mark of divine favour, for example Charlemagne in 814. It was also practical. In the 1100s, Henry I was embalmed so he could be brought back from France to England.

The anatomist William Hunter (yes, him from before) is generally credited in the early 1770s with being the first to propose, in any detail, arterial and cavity embalming as a way to preserve bodies for burial. A century earlier, however, English physiologist William Harvey had already discovered how blood circulates by injecting dye into cadavers and, subsequently, Dutch and German scientists are thought to have used similar arterial injection techniques to stop cadavers from decomposing. However, William Hunter's 'discovery' attracted much attention when in 1775 his brother, John, embalmed the body of Mrs Martin Van Butchell, whose will specified that her husband had control of her fortune only as long as her body remained above ground. So Mr Van Butchell had her embalmed, dressed in a fashionable gown and placed in a glass-lidded case in his sitting room. What a truly lovely man.

Embalming slowly became more popular in England and America as an option for bodies that had to be transported distances, but the public resistance to the idea of 'mutilating' the body after death remained strong. It took the American Civil War for enough people to overcome this aversion. The war was fought from 1861 to 1865 and, based on a recent examination of American census records from 1850 to 1880, an estimated 750,000 soldiers died. Compare this with America's ten-year war in Vietnam, during which 58,220 American military personnel died. During the Civil War, and irrespective of the newly established national cemeteries for war dead, many families wanted their dead sons brought home, so contracts were awarded to undertakers and embalmers to prepare bodies for shipment. This made embalming more culturally acceptable, and even seen as patriotic, especially after President Abraham Lincoln's son, Willie, was embalmed after he died of typhoid fever in 1862 aged twelve, followed by the president himself after he was assassinated in 1865.

In this story, Betsy dies of tuberculosis. So why doesn't Tatty catch it? Well, read on. Tuberculosis – also known as consumption, phthisis, the King's evil, and the white plague because of the pallor of those who contracted it – has long been (and remains) a common and frequent killer, and became an epidemic in Europe and North America in the 1700s and 1800s. It's caused by the bacterium *Mycobacterium tuberculosis*, is highly contagious and infectious, and is spread from person to person through the air, which wasn't even vaguely understood until the 1860s. During an epidemic the majority of a population will get infected with the bacterium, and it's been estimated that seventy to ninety per cent of the urban population of Great Britain was infected during the later 1800s. Most people with robust immune systems will be able to fight off the bacterial infection without ever knowing they have it – this is called latent tuberculosis. Tatty, Lorna and Mrs Seddon have latent tuberculosis. It might recur later in life or it might not. Other infected people won't be able to fight off the infection, especially without antibiotics, and will go on to develop what is called active tuberculosis. Using the example of a single year, in 1870 twenty per cent of the population of Great Britain died from tuberculosis.

After physician Jean-Antoine Villemin proved in 1865 that tuberculosis is an infectious disease, and scientist Robert Koch isolated the tubercle bacillus in 1882 and demonstrated its presence in the spit of tuberculosis patients, the message finally became clear – stop hoicking and spitting in public (on the street, into spittoons in the pub, etc.) and stay away from people with consumption. While this slowed down the spread of tuberculosis it did seriously victimise those who had it. It also gave rise to sanatoriums, where wealthy patients could go to rest in peace, quiet and fresh air and probably still die. If you were poor you could perish in far less appealing TB hospitals or fade away at home. It wasn't until 1921 that the 'BCG' vaccine, developed by Albert Calmette and Camille Guerin, was first used on humans in France as an immunisation against tuberculosis. Great Britain, however, didn't use the BCG vaccine till after World War II, and even then was slow to embrace it. Antibiotics have helped to lower rates of tuberculosis worldwide but the biggest contribution to its eradication post–World War II has been improvements in standards of living, although it's making a comeback. In 2020, an estimated ten million people worldwide fell ill with tuberculosis and 1.5 million died, despite the infection now being curable and preventable. The disease is the thirteenth highest cause of death in the world, and the second most infectious fatal disease, after Covid-19 (https://www.who.int/news-room/fact-sheets/detail/tuberculosis).

Titus Crowe takes Collis Browne's Chlorodyne for his stomach pain, as well as laudanum and morphine tablets. Chlorodyne contained morphine, chloroform and cannabis, while laudanum was a tincture of opium in alcohol. In Victorian times you could buy these medicines, and similar products, from any chemist, and from market stalls, door-to-door salesmen and quack doctors. Or you could get a prescription for them from a doctor, if you could afford to see one, which many couldn't. There were few cures for most ailments, even fewer successful surgical interventions, and not much was known about drug addiction (including alcoholism), so it's not really a surprise that a significant number of people of all classes became dependent on the medications they took to manage their pain.

The chemist might make up something specific for you containing opium, morphine, cannabis or cocaine depending on your symptoms, or you could buy a patent medicine like Kendal Black Drop, Dover's Powder, Dalby's Carminative or McMunn's Elixir, all of which contained opium or its derivatives. Children and infants were frequently given Godfrey's Cordial (aka Mother's Friend, and consisting of opium, treacle and water) to calm them when they were teething and/or wouldn't settle or sleep – sometimes to the extent that they did sleep but never woke up again. 'Teething' was quite often recorded as a cause of death by coroners (https://victorianweb.org/victorian/science/addiction/addiction2.html).

Cocaine was also frequently used to relieve hay fever and cold and flu, as well as in lozenges for sore throats, and as a local anaesthetic during dentistry, eye surgery and other minor operations.

But by the 1860s in the UK, after individuals and religious groups campaigned against the growing social impact of 'morally degenerate inebriates' (addicts), the *Pharmacy Act 1868* stated that only registered chemists could sell a range of poisons and dangerous drugs, including opium. This didn't stop department stores, including Harrods, selling gift kits of syringes, needles, cocaine and heroin to send to loved ones to ease the misery of being at the Front nearly fifty years later during World War I (https://www.bbc.co.uk/bbcthree/article/966b1bdd-69ff-4de0-9c39-d9276eba706b).

The situation changed in 1920, when the *Dangerous Drugs Act* established that only medical practitioners would be allowed to prescribe morphine, cocaine and heroin.

New South Wales introduced its own legislation to manage the indiscriminate sale of narcotics and poisons with the *Sale and Use of Poisons Act 1876*, which stated that only registered chemists could sell laudanum, opium, arsenic, strychnine, etc., which, to me, sounds like business as usual.

At the heart of Catie Gilchrist's book *Murder, Misadventure and Miserable Ends* is the work of Henry Shiell, metropolitan Sydney's coroner from July 1866 to January 1889. Coronial inquests (meaning an inquest relating to a coroner) were held more or less for every death that was considered: *strange, sudden or suspicious, violent or 'unnatural'*. *All such deaths in gaols, asylums and hospitals were to be reported to the coroner, and since 1861, the origins of suspect building fires also came under his remit.* The inquest was not a trial but a fact-finding mission, an investigative procedure rather than one looking to establish blame, although the coroner could refer the matter to the criminal court as a potential murder or manslaughter if he thought that was appropriate. He could also grant bail to a suspect or remand him or her in police custody according to the circumstances arising from the inquest. Murder occurred less frequently in colonial Sydney than you might think, although alcohol-related manslaughter was depressingly common, as were incidences of suicide and infanticide. If a death had occurred due to, for example, the negligence of an employer, an institution or a quack doctor, then the coroner could bring to light carelessness, corruption and abuse of authority, and make remedial recommendations. They weren't always followed, but sometimes they were and changes made for the better.

Inquests were open to the public and were usually held in hotels. The body in question was subject to a postmortem by a qualified surgeon when the cause of death wasn't obvious, then presented at the inquest to be inspected by the coroner, a jury of 'twelve good and lawful men' (essential at every inquest), and anyone else present who cared to look. The only time the corpse wasn't displayed was when decomposition was especially advanced. The coroner would listen to testimony relating to the death from witnesses, friends, family, plus the medical evidence, then sum up the facts and the jury would return a majority verdict on how the death had been caused, which was recorded on an official form. Only then could the deceased person be buried.

Henry Shiell, who was on call night and day, appears to have been a very busy person, sometimes attending up to five inquests in a day. These seem to have been organised virtually overnight — no waiting weeks, months or even years as happens now, which obviously would have been impractical with the requirement of inspecting the corpse. He did, however, as happened with Titus Crowe in the story, very occasionally order the exhumation of a body if information came to light suggesting there were more sinister aspects to a death than originally thought.

According to the *Act for Registering Births, Deaths and Marriages* of 1856, in New South Wales anyone could certify a death. Obviously a professional and qualified medical doctor would have been the most appropriate person, but a spouse could do it, or another relative, a midwife, a neighbour, the rat-catcher – anyone. Many of these people didn't have any medical knowledge at all and simply guessed at the cause of death, and some didn't want the real reason that their loved one had died to go on record. For example, syphilis or alcoholism could be recorded as consumption or some other more socially acceptable illness (*died of natural causes* was popular), and 'bashed across the head with a cast-iron frying pan' could be recorded as *fell over and hit head*. Also, a death didn't have to be registered with the Office of Births, Deaths and Marriages for thirty days, well after the deceased had been buried, thereby potentially concealing the true cause of death. These anomalies were apparently debated at length by a Select Committee in 1886, but looking online, the next revamp of the Act I found was dated 1899, thirteen years later.

In this story, when Titus's death is being investigated by the coroner, it occurred to me, well, would they actually be able to tell if he'd been poisoned back in 1868? Did they have toxicology tests then? Yes, they did. The 1800s were apparently known as the Arsenic Century because so many people died from it, though not all were murdered. Arsenic was a component in the beautiful bright green dyes known as Scheele's Green and Paris Green, which were used to colour fabric, paint, wallpaper, carpets, toys, food colouring – everything you might wear or have in your house. Over time the colour faded, leached toxins, made people sick and sometimes killed them. Arsenic was also used in a lot of medicines, as a bulking agent in bread, and in cosmetics. By the 1870s, it had become clear that arsenic was deleterious to humans and it was therefore used only in rat poison, though it was still easy to purchase – you just had to say to the shopkeeper you had loads of rats to get rid of and sign some sort of register. But by then there were toxicology tests to prove that arsenic had been the cause of death, so it was more difficult to go on a people-poisoning rampage.

While cyanide and strychnine were, and sometimes still are, used to deliberately kill people, arsenic was the 'go-to' poison in the eighteenth and early nineteenth centuries because it left no detectable trace. However, in the 1830s, James Marsh, a chemist working at the Royal Arsenal at Woolwich, developed a method to test for the presence of arsenic using body tissue or fluid. This was based on earlier tests developed by scientist Carl Scheele in 1775 (yes, the same bloke who invented the lethal arsenic-saturated green dye), and physician Samuel Hahnemann (the founder of homeopathy) in 1787. I'm not going to explain how Marsh's test worked because the chemistry is absolutely beyond me, but it was successfully used during the sensational murder trial of Marie Lafarge in France in 1840, which resulted in Lafarge being sentenced to life in prison.

This is interesting. For this series I've been doing a fair bit of research about social conditions in Sydney in the 1860s and 1870s, particularly for impoverished women and children, and they really were quite grim. I didn't expect to find much good news, so I was surprised to read about the Sydney Benevolent Asylum, where one of the city morgues was located. It was a place of refuge, not an asylum in the 'mental hospital' sense of the time, and was established in 1818 by the philanthropic New South Wales Benevolent Society to help the poor and needy.

The asylum was located on the corner of Pitt and Devonshire streets, adjacent to the old Devonshire Street Cemetery, and its primary purpose was to be of assistance to married women expecting babies, old single men, and families in dire straits. The Benevolent Society also operated another asylum at Liverpool Hospital, though that became seriously overcrowded, resulting in the government taking over its management and transferring some patients to a government asylum on Parramatta Wharf. From 1862 the Benevolent Asylum on Pitt Street stopped taking men and boys (who were sent on to Liverpool Hospital), and operated as a lying-in hospital for married and unmarried women, a foundling institute and a refuge for deserted mothers and destitute children. I really am quite surprised to discover there was a facility for pregnant unmarried women, given the social mores of the time, especially one funded by private subsidies and subscriptions.

In 1901 the Benevolent Asylum was demolished to make way for the new Central Railway Station. The New South Wales Benevolent Society used the compensation money they received for having their building flattened to purchase Flinton, a 1.6-hectare estate in Paddington, for a new lying-in hospital with free services and teaching facilities. It included a three-storey house which, in 1905, became the Royal Hospital for Women. The hospital remained there until 1997, when it relocated to Randwick where it continues to provide world-class women's health care and research programs.

Gladesville Hospital for the Insane, where Elias Nuttall ends up, started off as Tarban Creek Lunatic Asylum in 1838, on the north bank of the Parramatta River between today's suburbs of Putney and Hunters Hill. The asylum was designed by Colonial Architect Mortimer Lewis, who also designed the Australian Museum, Sydney Customs House, Darlinghurst Gaol and various courthouses, police stations and other public buildings.

Governor Bourke considered it would be impossible to find anyone in New South Wales suitable to fill the positions of superintendent and matron of the new asylum, so he arranged for John Thomas Digby and his wife to come out from England, both of whom had experience working in lunatic hospitals. But by 1846 it became clear there was a lack of expert medical direction at the asylum and on 1 January 1848 Dr Francis Campbell was appointed to administer the asylum.

In 1867 Colonial Secretary Henry Parkes invited visiting Englishman Dr Frederic Norton Manning to become medical superintendent of Tarban Creek Lunatic Asylum. Dr Manning was a general physician and naval surgeon who had seen active service aboard HMS *Esk* at the Battle of Gate Pa in New Zealand in 1864, during which the British suffered a serious defeat. Dr Manning said not right now, thank you, and went on an overseas tour to study methods of administration and patient care in asylums. He returned to Sydney and in October 1868 took up the position at Tarban Creek, and immediately reported that patients were cut off from relatives in gloomy, prison-like accommodation, there were no facilities for recreation or gainful employment, and the food was rubbish. In January 1869, the name was changed to Gladesville Hospital for the Insane, by which time patients were receiving proper treatment rather than being subjected to life in what Dr Manning had referred to as a 'cemetery for diseased intellects'. By 1879, radical changes in treatment and accommodation had been made, and the use of restraint minimised (https://adb.anu.edu.au/biography/manning-frederic-norton-4147).

The name changed again in 1915 to Gladesville Mental Hospital, and yet again in the mid-1960s to simply Gladesville Hospital. The facility was allegedly constantly overcrowded throughout its history (though perhaps not during Dr Manning's tenure?), until the emphasis changed from in-patient care to community-based services and psychiatric units in general hospitals. After that the in-patient population of dedicated facilities like Gladesville decreased, and on 29 January 1993, Gladesville Hospital closed. There are 1,228 people buried in the hospital cemetery, patients who died there over the years. Dr Frederic Manning died in 1903 and is also buried in the hospital cemetery (https://researchdata.edu.au/tarban-creek-lunatic-1915-93/164329).

Acknowledgements

As usual I have plenty of people to thank, because I'm not producing these books on my own, you know.

Thank you to my excellent agent, Clare Forster at Curtis Brown Australia, who always goes the extra mile to support me, my ideas and my books, and thanks also to the Curtis Brown team.

Another big thank you goes to Anna Valdinger, Fiction Publisher at HarperCollins Australia, for unfailingly championing my work, and especially this time really working with me to smooth out all the bumpy bits, and also to eagle-eyed and thorough Senior Editor Rachel Dennis, and to the editing, design, marketing and publicity teams. Ditto to Sandra Noakes and the hard-working crew at HarperCollins New Zealand.

There is always a stage when a new manuscript from me is more of a sow's ear than a silk purse. This is when Anna critiques it, I do a rewrite, then it goes to freelance book editor Kate O'Donnell for fine-tuning and polishing. Thank you, Kate – your expertise and insight are invaluable.

Then there's my friend and fellow writer Ngahuia Te Awekotuku, who provides a welcome ear for me to bend about my work. Thank you! Writing can be a lonely pursuit and it's good for authors to get together and have a whinge.

Almost last but never least are my family – my stepchildren, and my partner, Aaron, who supplies me with meals and cups of tea when I'm flat out working. This isn't because I'm so immersed in my art I can't tear myself away to cook some food; it's because I'm too lazy to do more than open a packet of biscuits. Thanks, Aaron!

Finally, a huge thank you goes to my faithful readers and Facebook followers. There's no point doing any of this without you.

Look out for the next Tatty Crowe novel,
coming from HarperCollins in 2025.
Read on for an exclusive extract.

Chapter One

April 1871, Sydney

Tatty Crowe, Sydney's only female undertaker, and a young one at that at the age of twenty-four, finished brushing her hair until it gleamed like anthracite coal then tied it back in a plain and tidy bun. As far as she was concerned, curls and ringlets were far too frivolous for a woman who dealt with death and grief daily. For the same reason she'd forgone coloured clothing and had worn black since beginning her apprenticeship as an undertaker six years earlier. Since before that, in fact, as she'd been in mourning for her parents.

'Come in!' she called in response to a knock on her bedroom door.

It would be the housemaid, Lorna, no doubt, with her morning cup of tea.

And it was Lorna, but without the tea.

'Something awful, Tatty,' Lorna said from the doorway, her eyes red as though she'd been crying.

Tatty wondered if the range in the kitchen had gone out overnight and now there was no hot water and they'd all have to have a cold breakfast. It did that sometimes and was very annoying. 'What's happened?'

'There's something in a box. On the back porch.'

Although Lorna was thirty-nine, she was a little simple and did tend to become overwrought at times. Tatty was occasionally tempted to tell her to just calm down and stop being silly but she never did because she'd known Lorna since she was born and she loved her. She would rather put up with an occasional bout of unwarranted panic than upset her.

'What sort of something, Lorna? Did you have a look?'

'Of course I did! It's a poor little dead baby, all blue and cold.'

Oh no, Tatty thought, her heart sinking, that's the third one. 'I'll come down now. Have you told Cora?'

Lorna shook her head.

'I will. Perhaps you could help Mrs Seddon to get on with breakfast? We've got a busy day today.'

'And the baby ...?'

'Don't worry: I'll make sure the right things happen.'

Lorna immediately looked relieved. 'Oh, I knew you would, Tatty. I feel so much better now.'

'Good. Off you go, then.'

Tatty was hungry for her breakfast and desperately wanted a cup of tea, but first she had to attend to the poor baby in the box. She went along to her assistant Cora Billings's room and knocked on the door. 'It's Tatty. Are you dressed yet?'

The door opened and Cora said through a tortoise shell comb held in her mouth as she twisted her hair at the nape of her neck, 'Lorna hasn't brought me any tea. I'm *gasping*.'

'Someone's left another dead baby on the back steps.'

'Have they? Bugger. That's sad.' Cora secured her bun with the comb. 'That's three now. Word must be getting out.'

Tatty said, 'I can't see how.'

Outside, in the morning shadow of the three-storey building that was Tatty's home and place of work, she and Cora stood looking down at the still, blue features of an infant. It had been wrapped in what looked like an old petticoat and laid in a wooden grocery box. A quick check revealed that the umbilical cord was still attached, indicating that the baby girl had only just been born, though whether she'd been stillborn or had died after birth, and whether that death had been natural, was impossible for them to tell.

'I'll talk to Reverend Cole today,' Tatty said. 'Let's have breakfast and then we'll tend to her.'

They took the baby in her box inside and placed her in the parlour, on an occasional table near the window where she could rest in the warmth of the early morning sun, then headed to the dining room.

The dining table seated ten and these days was practically filled by Tatty's staff, who all lived in. Apart from Tatty, there was Cora, who was almost twenty-six, and Robert Edmonds, both assistant undertakers, and thirty-seven-year-old Henry Dodds, who looked after the horses and drove the hearses. Cora, Henry and Robert had been with Crowe Funerals when Tatty's late husband, Titus Crowe, had been in charge. But Titus had died in 1867, after which Tatty had hired Benjamin Everitt as another assistant undertaker. He and Robert were both now twenty-six. Tatty knew it was all very well having lady undertakers like herself and Cora to provide the recently bereaved with compassion and grace, but the business still needed young men with plenty of muscle to heft bodies and coffins about. And finally there was Maggie Seddon, grey-haired at fifty-nine, and her niece Lorna Coates, who had been employed for years in London by Tatty's mother and father before they'd died, and who three years earlier had followed Tatty to New South Wales to work for her.

'Someone left another dead infant,' Cora said as she reached for a third piece of bread. 'A dear little girl.'

'Christ,' Henry said. 'Why can women not give their poor Godforsaken dead babies proper funerals?'

'Why can men not stop getting girls in the family way?' Cora shot back.

'The last I heard it takes two for that to happen,' Henry said.

Cora said, 'I think I just said that, didn't I?'

'Excuse me,' Maggie Seddon said as she sliced more bread. 'That's hardly a topic for the table.'

Tatty didn't think it was, either, though she did agree with Cora: men should take more responsibility for preventing unwanted babies, and she was learning that they seldom did. That task almost always fell to women. Avoiding pregnancy when Titus was alive had taken up a considerable amount of *her* time and effort, but had definitely been worth her while. It wasn't that she didn't like children – they just didn't fit into her plans and probably never would.

However, she didn't agree with Henry's initial comment. He knew that some women couldn't afford even the cheapest of funerals, and he was also aware of how ashamed most would feel handing over the bodies of their infants to be buried on the parish in a pauper's grave. Normally he was a benign and generous man, and she wondered what was making him so mean-spirited.

'Did you get out of bed on the wrong side this morning?' she said.

'No,' Henry said. 'Why?'

'Because that was a particularly unkind thing to say about women.'

'Well, I'm sick of all these dead babies turning up everywhere,' Henry said. 'It's shocking and disgusting and it goes against God. And now they're leaving them here.'

'Well, we're doing what we can,' Tatty said.

Henry said, 'I know, but it's a drop in the bucket, isn't it?'

'We can't give them all proper funerals, Henry,' Tatty snapped. She looked around the table at everyone's slightly alarmed faces. 'I'm sorry. I truly am. But we can't. We can make burial arrangements for some of the poor little things, but we just don't have the time to go about looking for abandoned dead babies. Most of them will end up on the parish or be lost forever. Henry? You know that, don't you?'

Henry sighed, then nodded.

'Good,' Tatty said. 'And don't blame the mothers. I don't want to hear comments like that again in this house. Is that clear?'

*

Tatty had planned to lead that morning's funeral procession and accompany the party of mourners out to Haslam's Creek Cemetery on the funeral train, but at the last minute asked Cora to take her place.

Instead, she stayed behind and tended to the dead baby. She washed the tiny body thoroughly, wrapped her in a small blanket, and settled her into the smallest of the white coffins Crowe Funerals had available for children. Then she harnessed Shadow to the dog-cart and headed west out of town towards Camperdown Cemetery in Newtown.

The cemetery was for Anglicans (and any other denomination happy to be buried using the rites of the Church of England), had been consecrated in 1849 and closed in 1868 to new burials, although people with pre-purchased plots could still be buried there. The reverend was Reginald Cole, whose church was St Stephen's on Stephen Street. It was too small now for the local congregation and Tatty understood that a new, much bigger church was to be built in the cemetery grounds, beginning later in the year. She very much liked Reverend Cole.

She went to see him at home, where she found him in the garden with a pair of scissors, dead-heading assorted blooms.

'Good morning, Mrs Crowe,' he said. 'Oh dear, don't tell me. Not another one?'

'Good morning, Reverend. Yes, unfortunately. I trust our arrangement still stands?'

'Of course. You have the hapless little mite with you?'

Tatty nodded.

'Then do come inside and have some tea. Gerrard can make us a pot, then attend to your horse and the child.'

Tatty followed the reverend into the house. At the door he stopped to divest himself of his scissors, his ratty old leather gloves, and the wide-brimmed straw hat he'd been wearing, which had seen far, far better days.

'Please, do have a seat,' Reverend Cole said, indicating a sofa absolutely covered in pale cat fur.

Tatty had fallen into that trap in the past, and Lorna had had to brush so much fur off the black dress she'd had on that she swore a whole new cat could have been knitted from it.

'Do you have a newspaper?' she asked. 'I see there are a few cat hairs on the couch. It's this black fabric. You know.'

The more pertinent question would have been, do you have a housekeeper?, but that was really none of her business.

'I do, yes, of course. Here you are,' the reverend said, passing her a copy of the *Sydney Morning Herald*. 'It's dreadful, isn't it? My cassocks sometimes!'

Tatty spread out the paper and sat on it. Of the shedding cats there was no sign. Probably spreading fur all over the soft furnishings upstairs, she thought.

Gerrard, the reverend's manservant, brought in tea and cake on a tray and served them. 'The ... delivery is in your dog-cart?' he asked Tatty.

'Yes,' Reverend Cole answered for her. 'Put it in the usual place in the pantry, thank you, Gerrard.'

Tatty knew some people might find the idea of storing the corpse of a dead baby in a pantry odd, but the reverend's food cupboard was the coldest room in his house, and therefore quite suitable for that purpose.

As Gerrard went off to fetch water for Shadow and to retrieve the little coffin, Reverend Cole cut several slices of cake.

'Would you like a piece,' he asked, 'or two? It's Madeira. Lovely icing. Gerrard made it.'

Tatty accepted a slice and it was in fact very good. They chatted for a while and when Tatty had finished her tea and cake, she reached for her purse, took out a five-pound note and passed it to the reverend.

'For the Parish Poor Relief Fund.'

'That's generous, Mrs Crowe. Thank you very much.'

It was what Tatty paid every time she brought a dead baby to Reverend Cole. The money really did go to the parish poor and in exchange, at night, a small grave was dug in consecrated ground at Camperdown Cemetery, and the baby was buried with full Christian burial rites pronounced by the reverend. These days Tatty truly did doubt whether heaven actually existed, but she hoped that if it did, these poor dead infants, who probably hadn't been baptised, might have a better chance of getting there if they'd been properly buried.

She'd brought nine babies to Camperdown now. Three had been left at her house. The other six had been quietly referred to her by Sydney's coroner, Henry Shiell. They had all been found over the past fifteen months around the city, floating in creeks, in alleyways, and hidden under rubbish on vacant lots, and sent by the police to Coroner Shiell for inquests. Afterwards, the coroner had asked her if she could arrange private burials for them, and she'd agreed. She wasn't aware if he'd approached rival undertakers for assistance to bury other abandoned infants, and she hadn't asked. Perhaps the majority were buried on the parish.

And over the past year or so there had been an increasing number of dead babies found abandoned in Sydney, so many in fact that the *Sydney Morning Herald* had taken to calling the situation 'an epidemic of infanticide'.

It *was* almost an epidemic, Tatty thought, but what was causing it?